Truth in the Smoke

Glamour Blind Trilogy Book 1

SP Neeson

18 STREET PRESS

Truth in the Smoke

Glamour Blind Book One

Cover by Nocturn Cover Art

Editing by Tracy Thillmann

ISBN: 978-1-7389875-0-4

Version: June 2023

For Krys, Steph, and Ryan
My biggest fans

CONTENTS

CHAPTER 1

When the woman walked into my tiny private investigator office, I knew something was off. First, she looked like a supermodel, and supermodels did not try to hire me. From the top of her golden blonde head to the tips of her purple, lace four-inch heels, she was perfectly put together. Her teal designer dress draped over her long lithe body and somehow the colors complemented her bronzed skin. It took me a moment to figure out the second, and more disturbing, thing wrong with the picture of her. Although the Vancouver sky had opened up a couple days ago and had yet to stop trying to drown its residents, she was completely dry.

"Hi," she said with a brilliant smile as she perched on the edge of my single guest chair. She set her handbag on my scratched and dented desk, pointing the Prada label in my direction. Then she slid one endless leg over the other, subtly showing off the red sole on the bottom of her shoe as she did.

I blinked slowly at the overt display of designer fashion, but didn't comment. "May I help you?" I asked.

"You're Calynn, right? The private investigator."

"I sure hope so. Otherwise, I paid way too much money for the sign and business cards."

Her laugh reminded me of a brook or stream, but she stopped laughing before I could consider the idea too long.

"I'm Meriel. I've been looking everywhere for someone who could help me. Most people are just looking out for themselves, you understand. There are no other investigators with the right background."

I had no idea what she was talking about, but I gave her a slight smile anyway. She took it as the agreement I thought she would and went on.

"Most of our people go into higher paying gigs, of course, like acting or modeling, or whatever."

By the way she said it, I guessed she was an actress. Not really a surprise. What surprised me was her saying *our people*, like we had something in common, like we were friends. People tended not to like me, which had the unfortunate result of my private investigator business being on the verge of bankruptcy. Of course, being a woman in a male dominated industry didn't help either.

"I bet you get a lot of business from the rest of us."

Since I still had no idea who she meant by *us*, I just smiled again and waited for her to continue.

"Of course, I'm sure you can't talk about your clients." She looked at me expectantly, like she thought I was about to tell her everything.

"I have a pretty strict confidentiality policy. Why don't you tell me about the job?"

"The job?" Meriel's pretty brow crumpled in confusion.

I pointed to myself. "PI." I pointed to her. "Client."

"Oh, right." She unzipped her handbag and pulled out a photo, sliding it over to me. The woman in it was even more beautiful than the one in my office, but in a more dangerous way. Her dark hair flowed past her shoulders in a wild, wind-tossed tangle as she turned away from the camera. Her dark red, lace dress covered her demurely from collarbone to below her knees, sheer sleeves reaching past her elbows. The longer I looked at her, the more I felt like I was suffocating.

I pushed the feeling aside to look at the other details of the picture. I noticed a large, antique key dangling from a chain so thin I wondered how the key didn't break it. I traced the necklace with my finger.

"I have a close-up," Meriel said excitedly as she passed me another photo from her purse. This one focused only on the key draped on a red lace background. The top of it looked like a silver snowflake superimposed over a gold sun. In the center of the snowflake-sun was a large green gem with deep, glittering black flakes. A silver and gold braid made up the stem and ended in the most intricately designed tooth I'd ever seen. What kind of lock could this key fit into?

"It's beautiful, isn't it?" Unconcealed longing dripped from her voice.

It was, but I couldn't understand why Meriel would be so interested in it. It wasn't the most expensive necklace I'd ever seen. Maybe some fancy designer made it?

"Yes, it is," I said. "So, what's the job, exactly?"

Meriel regarded me blankly. "I want you to find it." She said it like I should already have known what she wanted.

"It doesn't look very lost to me," I said, sliding the pictures back across my desk.

Her face brightened into a smile that almost blinded me. I found myself hoping she never tried to play poker. "Apparently, it was lost only a few hours after the picture was taken. I have it from a reliable source that almost no one knows she even came out of the Sidhe with it. So we would be the only ones looking for it."

"Right." I didn't try to explain to her that "reliable sources" were rarely as reliable as they seemed or that a printed picture didn't tell you anything about when or where it was taken. For all I knew, this picture could have been taken months ago. I also didn't mention I had no idea what "she came out of the *she*" meant.

She rolled her eyes. "Ugh. You're not one of those who believe the key is a hoax or cursed, are you? I know at least two others who have taken it back and received a full pardon."

I knew I was going to regret asking, but I did it anyway. "A pardon from what?"

If I was confused by what she had been saying, she looked more confused by my question.

"From exile."

"Right. Just so we're clear. You want me to find a key."

She shook her head. "Not just *a* key. *The* key. Don't you know what this is? Who this is?" She tapped the photo of the woman with her manicured finger. "This is the Queen of Air and Darkness. And she's lost the key to the Sidhe."

"Uh-huh." I'd always had a bit of a knack for knowing if someone was lying or not. It was some kind of instinct I had learned not to ignore, and it was part of what made me a good detective. That instinct hadn't gone off, which could mean only one thing. She believed what she was saying.

"Well, miss..." I trailed off. She hadn't given me a last name, and we stared at each other for a moment until I realized she wasn't going to. "Meriel. I'm very busy right now. Why don't you leave me your number and I'll get back to you if I can free up some time?"

"But this could be our chance. I've been searching for this key for the last fifty-five years. With the knowledge I've gained since then and your skills as a PI, we could find the key and go home. Don't you want to go home?"

There were so many things about what she said that raised an alarm, but I decided now was not the time. So I just answered her question.

"Considering I live in an apartment upstairs, I think I'm okay."

She couldn't have looked more heartbroken if someone had just run over her puppy. She said in a small voice, "But you're fae. I could feel the magic when I walked in the door. Why don't you want to go home?"

I was finally going to ask her what the fuck she was talking about when she straightened, the heartbroken look replaced by one of disdain. She stood, dropped a business card on top of the photos on my desk, and said, "Call me when you've come to your senses." Then she stalked out of my office and slammed the door.

I watched the closed door for a while, then I got up to get another cup of coffee. It looked like sludge now that it was about six hours old, but I figured, with enough milk and sugar, I could still drink it. There wasn't any left to make more anyway. I cast a longing look at the empty package of beans my friend Arial had bought me from our favorite place on Granville Island a few months ago while I heated my cup. I still couldn't bring myself to throw out the bag even though the beans were long since gone.

I returned to my empty office, Meriel's business card taunting me from my desk, and my mind whispered I could afford more of that coffee if I took the job. But she was crazy. She really believed the bullshit about a queen and exile and the key to something called a "she." I shouldn't care what she said about me. She probably couldn't pay anyway. That purse was probably a knock off. Probably.

The trouble with always being able to tell when someone was lying: it made it impossible to lie to yourself.

I tried to put Meriel and her crazy story out of my head. I opened my ledger, that I still kept on paper, and tried to focus on my finances. If I used all the money in my account, I was still two hundred dollars short on rent, and I also had to find a way to pay the electrical bill I hadn't paid last month. And that completely ignored what I would need for gas for my motorcycle and groceries. I wasn't entirely sure where I was going to get the money I needed in the next few days.

Some of what Meriel had said bounced around in my mind as I stared down at my ledger. The *us* and *going home*, like I was part of some kind of club she belonged to.

I set my teeth together, not quite clenching my jaw, frustrated that the only potential client to walk through my door in the last few days was crazy.

I took a sip of the coffee and grimaced. It really was terrible, but I had none left. My frustration started to boil over. I was supposed to go for dinner tonight with Arial. She would insist on paying. Again. And I would have to let her. Again.

This fucking life was little more than a cage.

All of a sudden, my mug shattered in my hand, spilling coffee all over my ledger.

"Shit."

CHAPTER 2

The day went pretty much downhill from there. I contacted a few people I'd done some work for in the past—lawyers, other PIs, the list was embarrassingly short—and no one had anything for me. No one else came in for the rest of the day and I didn't come up with any brilliant plans on how to make more money before the month was up and my rent was due. If I couldn't pay, I would lose my office and my home. The apartment above my office included a kitchen and living room area barely big enough for my little table and an armchair I bought from a thrift store. It also included a bedroom crowded with a twin bed, and a tiny bathroom I could almost turn around in. The best part about the apartment was the large balcony overlooking the neighbor's property on Williams Street. The office itself was also small, with the front room to host clients and a small back room with a safe, a filing cabinet, and my coffee maker. It was a dumpy little place, but it was *my* dumpy little place. And I would lose it if I couldn't get the money together to pay next month's rent in less than a week.

I glanced down at the business card and pictures on my desk.

Her full name was Meriel Jones. I had looked her up between phone calls and found out she was indeed an actress. A famous actress who I would know if I went to see movies ever. She could definitely afford to pay me. I had picked up my cell phone to call her three times already and stopped myself each time. I couldn't justify taking money from someone who wasn't in their right mind. It would be wrong. Even if she could afford to pay all my debts and bills for the rest of the year and still be able to afford a few new designer outfits for herself.

My day was almost over. Just for curiosity's sake, I typed "what is a fae" into my Internet browser and read the Wikipedia page about fairies and the different European cultures that believed in them. I spent some time reading through the Celtic entry about a race of gods who were called the Tuatha Dé Danann. The more I read, the faster my heart beat, but I couldn't have said why. Finally, I slammed my laptop shut.

"This is ridiculous."

I was about to get up to lock my door when it opened again. I looked up, hopeful an actual client was here to hire me, but one of the property managers for my apartment and office came in instead, shaking off his umbrella as he did. I repressed a groan when I saw him. He never brought good news.

"Good afternoon, Calynn. How are you doing?"

"I'm okay, Greg. It's good to see you. Do you want a coffee?" I said before I could think better of it. I prayed he said no. I might poison him if he tried to drink the stuff. If Stacy had come by, I would have gladly poisoned her, but I liked Greg.

"No, thank you. I came by to ask about the rent."

I forced myself to keep breathing. Slowly. In, out. "It's not due for another six days."

"I know that." He twisted the umbrella in his hands, spinning it around and around. "I just got a message from the company who owns the building. There's a couple of tenants who they're having trouble with. Trouble with payment. Unfortunately, your name came up. Stacy wanted to come talk to you, but after what happened last time, I thought it was better if I came. They said if you don't pay on time this month, they're going to evict you."

Stacy was one in a long line of people who seemed to hate me for no reason. And after twenty-nine years of bullshit, I tended to be pretty quick to snap back if someone was being a dick to me. Maybe that meant I got into more fights, which in turn made me more unlikable. I couldn't say.

"I've only been late a few times and only by a couple of days. And I always pay."

Greg looked like this conversation was physically painful. I felt sorry for him. I hated putting him in this position. "I know that, Calynn. And other than the sometimes late payments, you're a great tenant. You clean up after yourself. There have never been any complaints about you from the other tenants. But you've been late four of the past six months. There's nothing I can do." He spread his hands, the umbrella still in one of them. "If I'm going to be completely honest with you, I'm afraid they're looking for an excuse to evict people. I think they want to do some renovations and then put it back on the market at higher rents."

"There's been a lot of that happening around here lately," I said, absently. I tapped my finger against my desk, thinking furiously about what I could do to ensure I would have enough money in six short days. My gaze landed on Meriel's business card. I looked up at Greg with a sunny smile I didn't feel. "But hey, I just got a new client today, so it should be no problem. I'll be getting the advance tomorrow."

He looked so relieved and I realized how close I had come to losing my home and business. If I didn't get the money, I would be out.

"I should go then. I've got a couple other people I need to talk to. Have a good rest of your day."

"You, too," I told him as he left.

I opened my ledger again and stared down at the coffee-stained page without seeing it. I slid the business card off my desk and into my hand and picked up my cell phone in the other.

"You shouldn't call her," I told myself. "It's wrong to take advantage of someone not in their right mind." I tapped the card against the edge of the desk. "She can afford it. And you heard Greg. You need the money." I took a deep breath. "It's still a bad idea."

Then I shut up and dialed her number.

She answered after a couple of rings. "Meriel."

"Ms. Jones. This is Calynn D'Arcy. You came by my office earlier today?"

"Ah, Calynn. You've come to your senses and changed your mind. I just knew you would."

"Right. Well, I'll need an advance. A thousand dollars should be enough."

"Of course. I'm in the area still. I can bring you a cheque and some other notes I have with me. I can be there in about twenty minutes."

"That sounds great. I'll see you then."

"Oh, Calynn. You won't regret this."

We hung up, and I was certain I already did.

***

When she returned to my office, I noticed again she was completely dry despite the pouring rain outside. There was something weird about her and I considered the idea she wasn't actually crazy before I pushed it away. However she kept dry in this weather was none of my business. Especially if she was going to give me a thousand dollars.

"Hi, Ms. Jones," I said as I stood up to shake her hand.

She stared at my hand for a moment before I let it drop.

"Why are you calling me Ms. Jones? Just call me Meriel."

"Of course." I sat down and she took the seat across from me again, setting her purse in her lap and pulling an old, slim notebook from inside. She hesitated a moment and then handed it to me.

"I don't normally share this with people," she said. "I've kept this since I was forced out. For such a petty thing, too." She pouted and then sighed. "Anyway, everything I know about the key is in there. You'll be discreet about the rest of it, won't you?"

She actually looked a little frightened.

"What is this?" I asked her.

"It's my diary. I admit, I haven't kept it faithfully, but sometimes you just want to let all your feelings out somewhere. And my family has refused to visit me here, so I can't talk to anyone. Or at least I couldn't. Perhaps now..." she trailed off and stared into the distance and I could tell she was thinking of something that made her happy. I thought again how she really shouldn't play poker.

I flipped to the first page in the journal. The date said she started it in 1962. The yellowed paper was obviously old, but the woman sitting across from me was only twenty-three, if the information on the Internet was correct. She certainly looked closer to twenty-three than however old she'd have to be to start a journal that long ago.

"1962?" I asked.

"Yes," she replied with another sigh. "It's been so long since I was home. The only comfort I have is in the sea. Of course, the sea up here is too cold. But when I'm in California, it's nice to be in the warm ocean."

"Yeah. Of course." I was pretty sure if I let on I had no idea what she was talking about, she would leave and I wouldn't see a dime from her. I decided to play along with her delusions. And I felt like shit doing it.

"How long have you been here?" she asked.

I glanced back down at her journal and the 1962 written on the first page. I didn't want to lie to her, so I said, "Twenty-nine years." That's how old I was, so it was technically true.

She nodded like we were bonding over something. "The first thirty are the hardest. I don't know if you ever met Killian. Before Ronan, he used to be the strongest fae around these parts for a long time. I heard he's been here for a hundred and fifty years. Can you believe it?"

"Uh huh." I set the journal aside on top of my ledger and wished I didn't have to take this job. "What can you tell me about this key you want me to find?"

"Right. Well, I've heard a lot said about how the key is never lost and sometimes the Queens make it seem like it is to give us false hope. But I can't believe that's true. Some have also said it's never lost but is given to one exiled fae in particular to allow them to go home. They just have to know where to look."

"Right. And you said you know at least two people who have found it?"

"Yes. It has always been near one of the Ways into the Sidhe when it is found. Almost as if they key itself wants to go back."

I wrote everything down having no idea what it meant and I waited for some lie to trigger my instincts. None came. Meriel Jones, A-list actress, believed a place called *the she* existed that she could get into with a special key. She believed two other people had already gone there. She believed she had been away from there for around sixty years. Oh, and she believed in fairies.

The question was: was Meriel Jones insane? Or did she know something I didn't?

I set my pen down.

"Do something for me," I said.

"Anything."

"Tell me something you know is untrue."

She frowned at the request but said, "It's a sunny day."

Lie. My instinct rang as clear as day. She knew that was a lie and so she also believed every other thing she had said.

"Okay. I will look for this key, but I need you to understand something. Having a few pictures of someone wearing the key and then not wearing it does not mean it's actually missing." I thought about how to phrase my next question. "Why have you not found another investigator before now?"

"Well, they're all human, of course."

Which clearly meant she believed she was not and neither was I.

"And just for my reference, why do you think that is a problem?"

She rolled her eyes. "You know how humans react to us. They're either infatuated by our magic or hate us because of it."

Something clicked in me then. They say when you're about to die, your life flashes before your eyes and I wondered later if it was something like what I felt in that moment. *They're either infatuated by us or hate us.* Other than my best friend and a few others I had met here and there, that explained every interaction I'd ever had with people.

Could she really know something I didn't? Could I be like her? I glanced quickly around my office, the cheap trappings of a very human life. I'd always felt somewhat out of place. Could there be an answer to why I felt that way?

Meriel pulled me back from my existential crisis. "Oh. You said a thousand should be enough for the retainer? Though I don't know why you would need it with the Diaspora Corporation. I expected some other kind of bargain for your assistance." The cheque she handed me distracted me from asking what the Diaspora Corporation was. I took it between numb fingers, looking down at the one thousand dollars written on the little paper. This would solve all my problems. But how many additional problems was it going to bring me?

CHAPTER 3

M y mind continued reeling long after Meriel left. We planned to meet at her house the following morning to discuss where I thought we should go with the case. After she left, I wrote the name of the corporation she had mentioned so I would remember to ask about it. Then, I closed up and got my rain gear. I went out to where I parked my motorcycle and got on. It would be cheaper to take transit to meet my friend, but I needed the ride.

I purchased the shell of my 1986 Triumph Bonneville six years before and put every extra penny I had into getting it running and looking beautiful. I saved money by learning to build it myself, and over the years fixing it and riding it had become my meditation. I took some of the quieter residential streets to avoid as much of the traffic as possible. I loved riding my bike, even in the rain. Which was good, considering how much it rained in the city. We never got much snow, so I could ride pretty much all year, as long as I braved the wet weather and was careful to wear my reflective rain jacket when it was dark.

I left my bike in a parkade near the bar, swiped my credit card at the pay station, putting it a little further into the red, and then made my way inside. In a city with a lot of great choices for bars and pubs, this one was my and Arial's favorite. It didn't hurt that the bartender and owner, Sam, was hot. He was somewhere in his mid-thirties with blonde hair cut close to his head. He was fit and I'd seen him bench two hundred and fifty pounds at our local krav maga gym. Arial had a crush on him and I was pretty sure it was reciprocated, but he hadn't made a move yet.

The bar itself was made from a gleaming red wood with brass accents. Black stools with backs lined the bar and nine low-top tables dotted the floor, each with three chairs around it instead of the usual four. The lighting and the wood and leather interior always made me feel like I was somewhere warm.

Arial and I tended to sit at the bar so we could chat with Sam if he wasn't too busy. Though since we went on Fridays, he usually was. Tonight was no different, and all the tables were full. My usual seat at the bar was empty, so I sat down and ordered a Bushmills Black and a burger and fries, realizing too late I hadn't deposited the cheque Meriel gave me.

"Have you seen Arial yet?" I asked Sam as he set the glass in front of me.

He shook his head and went back to his work.

My friend arrived before my food.

She shook her umbrella out and stuffed it in the umbrella stand by the door before coming to sit at the bar. Arial was small and had to hop up on the stool next to me. At just barely five feet tall, I towered over her, despite being only five foot three inches tall myself. Her short blonde hair was dyed bright green this month and spiked. It matched the splotches of green on her short white dress she wore despite the rain.

"Hi," she said as she took her seat. She signaled Sam and he brought her a vodka and cranberry. She placed an order for a cheeseburger and fries.

Then she turned to me. "So, how are you?" Her green eyes sparkled over the rim of her glass as she took a sip.

I shrugged. "Good. A new client came in today. She's an actress."

Arial's mouth dropped open. "Seriously? Would I know her? What did she want?"

Arial was a hairstylist for celebrities and the more affluent people of Vancouver. She lived on celebrity gossip. And since we had an agreement that I would tell her about my jobs but not who the client was, I felt comfortable telling her about the weird vibes I'd gotten today.

"Yes, seriously. Yes, you'd know her. And she wants me to find a key. But she mentioned some weird stuff and I'm worried she might be a little insane."

"Like what?"

"Like a queen and being a fae in exile."

"Fae as in a fairy? Hm. A mystery. Sounds exciting."

I snorted. "Right."

"I'm terribly curious about who she is." She took another sip of her drink. "You took the job, right?"

I grimaced and nodded. "I wasn't going to. I didn't think it would be right to take money from someone who's had a break with reality. But shortly after she left, Greg came by."

Arial's eyes widened. "Oh no. What did he say?"

My best friend's skills as an audience were beyond compare. "He said the company that owns the building has noticed my late rents. They want me to pay on time or get out."

Arial thunked her glass on the bar top. "They can't do that!"

"Yes, actually. They can. I've been late more than once recently. And while I've paid, they can start the eviction process."

Arial sighed. "I know you don't want me to ask this, but do you need a loan?"

"No. I called the actress after Greg left and accepted the job. I told her I needed an advance. I got the cheque. I just forgot to deposit it on my way over."

"A crazy client is better than no client, right?" She held up her glass and I clinked mine against it. We both drank, enjoying the moment of connection. Then Arial sobered. "Calynn, I know you hate to ask for help. You always want to be the one to help others and that's great. Lord knows I've needed help before. But you don't have to do it all on your own. If you need a place to stay, you can stay with me. If you need a loan, I can loan you money. You're more than just my best friend. You're like my sister."

Sam saved me from having to respond by dropping off our food. Before we could get into our dinner, a couple of men came over and offered to buy us drinks.

Arial smiled and shook her head. "No thanks, fellas. We're just having a little girl talk tonight."

They didn't take the hint. The larger one said, "Come on. Beautiful girls like you shouldn't be alone. You want some company."

"We're not alone," I said.

"You seem to be here alone."

"We're here with each other. You need to sit back down before I sit you back down."

Arial shook her head and took another sip of her drink. This happened frequently when we were out together. She had seen it all before.

One man seemed to get the message we were not interested and took a step back, but the first man didn't want to give up.

"Come on, girls, you're obviously looking for some fun."

"The answer is no."

He finally started to turn away, but I heard him mutter "cunt" under his breath. He turned back when I stood up and I took the opportunity to punch him in the face as hard as I could. I broke his nose with a satisfying crunch and blood streamed out of it. I was glad the sound was so satisfying because the pain in my hand was not.

A hush fell in the bar as everyone stared at us.

"Bitch," he said, and stepped toward me. Sam took the bat out from beneath the bar and set it on the top with a distinct clunk. Not that he needed it. But the visual was a good threat that often resolved conflicts before they became fights. And one of the biggest rules of krav maga was to avoid any fight you could. It was a rule I was kind of bad at following.

The man looked at Sam and then back at me.

Sam said, "Next time you want to ask a girl out, listen to her answer and respect it."

I sat back down, and the two guys left the bar. Everyone else went back to their own conversations now the show was over.

"How's your hand?" Arial asked.

Sam set a glass of ice in front of me with a towel and a raised eyebrow. I grimaced at him. "I shouldn't have caused a scene. If you get me a mop, I'll clean up the blood."

He nodded at me and moved off to get the cleaning equipment.

My middle and ring fingers already had a bruise forming, but otherwise, it was okay.

"It'll be fine," I told Arial. I always healed really fast. I wouldn't be surprised if the bruise had mostly faded by morning. I put some ice on it anyway.

"I never understand why they can't take no for an answer. They can when I'm with my other friends, but with you, it's like there's something about the two of us together." She shrugged as she popped a fry in her mouth. "I guess we're just too hot to handle."

I snorted and started eating, but my mind wandered back to what Meriel had said. *They're either infatuated by us or hate us.*

Or both, I added.

Sam returned with the mop and I cleaned up the mess I had caused. Arial went on about her clients and a friend who had asked if she might be interested in going on a trip after Christmas. She could chatter on for hours and I enjoyed listening to her. Her skills as an audience were only eclipsed by her skills as a storyteller. We had been friends since we were ten years old. Despite having completely different personalities, and being in vastly different social circles—as in she had one and I didn't—we continued to be friends long after graduation. I let her talk the rest of the way through our food and until we finished our drinks. When we were getting ready to settle up, she announced it was on her.

"You paid last time," I protested.

She looked at me seriously and said in a low tone, "Do you have the money to pay?"

I set my teeth together and shook my head once. While I had a bit of money in my account and the cheque in my pocket, things would still be tight for a while.

She didn't look at me with pity, and that was the only reason I could allow it to go on. I still hated to feel like I was in her debt, and the look on my face told her so.

She smiled. "Don't worry about it. One day you'll win the lottery, and you can pay for all our dinners."

"Right."

After she had paid, she linked her arm with mine and said, "The rain has stopped. Let's go for a walk."

We walked out of the bar and started down the sidewalk to a nearby park. "What do you want?" I asked her.

"What makes you think I want something?"

I looked down at our linked arms.

She peered up at me ruefully. "I'm always so obvious." She took a deep breath. "I want you to come to my birthday party."

My head fell back as I groaned to the sky.

"I know, I know. You don't like parties. You don't like getting dressed up. You don't like my friends. But I want you to be there. It's my thirtieth and I'm having this big party. A couple of my clients are coming, and *all* my friends. As one of my friends, specifically my best one, you need to be there to ensure the *all* part."

"It's not that I don't like your friends. It's that your friends don't like *me*. Can't I just take you out for dinner like always?"

"This isn't a *like always* kind of birthday. This is thirty. And you're my best friend. *And* I just paid for your dinner."

"Okay, okay. You sure know how to lay it on thick," I said. Though she was right. I already felt better about letting her buy my dinner knowing that going to this party would pay her back for it.

She gave me a parody of an innocent smile. "It's next Saturday at my house, so we won't do dinner on Friday. Wear your red dress."

I groaned again. "Arial!"

"Do it for me?" She fluttered her eyelashes, pretending innocence. "And I'll do your hair, so be there early. It'll be great. You can bring Jeremy if you want."

"Jeremy?"

"Your boyfriend. You remember him, don't you? Tall, dark hair, dark eyes, gorgeous."

"Yeah, I remember him. But he's not my boyfriend. Calling us friends with benefits is even a bit of a stretch. We're not really friends." I'd been seeing Jeremy for three years now, off and on. He was practically perfect for me. A player with no intention of settling down. But lately he'd started changing. He seemed to want to spend more and more time with me, and I was starting to feel claustrophobic.

"I don't understand you, Calynn. You always have these guys crawling over themselves for you and you never seem to care. Just once, I'd like to have a guy fall in love with me."

Meriel's words came back to me once more about how humans were infatuated by us.

"It's only fun to have a guy fall in love with you if you fall in love with them back."

We found the park and started a slow circuit around it. Despite the rain finally stopping, it was still cold, so we didn't linger.

"You'll fall in love one day," Arial assured me.

I snorted. "Sure. The same day I win the lottery."

We walked back to the bar where Arial caught an Uber and I got on my bike. I took the long way home, so I could spend more time riding. The faster I moved, the further away my problems felt. Eventually, I would have to stop and let them catch up, but for a while, I kept going, riding through the quiet neighborhoods and then, eventually, back home.

It was around ten when I walked into my office to retrieve Meriel's diary to bring it upstairs. I flipped on the light switch, but nothing happened. I flicked it a couple times but still nothing. Great. All I needed was a burned out light bulb. I didn't think I had any extras, either. I went to the small room at the back to check and tried to turn on the light in there. More darkness greeted me.

"No."

I sat down at my desk and turned on my laptop. It was plugged in, but in the bottom corner of the screen, the little battery told me it wasn't getting any power. Since I had turned it off before the power was cut, it was still at 100%. I thought I was behind by a few weeks. According to my ledger, I'd made a partial payment six weeks ago, but it had been much longer since I paid it off completely. I checked my desk drawer, looking for the bill, and found the photos and Meriel's diary instead.

Then I sighed and turned my laptop off again, gathering the photos and diary and bringing them upstairs to my apartment. There was no power in my apartment, either. I stuffed the things for the case into my backpack so I could leave for my meeting with Meriel right when I woke up in the morning. I couldn't afford to be late.

***

M eriel Jones lived in one of the most expensive neighborhoods in West Vancouver. Her house was a mansion on the banks of Burrard Inlet, hidden from the street by a large hedge and a black wrought-iron gate. And today, also hidden by a bunch of police cars. Police tape blocked my access to her driveway, so I pulled forward and parked my bike a little way down the street. As I walked back, I checked the time to ensure I was still early for my appointment.

A uniformed police officer barred entry to the house, and I strode over to him.

"Excuse me," I said. "Can you tell me what happened here?"

"No, ma'am. There's an ongoing investigation and I can't divulge any information."

"Okay. I had an appointment with Ms. Jones. It was kind of important. Is it possible to speak to her?"

"No, ma'am. But if you wait here, I'll get the detective."

"I can wait."

About fifteen minutes later, the uniform came back with another man I recognized but couldn't place. He was dressed in a suit, and I could tell immediately he was the detective in charge of whatever was going on.

"Ma'am, I'm Detective Granger," he said as he came under the tape to talk to me. "You mentioned to the officer you had an appointment with Ms. Jones."

"Yes."

"Can you tell me what that appointment was regarding?"

I pulled out my wallet and handed him a business card. "I'm a private investigator. Ms. Jones came to my office yesterday to hire me. I was coming today to discuss the details of the case and get started."

"Do you usually wait twenty-four hours to start a case?"

I bit my tongue against the urge to tell him to mind his own fucking business. I can make good decisions sometimes. I also didn't want to mention anything about the notes she had left me in case he wanted to read them. How would I explain I almost believed she wasn't human? Instead, I said, "I wasn't sure at first if I could take the case. I freed up some time later yesterday afternoon, so I called her. By the time she was able to come by with the retainer, it was a little too late to get started, so we made an appointment for me to come here today."

The detective produced a cell phone in a plastic evidence bag from his pocket. He opened it and scrolled through the recent calls. "This you?"

I looked at the screen and nodded.

"Can you tell me the details of the case you were going to be working on for Ms. Jones?"

"I would prefer if she told you herself. I try to respect my clients' privacy unless I see something illegal. There was nothing illegal about her job."

"Unfortunately, that won't be possible, Ms." He glanced at my business card. "D'Arcy. Ms. Jones was killed last night. At this point, according to our information, you were one of the last people to see her alive."

"Shit."

CHAPTER 4

We arranged I would come to the station that evening to give my statement. I rode my bike home and flicked the light switch in my office without thinking.

"Shit." I was saying that a lot lately. I locked the door behind me and pulled my blinds so no one would try to come in. Then I went to my desk and sat down.

My client was dead. I hadn't cashed the cheque she'd written me and now I couldn't. I had no way to pay my rent or my electrical bill. My bank account balance sat at the same number as when I'd checked it yesterday. Not enough to pay my full rent and then nothing left over to pay for electricity, food, or gas. It was Saturday, so I didn't have to worry about being open for potential clients, though yesterday I'd planned to. That was before my power was cut.

And now there were also all these questions I had about myself. Was Meriel actually crazy? Or if she wasn't, who—and what—was I?

I sighed and put my head in my hands until it occurred to me, I did still have something that might have at least a few answers. I got up and found a candle. Though I'd always been able to see well in the dark, with the blinds closed and how cloudy it was, I didn't want to try reading.

The first entry in the book was dated August 2, 1962. I flipped to the last entry, dated yesterday. The handwriting was the same. I read through a few entries at random. The tone was the same. The language was similar, if a little less formal in the more recent entries. Everything I saw pointed to the whole diary being written by the same person. The diary was old, too. I had no trouble believing a single person had started writing it around sixty years ago. The troubling part was thinking it was all written by Meriel.

I flipped back to the beginning and started reading.

Mother always told me the best way to feel better was to talk about what was wrong. But I have no one to talk to in this wretched world. Not even Mother or Cinnia have come to visit me. I suppose I could find another fae to talk to, but Mother also said only our own kind could truly understand us. I haven't met any other selkies since coming here. So I decided to start writing in a journal. Maybe if I can tell someone what I am feeling, even if it is only myself, it will help me feel better.

So what do I feel?

I feel cold. Even here, in what is supposed to be a hot place in the world, I feel cold. I'm always cold here.

I feel lost. I don't know where anything is. I could retreat to the sea for a time, but I would face the same problem. The sea here (they call it the Pacific Ocean) is a foreign place to me. I have lived my whole life in the Muir and know nothing else.

I feel alone. There are no other selkies. I would even settle to befriend a kelpie if I could find one. But there are no other fae from the Muir in this part of the world. I could travel. I have received some human money. I could find some place where there are others like me. But what is the use? We are none of us allowed to go home.

I continued reading and found an entry about three years after the first that finally mentioned the key she was looking for. Shortly after that, she wrote about how someone else had found it and gone home. She was crushed when she realized this time it would not be her. The journal went on. Despite the occasional entry that made her sound like a stuck-up snob or a selfish brat, the undercurrent of every one was the same: sadness, loneliness, desperation.

I understood those feelings well. I had grown up in foster care and been shipped from one house to another, one family to another, never fitting in with any of them, never finding a place for myself among them. The only person I had ever maintained a relationship with was Arial. Somehow, even if I had been sent to a family at the other end of the Lower Mainland, eventually I would wind up back in Vancouver, near enough to Arial's house to go to the same school as her.

I think if I had even a slight chance of finding the kind of home Meriel had once had, I would cling to it for decades as well.

She went on and on, year after year, searching for the key. She would mention people, but only by initials. I made notes of all the people and where she said she was when she met them. She would spend half the year in Vancouver and the other half in California. I wrote down the types of fae she mentioned, not understanding what half of them were. However, the more I read, the more I believed what I was reading.

Then, a few months ago, her entries changed slightly. She mentioned meeting someone she called AS.

After that, she didn't mention going home as often as she had previously. Instead, she sounded like she was happy, like she had found a new home. I felt at once happy for her and sad for whoever she'd left behind.

Finally, I came to the most recent entries. Yesterday, she wrote:

It's back. Mad Mab has brought it out and lost it. I talked to AS about it at dinner last night. I told him if I found it and went home, I would invite him back and we could be together in the Muir. We could don our skins and swim together there. He asked if I'd slept with RDS again. I told him I hadn't, but he didn't believe me.

He just doesn't understand. He hasn't been here as long as I have. This new information comes from a reliable source. She gave me pictures and the name of another fae living here in Vancouver. One who could help me. I am going to visit this fae today. I pray to the Ancient Mother that she will help me.

I looked through the photos again this morning. There's one of the dark Queen looking at the camera. It makes me shudder to see it. Can I live under her rule?

I must. It's the only way home.

It was the last entry. I wrote down the last few initials and checked my notes. Meriel mentioned a lot of people in the diary who might be able to help answer the questions she had stirred about myself. But I had no idea how to contact any of them.

***

I t was still early when I left my office again, so I went to my krav maga gym for a workout, hoping to release some of the pent-up energy. Arial had bought me a year membership for my birthday for the last few years, otherwise I'd never be able to afford the fees.

After I'd gotten changed, I found Sam warming up as well. I was relieved to see him since most people at the gym either wouldn't spar with me or would make full contact, which in turn drove me to make full contact. And then I ended up hurting people. But Sam would give me a good fight that would leave us both tired, but uninjured. I walked up to where he was working and lifted my chin at him when he saw me.

"Getting in a workout before heading to the bar?" I asked.

"Yeah. You?"

"Gotta head into North Van in a bit for an interview. Wanna spar?"

He agreed and after we were both warmed up, we went into the ring. We nodded to each other, indicating we were both ready, and then began. He came at me with a push that I pivoted away from, sending an elbow toward his back. He continued moving and so I missed completely and then he turned and swung a punch toward my face, which I blocked easily.

"You'll have to be faster than that," I taunted him.

He grinned and we continued, pulling the punches and kicks we would have landed, though neither of us landed many. The idea in the practice ring is to have enough control to avoid being hurt and to avoid hurting. It became an intricate dance that I lost myself in for a good twenty minutes until Sam stepped back and held up his hands.

"I'm done," he said, panting.

We'd both been practicing for a few years now and were pretty good, so we drew a small crowd of the newer people who clapped at the end of our round. Sam, ever the showman, bowed to the crowd. The owner, Tony, came into the ring and shook Sam's hand.

"You ever want to start a new career, you're always welcome to teach a class," he said, completely ignoring me. I didn't mind.

We left the ring as Tony started the morning class, and spent some time stretching before finding a spot against a wall to sit and watch the others. We each pulled out water bottles and drank. As we watched, the thoughts I'd been working hard to distance myself from came floating back.

"You know anything about folklore and fae?" I asked. Then I grimaced. I shouldn't have brought it up, but Sam didn't notice my face. He just laughed.

"You pull a job for one of the wee folk?"

"Wee folk?"

"It's what my great-granny called the fae. She was from Northern Ireland. The Irish took that shit pretty seriously for a really long time. Even a hundred years back, a lot of people in the less populated areas still believed in the wee folk." He chugged some water. "Why do you ask?"

"A client of mine mentioned the fae. She seems to believe in them." It didn't matter she was dead. Meriel still felt like my client. "If I were doing a job for your granny that she believed involved the fae, what would she think I should know about them?"

Sam considered my question for a bit. Then he said, "She'd probably tell you to be careful when making bargains with them. They're tricky and will hold you to the smallest promise. Never thank them. It puts you in their debt. There's a lot of folklore about them not being able to lie, but in my granny's stories, she always said she wasn't sure about that one. She thought there was something to it, but it wasn't black and white." He shrugged. "My grandfather and my dad said it was all nonsense."

"Maybe so. But I want to be respectful. I need the money."

"You could always come work at the bar if you need to make ends meet."

"You remember that guy last night? I don't think I'd be very good for business."

Sam grinned at me. "I'd keep you hidden in the back doing dishes or something." He stood and offered me a hand up. "See you later, Calynn. Let me know how the case turns out. I'd love to hear if you meet any fae."

CHAPTER 5

After a shower, I made my way to North Vancouver for my interview. When I got to the station, I was led to an interview room and left to wait for fifteen minutes before the detective arrived. It wasn't Granger from the crime scene. Instead, it was a detective I knew really well.

"Jeremy?"

My not-boyfriend, Jeremy Lopez, looked surprised to see me. His long, lean body showed the evidence of his exercise regimen. His suit was a little more expensive than most detectives' and fit him impeccably, showing off the broad shoulders and narrow hips that first attracted me to him. He'd told me back then his parents had left him a little money. I knew he was lying, but not about what. I couldn't tell if he'd gotten his money another way, or if he had more than he was letting on. Since we weren't serious, I'd let all of his little lies slide, and there were a few. I'd never thought it worth it to push.

"Calynn. What are you doing here?"

"I came to give a statement. I was apparently one of the last people to see to Meriel Jones before she died. Wait, now I know where I've seen Granger before. He's your partner."

Jeremy nodded and sat down across from me. "For about five years now. He didn't mention the name of the person he asked me to interview. You know I can't take your statement, right?"

"Conflict of interest. If my statement leads to an arrest, you'll have a difficult time with the defense attorney. Though I don't know how what I have to say will help. I only met her for a short time yesterday."

"Still, you'll have to wait until Granger gets back. He shouldn't be much longer. Do you want something to eat? Some coffee maybe?"

"Your coffee is probably better than mine. And if you have something to eat, that would be great. I haven't had dinner yet." Or lunch, but who was counting?

"Coming right up."

"Oh, and could I use that plug over there? I forgot to charge my phone last night."

"Sure."

He was gone and back in about ten minutes with some coffee in a Styrofoam cup and a sandwich in a clear plastic container. He set them in front of me and I brought the cup to my face, smelling it before taking a sip. It was bitter and stale, but definitely better than the coffee I'd had at my office for the last few days.

"I never understood how you can drink that stuff black," Jeremy said as I set the cup down and took a bite of the sandwich.

I shrug. "I like coffee."

"I know you do. Even the shit coffee we have here."

"All coffee has its place. Even shit coffee. And to be honest, I like it enough that I'll take what I can get."

Jeremy and I sat in an awkward silence while I ate the first half of the sandwich until Granger came in.

"Ms. D'Arcy, sorry to keep you waiting," he said in a tone that said he wasn't sorry at all. My lie detector told me his tone was more truthful than his statement. He and Jeremy exchanged nods before my not-boyfriend left me alone with his partner. I put the other half of the sandwich back in its container and stuffed it in my bag. Then I wrapped my hands around the coffee cup and waited while Granger sat down and got ready. He placed a folder in front of him, along with a digital recorder. He turned it on and recorded the date, the file number, and who we both were. Then he said, "Ms. D'Arcy, you mentioned Ms. Jones had tried to hire you."

"Yes. She came to my office early yesterday afternoon. We talked briefly. We decided I would call her back after I'd had time to consider it."

"Which you did at 4:05pm?"

I shrugged. "I guess so. Sounds about right. She seemed fine when I talked to her. Excited to get started on the case. Since she was in the area, she even stopped by to drop off a cheque for my retainer. Which I didn't cash and now can't."

"When did she leave your office yesterday?"

"The first time she was there about ten minutes maybe. The second time, maybe another ten."

"Did she say where she was going after she dropped off the cheque?"

I shook my head. "She didn't."

"Where were you last night between seven and eight?"

"I had dinner with a friend at a bar near Stadium Skytrain Station. We left the bar and went for a walk for about another half hour. I guess I left her around nine. I rode my bike for a bit and then went home."

He wrote that down, and I told him Arial's information and the name of the bar.

"What was the job Ms. Jones wanted you to do?"

"She wanted me to find a necklace her friend had lost." On the way here, I'd figured he would ask me about the case and decided this was the closest to the truth I could come without sounding completely insane.

He opened the file and slid a photo across to me. "This necklace?"

I picked up a copy of the photo I had at my office, the one of the supposed queen wearing the key.

"Yeah, that's the photo she showed me."

No wonder she'd let me keep the photos. Meriel had copies. Judging by the file, she'd had more pictures, too. What else was in that folder? My hands itched to hold it, but I kept them around the cup of coffee.

"Who is the woman in the photo?"

I wasn't going to tell him she was supposed to be the queen of faeries. "I don't know. Ms. Jones never mentioned her name. We didn't talk about many details of the job when she came by the second time. It was already late."

"So you don't know who this woman is?" He pulled out another photo of the woman with the key. She was looking at the camera this time, her wild black hair framing the snow-white skin of her face. It looked as though she'd seen the camera when this picture was taken, and she stared right at it. Her dark eyes, almost as black as her hair, seemed to look right at me through the paper. I pulled my hands away from the coffee cup so Granger couldn't see them shaking.

"Ms. D'Arcy?"

I looked up at Granger and realized I'd stopped breathing.

"I've never seen her before except in these photos." I tapped the one of her profile, not wanting to look down at those mesmerizing eyes again.

"You're sure?"

I nodded, hoping I didn't look as terrified as I felt. I couldn't explain my fear. It was just a photo. And then Meriel's words came back to me, *You're fae. I could feel the magic when I walked in the door.*

***

If I hadn't thought it was real before, the possibility stayed with me now. Jeremy called to me as I left the station, but I pretended not to hear him as I got on my bike. I revved the engine loudly and started to ride, feeling pursued. Those dark eyes haunted me the whole time, and I had to keep reminding myself to breathe. It felt like the air in my lungs had gotten heavier and I struggled to drag in a breath and blow it out. I wasn't sure how long I'd been riding or where I'd intended to go. I started heading toward home, but passed my turn and kept going straight. Before I realized where I was going, I was there, pulling into the driveway, parking next to the tree in the front yard, and rushing toward the blue front door.

As soon as I opened it and stepped past the threshold, I gasped, finally able to breathe again. I took in a couple ragged breaths as I yanked off my helmet and set it on the table Arial had placed beside the door a few years ago. "Arial?"

She came down from the second floor in pajama pants and a t-shirt, her hair still wet from a shower. "I thought that was your bike. What's up? Is everything okay?"

I wasn't sure where to start. I figured the weirdness of the dark eyes was the wrong place, but it was most prominent in my mind. Instead, I said, "Meriel Jones is dead."

"The actress?" she asked. I could see the moment her confusion changed to comprehension. Then she said, "I think this is a sit in the living room with a glass of wine kind of conversation."

She went into her kitchen and grabbed two wine glasses and filled one with white wine. She was about to pour the second when she thought better of it and took a tumbler out of her cupboard and poured a generous shot of whiskey instead. She handed me the whiskey and settled into the corner of her couch beside the chair where I had settled. "Okay. Tell me."

I told her about how Meriel was my client and we had made an appointment for this morning. How I arrived at her house and found the police. How I'd read the diary and it made sense. It made me want to believe her. How I'd gone to the station and told them what I knew of her last moments, and how the detective in charge was my sort of boyfriend's partner. Then, I mentioned the picture.

"Meriel had shown me a few of the same pictures. She called the woman the queen. I really didn't think much of it or the other weird stuff she said. But then I saw a picture of the woman and she was looking at the camera. It seemed like she was looking through the picture right at me."

"Pictures are like that sometimes."

"It wasn't like that. I could feel her eyes on me, like a weight. And the air felt heavier, like stones in my lungs. It was creepy."

Arial smiled. "So you came here so I could protect you?"

Since it had always been the other way around, I could see why she thought that was funny. I tried to give her a smile back, but it felt more like a grimace. "I honestly don't know why I came here. I was riding and then I was here." I paused, hesitating. I wanted to tell her what I was thinking, but I didn't want her to think I was insane. "There's more, Arial."

She took a sip of her wine and waited for me to continue.

"When Meriel was at my office, she said some things."

"You said she was acting a little crazy. And that journal sounds weird."

I shook my head and took a deep breath. Arial was my best friend. If I couldn't talk to her about this, I couldn't talk to anyone. "I mean she said some things about *me*. She talked about all this stuff like I was already supposed to know it. Like I was *part* of it. The key is supposed to end some kind of exile and if she found it, she could go home. She asked if I wanted to go home, too."

Arial studied her wine, and I was scared I'd gone too far.

"What did you say?" she asked quietly.

"I told her I was home. She got upset. She said I was fae and she could *feel the magic* when she came in."

She looked back up at me, a concerned frown between her eyes. "What do you think she meant?"

"I have no idea. But I've been thinking about it since reading her journal and then seeing that picture. What if she wasn't crazy? What if she knew something I don't, something that could explain why I've always felt a little bit outside of everything else? She mentioned how humans either hate us or are infatuated by us. Doesn't that describe how most people react to me?"

I was a little worried about the way she bit her lip and the fear in her eyes. But she regarded me steadily, her glass held in front of her, all but forgotten. "What are you going to do?"

"I don't know. What can I do? I can't ask her about it now. She's dead. Her journal mentions other people I might be able to ask, but only by initials. If she had their contact information, she didn't give it to me. Fuck, she probably thought I knew everyone she mentioned. She *might* have more information at her house, but I'd have to break in to even look. And that's assuming the police haven't taken it already."

Arial shrugged one shoulder, the fear disappearing from her eyes as she took a sip of her wine. "You could give it a shot."

"Break into an active crime scene? You know how much trouble I'll be in if I'm caught?"

"More than you are now? You've got no money, no clients. You're about to be evicted from your office and home. You know if that happens, you can stay here. But that doesn't really solve your problems." She hesitated, looking into her wineglass again. "I admit to a selfish reason for wanting you to look into this. It sounds a lot like some of the things my mom used to say before she got sick." She looked up again. "I'd like to know the truth. Wouldn't you?"

I hadn't thought about that before, but she was right. Still. "It's a bad idea."

She gave me her most mischievous smile. "Maybe it's a bad idea. But aren't you the one who always says that's what you're best at?"

"I *am* really good at bad ideas."

"Come on. I'll make dinner."

CHAPTER 6

We ate dinner and chatted about Arial's day at work. She kindly didn't bring up the weirdness and let me dwell on it while she fed me gossip about the latest celebrities who were in Hollywood North. She also let me think without pushing me to contribute to the conversation. By the end of dinner, I'd made my decision.

As I got ready to go, Arial asked me, "Are you going to do it?"

"I'm not going to answer that question. Plausible deniability."

She laughed. "Right." Then gave me a hug. "If you need me for anything, all you need to do is ask. That includes bail money."

I hugged her back.

The truth was, of course I was going to break into Meriel's house. I had too many questions and no other way to answer them. If I could find an address book, some way of finding the people in her journal, I could figure out what she meant when she called me fae.

I rode my bike through the quiet streets back home. When there, I changed into black jeans and a black t-shirt. The clothes looked inconspicuous, but also would help me blend into the shadows if necessary. I went downstairs to my office, found my small case for quick jobs, and made sure everything was in it. The case held my Leatherman, a lock pick set, and a mini flashlight, plus a few empty slots. I pulled out the tiny flashlight and checked the batteries were still good. The light brightened the darkness of my office.

Before I left, I did a little research on Meriel Jones on my phone, which I'd fully charged at Arial's house.

According to the Internet, Meriel had been the daughter of a wealthy businessman. Her father died a few years ago and left her all his money. She had started acting around the same time her father died, and her career took off immediately. She was an overnight success. Everyone who worked with her praised her professionalism and talent. It was like she had been acting her entire life. She was a sensation at twenty-three and people expected her to continue on the rise for many years. Until she died.

I skimmed a couple articles. One was an interview after her big debut in some blockbuster film. "I've always wanted to act," she told the magazine. "After my father passed away, I knew I couldn't wait anymore."

Another article was about her two ocean-front mansions. One in West Vancouver, the other in California. According to the writer, her family had owned the estates for almost sixty years, and both included a salt-water pool steps from the beach. I rolled my eyes as I moved to another article.

I went through four more articles, all focusing on her life and career, noting any pertinent details, then sat back. Not a single word on the Internet talked about her being a little weird. Of course, there were the Internet trolls, but none of the things they said indicated they had ever even met the woman.

I wrote some questions under my other notes. *Is all this a lie? She hadn't believed it was. Was she really what she claimed? Was she crazy? Who was her father? Because she was so famous, wouldn't someone have dug into her past and found something if there was something to find?*

After writing out my questions, I had just about convinced myself the whole thing was ridiculous. Then I glanced at her journal and remembered the first date. Her family had owned the estates for as long as she had claimed to be exiled. That was quite the coincidence.

I checked the time. It was late enough now that people would already be out for the night or settled at home. I slipped into my leather jacket and tucked my small case into my pocket before pulling on my leather gloves. At the last moment, I grabbed the journal as well and stuffed it into my small backpack before going back to my bike. The ride out to Meriel's house was quick with little traffic clogging the roads. I rode through her neighborhood, where a single police cruiser parked on the street with two silhouettes in the front seat. The front gate had yellow police tape crisscrossing it. It wasn't going to be easy to get inside.

I rode a block away and parked under a no parking sign on a dead end street. Brush and trees separated me from the beach. It didn't look like I could get through that way. I left my helmet with the bike but kept on my jacket, riding gloves, and backpack. I stayed in the shadows, walking along the street back through the neighborhood, counting the houses I passed. Based on what I'd seen online, there were twelve houses between the side street where I'd parked and Meriel's house. When I got to the fourth house from Meriel's, I slipped into the backyard and started through it toward the beach.

I noticed a black cat sitting on the patio table cleaning itself. It stopped as I came into the yard and looked at me, its yellow eyes glowing in the moonlight. I scanned the area cautiously. Where there were cats, there could be dogs. And dogs were loud. This yard had a six-foot fence along both edges, separating it from the neighbors. At the end of the property, the fence was shorter and made of glass with a gate allowing access to Burrard Inlet stretching out beyond. I started toward the gate, figuring to take the beach to Meriel's property instead of hopping the fences from yard to yard. I stayed to one side in case the home-owners looked out their back window. They did something worse. About three quarters of the way to the back fence, the homeowner opened the door and let the dog into the yard. I heard the door close again, and the dog left the deck and moved to the grass. She sniffed the ground close to where I had come over the fence and then started in my direction. I looked at the gate and back at the dog. If I was going to make it, I'd have to run. She saw me move and started barking. I added as much speed as I could and made it to the gate before she caught up. The gate opened out to the beach, and I was through by the time the dog reached me. I slammed it closed on her nose, and she continued barking at me, following me along the edge of the fence until she couldn't anymore.

"Daisy! What are you barking at?" I heard someone shout.

I didn't stick around to see if the homeowner was going to investigate and fled down the beach.

I made it past Meriel's neighbors and to her backyard. She hadn't bothered with a fence or gate, preferring, I suppose, the unobstructed view of the water. I walked up through her property, past the Olympic-sized, saltwater pool which was surrounded by a glass fence. The crystal clear water steamed slightly in the chilly October night.

I worked my way around the building until I found an unlocked basement window. As I opened it and shimmied inside, I thought idly it shouldn't be considered breaking and entering if you didn't break anything.

I dropped into the basement and pulled out my flashlight, shining it around to see an at-home gym. A treadmill and elliptical machine faced a large flat screen while a full set of weights, a yoga mat, and stability ball waited in a far corner. I moved to the stairs and started up, noting as I went a complete lack of creaking. I opened the door to the main floor slowly. It swung open silently. I made a note of that: Meriel, or someone who worked for her, kept the house from making any noise. This would have been a benefit to the person who had killed her. The killer could have come in and killed Meriel before she had even realized she was in danger.

At the top of the stairs, I shone my light around Meriel's garage. A bright blue Porsche and a dark green Ferrari took up two spots in the three-car garage. Why have one luxury car when you can have two? I took out my phone and snapped a picture of the cars and their plates, strictly for thoroughness, before finding the door into the house and turning the flashlight off before I went in.

I made my way past a pantry into an enormous kitchen. Marble counter tops gleamed in a U-shape around a marble island. It was open concept with the dining room straight ahead of me and a great room to my right. Both dining room and great room had a wall of windows overlooking the patio, the pool, and Burrard Inlet beyond. It was a million-dollar view that matched everything I currently knew about the recently deceased actress.

The main living area would have been spotlessly clean except for all the dust and sticker markers where they had taken pictures of fingerprints. I tugged at each glove to make sure they were securely in place.

Starting in the kitchen, I opened drawers, looking for a junk drawer where Meriel might keep an address book. I found nothing useful. There was nothing interesting in the great room or dining room either, so I moved to search the rest of the house.

There was a hall to the right of the great room and another to the left of the dining room. I decided to start on the right and as I passed by the couch, I glanced at the pictures sitting on the table behind it.

Most of them were of Meriel. There were none of a man who could potentially be the father she claimed to love so much.

I continued to the hall, and it led me to a master suite that would have been luxurious if someone hadn't been murdered in there. The furniture included a bed, a chair, and a couple of side tables, neither of which held a drawer where I might find what I was looking for. But it was all beautiful. The bed was massive and faced the floor to ceiling windows and looked as though someone was about to climb into it. The chair looked cozy set by the windows on the far side of the room from a door leading to the patio, which was just to my left hand. Unfortunately, the plush white carpet in front of the chair was horrendously stained with a huge splotch of blood. Most of the blood spatter was on the chair and windows beside it, telling me Meriel had been standing at the foot of her bed, beside the chair when she'd been shot. The killer had stood right about where I was standing.

I noticed a small table beside the chair with a book on it. The police had left an exhibit placard next to the book but hadn't bagged it. I stepped over the blood patch to look at the book. The title was *A Selkie in Summer* and I noticed a bookmark halfway through. A wave of sadness washed through me with the realization she would never finish it. I could imagine her sitting in this chair, setting the book down to go to bed, and then standing only to be shot. As I turned away, I remembered that's what she had called herself in her journal. A selkie.

On one of her bedside tables sat a picture of Meriel with a man. They had their arms wrapped around each other and looked happy. Happier than I had seen her in the pictures in her living room. I took a picture of the picture, figuring the man was important to her. Potentially the AS she had mentioned in her journal.

I left the master bedroom; it contained nothing I'd need. I went, instead, into the master bathroom in search of a walk-in closet. I wasn't disappointed.

The bathroom looked like a private spa and beauty salon. The double vanity stretched the full length of the room, neatly organized with enough makeup and accessories to last me three lifetimes. I could almost swim in the soaker tub, and the shower would comfortably fit five people. Just past the shower and tub was the largest walk-in I'd ever seen. I moved around the closet, looking for anything that might be useful. All I found were designer shoes, glasses, handbags, and outfits. I couldn't have afforded a single item.

No boxes of papers on a top shelf or hidden on the floor beneath long dresses and coats. No hidden doors, nothing of interest. Again.

I was just about to leave the closet and search the rest of the house when I noticed a strange leather jacket. I wasn't sure what drew me to it as I pulled it off the rack and held it up. It was a pale brown, buttery leather and the lining was like satin, but the shape was weird. It had short sleeves and a really long back. Remembering Meriel's size, if she had worn it, the sleeves would not have quite passed her elbows and the back would have fallen to around her knees. It had no zipper or buttons to close it and no tags to announce the designer. Something about the jacket made me want to bring it with me, but I knew the police would have started an inventory and I couldn't risk it. Instead, I hung it on a hook, closed the door, and turned on a light. I took a few pictures, front and back, before putting the jacket back where I had found it. As I did, the smell of the ocean wafted up from the strange piece, salty and damp. I shook my head and turned out the light before continuing to search, feeling a little foolish for thinking a leather jacket so important.

The rest of the wing on that side of the house held nothing of value. There were two guest suites, one of which was actually a guest suite. The other had been converted into another walk-in closet, only bigger, but still with no papers or anything I might consider useful. In conclusion, Meriel had enough clothes to fill a shopping mall for a size two, but no clutter.

As I made my way to the other wing of the house, I compared my wardrobe to Meriel's: five pairs of jeans, three blue, two black; ten cotton t-shirts, white, blue, and black; one black leather jacket; a couple sets of workout clothes; and one nice dress for special occasions. I had one pair of nice shoes to match my dress, which I hated, and one pair of runners for working out. Otherwise, I wore my black leather boots. Some might say I was a minimalist. I'd probably just say I was broke.

I crossed the house and found a third guest suite. This one had been converted into a photo studio complete with camera equipment, back drops, fans, and props. Whatever the motive for her murder, it wasn't theft. The camera equipment alone would have been worth thousands of dollars. I still didn't see anything in there that could help me, so I moved toward the last room in the house.

The office. Finally.

Of course, the police had already searched here, as was evident since the rest of the house was tidy, while this room had drawers pulled open and cupboard doors left ajar. I sat at the desk—situated next to the door instead of across from it to take advantage of the ocean views—and searched each of the open spaces, finding nothing in the way of an address book. More of the photos of the supposed queen and key sat in a haphazard pile, the police having taken a few and left the rest. There had also been a laptop plugged in to the printer on the other side of the desk, the cord that had connected them lying uselessly next to the mouse.

I set my teeth together in frustration. The police had obviously taken whatever had been here to find.

The last place to search, a bookcase next to the desk, didn't inspire me with much confidence. But I stood to search it anyway. It held a few books, a framed poem, and a few other knickknacks. Since I was at the back of the house, and the police cruiser was at the front, I took the risk and turned my flashlight back on to read the book titles. There were a few books on Celtic myths, another couple on selkies. The framed poem was called "Seal Woman" and the first line talked about a selkie dreaming alone. The author had signed the poem thanking Meriel for her help. I took a few more pictures of the items on the bookshelf, noting the small seal statues set out among the books and the poem.

But none of the books on the shelf were an address book, or even another journal. Nothing useful. I had nowhere to go from here.

I moved to the floor-to-ceiling windows and gazed out at the water. "What am I even doing here?" I wondered out loud. The whole idea to break in here was ridiculous and a completely useless risk.

I leaned my forehead against the glass, considering my next move, when I noticed the reflection of a painting. The ocean superimposed over the real thing. Something tightened in my chest. My instincts screamed that this was the path to what I searched for. I turned around.

The painting was huge. I'd seen it when I came in but hadn't really paid attention to it. Meriel struck me as the kind of person who wouldn't skimp on decorative items. But as I looked at the painting behind the desk, I realized she hadn't put up any other paintings in the entire house. There were decorative features and photographs, but this was the only painting.

I regarded it closely, noting the detail in the waves and the rocks. A seal bobbed with just its head out of the water in the surf. The frame was ornate and heavy, it alone probably cost a fortune.

That instinct had me moving around the desk to get a closer look at it, lifting it up from the wall to see if a safe hid behind it. No luck. Then I looked down at the floor and noticed four of the hardwood boards weren't staggered like the rest. They lined up perfectly right below the ergonomic leather chair. I moved the chair out of the way and crouched down, feeling along the edge of the boards. They didn't seem to be connected to the boards in front of them. I tried to lift them up but couldn't get a good grip. They didn't do much more than shift against my nails. But since none of the other flooring in the whole house shifted or squeaked, I figured I was finally on to something.

My heart started beating faster as I stood up and found a fancy letter opener on display at the front of the desk. It slipped easily into the space, like it had been designed for this purpose, and I pried up the boards. They came up, attached with thin strips of wood and hinged at the wall. The tongue portion of the tongue-and-groove floorboards had been stripped where necessary.

In the cavity was a small safe, set into the foundation of the house. It really was the smartest place to hide a safe. Walls could easily be torn apart with a hammer. Setting a safe in a concrete floor protected the sides and kept burglars from stealing the safe and dealing with opening it later. The only way in would be to crack it.

It was an electronic lock that required a code. Since I was familiar with safes, I knew models like this one could be anywhere from a three- to eight-digits. To make it just a little bit more difficult, it was alphanumeric with an A and a B in addition to the numbers. I also knew, as cautious as someone could be with their safe, they wouldn't always wipe it down after typing in the code, leaving fingerprints behind. I grabbed some tape from Meriel's desk and placed a strip over each column of buttons. When I pulled each strip off, I was in luck. I found a notepad and pen on her desk and wrote down the numbers she had touched. The code included a three, four, five, seven, and A. I tried typing that in but the cursor kept blinking indicating I needed more digits. I typed in three again and then one more time before the safe beeped and flashed the wrong code message. A seven-digit code meant two of the numbers repeated. I tapped the pad of paper with the pen, thinking. These numbers would probably not be a date. I checked the time. I probably should get out of here before a cop did a walk of the property or something.

I could go home, consider the code, and return tomorrow with some possibilities. And the proper tools to break into the safe, if necessary. I stood and stared at the painting with the seal. Then the instinct that had driven me toward the painting began putting pieces together. I thought of the poem and the books. The word that came up again and again. Selkie. Six letters. It was what she claimed to be. That was why I was here, wasn't it? She thought she and I were both fae.

I found the keypad on my phone. Under each number were three letters. I wrote out the word and what each corresponding number would be. It matched the numbers I had. The only extra thing was the A. A for AS? With a shrug, I gave it a try using the A as the first digit. The safe opened with a beep and a clunk.

My heart pounding in my chest, I pulled the door open, and it swung on well-oiled hinges. I shone my light into the small safe. The first thing I pulled out was a roll of money, followed by a second and a third. I put all three rolls into my inside jacket pocket. There had to be at least a thousand dollars in each roll, maybe even as much as five. The police didn't know about it, obviously since it was still here, so it was safe to take it, along with anything else inside. And let's be honest here, I needed the money more than Meriel did. I pulled out a small notebook next. My breath caught in my throat. It was a contacts book with a bunch of names in it. I took off my backpack and slid it, and the notepaper where I had written her safe code, in next to Meriel's journal. I found an Irish passport for Meriel McTaves next, the picture of Meriel Jones looking bored on the first page. It followed the address book and note paper into my pack. The last thing in the safe was a small vial filled with water. It felt strange in my hand, almost as if it was humming and vibrating. My hand felt hot where it held the glass. Whatever it was, I needed to take it with me as well. I wasn't sure why, but I knew it as simply as I knew the strange leather jacket was special. It seemed well sealed, so I put it into the case with my supplies, into one of the empty spots secured by a small elastic band. I put away my flashlight as well and zipped the case shut, sliding it into my jacket pocket. Then I put my backpack back on and closed the safe.

The lock beeped again as it re-engaged and I shut the floor board door. If the police ever found the safe, they would find it empty. They might wonder about it, but they would never know I had stolen anything.

I was about to stand up and replace the letter opener where I had found it, leaving everything exactly the way the police had last seen it, when a chill ran down my spine. The room seemed to grow slightly darker, the shadows slightly heavier. Operating on instinct alone, I twisted, the letter opener already in my hand. It sank almost two inches into a man's knee and I left it there, rolling out of his way as he grunted from the pain and swung a gun toward my head.

As I put the desk between us, he fired a single shot that lodged in the wall. I noticed several things at once. The man was possibly the tallest man I had ever seen. He was also possibly the blackest man I had ever seen, dressed head to toe in black leather, skin like ebony where I could see it to the top of his perfectly bald head. He even wore black, wrap-around sunglasses, and I wondered how he could see anything in the dark. He practically blended in with the shadows and if I had ignored my instinct, I would be dead right now. The last thing I noticed was that he used a gun with a suppressor. While the police would definitely know we had been here now, due to the shiny new bullet hole in the wall, no one would hear it if he killed me. Not even the officers parked right outside. I was on my own.

"You cannot hide from me, changeling. Come out and I will kill you quickly."

I shuddered at the sound of his voice. It sounded like it was made from shadows, and I could all but feel the darkness of it as it caressed my skin. Crouching with the hard wood of the desk at my back, I said, "While that is an intriguing offer, I think I'll decline. I'm not much for the dying part."

A small clattering sound told me he had pulled the letter opener out of his knee and dropped it. I couldn't hear him moving, but I hadn't heard him as he came up the hall so that didn't mean anything. I pulled my case back out and took out the flashlight and Leatherman. I put the pouch away again and pulled the knife out of the handle. Talk about bringing a knife to a gunfight, but it was all I had. My best bet would be to somehow get the gun away from him.

I wasn't sure how I was going to accomplish that, but I knew I would never be able to while crouched on the floor. I had one chance. I psyched myself up, reminding myself I had been practicing krav maga for the past four years and had been training for situations just like this. I gripped the knife and light in my left hand, my thumb just touching the flashlight's on/off button. I tried to remember everything I had learned about explosive movement and how to disarm opponents in the space of a single second. Then I jumped up and turned in the same motion. I found the man in the dark and turned the light on, shining it directly in his eyes.

Considering the sunglasses, I wasn't sure how effective the light would be, so I was surprised when he grunted louder than he had when I stabbed him. He held up his hand to shield his eyes, and that gave me a moment to move in and grab the gun with my free hand. I grabbed in desperation. I couldn't allow him to get another shot off or I'd be dead. My hand wrapped around the barrel of the gun. I yanked it toward me with all the strength I could, but I was used to disarming with two hands and the light slipped down. As soon as it was no longer shining in his eyes, he seemed to recover and ripped the gun back out of my grip.

"You don't need to do this," I said as he aimed the gun at me.

Unlike all the bad guys in all the movies ever, he didn't respond. He just pulled the trigger.

And the gun exploded in his hand.

He tried to flinch away from the flying pieces of the gun, but they seemed to follow him. While he was still recovering, I struck out with my foot to the knee I had already stabbed. I heard it crack before he fell back into the glass window, shattering it. I followed him out onto the patio and started running toward the beach.

Sprinting on sand, especially sand covered in rocks and driftwood, was treacherous at best. I did it anyway, counting houses until I reached the spot of brush that separated where I parked from the beach. I pushed my way through and made it to my bike. I drove away as fast as I could, again feeling like I couldn't breathe.

CHAPTER 7

I made it back to my apartment in record time. I slammed the door and locked it behind me, leaning against it as I tried to work some of the adrenaline out of my system. I was fairly certain I had just met Meriel's killer. Why had he gone back to the crime scene? And why had he tried to kill me? Unless he had wanted one of the items in the safe that I took with me, he could have just waited for me to leave and then taken whatever he wanted from the house.

Setting my bag on the kitchen table, I went to my sink and turned on the hot water, letting it run for a bit to get it as hot as I could. I pulled my canister of instant coffee from the cupboard and ignored how my hands still shook as I spooned some into a mug. I couldn't boil water since my power was still out, but the hot water was heated for the building. I filled my cup and took a bunch of deep breaths as I slowly stirred the instant coffee into the hot water. I breathed in the coffee's scent and took a sip, letting it calm me even as I grimaced at the taste. Coffee had always made me feel a little bit calmer, more grounded. The steps to make it, the smell of it. It brought me back to the good moments of my childhood. I would be at Arial's house, before her mother's illness got really bad, and she would make coffee in the morning. I took another sip, feeling more like myself, and then set the cup on the table with my bag.

I found a few candles and lit them before taking things out of my backpack. I removed the pouch from my jacket pocket first and examined the small bottle of water again before setting it in the center of the table, figuring I had other, more interesting things to consider. I was wrong. The water caught the light from the candles and lit up the entire room.

I jumped. Maybe I yelped. A little. When my heart started beating in a regular rhythm again, I moved closer to the table and carefully lifted the bottle up out of the light of the candles. The light went out of the bottle.

I slowly brought it back toward the candlelight and as soon as the light touched the bottle, it lit up again. I set it down in the middle of the table and stared at it.

The bottle was about six inches of clear glass, including the round stopper. It had a rounded bottom and a long, thin neck. The liquid inside was also clear and filled the round part of the bottle almost completely to the neck. I had thought it was just water, despite it feeling warm in my hand. But now that it was glowing, I wasn't sure.

Even though I was a bit afraid to open the bottle, the light made me feel the way a night light makes a toddler feel when they're afraid of the dark. I left the bottle on the table, lighting up the room, as I took out the two notebooks, the passport, and the money.

The first thing I did was unroll the money. The woman may be dead, but I wasn't, and I had bills to pay. Each roll consisted of twenty-five hundred-dollar bills. Seven thousand five hundred dollars. What with the money and the attempted murder, I figured I was officially hired to investigate Meriel's death.

I set aside enough to pay my electric bill and next month's rent and then put the rest into the safe in my bedroom closet. Then I went back to the table and opened the address book.

I took out the notes I had written while reading her journal the first time. There were a lot of initials, but I noted a few I would have the most luck finding. She had said BB was her assistant and never mentioned losing her. I figured that would be something Meriel would have written about, so I looked BB up in the address book and found her entry.

Each entry had a name and a type of fae that seemed to account for the initials. BB was Bidina, Brownie, and it was a name I recognized from my research on Meriel. Bidina Evans had been her personal assistant. Each entry in the book also had either Summer or Winter next to it and then the phone number and address. I noted all the information Meriel had on Bidina and then moved on to find AS. His real name was Angor and, as she mentioned in her notebook, he was a selkie, like she was. Next to that was "Summer" and a heart. My own heart cracked at seeing the childish doodle, so I moved on quickly to Ronan and Killian, who Meriel had mentioned during our last conversation.

I found Killian first and wrote out that he was a dwarf and Winter. My hand slowed as I wrote his information. He lived in Squamish, a few hours north of the city. She had said he'd been exiled for over a hundred years.

Finally, I found Ronan's name. He was a daoine sidhe and Winter, whatever that meant. I recorded his address and phone number.

I tapped my pen against the page. Given how long she had been writing in her journal, these were the only ones I could be certain would still be at the addresses in the book. Though I believed I could contact any of them. The address book had a few updated entries, I assumed, from when the person had moved. She had even marked if a person had returned to the *Sidhe*, not the *she*. Including the lack of squeaking floor boards and the tidy house, everything I'd found told me Meriel had been a meticulous person.

I considered the four names I had noted. Bidina would likely have the most useful information about Meriel and why someone might have murdered her. According to Meriel's journal, they'd been working together for the past fifteen years. I should probably talk to Angor about Meriel as well. But the thought of talking to him and seeing him heartbroken wasn't something I was ready for. Seeing him *not* heartbroken would be worse.

When I read Ronan's name, that instinct shivered through me again. Logically, I could say he would be a good choice to talk to. Meriel had mentioned how he'd taken over for Killian. Taken over what? Regardless, he obviously held some position of authority. But even without logic, that instinct had never steered me wrong before.

I made some more notes and then read through the journal one more time. I felt strange reading the words of a woman who would never write again. But as I read further, I simply got pulled into her story. This time, I allowed myself to see the person behind the words. And she was a lonely woman. I had felt the same pain she felt, had lived the same loneliness. Outside society. Looking in. Wanting to belong. When I got to the part about Angor, I wanted to skip it. They had started to build something together, and now she had been taken away. I tried not to think about the loneliness *he* must be feeling now.

I was about to turn the page when my head started to ache. I checked the time to see that I'd officially been awake for twenty-four hours. The last bit of coffee in my cup had long since gone cold. I blew out the candles on the table to find the sun streaming through the bedroom window. I hadn't noticed it with the glow from the water lighting up the apartment.

I looked down at the notebooks again. The adrenaline from the fight had worn off. I felt like I'd been hit by a semi-truck and my eyelids were being drawn inexorably closed. I stood up and went to my bed, falling into it and into sleep. I didn't even take the time to close the curtains and so I slept bathed in autumn sunlight.

CHAPTER 8

About an hour's drive outside Vancouver, in a rural area of South Langley, I found Ronan's address from Meriel's notebook. I'd slept for about three hours, which didn't feel like nearly enough. I parked my bike on his property beside a small tree in front of his house that reminded me of the one in Arial's front yard. The tree was about six feet tall and covered in small green leaves and bright red berries, despite the late season. I paused next to it, reaching out to touch a leaf, rubbing it between my fingers. It felt familiar, like I had seen it before. Or one similar. I thought of the strange jacket in Meriel's closet. Then I shook my head. I had things to do. Questions to ask. It was just a silly tree.

The house in front of me was a small, blue, cottage-style house with a wrap-around porch and large white columns framing the wide steps. I climbed them and knocked on the white door.

The man who answered the door was dressed in black. He wore black jeans and a black t-shirt. Even his hair was black and looked as though he had spent the day running his fingers through it. He was over six feet tall, broad-shouldered and looked like he could work on the farm where he lived. Or at the very least, worked out religiously.

He was also gorgeous. My mouth went dry as I stared at him. I was glad of that fact because otherwise, I'd likely be drooling. I was close enough to him that his scent reached out, enveloping me in a pine forest. But it was more than just that. Something colder. The way the air smelled on a freezing winter morning when the sky was clear and the sun was shining. Something deep inside me unfurled and relaxed, as though it had been waiting to meet this man.

"What are you doing here?" he asked.

His sharp tone pulled me from my stupid thoughts of pine forests and glaciers. I couldn't think of how to respond at first. He spoke as though he knew who I was, but I was certain I would remember if I had met this man before.

"Do I know you?"

"Do I *look* like someone you know?"

I looked into his green eyes and realized he was angry. I'd never been more confused in my life.

"No."

He spotted my bike behind me. "Park your bike in the garage and then come inside before anyone sees you."

He slammed the door in my face. I went back to my bike as the garage door slid up. I walked it inside and found the man looking at me with a measure of resignation. The door started coming back down and he said, "Follow me."

I did without comment. He brought me through a mud room into a bright kitchen. He motioned to the dining table and went into the kitchen. "Coffee?" he asked as I sat down.

If I were a little less tired, a little less confused, I would have made some quip about him being my hero or something. Instead, I said, "Yes. Just black."

He poured two cups from the coffeemaker and brought them back to the table. I took the cup he gave me and smelled it, closing my eyes as the scent helped ease the tension I'd felt since arriving. I took a sip and set the cup down. He sat across from me and I tapped the cup with my fingertip, unsure what to say or do next. I waited for him to say something first. Finally, he did.

"How did you find me?"

I sighed with relief as my brain started moving again. The case. I took out my phone and showed him the picture of his address in Meriel's book I had taken when I'd woken up.

"You seemed like the most logical first person to talk to. Meriel mentioned you the other day. She made it sound like you might have answers. I need some."

He took the phone and scanned the image.

"Where is she now?"

"Dead."

He shook his head, but didn't seem too distraught. "May the Sidhe bring her peace."

He looked up at me again and I fell into his eyes. They were green like emeralds, dark and glittering and hard. I couldn't look away. I was having trouble breathing again, but it didn't scare me like it had before. This time, I felt safe, like when the strange water created the glow in my apartment. Startled at first, but safe.

It was more than the initial attraction I'd felt at the front door. I'd been attracted to men before. This felt more powerful, more stable, more right than anything I'd felt before.

He closed his eyes and bowed his head. He seemed just as shocked by our reaction to one another as I was.

He cleared his throat. "You mentioned you need answers. What are your questions?"

I hesitated for a moment before responding. I was here to find Meriel's killer. I should start with a question about her. But what I heard myself say was: "What am I?"

He looked up again sharply. "You don't know?"

I shook my head. "Meriel came to my office two days ago and called me fae. She seemed to think I was like her and asked why I didn't want to go home. She wanted me to find a key. I thought she was crazy, even though some things she said made a lot of sense—though she didn't really say much. I decided to take her case anyway, partly because I wanted to ask more questions about what she thought about me. When I went to meet her yesterday, she was already dead. Since then, strange things have been happening."

"Like what?"

"I saw a picture of a woman and felt like I couldn't breathe." I took out the photo of the Queen Meriel had left me and showed it to him. "Not this picture, but one of her, looking at the camera."

"The Queen of Air and Darkness."

"Meriel said that. What do you mean, air and darkness?"

"One thing at a time. What else strange has happened?"

"I broke in to Meriel's house and found this."

I showed him the picture of the strange leather jacket on my phone.

He nodded, validating my feeling the jacket was important.

"Then I found her safe and found this." I had also taken a picture of the vial of water this morning and showed it to him. "It glowed in the candlelight in my apartment. Lit up the whole place. She also had an extra passport and her journal starts in 1962."

"The year she was exiled. Anything else?"

"Just the guy who tried to kill me."

He arched his eyebrow. "You might have started with that one."

I shrugged. "That wasn't weird."

"People try to kill you all the time?"

"No. But I understand it. People kill people all the time. It's not weird. What is weird is a twenty-three-year-old girl doesn't start writing a diary around sixty years ago."

He looked down at the photo I'd brought him and the picture on my phone. He didn't say anything. He didn't call me crazy. My heart was pounding as I waited for him to say more.

"What do you think you know?"

I swallowed and took a deep breath. "In Meriel's address book, it says your name is Ronan. You're apparently a type of fae called a daoine sidhe." I said the strange words slowly, sounding out the letters.

He still winced at my pronunciation. "It's pronounced 'dee-nih-she'. But yes, I am a daoine sidhe from the Winter court." He pointed to the picture of the Queen. "This is my Queen."

Complete, untainted truth. Either he and Meriel were both delusional or I had to accept it was real. My breath caught in my throat, but I forced the question past it.

"Okay. So, am I fae?"

"Yes. You are also daoine sidhe. Which is why Meriel could sense that you're fae. She wouldn't have known what you were."

"Why not?"

"She was a lesser fae. She was a selkie."

"What's a selkie?"

He sighed, his eyes closing in frustration. "This is going to take forever. You know nothing about this world."

I set my teeth together as my frustration boiled over. Then I said, "You're right. I don't. How did I end up here? Why did I think I was human? Why did I not know I was different? Is any of this real?"

"It is real. And the short answer to the rest of your questions is you're a changeling."

"The guy who tried to kill me said that word. What does it mean?" I'd meant to look it up, but with the adrenaline rush followed by a lack of sleep, I'd forgotten.

"A changeling is a fae who has been exchanged with a human child. The fae grows up in the human world. The human grows up in the Sidhe. Both are considered changelings. Though humans can also be brought to the Sidhe in exchange for inanimate objects like pieces of wood. Obviously, as you are certainly fae but grew up here in the human world, you are a changeling."

I dropped my head into my hands. "None of this makes any sense. I don't even know if I believe in all this."

"What's not to believe?"

"That fairies exist. That there's a queen of the faeries."

"There's two, actually."

I glared up at him. "You're not helping."

He had the audacity to laugh at me. "Little changeling. You don't have to believe. It won't change anything. You just have to decide. Will you accept it and move on or deny it and stay as you were."

"I can do that?"

He nodded. "You can choose to stay human. Choose your human life. Or you can choose your fae life. Choose to be daoine sidhe."

"What happens if I choose my human life?"

"Things will stay as they are now. You will continue as you are. You will grow old, and you will die. Like all the other humans."

"And if I choose to be daoine sidhe?" I said it slowly so I got the pronunciation correct this time.

"Your life will change. You will meet new people and do things you never thought possible. Nothing will be the same for you ever again. It might be better. It might be worse. You won't know until after you've chosen. And once you choose to be daoine sidhe, you can never go back to being only human."

I regarded him for a moment tapping my finger against the coffee cup I held. I thought about what he had said and realized I believed he was telling the truth. Or at least *he* believed he was telling the truth. I hadn't felt a single lie.

"How can I make a decision like that?"

He shrugged and stood up. "You'll have to think of that yourself. I have work I must see to. Feel free to stay here and think until I get back, but if you do, you'll have to stay until morning or else the Queen could see you leaving."

He started toward the back door.

"How? And why does it matter?"

"She is the Queen of Air and Darkness. She can see what she chooses in the dark. And I do not want her gaze focused on me."

"Will she not see me here?"

"She can't look past thresholds. Stay or go. It's your choice. But you must make it in the next three hours. If you're still here when I return, we will talk more, and I'll answer your questions as best I can."

"But why is she looking at me?"

"I can't answer that," he said with a shrug.

"Where are you going?"

"To find the ranch foreman. I need to go over a few things with him. I'll be back around sundown."

Then he left.

I explored his house. It was an open-concept, modern farmhouse with a lot of wood and stone. The cupboards were green and the countertops were poured concrete. The appliances were old-style porcelain and gleamed in the light. The kitchen was a good size and flowed into the dining room, where I sat at a large wooden table. The living room had a cozy-looking couch and armchair set before a large stone fireplace.

I got up from the table and, after putting our mugs in the sink, moved into the living room. A wooden staircase led to the second floor and next to the stairs, a door stood open to a large office with a huge wooden desk cluttered with papers. I wanted to snoop—that was my job after all—but refrained and went up the stairs instead. On the second floor, I found a small guest bedroom and the master. The bed in the master was as big as Meriel's but this one had no elaborate frame and hadn't been made that morning. I thought of Ronan in that bed and decided it was time to leave the room. I went up some more stairs to a loft area. It had been set up as a library. A couple of cozy chairs faced a window looking South. I sat down in one and looked out over Ronan's land.

His property stretched in the distance, fields falling dormant as autumn came to an end. There were houses here and there, but I couldn't tell where Ronan's land ended and theirs began since there were no fences. It almost seemed as though they were all one. But who would live in them? The foreman he mentioned, possibly. But what about the others? I could see Ronan moving toward one of the houses in the distance.

He was fae. I was fae. Meriel was fae. How was all this real? I thought about my life, how I'd never really found a peaceful spot. The cage that my life felt like. How, while I loved solving the puzzles my job gave me, it never seemed to give me quite enough. Not enough challenge, not enough resolution, and definitely not enough money. I thought about how I'd never found love. I thought about how lonely I'd been. Arial was the only one I felt really connected to. I had been given up for adoption when I was still a baby and finding my birth parents several years ago hadn't been a good experience. If all this was true, those people hadn't even been my real parents. So, who were? And what happened to the girl who had been taken in my place? I already knew who I was as a human. This life felt confining, like it didn't quite fit. There really was never any choice for me once Ronan told me I wasn't human. I needed to figure it out. I needed to discover who I really was.

I curled up in a chair sinking into the cushions and breathing in the scent of pine and ice. The turmoil in my mind finally slowed until I drifted off to sleep.

CHAPTER 9

I was awake in an instant, somehow understanding I'd woken because the sun had set and there was no safety in the dark. I shivered as I recalled those black eyes, but it didn't feel like they were watching me here.

I heard a door open and close downstairs as Ronan came back.

"Little changeling," he called. "Come down when you want to talk."

I stood from the chair and stretched. Then I made my way down to his kitchen, where someone had made dinner. The table had been set with two places, and dishes of food steamed in the center. It smelled amazing.

"How did you know I was still here?"

Ronan was looking in the fridge and didn't look at me when he answered. "I could still feel you here."

"Oh."

"Plus, your motorcycle is still in my garage."

"Right."

He straightened with a brown bottle in one hand and looked at me, gesturing to the beer.

I nodded and then waited until he was sitting at the table across from me to say, "What does it feel like?"

"What does what feel like?"

"Another daoine sidhe. Or even just another fae. Meriel said she could feel the magic when she came into my office. You seemed to as well. Why can't I?"

"You probably can. You just don't recognize it. Meriel and I grew up surrounded by magic and the fae. This world has so little magic in it, it's easy to know when another person has some, even a little."

"Who made this food?"

"Aelwyd."

He certainly had an infuriating way of answering questions without actually answering them.

He took the lid off the first dish and started taking out some roast beef. Then he moved to the next dish.

"And is Aelwyd going to eat with us?" I hadn't noticed anyone in the house with me, but I'd been sleeping. Whoever Aelwyd was, she hadn't woken me.

"No."

"Why not?"

"Eat. I'm not answering anything until I've at least started my dinner."

My stomach encouraged me to do what he said. I dished some of the beef onto my plate before moving to the dishes of carrots and mashed potatoes. I poured some gravy over the potatoes and meat and started eating.

It was amazing. Everything was cooked perfectly. The carrots were still crunchy in the middle and covered in a pepper and butter sauce. The potatoes were creamy and the gravy added the perfect flavor of beef to them. The roast was medium rare and melted in my mouth. Everything on my plate was gone before I knew I had finished it and I started scooping more. I couldn't remember the last time I'd eaten food this delicious.

I stopped scooping when I noticed Ronan staring at me. I could tell by his eyes he was laughing at me.

"Don't stop on my account. I'll tell Aelwyd you're a fan. She'll be pleased."

I continued eating, but slower. "Who is she?"

"She's a brownie who lives here with her family. She takes care of this house while her mother takes care of their house."

"Why?"

He shrugged. "That's their way. They choose houses to care for and then they do." He drank from his beer.

"So, where do we start?" I asked him.

"What do you want to know?"

"Everything."

He arched an eyebrow. Then he thought for a moment. "I guess we should start with the Sidhe's social structure. It's likely the thing most fae would say is the most important feature of our culture. The Sidhe is mostly separated into two ruling courts: Summer and Winter. Though there are fae who do not belong to either court, most do. A queen rules each court."

"The Queen of Air and Darkness."

Ronan nodded as he took another bite of his dinner. "She is the Queen of Winter. Her sister queen is Titania, the Queen of Light and Beauty."

"They're sisters?"

"No. They're called sisters. It's complicated to explain and not something to get into on the first day. Anyway. The Queens are daoine sidhe, which is the ruling class of the entire Sidhe. There are nobles and non-nobles among the daoine sidhe but among other fae, they are the elite. All daoine sidhe have control over at least one element."

"Air and darkness, light and beauty."

"Exactly. There are eight elements. The main elements, air, water, earth, and fire, and the lesser elements, darkness, flora, light, and metal."

"Beauty isn't one of the elements."

Ronan shrugged. "It's what she's called and she is not my queen. I don't know a lot about her. But each daoine sidhe should have two gifts which are a combination of one or more of the elements. My uncle has only water as an element, but has two gifts. Whereas my father has two gifts which comprise four distinct elements. There is a main gift which is easier to use and a latent gift, which is more difficult. Though in the last thousand years or so some of the daoine sidhe have been born with only one gift. If you are born with only one, you are considered less. The hierarchy is incredibly important among the fae in general and among the daoine sidhe in particular."

I tapped my fork against my plate. "So what are your two gifts?"

He gave me a completely passive stare. "I have a single gift, a glacier fed stream."

There was more to the story. I wanted to ask, but something in his closed expression told me not to push this one.

"Why have I not noticed a... gift before?"

"You're young. It likely has not fully manifested yet."

"I'm almost thirty. I'm not that young."

He laughed again at me. I was getting tired of that, even if it was a nice laugh.

"Little changeling. I'm one hundred and three. And I'm still considered quite young by the fae."

I glowered at him. "Why do you keep calling me that?"

"Maybe because you never told me your name."

"Oh. It's Calynn."

"Well, little changeling," he said with a deliberate smile before starting back on his dinner, "I wouldn't worry about not having a gift. You probably have already used your main gift without noticing. You may even have used your latent gift."

"How do you know I'll have one?"

He shrugged. "Your aura is strong and intoxicating. You will have two gifts. And they will be strong."

"Intoxicating?"

I almost laughed at him this time. He looked up, embarrassed and uncomfortable. He cleared his throat. "Yes. But it's the same with most nobles. The more powerful they are, the more the lesser fae want to be near them."

"So you think I'm a noble, then. But why would I have been changed if I had been part of the nobility?"

"I can't answer that."

I rolled my eyes. "You could just say you don't know."

I finished the last bite of food and then stood up to bring the dishes to the sink.

"Aelwyd will do that," Ronan said.

"She made dinner, *and* she's going to clean up?"

"It's what she does. She'll be in later, after we're both asleep."

"I'm going to at least bring the dishes into the kitchen." When I finished, I joined Ronan in the living room.

He sat in the armchair, so I sat in a corner of the couch, tucking my legs underneath me.

"What are considered lesser fae?"

"Depends on who you are and where you are in the hierarchy. If you're one of the noble daoine sidhe, everyone is lesser fae. If you're a selkie, like Meriel was, I would not be a lesser fae, but Aelwyd, a brownie, would be. There are many types of fae. Selkies, brownies, leprechauns, goblins, many of the creatures you've heard of before. And the mongrels."

"Vampires, werewolves, wizards."

He scoffed. "They're part of this world, not mine."

"Isn't this your world since you live here?"

He stared at the empty fireplace, his face completely devoid of emotion.

"When a fae is exiled from the Sidhe, all they ever want to do is go back. This is not where we belong. It's why Meriel was looking for the key. If someone finds it and returns it to the queen in power, she must lift their exile. The queen grants them safe passage in both the Winter and Summer domains. It works for humans as well."

"Have you ever tried to find it? In her notes, Meriel said she had approached you about looking for it together, but you'd turned her down."

"It's an immensely powerful relic. I've always thought the price of finding it too high to pay for the reward it offers. So, no. I've never looked for it. My place is here now."

He got up from his chair and lit a fire. While he did so, I considered what he'd just said. He had contradicted himself. But neither statement was a lie. How could his place be here if this would never be his home? I wanted to ask why he'd been exiled. I got the feeling he didn't want to discuss himself personally, but it felt like an important question. That same instinct that had led me to Meriel's safe and then to Ronan's house begged me to ask. But a different instinct told me he wouldn't answer.

"Why are fae exiled?"

He looked back at me, a surprised look on his face, like he had forgotten I was there. It took him a moment to answer. "Could be any number of reasons.

Usually for breaking one of the queens' laws." The fire was small now, but growing, and he stood and made his way back to his chair.

"If the result is exile, and exile is so bad, why would anyone break the laws?"

He shrugged. "Same reason humans break laws, I suppose. Going to prison isn't pleasant, yet humans break laws all the time."

He made a good point, though it didn't tell me anything about why *he* had been exiled. But even as I was certain I wanted that answer, I was just as certain he wouldn't tell me.

"Do you know why Meriel was exiled?"

"I don't. She never told me. And it's rude to ask."

Which didn't help me either. I knew I had to leave it for now. Eventually I would come back to the question, but I needed his cooperation, and I didn't want to do anything to make him stop talking to me. I changed the subject instead.

"What is a selkie?"

"A selkie is similar to what you understand as a were-creature. They're seals who can remove their seal skin and become human, or an approximation of a human. They can put the skin back on and become a seal. The legend is, once they put the skin on, they can't take it off for seven years. I never asked Meriel if it was true, but whatever the truth, it can work well for an exiled fae. When she gets to the point that humans might notice she hasn't aged, she can slip into the ocean and come back when it's safe. That jacket you have was Meriel's skin."

"I don't have it. I just took a picture."

He looked alarmed. "Their skin is the source of a selkie's magic. It's incredibly important and her family should have it. We need to get it."

"We can't. It's at her house. I broke in yesterday, then the guy tried to kill me and we broke a window. He also shot the wall. The police will keep a much closer eye on the place now."

"Tell me what happened."

I told him about the black man and the struggle. When I got to the end, he said, "He wasn't black, he was the Dark."

"You didn't see him. He wasn't just dark. He was black."

Ronan shook his head, staring into the fire as he thought about my story while he talked to me. "I don't mean the color of his skin. I mean him. He is Darkness. That's why he was wearing sunglasses. His eyes are just as black as the rest of him. When you shone the flashlight in his eyes, you effectively blinded him. He can't see in the light."

"Have you met him before?"

Ronan nodded, still lost in thought. "Once. He's a mercenary for the dark court. He's about a thousand years old and terribly powerful."

"He's a noble, then?"

"Oh no. He only has one gift. Darkness."

"Like the Queen?"

He nodded. "Some have whispered he's a distant relative. Though the Queen usually kills people who speak too loudly about that possibility. While he only has the one gift, it is stronger than many others I've seen. He likely would have been a noble though. He can blend into the darkness, and it makes him a great assassin." He laughed. "Possibly the best assassin in the dark court and you, little changeling, broke his knee."

"I'm not sure that it's a laughing matter. I'm pretty sure I just pissed off the wrong guy."

He waved his hand. "If the Dark is after you, you're screwed either way."

"That makes me feel better."

He smiled at me, and it felt like the room lost some of its oxygen. He was beautiful when he smiled.

I looked away. "Who could he be working for?"

"Could be anyone. He'll work for the highest bidder."

"Could he be the one to have killed Meriel? I got the feeling he'd been in the house before."

"It's possible. It would make more sense that there's one killer running around, rather than two. But why would someone want to kill Meriel *and* you? And why would someone from the dark court want to kill Meriel?"

"Was she from Summer? Wouldn't the dark court want to kill off the Summer people?"

"She *was* from Summer, but that's not how it works. We are not rivals. We balance each other. Two sides of the same coin. Winter fae rarely have anything to do with Summer and vice versa."

"Am I from Summer or Winter?"

"It's not clear from your aura. Probably because you've lived with humans your whole life."

"So unless I'm from Summer, too, the only thing Meriel and I have in common is the key. She was looking for it and she asked me to help."

"That may be true, but it doesn't make sense. She wouldn't have been killed because she was looking for the key. She's been looking for it for years. A lot of exiled fae search for it."

"What if she'd found it? If it's as important as you say, someone could have found out she had it and killed her for it."

"In the time between when she saw you and when she was killed?"

"Okay. What if she was getting close then? Someone killed her to stop her from finding it."

"If someone was going to do that, they would be more likely to go with your first idea. They'd wait until she'd found it, kill her, and take it from her then. But an only exiled fae would do that and the Dark doesn't work for exiles."

"So why was she killed if it wasn't about the key?"

"I don't know."

"I guess I'll just have to interview some more people who *might* know."

"Why?" I could see the confusion in his eyes, though it was subtle, only visible as a slight tightening in his eyebrows.

"Why what?"

"Why look into this at all? You didn't know her. She's gone now. What's the point?"

"She was murdered. Someone should care."

"No one cares about exiled fae."

"It has nothing to do with her being fae. It has to do with her being murdered. Could a human have murdered her?"

He shook his head. "It isn't likely. She would have noticed if a human had entered her house, especially if she was keeping her skin there. If someone steals a selkie's skin, they have complete control over them. Other fae respect that and so she would be confident it would be safe from one of us. Fae do not trust humans."

"Then the regular police won't be able to figure out who killed her, right?"

"Likely not."

"So I'm the only one who is going to look into this, right? Unless there is someone else who investigates the murder of the exiled fae?"

"There is not. My job is to protect the living, not the dead. And I would be the closest to someone who would look into it."

"If it was your job to protect Meriel, why didn't you even know she had died?"

"It wasn't my job to protect Meriel. I only protect those who ask for it. Meriel was one of the exiled fae who decided they didn't need protection. And most don't."

I leaned forward. "Why?"

"In the Sidhe, most lesser fae will pledge fealty to someone more powerful. They offer service and loyalty in exchange for protection from any who would harm them. In the human world, there are fewer creatures who can harm us. I am the most powerful fae in this region, and so I am the one they come to for protection if they think they need it. Most who do are small creatures like brownies or puka or leprechauns. Selkies can pass for human with little to no glamour and so they tend to be independent."

I sat back in my seat. "So then, no one will look for Meriel's killer. I can't let that stand. She was a person who had been unhappy for so long. She had finally found someone who made her happy. She had a chance, and someone took it away. And I don't mean the Dark. If he was the triggerman, fine. But I want to know who hired him. That's the person who owes the debt for her life."

Ronan stared at me for a long time until I started to feel a little self-conscious about my fervent declaration. Finally, he said, "It's late. We should get some sleep. I take it you've explored and found the guest bedroom upstairs?"

"Yes. But I don't think I'll be able to sleep much."

"Can you still feel her watching you?"

"How did you know?"

"She is my queen, as much as I hate her. I served her for several years and have the scars to prove it. I have felt her gaze on me before." He grimaced. "My uncle often told me I should keep my head down, but I only vaguely got the hang of it. I remember how terrifying it can be to have that gaze following you."

"Can she actually see me?"

He nodded. "If you feel it, she can. It doesn't mean she is actually seeing you, but she could be. Concentrate now, can you feel it?"

I closed my eyes and considered what I could feel. I could feel Ronan looking at me. I could even feel his presence in the room in a way I'd never considered before. But I couldn't feel her gaze. Since I couldn't, I switched my focus to Ronan. His magic was cold and wet with just a hunt of the smell of pine. I focused more, getting closer and closer until I could almost see the stream he'd mentioned. The water was freezing. I kept moving toward it, not sure how I was doing it, when I realized I was actually moving toward a specific stone beneath the water, smooth and frozen in the middle of the stream. I needed to touch it, but I couldn't quite reach it without getting into the water.

"I can't feel her. But I can feel you."

I opened my eyes to find him staring at me. His emerald eyes were as hard as the stone they resembled. His jaw was clenched hard, and he looked strained. He had leaned forward like he was about to get off his chair and come to me.

"Did I do something wrong?"

He closed his eyes and swallowed hard before he took a deep breath.

"You are quite powerful, little changeling. I've never felt anything like that before."

"What happened?"

He seemed to struggle for a few moments to gain control of himself and finally opened his eyes again when his body was once more relaxed, leaning back in his chair. For some reason, the posture looked like a lie.

"When you concentrated, it felt like you were touching me, trying to pull me closer. I couldn't stop it."

"I didn't mean it."

"It's fine."

Another lie, but an understandable one, so I didn't bring it up.

"Can other fae do that?"

"None that I have ever heard of." He stood. "The point is, though, you can't feel the Queen's gaze here. You got here before dark, and she can't see past the threshold. You'll be safe tonight. If you can't sleep, there are plenty of books in the loft. You're welcome to any of them."

With that, he turned and went up the stairs. I sat staring at the dying fire for a while longer, worried I had scared him away.

CHAPTER 10

The window needed to be cleaned. I couldn't see through it.

I was trapped and I needed to see what was on the other side.

A female voice behind me said, "I am sorry you are so young. I had hoped you would have longer to prepare."

I had known she was there and so I didn't turn around. "Prepare for what?"

"We cannot wait any longer. We have run out of time."

I reached up without really wanting to. As soon as my hand touched the glass, it shattered into particles so fine they were almost sand.

I woke with a gasp, my heart pounding. I didn't know why the dream scared me so much. I lay still for a moment, trying to make sense of it. The woman said we'd run out of time. Out of time for what? And why was a person I hadn't even looked at so scary?

I made a disgusted sound. It was just a dream. It didn't mean anything. I wasn't out of time. There was no shattered glass. I pushed the blankets aside and sat up, swinging my legs over the side of the mattress.

The sun was shining in through the window, bathing the bedroom in bright, warm light. I didn't move right away, letting the morning light wash away the anxiety and fill me with a sense of peace. It wasn't something I felt often. At home, I usually got right out of bed, focused on how I was going to make money. But here, I didn't need to worry about that. I also noticed I could feel Ronan's magic, though not as clearly as I had when I focused last night. He had been right when saying I probably had been using the ability to feel other fae before now. I considered how I had felt something weird when Meriel came into my office and also when the Dark had tried to kill me. Now, I knew Ronan was downstairs with another fae. Careful not to focus too hard, I examined the other person's magic. It was damp and soft. Something that would easily grow flowers. Loam, my instincts told me.

Which of my other instincts had been magic? My ability to tell lies from truth? My ability to find things that were lost? All of them?

I went across the landing to the bathroom, running my fingers through my hair, trying in vain to straighten it. Faeries were supposed to be beautiful people of myth and legend, not people with bedhead and morning breath. I found a clean hairbrush and a new toothbrush, still in the packaging, set out on the counter. I touched first one, then the other, wondering how someone so annoying could also be so considerate.

I cleaned myself up as best I could and went downstairs.

Ronan was reading a newspaper at the kitchen island while a girl made breakfast. I could smell the bacon, eggs, and biscuits cooking as she set out a couple of plates on the island. I sat down beside Ronan.

"I found the toothbrush," I said.

He shrugged one shoulder and turned the page. "I have a bunch of stuff for guests. Fae will often come here after they've been exiled."

"Why?"

"As I said last night, I'm the most powerful fae in the region. They naturally seek protection or assistance from the stronger fae."

The girl set the food on the island in front of us and Ronan said, "Aelwyd, this is Calynn. Calynn, Aelwyd."

The girl had long, thick brown hair caught up in a ponytail on the top of her head and curling down her back. Her skin was the color of rich, fertile earth. She was only about four feet tall and looked human except for her large, canted eyes and slightly pointed ears.

"You're the one who put the dishes in the sink last night. It's unnecessary," she said.

"Calynn is not familiar with our ways. She's a changeling."

Aelwyd almost dropped the pan of eggs she was holding. "A real changeling?"

I looked between her and Ronan, confused by her surprise.

"Fae changelings are very rare," he explained. "They are not allowed without express permission from both of the faerie queens."

"Oh. So both of the queens had to approve me being changed?"

"If they do not approve, the one who creates the changeling is punished. Usually severely."

Aelwyd began dishing out the breakfast food. I noticed she didn't have any plate for herself.

"Aren't you eating with us?"

"Oh no. I eat with my family."

"So you cook for Ronan?" I asked as I ate.

"Yes. And I clean. My mother keeps our house, and together, she and I keep the houses of the other fae who live here."

"Does Ronan pay you well for all that work?"

Aelwyd growled and bared her teeth. They looked a bit sharper than I had thought they would.

"Brownies find payment offensive," Ronan explained. "They work because they want to and for no other reason. I offer them cream and honey and the protection of my home. That's as much as they will accept."

"I meant no offense, Aelwyd. I didn't know."

She finished serving breakfast, then took a mug from the cupboard and filled it with coffee before giving it to me. I restrained myself from getting up and kissing her and instead just took the mug, inhaling the rich steam before taking a first sip, my eyes closing involuntarily at the taste. It was just regular coffee, made in a drip coffee maker, but it was still better than all the coffee I'd been drinking recently. Aelwyd nodded to Ronan before she left the house to some other duty.

While I was hungry and the food in front of me smelled delicious, I continued to hold my coffee cup in front of me, trying to gain the strength to ask Ronan what I knew I needed to ask.

"What's on your mind, little changeling?" he asked, and I realized I'd been sitting too long. But I hated asking for favors, even small ones.

"I need to ask for something."

He set the newspaper aside. "And you're having trouble. You don't want to ask."

I shook my head.

"You've never liked to ask for things. It's difficult. And when you do, you feel obligated to pay the person back in some way."

I blinked, startled that he could know this.

"Yes."

"You're fae, little changeling. Favors are a currency among us. Bargains. Once a bargain is struck, you must follow through or else you will be forsworn, which is a fate worse than death."

I let out a breath I hadn't known I was holding. Another piece of my past clicked into place. "Everyone always told me I was rude. I would never ask for something. Sometimes I would state what I needed and if someone offered help, I would accept. But if they didn't, I would try to do it myself. A lot of my foster parents would tell me off for not being polite and to just ask for help." I paused, thinking. "And I never say thank you, please, or sorry if I can get away with it. They've always felt too heavy."

"I'm not surprised. There is an implied debt when you use those words."

Something eased in my chest as I realized Ronan wouldn't scold me for being impolite. I could just tell him what I needed and he would help or not.

"I need someone who knows about this world to help me navigate it. Someone who can help me set up interviews with the other fae I want to talk to and will help them feel safe talking to me. In order to figure out who killed Meriel, I need to talk to the people in her life who knew her best, the other fae. But I also don't know anything about what that life would entail. What would be commonplace versus odd behavior."

"I can freely help you with this. So, where do we start the investigation?"

"I need to get some things from my office."

"I'll meet you there?"

I thought about my office and the lack of power. I would have to take care of that first thing.

"Uh, no. It's better if we meet somewhere else right now."

"Why don't you want me to come to your office?"

I kept my head down, staring at my plate, as I tried to think up a suitable excuse. I couldn't think of one, so I stalled. "What makes you think I don't want you to come to my office?"

"You don't want to meet there, and you won't look at me right now."

I looked up and he smirked at me. I scowled. "I didn't pay my electrical bill. It was cut off."

He started laughing at me again.

"You know, you can be very annoying."

"Little changeling, in the Sidhe, there is no such thing as electricity. Going to an office without it will not bother me."

"Fine," I said, still scowling. "You can follow me. After I eat breakfast."

Chapter 11

I nstead of going into my office, I brought Ronan up to my apartment. All the things I had taken from Meriel's house were there. I opened the curtains to allow the meager October light to brighten the place. I pulled the books and passport out of my safe along with the weird water, but left the money inside. He didn't need to know I'd stolen it as well. Though I had a feeling he wouldn't care.

I came out of my closet, and he was sitting at my kitchen table. I handed him the vial first. I knew what the books were. I really wanted to know what the liquid was.

He touched it and the glass frosted over.

"What are you doing to it?"

"Nothing." He turned the vial around in his hand. "I'm surprised she was able to get this much out. And that she hasn't used more than this over the years."

"What is it?"

"Water."

"No way that's water. It glows in candlelight. It's warm."

He held up the frozen bottle, the liquid inside turned to ice. "It was warm when you touched it. It freezes when I touch it."

"Why?"

He set the bottle on the table and the frost started to recede.

"It's water from the Muir, the faerie sea. I've heard lore that our magic comes to us from the water that flows through our rivers and into our Muir. It reacts to whoever touches it. I'm from Winter. My magic is water that comes from a glacier. When I touch it, it freezes."

"So I'm not from Winter then."

"You've been living here so long it has affected how you see your world and how your world sees you. The water's reaction isn't enough to know if you are Winter or Summer."

My internal lie detector buzzed, a faint tingle almost easy to miss except I'd been paying close attention to whether or not he was lying since I met him yesterday. Usually, this feeling meant a lie of omission. Most often, a deliberate lie of omission.

"You're not telling me something."

"What?"

"There's something you're not telling me."

"If there was more I could tell you, I would."

Truth. Not even a buzz of something missing from the statement. I decided to let it go. For now.

"So, why did Meriel have the water?"

"She used to live in the Muir. When she left, she stole some of the water. It would have been a comfort to her. It would have been a comfort to many fae. Not to mention its healing properties. If she had wanted to, she could have sold this for a lot of money."

"Not that she needed it. Did you see her house?"

"Yes. I've seen it."

I grabbed a notepad and pen from my kitchen counter and sat down at the table with him.

"When was the first time you met her?"

"What are you doing?"

"Beginning my investigation. When did you meet Meriel Jones?"

"Just Meriel. Fae don't have last names. We adopt them when we are exiled because we have to if we are to interact with the human world. Aelwyd and her mother and father never bothered because they don't deal with humans at all."

"Okay. When did you meet Meriel?"

"About thirty years ago, I guess."

"When was the last time you saw her?"

"It's been a while. I think I last saw her a few months ago. She received money from the Diaspora Corporation when she was first exiled. As such, she must meet with a representative quarterly to discuss finances. When she's in Vancouver, she meets with me."

"In her journal, she mentioned you're powerful and you're hot. Did you have a romantic relationship with her?" The only relationship Meriel had mentioned in her journal was the one with Angor, but she had mentioned Ronan a few times and I'd wondered if there had been something between them.

"What does that have to do with her death?"

"Maybe nothing, maybe something. I won't know until I have all the facts."

His glower told me everything I needed to know.

"How long had you been sleeping together?"

"About thirty years, I guess."

"You don't seem heartbroken over her death."

"Why should I be? We slept together from time to time. I would have been to her what this water was. Something that connected her to home. I didn't know she had it, though I can tell you with certainty she would unstop that bottle and take a drop out from time to time. She would drink it or drop it on her skin, and it would be like she was home again for a moment. Sleeping with me would have had a similar effect for her."

"What about for you?"

"Similar, but she was a selkie. Her magic wasn't as powerful as mine. But she was a very beautiful woman."

"So that's it? You occasionally slept with her because she was beautiful? There are a lot of beautiful women out there."

"There are. But there are few who are also fae and in the Lower Mainland. There was Meriel, a few you haven't met, and you."

I felt myself blush and hated myself for it. I knew he said it to throw me off my line of questioning, since he didn't like discussing himself. I hated it worked. I tried to cover my embarrassment by standing and going to the sink and running the hot water. I pulled a mug out of my cupboard and the instant coffee.

"Do you want something to drink?" I asked as I prepared my cup. "I have water and instant coffee I could make with hot tap water."

"That sounds awful."

I cast a glance over my shoulder. "There's no such thing as awful coffee."

When I finished, I brought my mug back to the table. I smelled the coffee, letting the scent settle my nerves before I took a sip and grimaced. It was awful.

"So. You were sleeping with her. Do you know if she was sleeping with anyone else?" I was thinking about Angor.

"We never really talked about it. The only things we ever talked about were her finances, home, and sex."

"It wasn't love, then."

He smiled as though the very idea was funny. "No."

I passed the address book to him. "Do you know any of these people?"

He took it, slowly turning the pages. "Yes." When he got to the end of the book, he handed it back to me. "I know all the fae listed there who live in this area. Though she has a few who live in California, and I don't know them."

"All of them? How?"

"When I was exiled, I became this region's representative for the Diaspora Corporation."

"You and Meriel have mentioned that corporation. What is it?"

"It's a world-wide corporation based in Ireland. There are representatives in a few of the places where the fae who are exiled tend to congregate. Obviously, many choose to live in the old country, Ireland, Scotland, England, and Wales. But because so many people from there have moved to North America, there are pockets here where the fae like to live as well. Especially those who decide to have a career in Hollywood, like Meriel. The corporation is run by exiled fae to help other exiled fae. The representative in each region is always the strongest fae who lives there. The idea is, we give people the money they need to get started out here. They give a percentage of their income back to the corporation quarterly to continue helping other fae. The percentage is small, but when you make as much money as someone like Meriel, it can be a lot of money. If ever they no longer need the money, it goes back to the corporation. Additionally, we offer protection to the fae who don't want to involve themselves in human affairs. Meriel took money and not protection."

I lifted the passport and tapped it against the table before handing it to him. "You should probably take this then. Did you know Meriel had another passport?"

He flipped to the page with her picture. "I didn't. But it doesn't surprise me. If I remember correctly, this was her passport about twenty years ago. She should have destroyed it, but she could be sentimental."

I gestured toward the address book again. "Who are some of these people in this book? Who do you think I should know?"

He opened it to a page, pointing to an entry that said Evander and Family.

"Evander is Aelwyd's father. He's also Bidina's father, Meriel's assistant. Evander is the healer on my ranch and also the second in charge if something were to happen to me."

"Bidina worked for Meriel? I thought brownies found payment offensive."

"They do."

He didn't say anything else, but I could feel the weight in his statement. I cleared my throat. "Right."

He turned to another page and pointed to the entry there. "Killian was the Diaspora Corporation representative before me. He was the representative when Meriel was exiled."

"Is it at all possible that her murder had something to do with why she was exiled?"

He shook his head slowly. "I doubt it. She was exiled sixty years ago. Why would anyone wait that long to kill her? Besides, some fae, Meriel included, would prefer death to exile."

"Exile is that bad?"

"There is so little magic here. Magic to us is like oxygen. Imagine living up on the top of the highest mountain where the air is thin. You can never take a real full deep breath again."

"If I go to the Sidhe, will it become that way for me? Or will I still be able to come back to this world?"

"If you want to return to the human world, you would be able to. As for how you will react to the difference in magic, I don't know. As I said, fae changelings are very rare. I've never met one before you."

I looked down at the book and remembered something I had read before. I flipped to the back. My name was the last one, question marks next to the court and the type. There were still so many questions to answer. And then I added one more to the pile.

"You didn't know me."

"What?"

I pulled her journal toward me and flipped to the relevant entry, reading it out loud, "I have this new information from a reliable source. She gave me pictures and the name of another fae living here in Vancouver. One who could help me." I looked up at Ronan. "She's talking about me. Someone knew I was here and sent her to me." I turned Meriel's notebook to him and pointed to the entry. "She wrote everyone's initials in here. Mine, yours. But this reliable source didn't get initials. Why not?"

Ronan was quiet for a minute, considering. Then he said, "I'm afraid her death may have more to do with you than you want to believe."

The thought chilled me. I seemed to be tangled up in this mystery somehow. Someone had sent Meriel to me. The Dark had known I was a changeling. I'd been willing to believe before that he had tried to kill me for being in the wrong place at the wrong time. But as I continued putting pieces together, it became more and more obvious, he had been there to kill me specifically.

My phone saved me from the need to respond. I picked it up and saw Arial was calling.

"Excuse me." I went into my bedroom and closed the door. "Hey, what's up?"

"You never called to tell me what happened after you left here."

"Yeah. I've been a little busy. I took on a case. I can come by tonight and tell you all about it."

"Okay. Sushi for dinner?"

"Sure. And alcohol. I have a feeling I'm going to need it."

Arial laughed. "No problem. I'll make sure I'm stocked. See you around six?"

"Yeah. See you then."

We hung up and I went back into my kitchen. Ronan was flipping through the notebook.

"See anything useful?"

He shook his head. "She wrote detailed entries, but they're all about the key and how lonely she was. There's nothing here to explain why someone might want her dead."

"Too bad. But I agree. I read the whole thing the other night. I didn't see anything I thought might be a motive for murder."

"But you're right about this last entry. It's strange that she doesn't mention who told her about you."

"Who would have known I existed?"

"Killian would have been told. And the one who changed you. But beyond that..."

I wrote Killian's name down on my notes and then tapped my pen against the paper. What were my priorities here? I wanted to figure out who killed Meriel and why. I also wanted to figure out who I was. But I'd lived almost thirty years not knowing there was anything special about me. I could live a few more days without answers so I could focus on Meriel's murder.

"I'd like to go see Bidina. As Meriel's assistant, she would know more about her life than you do."

"Sounds reasonable."

"I'd like you to come with me. I think I'll have more luck if someone she knows is there."

He nodded. "Her office isn't too far from here. We can go there now. I'll call to tell her we're coming."

"Perfect. I'll ride my bike over and meet you there."

"It's going to rain tonight. You have appropriate clothing to be riding in it?"

I rolled my eyes. "Yes, Mom." We started toward my door.

"I just feel responsible for you. You have no idea the world you're getting into."

"I don't need you to protect me. I've managed just fine on my own for the last twenty-nine years. I think I'll be okay."

He turned to face me and looked into my eyes. He kept his face carefully expressionless, but I could see, behind the facade, emotions roiling. They were too far away to make out what they were, but I could tell he was hiding from me.

I wanted to ask why, but I wasn't sure I wanted to hear the answer. I stayed silent, and we continued to look at each other until the silence became heavy and I felt like something was going to happen.

Maybe he was going to kiss me. Maybe I should kiss him. Maybe I should shove him out the door. Maybe I should move closer.

While these thoughts were running through my mind, Ronan decided for both of us, breaking the eye contact. "I'll meet you at Bidina's office," he said, and then he left, shutting the door firmly, but not quite slamming it, behind him.

CHAPTER 12

D espite leaving second, I got to Bidina's office first. It had warmed up during the morning, so I took off my riding gear and sat on my bike in the parking lot, enjoying the bright sunshine. The clouds that promised the rain Ronan had mentioned threatened in the distance, dark and heavy. They would roll in soon and there wouldn't be many more nice days before winter settled in. It felt good to not have to feel the weight of the queen's gaze on my shoulders. I closed my eyes and tilted my face up toward the sun, soaking up as much heat as I could.

I felt it when Ronan arrived. His magic reached toward me like a river flowing toward an ocean. Still ever present was the stone, deep beneath the water, strong and immovable. I let the magic roll over me without trying to call to it. I shivered as the icy water washed away the warmth I had soaked up from the sun. It wasn't unpleasant as I had thought it would be.

When Ronan didn't say anything, I opened my eyes. He was staring at me. I smiled slowly. "Like what you see?"

He blinked and almost shook his head. "Come on. We don't have much time before it gets dark."

I rolled my eyes and followed him into Bidina's office.

She was at her desk holding a picture frame and crying when we came in. Her brown, canted eyes were red and puffy, her long brown hair, a tangled mess. Otherwise, she had a strong resemblance to Aelwyd. She looked up at us when we entered and immediately stood, rushing over to give Ronan a hug.

"Oh, Ronan. It's just so horrible. Why would anyone do this? What am I going to do now?"

"You can come home, Bidina. Your mother stopped me this morning before I left and told me, if I were to see you, to ask you to come home."

"How can I after everything that happened?"

"Your family loves you. Nothing you've done could ever change that."

I watched the interaction from the corner of my eye, not wanting to intrude on the moment. I felt jealous of Bidina for having a family who wanted her and at the same time felt a warm spot open in my heart for Ronan for being so gentle with her.

Bidina sniffed and pulled back from Ronan. "I'm such a mess. Come in. Would you like a coffee?"

"That would be nice. Bidina, this is Calynn. She's helping me find answers about Meriel's death."

It didn't feel right to correct him that *he* was helping *me*, so I kept my mouth shut. It made sense for him to seem like he was the one in charge of the investigation in front of the fae who didn't know me at all.

"Hello," she said. "Would you like coffee as well?"

"I always want coffee," I told her with a smile, instinctively knowing she needed something to do to feel useful. It also had the added benefit of being the truth.

Ronan and I sat down, and I spent the few moments it took for Bidina to pour the coffee and set it out with sugar and cream to consider the magic I was feeling. Bidina felt a lot like Aelwyd. I could feel the differences, but also that they were certainly related. When we were all settled with our coffees, I said, "I was hoping I could ask you a few questions about Meriel."

Bidina sat down again with her own cup filled with heavy cream and she mixed in some honey. "I suppose so. If Ronan thinks it's best."

He nodded.

"Okay. Do you know of anyone who may have wanted to hurt her?"

"No. I can't think of anyone. Everyone who met her loved Meriel. Well. Except for Coira, of course. But she wouldn't have killed Meriel."

"Coira is the one the news said was Meriel's best friend," I said.

"Yes. But you know how stupid humans can be. It was all for publicity. Meriel and Coira would never have been friends."

"Why couldn't they be friends?"

Bidina looked confused at my question, but Ronan answered. "Meriel was Summer and Coira is Winter. And they both cling to the old customs. Or current customs, I suppose, if you're in the Sidhe. We tend not to follow them so much once we're exiled."

"Can you think of a reason someone might want her dead?" I asked Bidina.

"I cannot think of any. Her skin was not stolen, and that's the most valuable thing she had."

"She had a lot of money."

"Human money is meaningless to the fae," Ronan said. "We use it here in your world from necessity, but most of it comes from the Diaspora Corporation."

"So now that she's dead, who will inherit her estate?"

"The estate in Vancouver will be liquidated and returned to me for use later to help other fae who are exiled. The one in California will be liquidated and returned to the corporation representative of that region. A redcap, I believe."

"So not only were you sleeping with her, you stand to inherit all of her money."

Ronan shrugged. "I had no reason to kill her."

"I just gave you two very human reasons."

"I am not human."

Bidina watched our exchange. "You sound just like the detectives who were here yesterday."

"The detectives working the case?" I asked.

"Yes. They asked me these same questions. Though I didn't tell them anything. What could they possibly do in any case? Even the ones with clear sight can barely see what's in front of them."

Ronan sat forward. "One of the detectives is a wizard?"

Bidina nodded and sipped her cream and honey. "He couldn't even see me, and I was sitting right here. He's useless."

A detective and a wizard. I hadn't considered someone who understood magic might already be involved in Meriel's murder case. I filed that away for further consideration later. For now, I had one more question for Bidina. "Did Meriel mention anything to you about her search for the key and meeting someone who could help her?"

"She did. She said she got a tip about someone here in Vancouver who might be able to help her. She said she was an investigator." She looked at me, obviously connecting the dots. "She went to see you."

"The day she died."

"Oh my. That's... that's very odd. She didn't call me that night. We were supposed to discuss an upcoming shoot for an endorsement... well, today's shoot, actually. I was organizing a few trips and more jobs. She loved to be busy. But the last time I talked to her, she was excited about some new information she had gotten. She said it could be extremely helpful."

"When was this?"

Bidina looked down at a book on the side of her desk and pulled it closer to flip back through the pages. "Thursday. The day before..." She trailed off, choking up as fresh tears rolled down her cheeks. "I called to discuss a few potential jobs."

"Did she mention who gave her this information?"

"No. And come to think of it, that's strange of her. She usually just says whatever is on her mind. But that day she was different. Like she was after having had sex with you, Ronan. Or after she had used a drop of her Muir water. But she hadn't done either of those things since she met Angor."

Ronan nodded as though he understood.

"She had come in contact with the Sidhe somehow," he said. "The magic had touched her."

"That answers a question then," I said. "Whoever told her about me must have come from the Sidhe. They weren't an exiled fae."

"Likely not," Ronan said. "That also explains why she thought the information was good. And why she may not have used initials in her journal."

"Can you tell me what her day would have been like that day?"

Bidina slid the book over to me. "This was her schedule."

7am – Wake up

7:30-9am – Work out

9-10:30am – Swim

10:30-11:30am – Shower and dress

12:30-2pm – Brunch at Cardero's with Coira

3-4pm – Home photo shoot

4-4:30pm – call from Bidina

4:30-6pm – Dress for dinner

6:30-8pm – Dinner at Gotham with Angor

9-10pm – Relax

10pm – Bed

"Was her schedule always so detailed?"

Bidina blushed. "I like things to be organized. I made up daily schedules. She would follow them for the most part, but sometimes she would change them. She isn't the most organized and was always late for everything before I started helping her. I know that day she followed the schedule, though. She had planned the brunch with Coira herself. They go out together about once a month. And she would certainly have gone to dinner with Angor. They probably went back to her house afterward."

"And you said she mentioned finding out about me on her call with you. So if she followed your schedule, she either met the person from the Sidhe at her house or while she was out for brunch. Do you mind if I make a copy of this schedule, Bidina?"

"Take it. I don't need it anymore."

"It would be better if I take a copy." I pulled out my phone and took a picture of the page. "If the police come back and ask for her schedule, you should still have it."

I stood up and Ronan followed my lead. "That's all for now, I think." I held out my hand to shake hers and she stared at me for a moment, slowly standing as well.

"You're different. What are you? I can't figure it out. You're not from the sea. You're not from the earth. You're not from the air. You're not of fire. And yet. You are all. You feel almost like daoine sidhe but still different."

I looked at Ronan. I didn't know how much I should tell her. He nodded slightly.

"I'm a changeling."

She gasped and fell back into her chair. "But... that's not possible. There hasn't been a changeling in... I don't even know how long. They are too powerful. And to make one from a daoine sidhe. It's not done."

"I don't know what you mean," I said.

"It is said that changelings are dangerous. They don't have the same rules as the rest of the fae," Bidina explained. "It makes them more powerful than any of us. And the daoine sidhe are already the most powerful."

"Is that true?" I asked Ronan.

"I don't know why fae changelings are not created. I only know they are not. If they are dangerous and don't have the same rules, it would make sense for the Queens to forbid them."

"What can I do that you can't?"

"No one knows," Bidina answered. "The Queens outlawed fae changelings long before I was born. I couldn't even say how long ago it was."

"So then, how was I changed?"

Bidina looked speculative for a moment. "There was a rumor. About thirty years ago. A fae was changed against the Queens' wishes. No one was sure if there was any fact in the rumor. I never paid it much heed myself. Father was interning with the Summer High Healer. I was just beginning my clothing business. We'd heard rumors before. This was nothing new. I assumed it was another thing to undermine the Queen's authority. I never heard much information, whether the fae was Winter or Summer, or whose family the fae had come from."

"Have there been many rumors that undermine the Queen's authority?"

"Oh yes. Some have claimed both of the Queens' power has been waning in the last century or so. Some claim it has been even longer. There are factions who wish to see the Queens deposed. But of course, that isn't done."

"Of course."

I was about to offer my hand to shake again and decided against it. Instead, I looked to Ronan.

"Remember what I said," he told her. "You can come home anytime. Your mother would love to have you."

Bidina stared down at her desk. "But what about my father?"

"He misses you just as much as your mother. But you know he won't say so."

She didn't look convinced. "I have to put Meriel's affairs in order. But once I am done, I will consider your offer. Her lawyer will be in touch with you soon."

That reminded me of something. "Bidina, when will you be going through her estate? Will you be able to get her selkie skin back for me?"

"I don't know. I can ask the police."

I nodded. "If you can get it back, it would be safer with Ronan than at her house."

"I'll try."

Ronan nodded and turned to leave, so I did the same. When we got back out into the sun, I said, "So that was interesting information."

"Yes."

"Did you ever hear these rumors?" I asked, putting on my jacket and zipping it up.

"Everyone knows about the Queens losing power. It's the worst kept secret in the Sidhe. But the rest." He shook his head. "I had already been exiled."

I pulled on my gloves next and picked up my helmet. "I'll go over my notes and let you know tomorrow who else we should talk to. Definitely Coira and Angor. But I'll make a list of anyone else."

As I pulled on my helmet, I could have sworn a flash of relief crossed Ronan's face, but I had no idea what he could be relieved about.

CHAPTER 13

Before I went to Arial's place, I went to the bank to deposit the money I had stolen from Meriel's house. Only enough that I could reasonably explain as money from a legitimate job. I'd have to write something in my books, and it couldn't be Meriel's job. After breaking and entering, then stealing, what was a little bit of money laundering? I paid my electrical bill on the ATM and then started for Arial's house. If I called them, they would probably get the power turned on pretty fast.

I felt the moment the sun set. The weight of those eyes settled on me again. The air in my lungs felt heavy and it became difficult to breathe. I moved through the evening traffic as quickly as I could to Arial's neighborhood, parked my bike next to the tree in her front yard, and rushed inside. As I crossed the threshold, the weight lifted and I sucked in a deep breath. I pulled off my helmet, breathing raggedly.

"Calynn?"

I didn't answer right away. Ronan had said the Queen would be able to see me if I could feel her eyes on me. But she couldn't see past thresholds. The door was still open behind me, but it didn't seem to matter. I stepped out the door and the gaze fastened to my shoulders immediately. I stepped inside again and the weight vanished. I closed the door.

"What are you doing?" Arial asked.

"Testing a theory. You have a drink for me?"

She held up the tumbler with a shot of whiskey in it, a wry smile on her face. "I heard you coming. I had it ready."

I took the drink and tossed it back. "I think something weird is going on."

I moved further into Arial's living room, where she had already set out the sushi on her coffee table. A bottle of Bushmills sat on one side and a bottle of some local white wine I knew she loved sat on the other in a bucket of ice.

"Figured it was a night for the good stuff."

"You can say that again."

I sat down on the floor near the whiskey and poured another shot. This one I sipped slower. As I did, I noticed something I hadn't before. I could feel magic here. It felt fast, like a brisk wind, and smelled like a hint of smoke and flowers in the spring. Hyacinths. I had no idea how I knew which flower, considering my knowledge of plants was pretty much limited to the produce section of the grocery store, but no sooner than I'd thought the word, a picture of the small blooms formed in my mind. Pink and purple and white.

"Do you know what a hyacinth is?" I asked.

"Of course I do. They're my favorite flower. They were my mom's favorite, too."

"Do you have any here?"

"In the spring. It's October, Calynn. They don't grow this late in the year. What's wrong?"

"I have no idea."

"Well, start with what happened when you went to Meriel Jones' place."

So I told her. About exploring the mansion, finding the weird jacket, guessing the code on her safe, taking the contents inside, and finally, the attempted murder.

"Someone tried to kill you?"

"Yeah. He seemed pretty intent on it, as well. Like it wasn't opportunity, or wrong place-wrong time. He wanted to kill me specifically."

"That's scary."

"There's more." I went on about the notebooks, how Meriel had started the journal around sixty years ago. How she'd mentioned Ronan when she came to see me and also in her book. How I went to visit him the day before.

"Someone with answers," Arial said.

"Yeah, but they're hard to believe."

"Try me."

I took another sip of my whiskey, delaying the moment. "He says the jacket at Meriel's was her seal skin. That she was a selkie, some kind of mythical creature. He's apparently something called a daoine sidhe, which is like the royalty of the faeries, and he lives with brownies. Not the food. The little fae creatures. Except they're not that little."

"And you believe all this?"

"It's hard not to. All this weird stuff has been happening. I could tell the jacket was special, even before I knew what it was. When I met Ronan, I could feel the magic. He feels different from humans. And then there's the queen."

"What queen?"

"Mab. The Queen of Air and Darkness. Ever since I saw the picture of her, I feel like she's watching me. He said she can't see past thresholds. That's what I was testing when I got here. Outside your house, I can feel it. Inside, I can't."

"So what does that make you? Part of this whole thing? Faeries and queens and brownies?"

"Yes. He said I'm a changeling. That I was changed when I was a baby. That's why I didn't know about any of this."

We had finished eating by this time and Arial poured her second glass of wine.

"I have to say, Calynn. This is a very strange story."

"I don't expect you to believe it. I hardly believe it myself. I'm going to meet another selkie tomorrow. She can turn into a seal, Arial."

Arial started laughing. I couldn't help it. I did as well. The whole situation was ludicrous. If it all hadn't been happening to me, I wouldn't believe any of it. But I had no other explanation for the queen's gaze, or the magic I was feeling.

When the laughter subsided, I said, "It's not possible, right? This stuff isn't real."

Arial took a sip of her wine, staring at a photo of her mother. "I'm not going to say I don't believe it. My mother believed in faeries. She used to tell me stories about one who came to visit her before I was born. When I was little, I believed she was telling me the truth. Later, when she got sick, I think I stopped believing her stories, but she was convinced it was all real. Maybe she wasn't wrong."

I thought about it for a moment. I knew how hard it was for Arial to talk about her mother's illness. She had been diagnosed with schizophrenia when Arial and I were fifteen, and her health deteriorated rapidly after she went into the hospital for treatment. She died only five years later. It was almost like when she went on the medication, she gave up living.

Arial brought me back from the past. "What are you going to do now? Shouldn't you give the notebooks to the police? It could have something to do with her death. Or at the very least, it could help them put together a suspect pool."

"I know. But I don't think I can. I can't imagine it's safe to have all this information about who is fae in Vancouver and parts of California written in one spot. If there are fae in this world, I'm certain there will be people who will try to take advantage of them. Otherwise, why wouldn't it be more common knowledge? Besides, I don't think the police will solve this one. I can't help it. I believe what Ronan has told me. I don't think Meriel was human. And I don't think a human killed her."

I didn't mention the fact that one detective was also a wizard. Whoever that was might be able to help me if I could figure out who it was. Since I didn't know, it wasn't something I was going to rely on.

"Did Ronan say anything about this guy who tried to kill you?"

"Yeah. He's apparently a professional assassin. I think he killed Meriel. But he was only the trigger man. Someone else would have ordered the death."

"And you're the one who needs to find the person responsible."

"Who will if I don't? Someone needs to bring her killer to justice. The police can't. And it seems like the fae or whoever won't. They don't care about exiled fae. Someone should care."

"I know you, Calynn. I already knew you would look into this. You can't just leave stuff like this alone. If you could, we wouldn't be friends."

She was right. I had been the one to stop people from bullying her back when we were kids. None of the teachers seemed to notice it was happening, but Arial had been picked on every day for a month before I stepped in.

I poured some more whiskey. Talking it all out helped me put everything into perspective. It was still hard to believe. But it was getting easier. Putting all the pieces together showed me a whole that all pointed the same way. Occam's Razor said the simplest explanation was likely the right one. Even if the simplest one included faeries.

CHAPTER 14

The darkness kept me at Arial's house that night. I told myself I stayed because it was warmer and I could use her Internet to do some research and her electricity to charge my laptop and phone. I told myself that I was not afraid to go outside in the dark.

The Internet had a lot of information about the fae. So many people still believed in faeries and goblins and elves. Or wanted to believe. I had no way of knowing what was real and what was not. If you had asked me a few days ago, I would have said none of it was real. I took a few notes on daoine sidhe, brownies, and selkies, intending to ask Ronan about it all later.

Then I switched my focus and tried to research Meriel a bit more. I figured I could safely rely on this information, until I read her birthdate and realized it would all be a fabrication to allow her to pass for human. It would at least give me something, though, so I kept looking.

I didn't find much more than what I had noted before. I sorted my notes and tried to make sense out of them. Likely, the father who "died" was complete fiction and just a way for her to get the money that had already been hers in a way that didn't create questions. She was so talented at acting likely because she had been doing it for years under a different alias.

When I finished my research, I found there were more questions than answers. What of the fae research was real and what was not? How had Meriel hidden the fact that she had been around before? What had she been doing before her fictional father's death? Maybe she had been living as a seal at that time. Was any of this relevant to why she was killed? If not, why would anyone want to kill her? She was rich, but nothing had been stolen from her place.

I woke just before sunrise and left as soon as the sun broke the horizon. In late October, the sun rose around 8am, something I hadn't paid much attention to before but seemed to be instinctual now. I knew when the sun rose and set like I knew how to breathe, even when the clouds were thick in the sky and I couldn't see the it at all.

Ronan had sent me a text message last night saying he and Coira would meet me at my office. He promised she wouldn't notice if I didn't turn the lights on during the day. I should have called the electric company before and told them I'd made the payment. But after talking with Arial, I'd forgotten. I could call before they got here.

I went into the office and set my riding gear in the back, wishing I could make some coffee, but I didn't keep any instant coffee here. And even if I did, I didn't want to offer Coira instant coffee made with hot tap water. I opened all my blinds, letting the light from outside filter through the windows. I turned back to my desk, intent on finding my cheque book to write my rent cheque, when I got a familiar feeling of being watched. I checked out my window but couldn't see anything or anyone suspicious. Perfect. I was officially jumping at shadows.

I reminded myself that the Queen could only see me after sunset. I picked up my phone to call the electric company. Before made the call, Ronan came in.

"Hey," I said. "Have a seat. I have some water. I don't have anything else to offer Coira."

"That's fine." He sat down in my guest chair but then stood again as Coira entered, coming through the door like she was floating.

She reminded me of Meriel. They had the same air of pretentiousness, and I could smell the sea as she settled in my office. It was like the smell from Meriel's jacket, but colder. Everything about her was colder than Meriel, in fact. Where Meriel's looks were bright and warm, Coira was white and freezing. Her eyes were ice blue and her shoulder-length hair was white-blonde. Any color on her was color she had added herself, like her bright red lips and matching dress. She perched on the edge of the chair and turned her body to face Ronan.

"Oh, Ronan. Tell me you know what's happening. It's just so awful that Meriel's gone."

"There are no cameras here, Coira. You can drop the act." He settled his hip against the edge of my desk and crossed his arms over his chest.

She blinked and then smiled. "Of course. I forget myself sometimes."

She looked at me and her gaze traveled up and down quickly, sizing me up. I could tell she didn't much care for what she saw. I'd seen the look enough times before to know what it meant. I liked to think that people were constantly underestimating me.

"Coira, it's nice to meet you. I'm Calynn."

"Mm-hm." She turned back to Ronan. "I really would like to know what's going on. Am I in any danger? Or is this a Summer thing?"

The derision in her voice when she said Summer was so thick I could have cut it with a knife.

"We're not sure," I answered, trying to get her attention back to me.

"Who are you?"

"Coira, this is Calynn. She's helping me investigate Meriel's death."

I arched an eyebrow at him, but didn't correct him again. He regarded me steadily while Coira responded.

"I see. And why do you want to talk to me?"

I turned my attention back to her. "You saw Meriel the day before she was killed. You went for lunch at Cardero's?"

"Yes. We would meet occasionally. For the cameras, you know. We wouldn't be caught dead making friends with humans. So we only had each other. Though of course we weren't friends either. More like... what's the term humans use? Frenemies? Whatever. We used each other to get publicity. It was a mutually beneficial arrangement."

"Right. Well, the day you met for lunch, Meriel met with someone from the Sidhe and it seems connected to her death somehow. I wanted to know if she had been acting any differently that day."

Coira shrugged and rolled her eyes. "She was from Summer. She was always different."

"More different than usual."

She heaved a sigh. "No. I don't think she was. She was the same sunny Meriel as she always was. We talked about upcoming movies and discussed doing another together soon. They always went over very well."

"Why is that?"

She laughed. "The magic, silly. Humans can't say no to that much magic in one place. It's like compounding interest. I'm sure you've noticed it when you're out with other fae in public."

Considering I hadn't been out with any other fae except Ronan, I hadn't noticed. But it brought to mind the times when Arial and I went out and guys wouldn't leave us alone.

"Now, if that's all your questions, it's Meriel's funeral today and I really must be seen there."

Ronan straightened as Coira stood. "Of course."

"Anything for you, Ronan," Coira said, as she draped herself over him to kiss his cheek. "Say the word and I'm there."

I rolled my eyes and told myself I wasn't jealous.

He smiled down at the woman, but also set her away from him. "Not this time, Coira."

She looked from him to me with a little pout. "I see. Well, when you change your mind, you know where to find me." Then she turned and started for the door. Before she left, she turned back. "Oh, I just remembered. As I was leaving, I noticed a human woman approach Meriel. Golden hair like yours." She pointed to me. "Kind of short, wearing a lovely dress, or else I probably would have forgotten completely."

"You're sure she was human?" Ronan asked.

"I was too far away to notice if it had any kind of magic, but it was definitely a human."

Ronan nodded and opened the door for Coira, who left my office to get into a stretch limousine. Of course she would come to my office in a limousine. After the door closed behind her, I said, "So you're sleeping with her, too." And immediately wanted to slap myself.

"That's a little too present tense for my and Coira's relationship," he said as he took the seat Coira had vacated.

"What happened?"

"Like humans often do, Coira got too attached. I had to stop for her own good."

"You don't think you could have ever had real feelings for her?"

He paused for a moment, as if weighing what to say. Or how much.

"I know I wouldn't."

His certainty was absolute. And there was more to this story as well. But he had erected a wall between us that told me I wasn't permitted to it. I wondered if he had feelings for someone else and was surprised by how much the idea bothered me. I didn't linger on the thoughts.

"Okay. There's two things I want to discuss from that conversation."

"The human."

"That's one. Are there humans in the Sidhe?"

"There are a few, yes. They're changelings."

"Like me."

He shook his head. "Saying you and the human changelings are alike is like saying a rocket ship and a bicycle are alike because they are both modes of transportation."

"Am I the rocket ship in this analogy?"

He arched an eyebrow, then just continued. "Most human changelings are changed as babies and are changed with inanimate objects like pieces of wood. The parents don't usually notice the switch at first, but the object will eventually fade and they think their child has died. It doesn't happen often anymore."

"What happens to the humans when they're brought to the Sidhe?"

"Any number of things from being tortured and killed to being kept as beloved pets."

"Neither of those options sound good to me."

He shrugged. "Being a beloved pet can be nice. It's better than being an unloved pet, little more than a toy to play with from time to time. And if *that's* to be your fate, being killed is often better."

"You're not really selling me on the whole magical other world idea."

"It can be a harsh place. The way we live is different from humans. Some things are better. Some things are worse. And where it is worse, it is a lot worse. There is an imbalance in the Sidhe. Many people speak of it, but always in hushed tones. Some believe, if the Sidhe can be brought into balance again, life will be better for all. Though don't mistake me, we are still predators, every one."

We sat there in silence for a moment. I wondered if Ronan had a bit of experience being the unloved pet. The way he spoke of it certainly made me think he had. I knew a little something about being unloved. I wanted to reach out to him, but I didn't think he would accept comfort from me. I knew I never wanted comfort from people who didn't understand what I was going through. It felt too much like pity.

"So could a human changeling have the same effect on Meriel that being with you or using the fae water could?"

"It's possible. But the human would have had to be in the Sidhe for a while. A decade at least. But also be young enough that coming back to the human world wouldn't undo them."

"What does that mean?"

"If a human lives in the Sidhe, they stop aging at a certain point. Children will grow to adulthood, but then they age like we do, slowly. Humans can live to be a few hundred years old in the Sidhe. Not as old as the fae, but certainly much older than they could in the human world. However, if they were then to leave the Sidhe, the magic would no longer work and they would risk aging at a very rapid pace until they catch up."

"So if someone would have been a hundred years old in the human world..."

"They would exit the Sidhe only to age quickly and likely die from the shock. I've heard it can take an hour or less. Possibly minutes. The fae don't care enough about humans to pay close attention to it, though."

"Okay. Well, it's something to keep in mind. I'll go to the restaurant where Coira and Meriel had lunch and ask the staff about it. See if anyone else saw this meeting."

Ronan nodded.

"I'd like to visit Killian tomorrow. You said he was the Corporation's representative before you, so he would have met Meriel when she was exiled."

"That's right. He lives in the Chief. You know where that is?"

"You mean the most popular hiking spot in the Vancouver area? Yes. I'm familiar with it." I refrained from rolling my eyes, but couldn't contain the sarcasm. I was only human after all... Or, well, something anyway.

He studied me for a moment, his expression carefully blank. "If you want, we can drive together. You can come to my house and stay the night. Then you can inundate me with questions on our drive out there."

"I'm not that bad."

He didn't respond.

"Fine. I'll come out to your house. We can go together. I'll come by after talking to the Cardero's staff."

He stood as if to leave.

"Wait, I have one other question based on what Coira said. She mentioned humans not being able to say no to that much magic in one place and being out with fae in public." I paused, wondering if this was one of those questions I didn't really want an answer to. "Is it possible that Arial is fae?"

"Your friend? She is not true fae or else I would know her, but potentially a mongrel, or part fae. And certainly possible that it was recent in her family history. Did she know her father?"

I shook my head.

"Her father could have been fae then. Or a grandparent. You would have had trouble making friends with humans. They would have sensed the difference in you. It would make most uncomfortable and others would become addicted. But if Arial is fae, the fae in her would be drawn to the fae in you. Especially given your magical strength. She would have looked to you for protection."

"That... explains a lot." I thought about what that meant, to me and my past, what it would mean to Arial. Her mom might have been telling the truth after all. "If you met her, would you be able to tell?"

"I would."

"Would you meet her, then?"

"Do you really want me to?"

I looked down at my desk and moved some papers around, pretending to be looking for something, but I couldn't think of what I might possibly be looking for. "Well, she's having a party on Saturday for her birthday and said I could invite someone. If you wanted to come, you could."

"To your friend's birthday party?"

"Yeah. There will be food and music. A bunch of her friends will be there and I'm not really so comfortable with them. It would actually help me out if you came. I'd at least have someone to talk to most of the night. Or we could just scowl at each other." I finally glanced up at him, giving up on the pretense of looking for something.

He was smiling and I got the distinct impression he was about to start laughing at me. Again. "Okay. I'll go to your friend's birthday party. But only to scowl."

"Deal." I swallowed. "And if you think she's part fae, don't say anything. I'll tell her if I think she needs to know."

I sat at my desk for a long time after he was gone. I had been alone for most of my life. I had trouble finding people to talk to, who I could relate to. I wondered sometimes if something was wrong with me. Turns out, I was just living in the wrong world.

CHAPTER 15

I got to Cardero's and paid far more than I wanted to spend to park my bike on the street outside. I'd never been to this restaurant, but Arial told me it was really nice. I had to walk down a dock to get to it as it floated on the water of Coal Harbor surrounded by millions of dollars' worth of boats.

The hostess greeted me, introduced herself as June, and asked if I wanted a table for one.

"Actually, I'm wondering if you or anyone else here worked on October 23rd? Meriel Jones was here for lunch with Coira Winters." I showed her my private investigator license. "I was hoping to ask someone some questions about what happened that day."

"Oh yes. I loved that movie the two of them were in last summer. It was so awesome to see them. And so horrible what happened just the next day. I was hostess that day and Bethany served them. She's not in until later tonight."

"That's okay. Do you mind if I just ask you a few questions?"

She gasped. "Is this about the murder?"

"Uh, no," I lied. "Ms. Winters hired me to look into something for her."

"Okay."

"I know they were here from about 12:30 until 2. Did you see anyone talk to them?"

"I saw them both to their tables. Neither talked to anyone before they sat down. I poured them both some water and gave them menus. Then I didn't see them until they left. When they did, they said good-bye to each other. Ms. Winters' driver arrived, and she left. She didn't speak to anyone that I saw. But Ms. Jones talked to someone for a few moments after Ms. Winters left. Her driver was waiting, too, but it looked like an important conversation. Ms. Jones talked for about five minutes and then she left, too."

I nodded and made a few notes. "Ms. Winters noticed the woman as well. She said she'd like some more information on her, if I can find any. She thought she might have been one of Ms. Jones' friends and now, Ms. Winters is hoping to connect with her. Could you tell me more about the woman?"

"Well, I wasn't close enough to hear what they were saying, but it looked like she was giving Ms. Jones some really good news. She seemed to get very excited when she heard what the woman was saying. The woman was shorter than Ms. Jones. About your height, I would say. She had dark blonde hair, medium-length, I guess. She was pretty unremarkable, to tell the truth. Especially next to Ms. Jones."

"When she left Ms. Jones, did you see where she went?"

"Yes, actually. She went down one of the docks. I assumed she owned or rented a boat in the harbor. Though now that I think about it, that's kind of weird for October, isn't it?"

"Which dock did she go down?"

June pointed to a dock that stretched out into the harbor and I started in that direction. No gate prohibited people from walking onto it, so I started down, wondering what I was looking for.

When I began my career as a private investigator, I quickly found I was good at finding things. Sometimes that meant a clue for what my clients needed. Sometimes that meant a particular object. Now that I knew I was fae, I figured my gift had something to do with whatever magic I possessed. I always seemed to intuitively know where to go. I felt that way now. I was on to something. The further down the dock I went, the more certain I was. I allowed that instinct to direct my feet until I got to a spot about three quarters of the way down. I stopped and glanced around. Other than the boats, there was nothing. No people, nothing suspicious, but my instincts had never steered me wrong before. I focused on the magic and immediately felt something.

I could almost feel another path ahead of me. I couldn't see anything but water in that direction. I took a step and stood at the edge of the dock. I reached a foot out and felt around where my instincts were guiding me. Instead of feeling empty air, I felt something solid beneath my foot.

"You'll want to be careful if you go in there."

I started at the voice but couldn't see who had spoken.

"It's the Sidhe, isn't it?"

"A direct door to the heart of Winter."

"Who knows it's here?"

"Very few. It's a secret Way. The Sidhe built it only a few decades ago."

"Where are you?"

"In the Space Between."

"*Who* are you?"

"This Way's Guardian."

"You make sure only those who are allowed can enter here."

The voice didn't respond. I took that as assent.

"So if I were exiled…"

"An exiled fae may not enter the Sidhe without invitation. If one were to try, I would have to dissuade them from the attempt."

I shuddered at the malice in the Guardian's voice. I could guess what it meant by "dissuade." I doubted any exiled fae made it out of the situation alive.

"This has been enlightening information, Guardian."

"It was a pleasure, Changeling Calynn."

"How did you…" I trailed off because I could feel whatever had been talking to me was gone. The Way was there, but closed. I knew I could open it again, but I wasn't sure why it had been left open in the first place.

***

As I drove out to Ronan's property, I thought about what I had to do next. I needed to talk to Killian. Since he'd been the contact for fae when I'd been changed, he would almost certainly have answers about me. Though probably not any about the case. Still, it wouldn't hurt to ask him for his advice.

I needed to talk to Meriel's lover, Angor. They'd had dinner after she met the human from the Sidhe. At this point, I was certain that was who had sent Meriel to me. But why?

Meriel might have told Angor who it was she had seen, which would help me figure it all out. But a large part of me didn't want to talk to him. I didn't want to see his grief. I didn't want to be reminded, when Meriel had finally found what she'd been looking for, something she hadn't even known she *should* look for, she'd been killed before she could truly enjoy it.

I was almost at Ronan's house when the ground seemed to explode from under the front tire of my bike and I careened off the road. I managed to stop without falling off. When I looked back at what had happened, a monstrous creature stood there. He was about seven feet tall—maybe more—and had tusks that jutted out from his bottom jaw about six inches. He held a club in one meaty hand, though his claws made the club seem a little redundant. Short, bristly black hairs covered his body, and he suffered from a major hunchback. A mossy loincloth draped around his hips and hung down past his knees.

"Can I help you with something?" I asked him, getting off my bike and shrugging out of my pack. I tried not to notice how my hands were shaking as I dropped it on the ground and searched for anything I could use as a weapon.

The creature started stomping toward me. Or I guess he walked normally. It just seemed like stomping because his bulk shook the ground with every step.

"You have offended my mistress. She wishes I should punish you." His voice was gravelly and deep, like the earth he had just emerged from. I actually liked the way it sounded. I was sure it would grate on most people's nerves, but I could hear the magic behind it, and it made the creature sound as powerful as he looked.

"Ah. I see. Can you tell me who your mistress is and what I did to offend her?" I stepped away from him toward a cluster of trees. There had been a windstorm about a week ago, and a bunch of branches had broken. Instead of clearing them up, the city had simply pushed them off to the side of the road.

"It is not my place to ask questions of my mistress. It is only my place to obey."

"Of course. That sounds quite reasonable. But you understand, if I don't know what I'm being punished for, I'm liable to do it again." One of the first lessons of krav maga was you didn't have to participate in every fight you were invited to. The best way to win a fight was to avoid it altogether. And I wanted to avoid this one if at all possible. But the creature was still advancing toward me and there really wasn't any place I could go without putting myself in danger by turning my back on him. I knew I could never outrun him since his legs were far longer than mine. He wasn't leaving much choice. I found a large branch, about four feet long and thick enough that I *might* be able to use it to defend myself against that massive club.

"That is also not my concern."

I was now within swinging distance of the creature's weapon. I gripped my branch. Ronan only lived a bit down the road, but he would have no idea I was in trouble. And I couldn't exactly pause to make a phone call.

"Before we begin, could you tell me what this punishment is?"

"I will strike you with my club five times, as my mistress directed."

"Right. Well, you know that'll likely kill me."

The creature stared at me.

"Got it. Not your concern. Well, then you should also know, I'm going to have to defend myself. To the death. Yours or mine." I raised the branch into a guard position. I'd learned how to disarm opponents and how to use a person's size against them, but this creature looked carved from stone. I wasn't sure how much of my training would help me in this case.

He lifted the club, getting ready to deliver the first strike. "If that is what you must do, I accept your terms. But my duty is to my mistress and I must obey her."

I dropped the tip of the branch and asked out of genuine curiosity, "Why?"

The creature faltered. "I do not understand your question."

"Why must you obey her? Look, pal, I'm new to all this stuff. I don't understand why you have to do what she says. I mean, do you *want* to strike me five times? You never even met me before today."

"I offered her my oath that I will fulfill this request."

"Right. But you don't need protection. I mean, look at you. So why are you sworn into her service?"

"I am not sworn into her service," he growled, then paused. "You are trying to stall me."

"Maybe a little. But I really am curious. Your world doesn't make sense to me."

"It is not my job to educate you." He lifted his club again and I knew I had delayed as long as I could. I set my teeth together, lifted my branch, and prepared to die.

The creature swiped at me, and I caught the swing on the branch, stalling some of the momentum. I heard a crack from the branch and was thrown to the ground under the strike. My shoulder and wrist felt like they had been ripped out of the sockets. I could still move, though, and I used the time it took for the creature to heft the club for a second swing to roll back onto my feet. I'd be dead in seconds if I stayed on the ground. I tried to lift the branch to guard against the next strike, but my shoulder was no longer obeying my commands. If I took another hit on that side, I'd be toast.

"Nice swing," I said.

"Nice block," he responded.

He came at me with a backhanded swing and I tried to run away from it. Because of that, the club hit my left side with a little less force than if I had just stood there and taken it. I still ended up on the ground again, wondering if my left arm was broken. I didn't have the time to find out because the creature was already preparing for another strike.

"You really ... take your job ... seriously," I said, panting a little from the pain.

"My mistress requires nothing less. She expects her word to be carried out. To the letter."

I didn't move quite fast enough and this time, when the club came down, it smashed my left hand, and I *knew* it was broken. I screamed from the pain, distantly surprised to find my hand still attached to my arm when the club lifted again. I climbed to my knees, still gripping the branch in my right hand, my left arm cradled against my body. I flailed back from the creature as he took a swing and this time, the club only grazed my back. Pure luck, I was sure.

Still on the ground, I turned to face him again and held the branch out in front of me. Though I wasn't sure how exactly I'd held onto it or what I was going to do with it now or how much good it would do. At some point, it had broken and was now only two feet long.

The creature chuckled. "You also take your job very seriously, young one. You do not give up, even in the face of defeat."

"Well. I can be... pretty stubborn."

"So I see. It has been a pleasure, young one." He hefted the club and started to swing it down toward my head. At the last moment, I got the branch between me and the club, holding it up in sheer desperation and yelling in defiance. I didn't know what happened next. Maybe it was the desperation, maybe the club had some structural deformity, but when the club hit the branch, they both shattered. Splinters of wood rained down on me.

The creature looked at me, startled. "You broke my club."

I wasn't sure how that could be true, but I just said, "You broke my hand."

"No matter. That was the fifth strike. Your punishment is complete."

The creature turned and started stomping back to the hole he had created in the road.

"That's it? You're not going to try to kill me some more?"

He turned to look at me. "My mistress asked me to punish you. Bugganes do not kill for punishment. She asked for five strikes from my club. Perhaps she believed it would be enough to kill you. Perhaps not. But I have delivered the five strikes, and every one hit you in some form or another. My job is complete."

"What's your name?" I asked the creature.

He tilted his head to the side. "Why do you want to know?"

"I respect you. I'd like to know who you are."

He nodded once. "I also have come to respect you, young one. My name is Deegan. It was a pleasure to deliver your punishment."

"I'd say it was a pleasure to receive it, but it really wasn't."

Deegan laughed and I decided I liked this guy, even if he did just almost kill me. I pulled my phone out of my pocket and sent Ronan a text. By the time he got there, moments later, and got out of the truck, Deegan had already gone.

"Hey," I called to him, cradling my arm as my hand throbbed. "Took you long enough."

Ronan ran to me. "Are you hurt?"

I lay back, relieved someone was here so I could relax and let the waves of pain distract me from the world.

"That is the dumbest question I've heard all day."

CHAPTER 16

Ronan drove me back to his house in stony silence. I wasn't too worried about it, focused instead on the throbbing in my body. I rested my head against the glass of the passenger side window with my eyes closed. Everything from my hips to my head hurt in some way. I couldn't move my left hand at all and though I hadn't taken any other direct hits, the rest of my body protested all movement.

Ronan parked outside and came around to help me out of the truck and up the stairs into his house. Aelwyd was putting together dinner and startled as we came in the door.

"Go fetch your father," Ronan said. "And Carrick."

The girl hurried out of the house.

"Who's Carrick?"

"Don't you ever get tired of asking questions?"

He helped me up the stairs and into the spare bedroom. When I was lying on the bed, he smoothed the hair out of my face and stared hard into my eyes, his emerald eyes filled with emotions that didn't cross his face.

I squirmed under his scrutiny. "What are you looking at?"

"I'm looking for signs of a concussion."

"Deegan never hit my head. Just my arms and hand and back."

A door downstairs closed, and footsteps approached. Ronan pulled away from me as a brownie and another fae creature entered the room. Ronan introduced the brownie as Evander and the other as Carrick, who he sent after my bike. Evander came closer to the bed, holding a case and pulled a bunch of things out of it. Ronan moved to the door and watched as Evander checked me over.

The brownie tsked as he noted my bruises and my broken hand. "We should remove your shirt to see the full extent."

I looked at Ronan, surprised by the heat uncurling in my belly.

"I'm going to discuss dinner with Aelwyd," he said before leaving the room.

Evander helped me with my shirt.

"He's not too happy with me," I said.

"You misread his emotions, child. An easy thing for one as closed as him. He's upset he wasn't there to protect you."

"Why would he need to protect me? I've been protecting myself just fine for the last twenty-nine years."

"It is in his nature to want to protect you. You are one of the high fae. We all feel drawn to serve you."

He spread some salve on the bruises on my back and it felt warm wherever the gooey mess touched it. Then he spread the stuff down my arm and onto my hand, gently touching where the bones were definitely broken. Then he set my hand on a board and wrapped it tightly in bandages, using the board as a kind of splint.

"I thought the stronger fae were supposed to protect the lesser fae."

"It works both ways. We protect you from harm so you can protect us from harm."

"But why? Deegan said something like that. Do you know who Deegan is?"

"I do, though I never met him. He is the captain of Queen Titania's dungeons. I have often wondered about his loyalty, though."

"He said wasn't in service to her, but had offered his oath. But he couldn't or wouldn't explain why."

Evander sat back and began packing up his things. "In the Sidhe, the lesser fae will often choose a liege. If a fae swears fealty, they *must* do as is requested or else be forsworn. When Deegan arrived in Lumina some years ago, he offered my Queen his loyalty but did not swear fealty. He can accept or refuse requests from his mistress. But if he offered his oath that he would complete a task and then did not complete that task, there would be terrible consequences."

"Like being exiled?"

"No. It is much worse than that. If someone breaks their oath, their magic is forfeit. It is torn from them and they fade into nothing. It is a terrible fate. One no fae would ever choose."

"Like, they'll die?"

He shook his head. "If a fae dies, their magic is reborn through the Sidhe into something new. If they break their oath, it is stripped and never seen again."

"But you said Deegan hasn't sworn fealty."

"Not while I lived in the Sidhe."

"Why would he swear loyalty but not fealty?"

"Fealty comes with a thirty-year term. It cannot be broken unless the master allows it. Your loyalty is something freely given and can be lost at any time if it is no longer deserved. The Queen believes he offers his loyalty because she deserves it. Many others believe he offers it so he can spy for his people."

Evander shrugged as though none of this concerned him anymore. And it probably didn't since he now lived in the human world.

"I will return to check on you throughout the evening. And I'll make some fresh salve so it's more potent. You should feel better by tomorrow, though the hand might take a bit longer. And you'll need plenty of rest."

He fell silent and stood, his case of medical supplies in his hand, but he didn't turn to leave the room.

"Is there something else?" I prompted after a minute of silence.

He didn't look at me when he said, "I know you went to see my daughter. Bidina. I wonder if I might inquire as to how she is faring?"

"Oh." I wasn't sure what he wanted to hear, that she was doing well out there on her own, or that she wasn't. I decided on the truth. "She seemed okay to me. She was sad. I guess she really liked Meriel."

Evander nodded and breathed a sigh. As he turned to leave, I noticed the gleam of tears in his eyes. Just before he left the room, I heard him say, "I just wish she would come home."

***

A elwyd brought me dinner in the spare bedroom, where I had been told to rest and recuperate. I hated being told what to do and not being allowed to move, but I hated more that Evander had been right. I needed to rest. I spent most of the day reading Meriel's journal again, which I had begun carrying with me, along with my notes on the case. I was more familiar with her story by this point than I was with my own. Then again, I had no idea where I came from, so that wasn't really surprising.

I had just finished eating when Ronan appeared in the bedroom doorway. He stood there awkwardly for a moment before he said, "I wanted to tell you I'm going out to help Evander. Aelwyd is downstairs if you need anything."

This time, the lie was clear. It rang as a discordant note through every word.

"You're lying to me."

"What?"

"You didn't come up here to tell me that. So why did you come up here?"

"How did you know I was lying?"

"I just do. I've always been good at telling if people are lying or not. Why do you think I've believed everything you said? Some of it sounds quite ludicrous, but you believe everything you're telling me. Though I can also tell there are things you're not telling me. Lies of omission are more difficult to spot, but I still get them sometimes. What you said just now was an outright lie. Those are easy to hear."

Ronan regarded me for a moment like I had just grown an extra head. Or like he was going back over everything he had said to me and wondered if his secrets were still safe. Whatever he was thinking, he quickly schooled himself and was again the unreadable mask I had come to know.

"I came up here to check on you. See how you were doing. But you don't like people worrying about you, so I gave you a different reason."

Regular old truth. No lies present. But it did bring up another question. How does he know I don't like people worrying about me? We've known each other for a few days. He shouldn't know me that well this soon.

"Before you go, we should talk about the next steps in the investigation." I'd made some more notes on what I wanted to do next while reading through Meriel's journal again.

"The next step is for your hand to heal."

I rolled my eyes and was about to argue when someone knocked on the door downstairs.

"Humans," Ronan said.

"What?"

"At the door. I have to go."

Aelwyd appeared in my doorway with an alarmed expression on her face.

"Don't worry," Ronan told her as he passed. "I'll take care of it."

As he went to answer the door, I motioned Aelwyd over. "Help me to the top of the stairs. I want to listen."

She did as I asked, but I could tell she was reluctant to do so. I sat down, out of sight of the lower level of the house but able to hear everything. "Go ahead to the loft," I told Aelwyd, and she didn't need any more encouragement.

"Can I help you, gentlemen?" I heard Ronan say when he opened the door.

"Mr. Smith?"

I knew that voice.

"I am. Call me Ronan."

"I'm Detective Jeremy Lopez. This is my partner, Detective Mack Granger. We have a few questions for you regarding the murder of Meriel Jones. Do you mind if we come inside for a moment?"

My world narrowed to the voices downstairs. I held my breath. And a thought I hadn't spent enough time considering pushed forward in my mind.

"Of course, detectives. Would you like some coffee?"

"No thank you," Detective Granger said.

"I'll have a cup," Jeremy said.

"I was sorry to hear of Meriel's death."

"Were you close?" Jeremy asked.

"Not very. I assume you're here because I am the beneficiary of her estate."

"Can you explain to us how that came to be, Mr. Smith?" Granger this time.

"Of course. I am the West Coast representative of the Diaspora Corporation, a non-profit organization. We give loans to individuals who meet certain requirements. The individuals then pay a percentage of their yearly income back to the corporation. If they were to die and leave no heirs, their estate reverts to the organization. To help future individuals, you see. We gave one such loan to Meriel's family several years ago. About sixty, I believe. But that was before I was the representative here. I can find out exactly when and get you the paperwork, if you would like. It might take me a couple days to dig it out of our files."

"That would be very helpful, Ronan," Jeremy said.

"Of course. Do you have any other questions for me?"

"You said you weren't close to Ms. Jones. What did your relationship look like?" Jeremy asked.

"She would meet with a representative once a quarter. There is another in California who she would meet with as well, but if she was in Vancouver, she would meet with me. I saw her two, maybe three times a year for the past few years."

"So you didn't know any of her friends? Any acquaintances?" Granger asked.

"I knew her assistant, Bidina. And her lawyer, Mr. Avery. I'm afraid I can't be more helpful."

"If you think of anything else," Granger said.

"Of course. I'll have the documents sent to you as soon as I can."

I heard the detectives start to leave, and then I heard Jeremy's voice again. "Oh, I think I left my jacket inside. I'll just be a minute." A pause and then Jeremy said, "What's going on here?"

"What do you think is going on here, detective?"

"I think my partner and I are in a little over our heads. Meriel wasn't human, was she?"

"You're not as blind as Bidina thought, after all."

"What are you?"

"Can you not guess?"

"Sidhe."

"We prefer daoine sidhe. Or tylwyth teg."

"Exiled?"

"Not that it's any of your concern, but yes."

"Who killed Meriel Jones?"

"Likely the Dark."

"Jesus."

"You've heard of him."

"Who hasn't?"

My mind was reeling. Jeremy. The Jeremy I had been sleeping with for the last three years was downstairs and knew about this world I had stumbled into. I remembered what Bidina had said. *Even the ones with clear sight can barely see what's in front of them.* I'd been so focused on who Meriel had met with from the Sidhe I hadn't considered if the wizard who interviewed Bidina might be relevant. He probably wasn't relevant to the case. But he was certainly relevant to me.

"I guess we'll have an unsolved murder. Shit. Send the paperwork anyway. I'll see what I can do to close the case as quickly as possible."

"That would be appreciated, detective."

"Of all the cases in West Van."

I heard the door close, and Ronan come up the stairs. I didn't look up at him. I was still trying to make sense of what I'd heard.

"I should have known you would be eavesdropping."

My best friend was probably partly fae. Jeremy was a wizard. How many other people in my life had some kind of magic?

"Calynn?"

"Jeremy is the wizard."

"He is certainly a magic user."

I looked up. "Magic user?"

"Humans have different names for different types of magic users. I don't know what kind he is. What's wrong?"

"I've been seeing him. For a few years. Very casually. I'd just decided to stop. But I haven't told him yet."

Ronan reached down and helped me up and back to bed.

"Why did you decide to stop?"

"He seems to be getting feelings for me and I don't have any for him. I mean, other than like... well..."

"Sex."

I glared at him. "I wasn't going to be so crude, but yes." I sighed as I settled back into the bed and pulled the covers over myself with my good hand. Ronan helped me. "I've been in this position before. Guys tend to feel more for me than I do for them."

"That's not surprising."

I rolled my eyes. "Why? Because I'm so irresistible and intoxicating?"

"No. Because you're fae. Humans can become addicted to the magic in us. Only those with a bit of magic themselves can hold off, but usually only for a time. I'm surprised he lasted as long as he did. He must be a powerful magic user."

"Great. So now I'm this fairy creature and my boyfriend's a wizard. Can my life get a little bit more weird?"

Ronan laughed and I smiled at his laughter. I forgot how nice it was when he wasn't laughing at me.

"Don't tempt the Ancient Mother, little changeling. She likes to grant wishes at the most inconvenient times."

Our hands rested right next to each other on the bed and it occurred to me that Ronan was sitting on the edge of the mattress. He was close enough for me to touch if I simply adjusted the placement of my hand. He might have realized the same thing because he stood up quickly and started toward the door. "Get some rest. You'll heal faster."

He left and I relaxed against the pillows on the bed. I didn't realize how tired I was until then. I was asleep before Aelwyd came down from the loft.

***

By the time I woke up in the morning, I could move my hand, though it was still covered in a rather ugly bruise. I went downstairs to find Ronan at the island eating breakfast, a newspaper and a cup of coffee in front of him while Aelwyd bustled around the kitchen.

"So, what time are we leaving?" I asked as I sat next to him.

He blinked slowly at me and I noticed the confusion in his eyes, though his expression remained the same. "Leaving for where?" he asked.

"We're going to visit Killian today," I reminded him.

Aelwyd set a coffee in front of me and I smiled at her before lifting the cup to smell the brew and then taking a sip.

"You could have died yesterday."

"Mm-hm. But I didn't. You can drive if it makes you feel better."

"Killian lives up on the side of the mountain. We'll have to hike to get there."

"I broke my hand, not my foot. You want to leave right after we eat so we can try to leave there before dark?"

He continued to stare at me. I ignored him as Aelwyd set a plate of scrambled eggs and bacon in front of me and then started for the back door. Ronan's food was already steaming in front of him, but he didn't pay any attention to it. As she went out, Evander came in with his medical case. I finished everything on my plate before I let him look at my hand.

While he was examining it, Ronan said, "She wants to visit Killian today."

Evander glanced up from his examination. "All right."

"How is she supposed to get there?"

"I would imagine you would drive her and then you would walk up. Her hand is broken, not her foot."

I should be awarded a medal for not laughing. I took a sip of my coffee instead.

The brownie stared again at my hand, turning it this way and that. "Hm."

"What's wrong? Is it not healing right?"

"No, no. Nothing like that. It seems the bones are no longer broken."

"Excuse me?"

"They aren't broken any longer. I have a touch of water magic. I can feel where the major breaks were yesterday. They have become little more than fractures today. Hairline."

"How is that possible?"

"You have magic of your own. You're healing yourself."

I looked between Evander and Ronan. "Is that normal?"

Ronan shook his head and turned away before I could see what emotions he was hiding. Evander answered.

"A person's magic will help, of course, but not this fast. You would need to have healing magic of your own for it to be able to do this. But I don't feel healing magic within you. At least not healing magic like I understand." He looked at Ronan. "In my opinion, she should see Killian if only so he can see her magic."

"Seeing magic. Is that something dwarfs can do but other fae can't?"

Evander spread more of his salve onto my hand and then wrapped it again so it could finish healing. "Not dwarfs. Just Killian. And even then, he has spent the last hundred or so years honing the ability. It was not a skill he was born with."

When he was finished and packing his things, I shoveled more food onto my plate and began eating again. I was starving. Though if my body was healing that fast, it wasn't really a surprise I was so hungry. "So we'll leave after we're done eating," I said between mouthfuls.

Ronan didn't answer, but the tightness in his glance told me we would go, but he wasn't going to like it.

CHAPTER 17

I t took about two hours to get to the day-use parking lot at the Stawamus Chief Provincial Park. Traffic wasn't great as people drove from the suburbs into Vancouver for work. While he drove, I peppered Ronan with questions. He told me about bugganes and how they were subterranean creatures who tended not to be from Winter or Summer but were considered wyldfae. Though individuals could have magic that was more Winter or Summer. I already knew Deegan worked for the Summer Queen since Evander had mentioned it, but I hadn't noticed if his magic felt more one than the other.

Ronan said there were many creatures like that in the Sidhe, wyldfae who belonged to neither Summer nor Winter and could move between the domains and through the area of the Sidhe known as the Fréimhe. He gave me the names of a bunch of creatures like redcaps, kelpies, clurichaun, and will-o'-the-wisp. I wrote them down to look up later. By the time we parked, my head was pounding with all the information he had given me.

I'd been to the Chief to go hiking before, though usually not at the end of October. I enjoyed hiking and had taken advantage of the amazing trails in and around the Lower Mainland a lot over the years. I'd done the six-hour hike to all three peaks at the Chief a few times in the past and hoped we wouldn't have to go all the way to the top to get to wherever Killian lived. My hand and the rest of my body might be almost healed, but I was still pretty exhausted. And I was hungry again. I should have brought the leftover breakfast with us.

"Where is his place?" I asked, as I got out of the truck and put my leather jacket on.

Ronan pointed up toward the mountain.

"How far?" I went to the back of the truck to check on my motorcycle that I had convinced Ronan to bring with us so I could go home after this instead of back to his place. It was still standing with the braces we had put together and looked secure.

"Not too far. It's before the first peak, but off the main trail."

"Not really interested in visitors, is he?"

"Killian? No. He's happiest when he's left alone. He was thrilled when I came to BC and took over as the Diaspora representative."

Ronan opened the back door of his truck and pulled a long umbrella from under the seat. I was about to ask if he thought it was going to rain again when my vision went blurry. I squeezed my eyes closed and when I opened them again, he had a gigantic sword resting against his shoulder.

"What the fuck?" I stumbled backward for a moment before I regained my balance.

"What?"

"You're carrying a sword! It was an umbrella. But now it's a fucking sword."

"You can see through the glamour?"

"See through the what?"

He was looking at me strangely, but answered my question anyway. "Glamour is a magic that makes things appear differently to their true form. You can see the sword?"

"Yes, I can see the motherfucking sword. It's right there, isn't it?"

"It is. But I don't know anyone who can see through glamour. It should just look like an umbrella."

"Well, it doesn't. Don't you have a scabbard or something for that thing?"

"Yes. But it's much faster to use it if it isn't in a sheath. And if something is trying to kill you, speed is rather important."

The shock of the umbrella changing into a sword was wearing off, and I became more curious about the weapon. I'd used a few weapons in training, but never a sword, and especially not one of that length. "I thought swords were carried on the side."

He settled the flat side of the sword against his shoulder so the point stuck up in the air past his head and the handle—hilt?—rested in his hand. He started walking and I fell into step next to him. "Sometimes. But when there is a possibility of having to use it, broadswords are more often carried like this. If I need to use it quickly, it's already in my dominant hand, ready."

"Do you think you'll need it?"

"Hard to say. The Dark attacked you four nights ago. By now, he will have reported that he failed his first attempt. Yesterday, a buggane attacked you. He also will have reported that he didn't kill you. Something else could be after you."

We started along the Chief Peaks Trail but only for a few moments before Ronan checked behind us and then stepped off it. Since it was a weekday morning at the end of October, I doubted anyone else would be hiking today and see us. I followed him off the trail and quickly it became too narrow to walk side-by-side. There were moments when I thought we were lost, but Ronan seemed to know where he was going.

"Speaking of you being in danger," he said over his shoulder, "I should have mentioned before: it will be dangerous in your apartment. Your threshold is weak. You live alone in shared accommodation. The Dark will be able to find you if you are there after sundown. Likely others as well."

"So now I have to be indoors after dark *and* I can't be in my own home?"

"You don't know how dangerous he is."

"He's already attacked me once and I survived."

"You got lucky."

"Nice vote of confidence."

"You don't understand this world yet, little changeling. You don't know the dangers. Do not underestimate the Dark."

"Fine. Has anyone ever told you how annoying it is when you tell them what to do?"

"No."

"I figured. Tell me more about Killian."

"He is a dwarf from Winter. What more do you want to know?"

"Well, let's start with what is a dwarf?"

Ronan stopped and looked back at me. The look of complete shock Ronan threw at me made me roll my eyes.

"I'm not stupid," I said. "I know what humans *think* a dwarf is. I did some research and I read a bunch about them living in mountains and underground. I know they're known for being blacksmiths and miners and they're usually portrayed as short, ugly, and with lots of facial hair. Lots of hair in general, actually. What I want to know is what are they, really? What do the humans have right, and what did they get wrong?"

Ronan didn't respond right away. He started forward again, navigating the path expertly, even though I could barely see it, and we were making good time. Eventually, he said, "Dwarfs tend to be shorter than the daoine sidhe. Height, or size really, is a good indicator of the strength of someone's magic." He paused, his step hesitating for a moment before he continued on. I wanted to ask what he'd just thought of, but he was already speaking again.

"Usually, anyway. But dwarfs are not ugly. I suppose human standards may label them ugly, but humans are weird. Dwarfs are often scarred, burned, or otherwise disfigured from working. They primarily work with metals, but some also work with wood and stone. They are blacksmiths and miners, but also craftsmen. They do live in mountains and underground because that is where the metal is."

"I read a lot about iron being bad for fae."

Ahead of me, Ronan shook his head. "I told you humans are weird. They're so superstitious, coming up with ideas for things that are supposed to protect them. Iron is an element of the earth, just like other pure metals. And the fae's magic comes from the earth. It doesn't bother us any more than gold or silver. But somewhere in the past, humans decided that cold iron would protect them from us."

"So it's just a myth?"

"Like many things humans believe about us."

"You said Killian is from Winter."

Ronan nodded.

"You're from Winter. Did you know him when you were there?"

"No. He was exiled before I was born. If I'm not mistaken, Killian is around a thousand years old, and he's been living in this area for about a hundred and fifty years. He's always preferred his home in the mountain, but only moved here permanently when I came."

"Why was he exiled?"

"It's rude to ask why someone was exiled."

"Oh. Right."

I wasn't sure what to say next. Some people called me curious. More often, I was called nosy. And if I was being honest, I didn't really want to ask why Killian had been exiled. I wanted to know why *Ronan* had been exiled. My instincts screamed to ask, to dig until I got the answer, but I knew he wouldn't tell me. At least not yet.

The path got steeper and I focused on making it up the hill instead of asking more questions. It only took another twenty minutes to reach Killian's home. If I hadn't been with Ronan, I would have completely missed his door. It looked like it was part of the rock face and when Ronan knocked on it, I had no idea why. But before I could question him, the rock moved, and a short man stood in the opening.

He was about five feet tall and solid. He looked like he'd been carved out of the rock he lived in. His coarse, long, dark hair grew into a longer beard, covering his head, face, and shoulders. He leaned on an interesting staff made from twisted and spiky black wood, a smooth ball on the top, under his hand. He sniffed the air a few times and then said, "Ronan." His voice sounded like rocks tumbling down the mountain. "Come in."

He turned his back on us and walked into his cavern, where a fire was crackling in front of a couch and two over-stuffed chairs. A pot of tea waited on the small table, three cups set out ready for us. Next to the tea, there were small squares of sandwiches. My stomach rumbled at the sight.

Killian settled into one chair and motioned for us to join him. "I knew to expect guests today, but I didn't expect it to be you. What has gone wrong?"

Ronan sat on the couch, and I took the second chair.

"Meriel has been murdered."

Killian sighed and seemed to stare into the fire. "May the Sidhe bring her peace. I told her to be more careful. She never would listen. Have you retrieved her skin?"

"No. I'm not sure it will be possible for a while. The human police are investigating her death. They won't release her estate for some time."

Killian sighed again.

"Why is the skin so important?" I asked. "Neither of you seem to care about who killed her. Only about her skin."

Killian sniffed again and turned in my direction. He didn't look at me, but through me. "The young changeling. You have found Ronan at last."

"Do you know me?"

"No. But I was the Diaspora representative of this region when you were changed. I was informed at the time it happened."

"But you didn't tell Ronan about it when he took over."

"Of course not. Pour the tea, Ronan. It is ready. And give the girl a sandwich." He paused. "Or two."

Ronan did as he was told and started pouring tea as Killian continued, handing a cup to the dwarf first and then one to me with two sandwich squares. I ignored the tea and just ate the sandwiches.

"The one who changed you said you would be safer if no one knew about you," Killian continued.

"Even the new representative? Isn't it his job to protect the fae in the human world?"

"The one who changed you is protecting you. You needn't fear about that, child."

"Who is the one who changed me?"

"It is safer if you, like everyone, do not know."

Frustrated, I took another bite of the sandwich, stuffing the rest of the thing in my mouth and picking up the second one. "Do you know why I was changed?"

"Of course. Can't you guess by what I have already said?"

I took a deep breath. "To keep me safe."

Killian smiled. "You are a bright young girl. Your time with the humans didn't change that."

Killian took a sip of his tea and then set it on the table beside his chair. He faced the fire again, but I realized he wasn't seeing it.

"You're blind," I said.

He didn't bother to turn back toward me. "Aye," he said. "My Queen saw fit to take my sight from me. But I manage just fine without it."

It didn't sound like he had said that for me or for Ronan, so I just let it slide.

After a moment of silence, Killian said, "You ask why we do not care about who killed her. It is because her magic still lives. It lives in her skin. It is possible, if her skin is returned to her family, for a new selkie to be reborn from her magic."

"Like reincarnation?"

"Similar, aye. It must be returned."

"I'll make sure it is."

Killian turned his head toward me and tilted it to one side, as though he was considering me. Which was weird since his eyes seemed to look right through me.

"You are clever. But there is more. Perhaps your time among the humans has not made you weaker, as some feared, but made you stronger."

"I don't understand."

"You will, child. Unfortunately, more than that, I cannot say."

I tried to remind myself I was here to figure out who might have killed Meriel even though everything inside me screamed to know more about myself and where I came from.

"Do you have any idea why Meriel might have been killed?" I asked.

"I do not. She didn't engage in the petty gossiping many fae take part in. She would host parties and she acted and modeled. She searched for the key. She was not quiet about the search. She wanted to return home from the moment she was exiled. Most fae who are exiled accept it for many years before they begin to yearn for home. To go back would mean death, or worse. But Meriel was willing to trade anything to return to the Sidhe. Even if it meant returning to Winter instead of Summer."

"Why would that have mattered?"

"She was a Summer fae. She would not have been able to survive in the icy waters of the Winter Muir. But she always believed Winter would be a better place than the human world."

"That's why she had a saltwater pool. It was heated."

Killian nodded. "The Pacific Ocean is cold in these parts. The pool would have been better for her."

"Why didn't she live in a warmer place?"

"She had a home in California, but the Queen of Light and Beauty only comes out of her domain in the summer. During winter, the Queen of Air and Darkness would come out here or in other Northern climes."

"So she lived where she would have a chance that a queen would be. Because they're the ones who would bring out the key." I paused, organizing my thoughts. "So she wouldn't have been happy in Winter. And she couldn't be friends with a Winter selkie. But she was sleeping with Ronan and he's Winter."

"Ah, but Ronan is daoine sidhe. He is much higher than she is in the hierarchy. To be with a daoine sidhe, it would not have mattered to her if he was from Winter. His magic would have been intoxicating to her. Like a drug."

Ronan had begun shifting in his seat the moment I brought him up. He rolled his eyes and stared at the fireplace.

"Is something wrong?" I asked him.

"You're speaking about me as though I'm not here."

"Do you dispute anything I have said, boy?" Killian asked sharply.

"No, sir."

I hid my smile and the dwarf took a sip of his tea while I considered what he had said.

"The people who worked for her couldn't all be fae, could they?"

"Most likely they too would all be at least partly fae, whether they knew it or not."

"Partly fae?"

Ronan spoke up. "The fae in the Sidhe call them mongrels. Some humans are half fae or their parent was half fae. They don't necessarily know it. If the half-fae lives here, the human parent is usually the mother. In the Sidhe, the human parent is usually the father."

"Why?"

"In human-fae relations, the woman carries the child," Ronan said. "The fae do not choose to live here, regardless of any child they may have."

I thought of Arial. "The child stays with the mother."

"The ones who live in the Sidhe end up with the longer lifespan of the fae and a stronger connection to their magic. Unfortunately, their existence is often far worse than even the lowest fae's."

Both Ronan and Killian looked sad.

I decided it was time to change the subject back to Meriel's case.

"Yesterday, I went to the restaurant where Meriel met Coira. The host was the same one from the day they were there, and she said a woman met with Meriel and then disappeared down one of the docks. I assume it's the same woman Coira saw talking to Meriel. The host thought the person was going to one of the boats. I went down the dock and I found what I think was a Way into the Sidhe."

"You didn't mention this to me."

I turned back to Ronan. "I was a little distracted, what with the buggane trying to crush me with his club and all. Anyway, the host said the woman talked to Meriel for only about five minutes. Coira said Meriel had been acting the same. Bidina said she had been acting weird. The woman probably disappeared back into the Sidhe after their conversation. That must have been the woman who told Meriel about me and that I could help her find the key. What I don't understand is why anyone would send Meriel to me. All she had were a few pictures of Queen Mab wearing the key and then not wearing it. That doesn't tell me anything. Besides, I don't need the key to get into the Sidhe, right? I'm not exiled."

Ronan nodded once in answer to my question, but both he and Killian looked concerned.

"Meriel would have created a risk to you," Killian began slowly. "If you're around another true fae, it would create enough magic to draw one of the Queens' attention. Your protector has spent your life keeping the true fae away from you to prevent just such a thing."

"What about you guys? You're full fae. Wouldn't you do the same as Meriel?"

"More, in fact," Ronan said. "Killian and I are both more powerful than Meriel had been. But the damage has been done. The Queens already know you're here."

That was a good point. I'd felt Mab's gaze on me enough times lately she had to know where I was. And the Summer Queen had to have been the one to send Deegan.

"Could my protector have sent the Dark after Meriel? To try to prevent this situation."

"It is not his way," Killian said. "In the past, he has simply told any others to leave if they got too close. If there had been more of an issue, he would have killed them himself."

"Has he ever done that?" I asked, alarmed.

"Not to my knowledge. Regardless, he certainly couldn't have hired the Dark because the assassin doesn't work for exiled fae."

"My protector is exiled?"

"Of course he is." Killian paused to drink his tea, and I wondered if he was stalling. Then he nodded. "Fae changelings are forbidden. If he changed you and then returned to the Sidhe, he would be immediately executed, or worse. If he didn't return, he would have been exiled so he never could."

I recalled my conversation yesterday. "Unless he had an invitation. The Guardian of the Space Between mentioned that."

"You spoke with the Guardian?" Killian asked sharply. Ronan was staring hard at me, and I wondered what I'd done wrong.

"He talked to me first."

"What did he say?" Ronan asked.

"The Way was open when I got there and I put one foot inside, just to test it. He told me to be careful and that it was a secret Way not many knew about to the heart of Winter." I paused. "So that means the person who told Meriel about me would have come from Winter. Can people move between Winter and Summer easily?"

"We can get back to that," Ronan said. "What else did the Guardian say?"

I narrowed my eyes at him, but gave him the information he wanted, anyway. "He told me about what would happen if an exiled fae tried to go into the Sidhe and then said it was a pleasure to meet me. And he seemed to know who I was."

Ronan stood as though he couldn't contain himself anymore and paced to the fireplace, where he stopped and leaned against the mantle.

I looked at Killian. "Is it a bad thing that the Guardian knows who I am?"

The old dwarf looked pensive as he held his tea. Finally, he said, "It is not bad. I am certain the Guardians know everyone who passes through their Ways. It is simply unusual that one would speak to someone."

"Why would he talk to me then?"

"I do not know."

Ronan was still holding on to the mantle, apparently not going to answer.

"Evander mentioned you could tell me more about my magic."

"I could, but magic doesn't usually manifest until a fae matures. And that is not until the eve of their third decade."

"My thirtieth birthday?"

"Even so."

"Well, I'm twenty-nine. My birthday is in less than six months. Isn't that close enough?"

"Not usually for me to be able to see it."

"Fine. Then back to my question about the fae moving between the domains. Is it possible?"

When Ronan continued to not answer, Killian said, "Winter fae have a lot of difficulty being in Summer and vice versa."

"But the person she met with was human."

"A human changeling?" Killian said. "They are common enough in Winter. Or were before I was exiled."

Ronan finally turned back to the conversation. "They were less common when I was exiled. Mongrels had mostly replaced any human staff. And children are never taken anymore. It is usually adult humans who make a bargain. The fools."

"They would have to know how to open a Way and have enough magic to do so. I would suspect a changeling who had been in the Sidhe for no less than ten years and no more than twenty."

Ronan nodded his agreement before sitting down again.

"But why?" I asked. "Why would they tell Meriel about me? What was the point?"

Ronan didn't look at me when he didn't answer. Killian seemed to consider my question for a long time before he said anything. Then he stood and said, "I am not sure what I can say without endangering your protector. I will discuss the matter with him and meet you tomorrow at Ronan's house."

Ronan and I stood as well.

"I will have the guest room prepared for you, Killian." Ronan bowed to the old dwarf, even though Killian couldn't see him.

I started to do the same and Killian stopped me. "No, young changeling. I bow to you." And he did so. Then he took my hands in his. "Be careful. You do not know the forces working against you. I may have more information for you tomorrow."

CHAPTER 18

The path back down from Killian's place was more treacherous than the way up. It was steep and narrow, little more than a game trail, and I slipped a couple times in the first few steps.

"Are you going to be able to get down?" Ronan asked.

"Yeah, yeah. I'm just... finding my footing."

His sword was again resting on his shoulder, and I was glad of it when an eerie howl split the air. Ronan stopped and looked back the way we had just come.

"What was that?"

"Cu sidhe," he said, like I was supposed to know what that meant.

Above us, Killian came out of his home in the rocks with his staff in one hand and a sword in the other.

"Ronan?"

"Here. You heard the howl?"

"Aye. Come inside, quickly."

A second howl pierced the quiet of the mountain, closer than the first. We started back up the mountainside, Ronan holding his sword in front of him now.

"We must get inside before the third howl. Once we've heard the third howl, there will be no escape. We'll have to fight."

"I don't have anything to fight with." I reached for a tree branch, about to break it off, but Ronan stopped me.

"That will be no use against the cu sidhe. He will keep coming until his head is severed from his body. His loyalty to his master is complete and so anything less than decapitation will not stop him."

We were just about at Killian's door when the third howl reached us.

"Changeling," Killian said, before he tossed me the short sword he held.

I caught it and immediately felt both better and terrified. I had a weapon, but I'd never used a sword before. The closest I came was using a staff in my martial arts classes. I tried to mirror Ronan's stance and grip as we watched the trees in the direction the howls had come from.

It emerged from the bushes and the first thing I did was scream, "What the fuck is that?"

"Cu sidhe. Fairy dog." Ronan's response seemed far calmer than I thought it should be.

The dog was as big as a bear with black shaggy fur and red, glowing eyes. Her ears were larger than what seemed natural and pointed toward us. The claws on her paws dug into the ground, the sharp points cutting through the dirt like it was water. But the worst part was her mouth. It was full of sharp, white teeth and dripping with saliva.

"What do we do?"

"Stand our ground. Fight to the death."

The dog seemed to agree as she growled and charged. I thought for sure Ronan would be dead with the first assault, but then the dog back away after a swing from his sword. The dog had a shallow cut across her chest. She growled again and then began to turn toward me.

"No. You deal with me first," Ronan said as he advanced toward the dog. The fight was vicious and brief. Ronan swung his great sword again and cut the dog, but that seemed to make her even more mad. The dog swiped at him with one of her huge paws and smacked aside the next thrust. She then sank her teeth into his leg and tossed her head, throwing him to the ground. The dog then stalked toward me. Ronan tried to get up to come after her, but his wounded leg buckled beneath him.

As Ronan continued to try to stand, the dog advanced. Killian stepped beside me, his staff raised to defend us both. I wasn't sure what the blind dwarf hoped to accomplish, but as the dog made another lunge, Killian stalled her with a swift thwack on her nose with the pointy end.

"Keep your sword in guard position," he said to me as the dog regrouped. "Feel the charge. You will know when to swing."

"How?"

"It is using its magic. Feel it."

I set my teeth together and did as he said. I could feel Ronan still struggling to rejoin the fight and Killian's solid presence, like a rock, next to me. In front of me, the dog seemed to gather magic from the surrounding air, getting ready to strike again. I felt her feet on the ground as the magic flowed into them. When she couldn't contain any more, she pounced toward me, mouth open, aiming a bite at my throat. I waited for the last possible moment, and then thrust the short sword into the dog's mouth and out through the back of her head. Her teeth struck my hand as I pushed the sword through its flesh.

The dog fell at my feet and I looked down at her, realizing my eyes had been closed until then. She was still breathing, though laboriously. She struggled to stand and come after me again, the sword still sticking through her skull.

Killian stepped next to me, and Ronan finally managed to stand up and limp over. Killian handed him the staff.

We stood around her as the dog died at our feet. Her blood leaked into the ground, as black as her fur. The strange liquid covered me. It had spilled all down my shirt when I stabbed the creature.

"I thought you said it needed to be decapitated to be stopped."

"That wound isn't much short of decapitation."

Killian bent to retrieve the sword and lingered to examine the dog's neck. He touched the entry and exit points and then snatched his hand away as though he had been burned.

"Mother, be merciful," he whispered as he stood up.

"What is it?" Ronan asked him.

"Her gift has manifested."

"I didn't feel anything," I said.

"Nor did I. Killian, are you certain?"

Killian made a disgusted sound. "Of course I am certain, boy. I know the feeling of magic when I touch it."

"Magic doesn't fully manifest until after the third decade."

"And yet, here we are. Ours is not to question the whims and designs of the Ancient Mother and the Sidhe."

"Well, what is it?" I asked him.

"Come inside. I must treat Ronan's wound. You are bleeding as well. And I believe this is a subject best discussed behind a threshold."

My hand seeped blood where the dog's teeth had punctured the skin slightly. We went back into Killian's home, and he busied himself getting some water on to boil and some bandages ready to bind the bite wounds. I waited impatiently while he prepared himself.

When he finally sat in front of Ronan, tending the wound, I said, "Can you tell me now? It's my magic. I should know what it is."

"The fact you do not even know you are using it shows how powerful it is." He pinned the dressing closed and turned to me. "Sit, child. Let me see your hands."

"My hands?" I sat slowly in the chair Killian had been sitting in during our first conversation.

"Your magic flows through your body," Ronan explained. "The easiest and most clear way to see it is through touch."

I held out my hands to the dwarf, and he took them into his own. My right hand had been punctured by the teeth, my left broken by Deegan's club. But both were already almost fully healed.

"I have never seen magic such as this."

"What are they?"

"Your latent magic is creative, while your main magic is mostly focused on destructive forces. It is this magic you forced through the blade into the dog, destroying his ability to heal himself."

I looked at my hands. "But how? I thought the magic was supposed to be elemental."

"What are destruction and creation but elemental?"

Ronan inhaled sharply. "Killian. Are you saying she has multiple elements?"

"Indeed. There is some of every element in her magic. And more besides."

"But that's not possible. No one has more than four elements. And even that is almost unheard of."

"You think I'm going mad in addition to being blind?"

"No, sir. I just... How is this possible?"

Killian dropped my hands and shrugged. "I know not *how* things are, only *what* they are. I've been using my magic to see for these past hundred and fifty years. I can see clearly with it. As I suspect you will be able to do." He nodded toward me.

"But I didn't even know I was doing it."

"You've been using it instinctively. I'm sure this is not the first time."

I considered that. "I broke a mug a few days ago, right after I met Meriel. I hadn't been holding it that hard, but I was really frustrated. It seemed to just shatter in my hand. And then the Dark's gun sort of exploded when he tried to kill me. I had been holding it, but he took it back and when he fired it... I just thought a bullet had gotten lodged. And Deegan said I broke his club, but I wasn't sure how. Could that have all been me using my magic?"

"Most likely," Killian said.

"But I never touched Deegan's club. I'd been using a branch to block, and they both shattered at the same time."

"But wood is one of the elements," Killian said. "Your magic would easily travel through it. Especially in times of great stress. Like someone trying to kill you."

"Well. He wasn't trying to kill me, exactly." I liked Deegan. I didn't want people thinking badly of him when he didn't deserve it. "Can I hurt someone?"

"Most definitely. Though not by accident, I do not think. You seem to use it when frustrated or desperate."

"How do other daoine sidhe use their gifts?"

"They must focus on what they want to do. You will learn to do this eventually, as well, to use your gifts consciously instead of unconsciously."

"What do I use creation for?"

"I have never seen gifts like these before. I cannot tell you what to use them for. But the Ancient Mother will have a reason for giving you such powerful tools."

"Who is the Ancient Mother?"

"She is the mother of all Faerie. She is the heart that beats through the Sidhe. She contains all the magic and distributes it to maintain balance among the fae."

"Is she like one of the Queens?"

"Oh no. She is much more powerful than the Queens. But she also does not walk among the fae. She lives deep in the Fréimhe, a place neither Summer nor Winter. There are pilgrimages to her domain, but she no longer shows herself."

"Some fae think she is just a myth," Ronan said. "Others think of her as our deity."

Killian stood up and Ronan and I did as well. "You must get home, Ronan. Sunset approaches quickly this time of year. Evander will fix your leg for you. And ensure our changeling is safe for the night. She is more precious than any of us have realized."

"I don't feel precious. I don't understand why this is all happening to me. I was willing to accept I was this different creature from a different place. Weird things have happened to me during my life. And I've always been kind of a loner. So if fae are generally unaccepted by humans, it all makes a sort of sense. But now you're saying I'm special, too? Why would they have changed me if I'm so special?"

"Do you not think they changed you *because* you are special?"

I stared at the dwarf for a moment. I didn't know what to say to him. I was tired and covered in some weird blood. I wanted to go home and go to sleep. I grabbed the sword and handed it back to Killian.

"No, child. You bloodied it in battle. The sword belongs to you."

"Killian," Ronan said.

"You will teach her to use it, boy."

"But it's..."

"I know what it is. When I heard the howl, I went for my weapons, and it called to me. It told me it was to go to her. You keep the shillelagh as well. I will get it back from you later."

We left Killian's house a second time that day and again started down the mountain. "What's a shillelagh?" I asked.

"This staff. It's made from blackthorn, a very tough wood, and can be used as a cudgel if necessary."

Ronan leaned heavily on the staff, but still carried his sword on his shoulder *and* didn't trip once going down the steep mountain path. Despite the injury, his strength seemed endless. Maybe I only felt that way because my own strength was flagging. After the healing, the hike up, the fight, and the hike down, I wanted to stuff my face with massive calories and then sleep for a week.

"And what was that about this sword he gave me?"

"Killian was known as one of the greatest swordsmiths in the Sidhe. That short sword is the best sword he has ever made. Even though the story is incredibly old, it is still told, or was before I was exiled. Killian created the sword and was offered immense sums, but he wouldn't part with it. He said he had made it for someone, and it would not go to anyone except the person he made it for. When questioned, he said he didn't know who it was for, but one day, the sword would tell him. This did not sit well with the Queen. She tortured for days before finally deciding he was willing to die to ensure the sword went only to the proper owner. She often gets bored with torture when she realizes her victim is willing to die. Plus, if he died, all the weapons he created and had not given to someone would lose their magic anyway, so it wasn't worth killing him. Years later, when she exiled him, Mab offered him a deal. She would allow him to stay if he would finally part with the sword. He declined. So she blinded him and he left the Sidhe with all the weapons he still had."

"And now he's given it to me."

"It seems you were the one he was waiting for the whole time."

"How old is this sword, then?"

"I'm not sure. If the stories are accurate, probably about two hundred years or so, maybe more."

The sword in my hand hummed with magic in my grip.

"It was waiting for someone with your magic, little changeling. It couldn't go to anyone but you."

Chapter 19

We reached the vehicles with only minor stumbling down the steep path. I got my backpack out of the truck and found the shirt I had worn yesterday. It was dirty from the fight with Deegan, but cleaner than the one I was wearing. I changed into it, smirking when Ronan turned away as I undressed. Given we'd both almost died, I decided to take pity on him and not tease him. Even though I wished he had watched. I certainly wouldn't have turned away if he'd taken off *his* shirt.

The smirk faded when I regarded my leather jacket. It also had that strange blood on it. I put it back on, determined I could clean it when I got home.

After I changed, I set up the board we had placed in the truck bed to get my bike out and Ronan said, "I could drive you to Vancouver if you want."

"That's fine. I want to go for a ride, anyway." After the last two attempts on my life and what I'd just learned about my magic, a long bike ride would help ease the tension wracking my body.

I got my bike down and grabbed my gear from the back seat of the truck. Then I helped Ronan put his sword under the seat where it had been before, since he was leaning rather heavily on the shillelagh.

"You shouldn't stay at your apartment tonight. It's dangerous."

"I'll be fine." I tore my bloody shirt along the seams, dropping the front half on the floor of Ronan's truck, trying to suppress the shudder. Then I took the back half and wrapped my new sword in it. It fit into my backpack with only the hilt sticking out of the top.

"The Dark will be able to find you there."

"I broke his knee just a couple days ago."

"He's likely healed by now. Look at your hand if you think I'm wrong."

I didn't look at my hand. I knew he was right. If I could heal myself in about twenty-four hours, he could likely find someone to help him heal just as quickly. "I thought you said he can't get past my threshold?"

"Magic can't get past your threshold. So he can't appear inside your place or kill you with his magic. But if he can find you, he will be able to physically get through the front door. Plus, your threshold is weak. You live alone and the building is your business as well as your home. He will be able to break through that protection with enough time."

"But you also said he can only come out while the sun is down. That's only a few hours I'll need to worry about. I have this sword now to protect myself. I'll be fine."

"You barely know how to use it." He took a deep breath. "Calynn. You were just attacked by a cu sidhe. A buggane attacked you yesterday. I might have believed the Dark tried to kill you because you were in the wrong place at the wrong time. But someone sent the other two after you. They only attack on their masters' orders."

I'd already thought of that, and I hated he was right. If someone from Winter had sent the Dark, and I knew Deegan worked for the Summer Queen, that was at least two people after me. "Who was the cu sidhe's master?"

"I don't know. It felt more Summer than Winter, but the noble daoine sidhe like to use the cu sidhe as status symbols. They are difficult to control and to gain their loyalty. You need to stay safe."

I sat on my bike and put on my helmet. "I've managed on my own for twenty-nine years. I'll be fine one night in my own home. I don't have to take orders from you." Then I started the bike and revved the engine loudly before I rode out of the parking lot.

I wasn't sure if I was mad because he had been telling me what to do, or if it was because I was still shaken by the fight with the dog on the mountain. If I was going to be honest, it was likely both. If there was anything I hated more than feeling vulnerable, it was having people worried about me.

It didn't take long for the joy of riding my motorcycle to melt the tension away. I took comfort in the solid feel of the bike, the vibration of the metal, the roar of the engine, and the wind ripping at my leather jacket. It soothed the ragged edges of my temper that were threatening to tear away completely. I just needed to escape it all for a little while.

Since I was already halfway there, I rode my bike up to Whistler before going back home. The sky was gray and dark, despite the early hour, but it didn't look like it would rain until tonight or tomorrow morning. The Sea-to-Sky Highway was dry at the moment, and I wasn't likely to get another chance like this for months. Plus, riding helped me organize my thoughts.

Something had been bugging me since I found out I wasn't really who I always thought I was, but I had refused to let myself think about it. I figured the ride would be a good time to sort through my messy thoughts of the people I'd assumed were my human parents. They had given me up for adoption when I was still a baby, but no one had wanted me. So I ended up in the foster system. I moved from house to house, always feeling a sense of animosity from whomever was supposed to take care of me, regardless of anything I did to try to make them like me. When I was sixteen, I went searching for the people who had given me up for adoption. I hadn't liked the answers I found. Now, I was in a similar situation, looking for answers and not sure if I was really going to like them. I thought I'd learned my lesson about asking those kinds of questions. It was a bad idea to look for answers if you weren't sure you could handle them.

As I reached Whistler and stopped for gas, I realized it didn't matter that it was a bad idea. Everything in my life felt like it didn't quite fit. I felt trapped. I felt lonely. But I couldn't make things better unless I figured out what was wrong, starting with who my real parents were and why they had sent me away. As I got on my bike to head back to Vancouver, I already knew I was going to regret these answers.

Night had completely fallen by the time I got home. The Queen's gaze had been on me for the last half hour, pushing me to go faster than was entirely wise. I rushed into my apartment and locked the door behind me, feeling the pressure lift as soon as I was in my kitchen.

Ronan had been right. I had no threshold at the door of the building. It was only inside my apartment that the pressure of the gaze eased.

I briefly considered calling the electric company to ask them to turn my power back on, but I'd put it off for so long, it was hardly worth it. I'd rather just get my power back tomorrow sometime than wait on hold to get it on right before I went to bed.

I unwrapped my new sword from the shirt and set it on my kitchen table. That was something I never thought I'd do. I considered how I was going to carry it as I threw the shirt into the garbage. The sword fit okay in my backpack, but it was also sharp enough to cut through the bag if I didn't wrap it in something. I found an old towel that would do for now.

I'd never been afraid of the dark before, but I grabbed the vial of water from my safe and a candle and set them on my kitchen table. The shadows disappeared when I lit the candle and the water caught the light. I breathed out a sigh as I sat down to write out everything that had happened that day. Everything Killian had told me and the attack from the cu sidhe. The sword and the gifts I apparently had running through my body. I didn't know what to do with all the information, but I figured eventually things would start to make sense. It couldn't stay confusing forever, right?

I finished eating my dinner of a peanut butter and jam sandwich just as my cell phone rang. I figured Ronan was calling to tell me to go somewhere safer, so I was surprised when I answered and heard Detective Granger say, "Ms. D'Arcy?"

"Speaking."

"This is Detective Granger calling. I have some more questions about Meriel Jones' murder. Are you able to come into the station tomorrow morning?"

"I have an appointment tomorrow at noon in Langley. It would have to be early."

We set a time to meet, though I was annoyed I had to go all the way back out to North Vancouver before going to Ronan's place. "I don't know what more I can tell you, detective. I only met her the one day."

"That's okay. See you tomorrow."

The abruptness of his ending grated on my already frazzled nerves, and I stifled a sudden urge to throw my phone against the wall. The motorcycle ride that had helped soothe those nerves now rendered completely irrelevant.

I took a deep breath and set the phone down on the table with exaggerated care, remembering the mug I'd shattered when I was feeling this stressed before. I didn't want to break my phone and have to get a new one.

I looked at the strange assortment of items on my kitchen table. A centuries-old sword made for me by a dwarf long before I was born. A bottle of faerie sea water that glowed in candlelight, felt warm to my touch, and froze in Ronan's. Notebooks full of content that did not make sense. What was I going to say to a regular police officer about Meriel and the world of fae that I belonged to? And if his partner was a magic user, what did he already know?

CHAPTER 20

*T*he *window needed to be cleaned. I couldn't see through it.*

I lifted my hand to try to clear a spot so I could see out. Just as my fingers touched the glass, it shattered beneath them, particles as fine as sand piling at my feet. Startled, I jerked away from the window and as I did, I heard—

I gasped and sat up, breaking the same dream I had a couple nights ago before the woman in it could speak. I didn't want to hear her voice again. The candle still burned on the table next to me where I had set it the night before, casting the room in a strange glow as the light reflected off the faerie sea water. I hadn't felt comfortable falling asleep in the dark, despite the sword within easy reach under my pillow, so I lit a pillar candle and slept in the light.

It only took a second to realize something was wrong. I was still gasping. It felt like it did when the Queen's eyes were watching me, but they shouldn't be able to see me here. I was behind my threshold and bathed in magic light. I reached for my sword while I felt for someone else in the room. That's when I noticed him.

The Dark was standing off to my right, in my kitchen, well out of the light. His magic felt like the darkness of death. Having never died before, I wasn't sure how I knew that is what death would feel like, but I was certain. It felt like what being buried alive must feel like, a suffocating darkness where the sun would never be allowed to shine again. I could also feel this was not how he had always been. I noticed scars in his magic, and I wasn't sure how that was even possible. But someone had done something to the Dark to make him who he was today.

"I know you're there," I said. "Why haven't you shot me already?"

"You broke my gun."

He seemed angry about that. I didn't ask why he hadn't just bought another one. I didn't think it would be smart to give him any ideas.

"So you're just going to stand there in my kitchen like a creep?"

"You were smart to sleep in the light of the Fae. I cannot touch you there with my magic. But you will not always be so careful. And I will be waiting. I have never missed a contract."

Between one breath and the next, he was gone. I don't know how he left or where he went, but the next moment, I felt the lightness of the sun rising above the horizon behind the clouds that lined the sky. I would be safe from him for the next few hours. It still took me about ten minutes before I could convince myself to get out of bed.

After only a few short hours, the Dark has somehow broken past my threshold. He'd broken it enough that he could use his magic inside, uninvited, and the Queen's gaze could find me. My apartment was no longer a safe place. I set my teeth together. Just like Ronan had warned me.

It took longer to get dressed than normal. My hands were shaking so hard it took three tries to do up the button on my jeans and another two tries to get the zipper up. I stuffed the notebooks into my backpack, glad I had brought them to bed with me and left them on my nightstand in the fae water's light. The Dark could have taken them when he broke in. I took my cell phone and laptop and stashed them in my backpack as well, along with a couple changes of clothes and my red dress. I wouldn't be coming back here tonight, or possibly even tomorrow.

I wrapped my sword in the old towel I'd found and then finally went back to my room, where the candle still burned. I didn't blow it out until I was about to leave the apartment. Before I left, I locked the water in my safe, just in case.

The attacks were coming too frequently for me to risk leaving anything of value where an intruder could take it. Especially since the Dark had destroyed any protection my threshold had given me.

Just before I left, the light in my kitchen came on and my fridge started humming, telling me my electricity was back on.

"A little late now," I muttered as I locked the door behind me.

*****

I made it to the station with a few minutes to spare and went in after moving my sword from my backpack to my bike's saddlebag. No need to bring a sword into a police station. Detective Granger met me pretty quickly this time.

"I'm not sure what more I can tell you, Detective," I said by way of greeting. "I only met Meriel that day. I don't know much about her."

Granger had a file in his hands like last time. He set it down in front of him as he sat across from me and pulled out another picture. I prepared myself to see the Queen of Air and Darkness again, but instead saw a picture of myself riding my motorcycle.

"Is this you?"

I took the picture and examined it, figuring out where it had been taken. I considered lying, but my bike was pretty unique, and Jeremy knew what it looked like.

"Looks like it," I replied.

It was a still from a convenience store security camera taken the night I'd broken into Meriel's house when I was on my way back home.

"It was taken near Ms. Jones' residence."

"Yeah. I went for a ride that night. I wanted to see her place."

"Why?"

I considered the detective. The good thing about knowing when people were lying was I became pretty good at it myself. The trick was to stay as close to the truth as possible.

"I was curious. She came to me for help, then she was killed. How do you think that makes me feel?"

"Her house was broken into that night."

"Was it? Was anything taken?"

"A sliding glass door was broken and there's a bullet hole in the wall in her office. You wouldn't know anything about that, would you?"

The other trick to lying was to answer a lot of questions with questions.

"Why would I go into Meriel's house? I barely knew the woman."

"That's what I keep asking myself. And yet, here you are, that same night, passing by her place."

"I'd just learned she was murdered. I'd been questioned about her death. I'm also a private investigator. I'm curious by nature. But riding through that neighborhood, seeing the houses of the people who lived there, seeing Meriel's house, I realized she was probably as stuck up and entitled as I thought she was the moment I met her. I decided you could handle the job of finding her murderer and I left."

"So you went past her house because you thought you might solve her murder single-handed?"

I studied the picture of me riding past the convenience store. I hadn't gone that way to get to her house, so they obviously had no other pictures of me or else he would have shown me those as well. They had no idea how long I'd been there.

"You want to know the truth, Detective Granger?"

"That would be nice, yes."

I took a deep breath and looked back up at him. "When Meriel came to my office, I thought she was a stuck-up bitch. I didn't want to take her case. She had a few pictures and some information, but nothing I could really run with. But on reflection, I decided to take the case, anyway. I haven't had many clients over the last couple of months and I needed the money. I knew she could pay. So I called. She told me to meet her in the morning. But after I found out she had been murdered, I couldn't help thinking if I had told her to meet me that night, she might still be alive. So I went for a ride because I felt guilty. I often ride my motorcycle when I feel bad or stressed. It helps. I drove past her house. When I got there, I knew I couldn't do anything you weren't already doing, so I went home. I had a terrible sleep and I tried to put the whole mess behind me. Now here you are, bringing it all up again."

Granger took the picture back from me and slid it into his file. "If I find out you're messing with my investigation..."

"I'm not. I don't care about your investigation. Now, if there's nothing else, I have an appointment with a client who might actually be able to pay me."

He glared at me for a moment before nodding.

I stood up, grabbed my helmet and started for the door.

"D'Arcy?"

I stopped but didn't turn around.

"Don't let me catch you near her house again."

I started walking quickly out of the police department when I heard my name called again. This time it was Jeremy, and it floated through my mind that he was a wizard, or some kind of magic user. What even were the other kinds of magic users? He would understand at least some of what I was going through. He was part of the magical world I found myself drowning in. But the thought of using him for a lifeline felt as shitty as using him for sex when he had started to have feelings for me. I also figured I shouldn't blow him off like last time, so I waited for him to catch up.

"I have to get to a client," I told him. "Can you walk with me to my bike?"

"Yeah, sure. How have you been?"

"Fine. If your partner stops accusing me of things, I'd be even better."

"I told Granger you had no reason to go to Ms. Jones' house. I know you had nothing to do with her murder. He said we had to talk to you, anyway." He shrugged. "He was right. We have to ask the questions. Even if we know the answers already. Hey, what are you doing Saturday night? Do you want to come over to my place?"

"Oh. I, uh, don't think I can. It's Arial's birthday and I was going to hang out with her."

Even before all this faerie craziness began, I'd been thinking I should break things off with Jeremy. Now, knowing his secret of being a wizard or something and mine of being fae, I was certain I had to do it. I should do it right now. I shouldn't let this go any further.

"Well, if you change your mind, I won't be going out anywhere that night. This case is taking up a lot of time, so I'll be working all day Saturday and Sunday. Probably just hang out at home for a bit between my shifts."

"Okay. Maybe. I'll talk to you later."

What can I say? I was a coward when it came to emotional shit. So instead of breaking up with him, I put my helmet on before he could try to kiss me—though he probably wouldn't have in front of the station—and started my bike. I was sure even the long drive out to Ronan's ranch wouldn't ease the guilt.

CHAPTER 21

Ronan's ranch spread out on either side as I rode my bike down his driveway. I'd swung by Arial's to drop off my things and sent her a text saying I was going to stay with her for a few days and I'd explain when I saw her. I still managed to get to Ronan's place early. He and Killian were already sitting on his porch in rocking chairs, waiting for me, when I came to a stop in front of the house.

"That is quite a motorcycle," Killian said as he blew smoke from his pipe. "1986?"

"How did you know?"

"I know machines," he answered cryptically. "Did you build it yourself?"

"Re-built it myself. The only way I can afford it. There's this great little garage near where I live that lets me work on it, use their tools and the lift. They only make me pay if I need help."

Killian's smile told me he liked my answer.

"You spoke with my protector? The one who changed me?"

"I did. He cannot give much information. His orders are to keep you safe and to tell you nothing."

"His orders?" I climbed the steps and leaned on the railing across from Killian.

"You think your protector is the one who made the decision to change you?"

"I guess I hadn't considered it. So someone gave him the order and he carried it out. He can't tell me anything, but couldn't he tell you and *you* can tell me?"

"It does not work that way. If the knowledge comes from him, even circuitously, he can be forsworn."

"Who is this guy? Maybe I can talk to him myself."

"I cannot tell you. That, too, would make him forsworn."

"But he has all the answers I need."

"Indeed he does. And you will receive none from him. If he tells you, he will be destroyed. And then he can no longer protect you."

I set my teeth together. I wanted to argue. The answers were all right there. I just needed to find the guy who changed me. But the tone Killian used warned me this was not an argument I would win against him. I remembered what Evander said being forsworn meant, magic ripped from you, not to be reborn. That would be a poor response to someone who had spent my life protecting me from the shadows, even though I never asked him to.

"So what do I do now?"

"The answers you seek must come from the person who ordered you changed."

"And that person is in the Sidhe."

"Indeed."

"So I'll have to go there."

"Yes," Killian said.

"What about answers regarding Meriel's murder?"

"Your protector believes Meriel's death is connected to you, but cannot explain how. Thus, those answers are most likely also in the Sidhe."

"Can't explain. As in, he isn't able to because of his orders or because he doesn't know?"

Killian smiled but didn't say anything.

I nodded. "Isn't allowed to explain. Fine." I took a deep breath, steeling myself. "So I go to the Sidhe." I looked away from the dwarf, my eyes finding the rowan tree in the front yard. I picked out individual leaves as I tried to calm the anxiety racing within me. I wasn't ready to go there yet. I knew I would have to eventually, but the thought of going somewhere so foreign was terrifying.

Killian gave me the out I was hoping for. "Your protector suggests not hurrying to the Sidhe. Many dangers wait for you there. Many deceptions as well.

More enemies than he knew of before he changed you almost thirty years ago. He suggests staying here and learning all you can before venturing there."

I returned my attention to Killian. "It's not exactly fair I have enemies I haven't even met. And they've been my enemy since I was a baby."

Killian looked sympathetic but didn't offer any more.

I shook my head. "It doesn't matter. I still want to talk to Angor. He saw Meriel right after she met the person from the Sidhe. He might know more about who it was." I thought about the meeting with Detective Granger earlier and how he'd told me explicitly not to go to Meriel's house. "And I have to get her selkie skin back."

"What?" Ronan said, speaking for the first time since I'd arrived. He'd remained completely still while I'd been talking to Killian, so much so that I'd almost forgotten he was there.

"You said if we return her skin to her family, her magic can be reborn into a new selkie."

"Well, yes, but..."

"You heard what Killian said. My protector believes her death is tied to me somehow. Even though I'm not to blame, I feel responsible. The least I can do for her is find out who killed her and why and return her skin to her family. All she wanted was to go home. At least part of her will be able to do that."

"Eventually her belongings in Vancouver will come to me."

"How long will that take? The police won't release anything until they conclude their investigation. And that's going to take a while since the killer isn't human. And how exactly do you intend to get her skin back into the Sidhe? You're exiled. I'm not. I'll be going there. I'll get it back before I go and bring it with me."

"You said yourself it would be difficult now to get the skin out of her house. You'll have to go at night and the Dark will be able to find you there. He'll be waiting for you to go back."

I couldn't repress the shudder at the mention of the Dark, remembering him in my apartment that morning. Unfortunately, Ronan noticed.

"What."

I looked away from him, back to the tree. I didn't want to answer.

"Calynn. What happened?"

Fuck. He had to be serious if he used my actual name. "When I woke up this morning, he was in my apartment."

Ronan exploded with anger, standing from his rocking chair and taking the two steps toward me. "When did you think you were going to tell me about this?"

"I wasn't."

Killian laughed.

"You think this is funny?" Ronan wheeled on him. "She could have been killed."

"But she wasn't. She has learned her lesson, has she not?"

"I have. I'm going to stay with my friend Arial for a few days. I already dropped off some clothes and stuff. And," I looked at Ronan so he would understand. "I want to learn how to use the sword Killian gave me."

He stared at me for a long time before nodding, accepting my request for help without me needing to give him something as recompense. "We'll get started after lunch."

Then he stalked into the house and left me outside with Killian, who was still chuckling.

"What do you find so funny, old man?"

"You and Ronan are more alike than you think."

"You mean I'm pushy and overbearing? A bit of a know-it-all? Over-protective when I have no reason to be?" I thought about it for a minute. "You're probably right, actually."

I went to the seat Ronan had vacated and sat down next to the dwarf.

"Will you tell me more about him? I know you can't... or won't tell me details of his past or anything. But what do you think about *him*? Do you trust him?"

"I think the question you're really asking me is, should you?"

"Well, should I?"

"And why should you trust my judgment before your own?"

I stared at the tree. Something about it eased an ache I'd long forgotten was in my chest. I traced the bright red berries and dark green leaves with my eyes. "I've not always had the best luck with people. I tried to trust people in the past, but it didn't work out well. So I kind of stopped. And now it's hard to start again."

Killian nodded and smoked his pipe. "Ronan has always been a good man to those who rely on him. He has been fair and helped when it was necessary and stood back when it was not. He has been a good leader to the exiled fae. I couldn't have asked for a more capable replacement. Though he has much he is responsible for, and it weighs on him, I think."

"Does he not accept help from anyone?"

"Who would offer? It is expected of the daoine sidhe to rule. There are no others in this area. Most exiled daoine sidhe do not choose North America to make their home."

"Why did Ronan?"

"That you would have to ask him."

And I knew exactly what kind of answer I'd get. Stony silence.

Aelwyd interrupted us to announce lunch was served.

"Come, child," Killian said as he rose from his chair, setting his pipe down on the table next to him. "You will need some energy if you are going to learn the sword."

CHAPTER 22

A elwyd had the food laid out on the table for us when Killian and I went inside. Simple sandwiches with roast beef and salad on three plates. I ate quickly, since I knew Ronan would make me leave long before sundown. We were out in the field in less than an hour.

Ronan changed his long sword for one about the same length as mine.

"The first thing you need to learn is the stance. Stand with your feet shoulder width apart. You hold the sword in your right hand and so your right foot should be slightly forward. Stand on the balls of your feet with your knees slightly bent, so you can move any direction as quickly as possible."

I did as he said. I held the sword in front of me and realized it felt heavier in my hand than it had yesterday.

"Will I be able to hold this for a long time?" I asked.

"If I was training you from the beginning, we'd work on arm strength. But you need to know the basics in case I'm not there to protect you."

"Excuse me. Who killed the cu sidhe? Oh, right. That was me."

He glared at me. "Luck. I'll teach you the basic moves, so if you need to defend yourself, you can. Then we'll work backwards and work on your strength and stamina."

We spent the rest of the day working on perfecting my stance, my weapon control, and the different guard positions. It wasn't so different from parts of my krav maga training and I picked it up quickly. While he didn't say anything, I could tell Ronan was impressed. Despite not moving around much, I was sweating by the end.

"We'll leave it there for today," Ronan said. "Come on, I'll give you a scabbard."

"You don't use one for your sword," I said, falling into step beside him as we made our way back to his shed.

"I do sometimes. Short swords can be drawn quickly from a side scabbard. Besides, are you planning to carry it around in the towel?"

We went back to the weapon shed and he went in. I followed him, finding several weapons, from swords of varying lengths and styles, to different shaped axes, and even a few longbows and crossbows. "No guns?"

"The fae made a few when humans started using them, but guns don't work well on us. If you shoot one of us, we tend to heal quickly. There is no magic in a gun. These weapons were all made with magic as part of their forging," he motioned to the bows, "or creation. They will wound the magic as well as the body, making it more difficult to heal."

"When the Dark was at Meriel's house, he tried to shoot me. He did shoot Meriel. And last night he didn't shoot me because I broke his gun the other night."

"I remember hearing he had a gun. And I don't know if there is magic in it, but I recall there is magic in the ammunition. If he had contracts for fae in this world, I can see the usefulness of having one. A gunshot wound is a lot more common than a sword wound."

He handed me a scabbard with a leather belt.

"You can add a glamour to it. So when someone sees it, they would see something other than a sword."

"I don't know how to do that," I said as I slid my sword into it.

"Consider what it is you want it to look like and then see it happening."

Though the instructions were rather vague, I gave it a try. I concentrated on the scabbard, trying to imagine it looking like an umbrella, like Ronan's sword had before I saw through the glamour. Nothing happened.

Ronan took the sword from me. "Feel the magic I use when I do it."

That I could do. I felt the magic as it flowed out of him and into the object. As I watched, it changed from a sword in a scabbard to a tree branch. But the branch was blurry and I squinted to try to get it to come into focus. When I did, the glamour faded away and I saw a sword and scabbard again. I could still feel the magic Ronan had used.

"It has the glamour on it, right?" I asked.

"Yes."

"I can't see it. I just see the sword."

I could even feel the magic dissipate as he dropped the glamour and handed the sword back to me.

"Try again."

I thought about what I had felt Ronan do and tried to emulate it. But nothing happened. The sword stayed stubbornly a sword, and no magic flowed from me. "I can't do it."

Ronan was looking at me oddly. "I'll discuss this with Killian tonight. You should get going. It'll be sunset soon. Unless you're going to stay tonight. But Killian is, and he's already called the spare room."

An image of Ronan's rumpled king-sized bed flashed through my mind. I noticed he was standing only a few inches away, and the shed felt cramped, like I needed to step even closer to him. I peered into his eyes and tried to read them, but as usual, he was completely closed to me.

"And endure hours more of your charming personality? I think I'll just go to Arial's."

"At least you'll be safe there." He turned and started back toward his house.

"Okay, okay," I said, following him. "I should have listened to you. I said you were right, didn't I?"

"No. You didn't."

"Right. I said I'd learned my lesson. But it's the same thing. I'll be more careful. I just..." I trailed off and slowed down to a stop.

He stopped as well. "What?"

"Everything is changing so fast. One minute I'm who I've always been. A loner, a private investigator, an owner of a failing business. I have one friend. I ride a motorcycle. I drink way too much coffee. And then suddenly, there's this whole other me who I didn't know I was. It would be hard to believe if it didn't answer so many questions."

For a moment, it seemed as though he softened, sympathy crossing his expression for just a second before it was gone.

"You'll figure it out."

"That's not very helpful."

"It's not my job to be helpful. It's my job to keep you safe."

"Since when?"

"What?"

"Since when is it your job to keep me safe?"

"Since you obviously can't. It's my job to keep all the fae in the Lower Mainland safe."

There it was again. Lie. So faint I could barely feel it. Something was missing from his statement.

"Those who ask for your protection. Meriel didn't. And I haven't. So it's *not* your job to keep me safe. It's *my* job."

He stared at me for a few moments, not saying anything. Then he said, "You're infuriating, you know that? I thought you wanted me to help you figure out who killed Meriel."

"I do. And I need your help to figure this all out. I have no idea what it means to be fae. I don't feel any different than I did before, but I am. I've always thought I was Calynn D'Arcy. Now I don't even know if my birthday is actually my birthday. Maybe I am thirty and that's why my magic has manifested already. Calynn D'Arcy isn't even my real name. If I'm not Calynn, who am I?"

"Your birthday is your birthday. In order for a fae to be changed with a human, the human they are changed with must match. The human must have the same birthday, and must be of Celtic descent."

"I thought fae changelings were rare. How do you know this?"

"It's fairly common knowledge in the Sidhe. The point is, you *are* the same person you've always been. You've always been fae. You've always been a changeling. You just didn't know it. You're not different. You're still you."

He looked a little too closely at me. Almost like he knew me better than I knew myself. No one had ever looked at me the way he was now. Not Jeremy, not any of the other boyfriends I'd had in the past, not even Arial had ever looked at me like they were really seeing *me* before. Maybe it was because Ronan and I were the same. Like a wolf seeing another wolf after living its whole life among dogs. My heart pounded in my chest and I needed to put some distance between us.

"If I'm not different, then I don't need you to protect me. I need you to teach me how to protect myself."

He continued to stare at me for a long time before he finally said, "We'll continue tomorrow. Come on. Sunset approaches."

Chapter 23

We planned to meet in the morning at his house to continue training and then I rode back to Arial's house. I had to ride slowly once I got into the neighborhoods to avoid the children running all over the place in their Halloween costumes. I'd completely forgotten what day it was. I still made it into her house before darkness set in and so didn't have to feel the weight of the Queen's gaze.

Practicing the sword at Arial's wasn't as productive as it had been with Ronan, but YouTube was more helpful than I had thought it would be. I found a video of a guy talking about a lot of the same things Ronan had shown me that day and watched it about a dozen times while practicing the stances and guards I had been learning. When I heard Arial come in, I put the sword away and met her as she was coming up the stairs to the bedrooms.

"How was your day?" she asked me.

"Not bad." I sat on her bed while she changed from her dress into some pajama pants and a t-shirt.

"You want to tell me what's been happening and why you're here?" she asked.

"I'm here because someone scary broke into my place last night and I decided it wasn't safe to stay there."

She turned to me, eyes wide. "Why didn't you say anything before?"

"I didn't want you to worry, since I'm fine."

She pursed her lips and stuck her hands on her hips. "Calynn. You know how much I hate it when you do that. And we've discussed this. I am *allowed* to worry about you. I have more than earned that right."

"I know." I looked away from her. "Then you should probably also know I was attacked the other day and the creature broke my hand." I held it up, the bruising mostly gone. "But I heal fast, so I'm fine. And I was also attacked yesterday but killed that creature and I'm still fine."

She was silent for a long time and so I looked back. "How many times have you been attacked?"

"Well, there was the Dark in Meriel's house, which I told you about. Then there was Deegan. He was the one who broke my hand. He's cool though. Then the cu sidhe attack on the mountain when I went to visit Killian. I killed it. And last night, the Dark broke into my place, but he wasn't able to attack me."

She closed her eyes and seemed to pray. "You've been attacked four times in the past week?"

"It sounds worse when you say it like that."

She sighed and started out of her bedroom and down the stairs. "How else should I say it? Are you sure this is a good idea? I know you can take care of yourself, but four attacks in a week, Calynn."

I followed her down and through the living room to the kitchen, where she pulled a bottle of white wine from the fridge and poured a glass for herself. She looked at me and I shook my head, so she put the bottle away.

"I know it's a lot. And it's absolutely a bad idea. But I don't think I can do anything about it. It feels like the only way out is through, you know. I can't quit now. The danger won't just go away. I have to figure out why someone wants to kill me before I can figure out how to stop it."

She leaned against the counter with her glass and regarded me. "You're right. So what else has been happening?"

"Why don't you sit down and I'll tell you about it while I make dinner?"

Arial rolled her eyes. "Will I be able to eat it?"

We laughed. "I can't promise gourmet, but you will be there to supervise, so I shouldn't be able to mess up too much."

I'd already searched her cupboards and fridge when I got back and found the ingredients for spaghetti and had set them all out on the counter. While I worked, I told Arial about meeting with Coira.

"Coira Winters is fae too?" she interrupted.

"They're everywhere, apparently."

"What kind of fae is she?"

"Same as Meriel was. Selkie. But they weren't friends. When they lived in the Sidhe, Coira was from Winter and Meriel was from Summer and apparently that's some big deal. I'm still not real clear on why."

Arial squealed with delight. "Oh, this is so exciting. There's this whole new world to learn about. Wait," she grew serious for a minute and leaned forward before whispering, "are there more things in this world than just the fae?"

I nodded. "If you can think of it, it probably exists. But according to Ronan, some are of this world and not the Sidhe."

"What does that mean?"

"I think it means wizards are human and I'm not." I let that sink in for a minute for both of us.

I cooked some chicken I'd had defrosting for the last couple of hours and added it to a rosé sauce I'd found in Arial's cupboards. She watched and then got up to get some vegetables out of the fridge. When she sat back down to chop them for the sauce, I continued with my story, telling her about the interview with the host at Cardero's and when Deegan attacked me. Then how I learned about Jeremy being a wizard, or some other kind of magic user.

"Wait, what?"

"Yeah. Apparently."

"But if he's a wizard, that means he's human."

"It does, yes."

"Are you going to invite him to my party? It's in two days, you know."

"I know when Saturday is, and no. I'm not going to invite Jeremy."

Arial sighed. "You're going to break up with him, aren't you?"

"To break up with someone, you have to start going out with them first. Jeremy and I never had that kind of relationship. But yes. I don't think I should see him anymore. I mean, like you said, he's human. I'm not."

"Is this because of Ronan?"

I paused in stirring the sauce, a shiver of cold and then heat running over me. "What do you mean?"

"The way you talk about him. I can tell you like him."

"What? I do not."

"Maybe you don't think you do, but you always seem to be the last to realize these kinds of things."

She was right. But I didn't think she needed to know that. "Regardless, I don't like him. He's bossy and overprotective and a complete know-it-all."

She blinked slowly. "You mean he's a know-it-all about the fae world of which he's a part?"

"Don't try to make excuses for him. He's helping me with the case. That's all."

Arial handed me the chopped mushrooms, celery, and onions and I added them to the sauce.

She shook her head. "Maybe I'm wrong about you liking Ronan. But you could invite him to my party if you want. The more the merrier. And I'd like to meet him."

I stirred the sauce, watching it carefully. "I already did."

She started laughing and I couldn't help but look up at her and smile.

"Right," she said, wiping the tears of laughter spilling from her eyes. "You don't like this guy at all. Inviting him to my party, spending every day with him."

"For the case. After this is over, who knows if I'll even see him again." I considered that for a moment. "I really have no idea what life is going to be like after this is over."

"What do you mean?"

"Well, I have to figure out the answers to all these questions. Not just about Meriel's death, but about my past. Who I am, where I came from. My magic is apparently really special, like never-been-seen-before kind of special. And I don't know how to use it. I have parents somewhere. What will they want from me when I go to the Sidhe? Am I willing to give it to them?"

The enormity of what all this new information meant settled on my shoulders and I felt like the Queen was watching me again, but it was myself who was creating the pressure this time.

"Hey," Arial said. She stood and came around the island where she'd been sitting and placed her hand on my arm. "I got you. They can't be worse than the parents you found a few years ago. No matter what happens. You are my best friend and I'm yours. We're sisters. That won't change."

"How are you so cool with all this?"

"Well," she mocked flipping her hair back and fluttered her eyelashes. "It's just because I'm awesome."

We laughed for a few minutes and got dinner on the table.

She tried a bite. "Not bad," she said.

"They make it idiot proof these days." I spent a moment twirling the spaghetti onto my fork, taking my time. "I'll remember what you said, Arial. No matter what happens in the next few weeks, I'll remember."

CHAPTER 24

The window needed to be cleaned. I couldn't see through it.

I needed to see what was on the other side. I reached up to clean a spot on the glass but as my fingers touched it, it shattered into a pile at my feet, the glass so fine it was practically sand. I startled away from the window, staring at the pile.

"It's broken," I said.

"It's clean," the woman behind me replied.

I woke with a gasp and stared around the room for a moment, trying to get my bearings. I reminded myself I was at Arial's house in her spare bedroom. My red dress hung on the closet door, in need of an iron from being stuffed into my backpack. My sword lay on the bed next to me in its scabbard so it was close at hand.

It was just a dream. A dream that felt more and more real every time I had it. My heart rate slowed down back to normal, and I got out of bed, got ready for the day, and made my way downstairs.

Arial was in the kitchen making coffee and eating a bagel for breakfast. She moved so I could make one as well.

"What's on the schedule for today?" she asked.

"I'm going to the gym to work out, then going to Ronan's house to practice sword fighting some more. I'll be home for dinner again."

The coffee was ready, so she poured some into two mugs, handed me one, then added a bit of cream to her own.

I smelled the coffee before taking a sip, my eyes closing as the strong flavor hit my tongue. "You make the best coffee. It tastes like home."

Arial laughed. "It's just a regular coffee."

"Made with fresh ground beans in a pour over coffee maker. That's the best way to drink coffee."

"If you say so." She took her cup to the stools at the island and sat down. "I'm on until six tonight so we can have an early night and I'll paint your nails for tomorrow. I have the perfect color that will match your dress. It's a dark burgundy."

I smiled at her. "If you say so."

After I finished my coffee and bagel, I packed up my gear and rode out to the krav maga gym. Sam was there as he usually was in the mornings and we sparred for a while before sitting down for a break, drinking water and chatting about the bar. He had hired a new server recently who seemed to be working out well. While he talked, I realized he was one of the few people I felt comfortable around and who also seemed comfortable around me. He'd never tried to hit on me or Arial, much to her frustration, and always treated us well. I considered him for a moment and felt a faint hum of magic. It was more faint than what I'd felt with Arial, so I wondered if he was like her, but the magic was even further back on his family line. It was none of my business, though, so I didn't say anything. Instead, I stood up.

"I gotta head out. I have to meet a client. It was good to spar with you, though."

"Anytime," he said, standing as well. "You and Arial coming in tonight?"

"No. It's Arial's birthday party tomorrow, so we're going to stay in tonight and watch a movie. She said she's going to paint my nails."

He grinned. "You don't strike me as a painted nails kind of person."

"I'm not. But what Arial says goes. Especially for her birthday."

He watched a few people who were going through a circuit training session. "Yeah. Tell her I said happy birthday."

"I will."

I rode out to Ronan's ranch and made it just before the rain began, parking my bike under the rowan tree to keep it from getting soaked.

I felt for the magic in the house and knew Killian was gone and Ronan was in his office. I set my gear down and went there, leaning against the door frame.

"Would I be able to feel someone's magic if it wasn't from the Sidhe?"

He didn't look up from his paperwork. "You would, but you'd also be able to tell the difference. Why?"

"Just a guy I know. He's always been nice to me and I realized today that he has magic as well, like Arial. But fainter."

He looked up at me. "Who?"

I smiled and sat down in the chair across from him. "Why? Are you jealous?"

He arched one eyebrow. "What would I have to be jealous of?"

"I don't know. You tell me."

We stared at each other for a long moment, and I felt like I was daring him to admit he found me as attractive as I found him. Fuck. Arial had been right. I liked the guy. I wanted him to be jealous. I wanted him to want me.

When he never responded, I said, "Are you ready for training?"

"Yes. I was just pulling the files on Meriel for the police. I'm hoping they will release the contents of her house to me so you won't have to go back there."

"You know that's going to take a long time. Even if you give them the files, it's still going to take weeks, if not longer, for them to allow things to be taken."

"I can still try."

I rolled my eyes. "Let's go. You have anywhere to train that's not in the pouring rain?"

He got up and I followed him out to the arena where we'd practiced yesterday. The arena was half open and half covered. He called the covered section a barn, though it only had three sides and was open to the front.

We worked on the stances again and this time he switched out my sword for a similar one that was heavier. It felt wrong in my hands, but I didn't complain. The idea was to get used to the heavier weight, making my lighter sword easier to wield for longer periods. After Deegan's attack, followed so closely by the cu sidhe, I realized how hopelessly outmatched I was. I needed to get better as fast as I could. By the time we finished, I was aching and drenched in sweat.

"Do you mind if I take a shower before I head to Arial's house?" I asked Ronan as we put the weapons away. I hadn't showered after sparring with Sam earlier and now my hair was itchy.

"Go ahead."

I turned the water as hot as I could stand it and rubbed my arms and back where I could reach, trying to ease the aching muscles from the exercise. I felt better when I got out and dressed again in new, clean clothes, but my neck and shoulders were still sore. I stopped in the middle of putting my boots on to stretch just as Ronan returned from outside.

"May I?" he said.

I stared at him and hoped he couldn't hear my increased heart rate.

I nodded and he stood behind me, settling his hands on my shoulders and rubbing away the soreness. I could feel the heat of his hands through my thin t-shirt. That heat spread through my whole body and I closed my eyes to bask in it. His fingers moved up to rub the spots behind my ears and then back down the sides of my neck and goosebumps broke out on my skin at the feel of his skin touching mine. I didn't want him to ever stop and when he did, I couldn't contain the slight sound I made that was certainly *not* a whimper.

"You should go," he said, his voice just a little huskier than usual. "It's getting late."

I should just leave. I should get up, say good-bye and walk out the door to my bike. I shouldn't look at him and try to figure out if he was feeling anything close to what I was feeling. So, of course, I turned around and searched his eyes. In the second before he pulled up his wall of emotionless distance, I saw the same need I felt.

"I'll see you tomorrow?" I asked. "At Arial's party?"

He nodded.

"I'll text you the address."

I walked away at a pace that made it clear I wasn't running.

CHAPTER 25

I was back at Arial's house before the sun set again, even after a quick stop. Another day without the Queen's gaze on me. Arial picked up take out from our favorite Greek place on her way home. We set it all out on the living room table with a bottle of white wine for her and a bottle of whiskey for me. She had a bunch of nail polishes set out in varying shades of red. I knew she would have gone to a salon to get her own done, so this was all for me.

I rolled my eyes but told her the color she had picked out was fine and I didn't need the rest.

"How was your day?" she asked.

I settled on the floor and loaded my plate.

"It was good," I said. "No one tried to attack me I wasn't expecting."

"You were expecting attacks?"

"Training. Also, it turns out, you may have been a tiny bit right."

She laughed. "Of course I was. I'm always right. What was I right about?"

I took a small container of tzatziki and dipped some pita bread into it, staring hard at the white dip.

"It could be possible that I kind of, just a little bit, like Ronan."

I winced at the high pitch squeal that came from my friend.

"Ha! I knew it! I knew it. What happened?"

"Nothing." I shrugged and kept eating.

"Calynn D'Arcy, you tell me what happened or so help me..."

"Fine, fine. I worked out all day today and that plus all the injuries lately, I was feeling kind of sore. And he gave me a massage and there was a moment."

She heaved a swoony sigh and I finally looked at her, one eyebrow raised in disbelief at her antics.

She laughed. "Come on, Calynn. You have never had a crush on anyone in the entire twenty years I've known you. You gotta let me have this one."

I managed a wry smile. "Whatever."

"There's a problem."

"How did you know?"

She lifted her wineglass and took a sip around a smile. "I know you. I can tell when you have a problem. So let's have it."

I heaved a sigh and pushed some food around on my plate. "He just plays it so hot and cold. I think he's interested, but for some reason he keeps holding back. It's messing with my head. I'm starting to wonder if my instincts are right or not. Maybe I'm reading the whole thing completely wrong."

"You know, there's a simple solution to this problem." She took a bite of her chicken and chewed slowly. I waited for her to finish. "Ask him."

"I can't do that."

"Why not? Sweetie. You're a private investigator. You ask uncomfortable questions all the time."

"It's different when it's about me. What if I don't like the answers?"

"Then at least you'll have them."

I sighed again because I knew she was right. Again.

"Other than Ronan. How have you been feeling? Dealing with all this new stuff."

I considered her question for a moment before answering. "You know, better than I expected. It was almost like I'd been waiting for something like this. Like I knew everything that had been happening to me up to now had to be for a reason. There was a reason my parents gave me up for adoption. There was a reason they didn't want me. There was a reason I could never make any friends."

She whacked me on the shoulder.

I glanced at her and smiled. "Except you, of course."

"Of course."

"Even if what's happening now doesn't make my life better, I'll still understand the reason, you know?"

"I get it. It helped to know my mom was sick, and that's why she had been acting the way she had been. It didn't make it better. But it was kind of a relief to know what was wrong."

I reached over and squeezed her hand. We sat like that for a few seconds before Arial waved both her hands in the air, as if shooing away the conversation. "Enough of all that. Let's get started on your nails and we'll turn on a movie."

She painted my nails while we watched the movie and drank wine and whiskey. When it was over and we were finished tidying up the dinner things, I said, "Oh. I saw Sam at the gym today. He said to say happy birthday to you."

"That's sweet of him. I thought about inviting him, but figured he'd be working."

"And I got something for you on the way back from Ronan's place."

I took a small box from where I'd set it behind my helmet, out of view. I set it on the counter and opened it to reveal a single-serving piece of strawberry shortcake. "Happy birthday, Arial. I know you said me coming to your party was all the gift I had to get you. But you also said, this isn't a *like always* kind of birthday. You only turn thirty once."

She looked from the cake to me and I could see the tears standing in her eyes. "It's perfect, Calynn."

We shared the small cake and stayed up late chatting, wondering about the future, making plans and dreaming dreams together. We eventually went to bed, and I woke up early and left her a note saying I was going to work out before the party. I went to the gym and was not surprised to see Sam there. I wouldn't be surprised if he was there every morning.

After we sparred, we chatted about his work and he said it had been a quiet night since Arial and I hadn't been there to cause a ruckus. I told him it was too bad he couldn't take the night off because Arial would have loved to have him at her party.

He shrugged. "Maybe I could leave someone else in charge for a couple of hours."

I left him and went back to Arial's house, climbing the stairs to find her in the bathroom, the straightener, curling iron, and makeup already spread out on the counter. I rolled my eyes but also couldn't help smiling at her obvious enthusiasm.

"Go for a shower and then we'll get started," she commanded. "You won't even recognize yourself when I get through with you. And Ronan won't be able to keep his hands off you."

***

Arial knew what she was doing when it came to makeup and hair. There had been a time when she'd considered becoming a makeup artist instead of a hairdresser. She'd decided on the latter because it had a better business model. By the time I was done and dressed in my red dress, I felt like a completely different person. I looked like one, too.

My hair was up in an elaborate style I could never have achieved on my own. As promised, Arial didn't use too much hairspray, so I could take it down on my own whenever I wanted. The makeup she used was light and focused mostly on my eyes to bring out the silver color of my irises. The dress was a deep red that complemented my olive complexion and golden hair and went well with the darker nail polish Arial had used last night. The spaghetti straps and V-neck showed just enough skin without being too obvious, and the fabric hugged my curves in all the right places. The skirt flared at my hips and was short enough I had trouble sitting down. The gold chain belt at my waist was for show only and matched the borrowed necklace and earrings I wore. Arial had picked the dress out for me a couple of years ago, stating I needed one for special occasions and I had to say, I did love it. Except I wished the skirt was about three inches longer.

I helped Arial get everything ready and guests began to arrive as the sun sank below the horizon. I let people in. Arial introduced me to some people I hadn't met before. And then no one spoke to me. It wasn't odd. And now that I knew what I was, it made even more sense. It didn't bother me anymore.

What did bother me was the fact that an hour later, Ronan hadn't arrived yet. I started to feel a little disappointed, sure he wasn't coming, when a cold calm washed over me and I felt a glacial river come closer, almost pulling me toward it. I opened the door before he could knock. He was dressed in clean, dark blue jeans and a white button-up shirt with dark green pin stripes. He'd combed his hair away from his face, and his emerald eyes scoured me from head to toe.

As much as I hated getting all dressed up, the look in his eyes when he saw me made it all worth it.

"Hey. I wasn't sure you were going to make it."

"I had a few things to take care of."

"Of course. Come in. I'll introduce you to Arial. Do you want a drink?"

"Sure. Just a beer is fine."

I led him to the kitchen and opened the fridge for him to choose one of the local brewery beers. He chose one as Arial came into the kitchen.

"Arial, this is Ronan."

"Hello," he said, holding out his hand to shake hers. "Calynn has told me about you."

Arial stared, her mouth open a bit as she did. After a second she said, "Whoa." Then she blinked and shook her head as though coming out of a dream. "Sorry. You're just really hot." She shook his hand as he laughed.

"You are also stunning."

Arial blushed at the compliment. "Uh. What did I come in here for?"

"Drink?" I offered, motioning to her empty wineglass.

"Yeah. Right. And ..." She hesitated and then lowered her voice. "I was going to thank you for coming, but I guess, if you're like Calynn, that would make you uncomfortable."

Ronan nodded.

"Right. Well then. It's nice to meet you. And I am glad you could make it. Calynn doesn't really like these kinds of parties, so hopefully you'll make this one enjoyable for her."

Someone new knocked at the door and Arial smiled at us before going to answer it. Ronan and I took our drinks and went to the dining room, sitting on chairs next to each other between the table and the wall. From our spots, we could see the whole lower floor. Most of Arial's guests were in the living room, with a few in the kitchen. Every so often, people would cast a surreptitious glance our way and I understood it was because of the magic.

"You didn't bring a jacket," I said, feeling a little awkward.

"Why would I?"

"It's the beginning of November and cold outside."

"I'm from Winter. This weather is not cold."

"Oh." I spun my bottle in my hands. If he didn't find this weather cold because he was Winter, I wondered if that was proof I was from Summer. But I had a more pressing question at the moment.

"So that was Arial." I crossed my legs in a way that felt supremely uncomfortable, but would ensure I didn't show off my underwear. My knee brushed Ronan's leg as I did.

"So I gathered."

"She doesn't really have an embarrassed button. She kind of says what's on her mind and doesn't care what people think."

"It's refreshing."

"It is. Except when it causes trouble. But that's why she has me."

"You protect her."

It wasn't a question, but I nodded.

"It's in your nature to protect the lesser fae. Though many of the daoine sidhe have lost that aspect of their nature."

I stared down at my drink. "So is she..."

"Yes. Half pixie. Which is uncommon."

I looked up. "Why?"

"Pixies are small. Few have the size to create a child with a human. Only the most powerful can achieve that kind of size. But that much power comes at a terrible price."

"What happens?"

"A fae's size is in direct correlation to how powerful it is. For pixies, if one gets too powerful, too big, its wings can no longer keep it in the air. They lose the ability to fly."

"Her mother was diagnosed with schizophrenia. She said she saw some things no one thought were real. But they were real, weren't they?"

"They may have been. But it's not uncommon for humans who are close to the fae for too long to suffer afterward."

"What about the men I've slept with?"

"It's different for you. You're young and a changeling."

"You say that like I'm supposed to know what you mean."

"Being young, your magic shouldn't have manifested yet." He paused and gave me a look like it was my fault I'd done things wrong. It was completely unfair, but he continued before I could call him out on it. "Prior to your magic manifesting, that alone would have protected your lovers. Being a changeling, you still have the option to stay human. That also protects them. Though your magic can still create an addiction regardless of what you choose."

"When will the option to stay human disappear?"

"I don't know for certain. There aren't a lot of details about fae changelings. But if I were to guess, I would say the first time you step into the Sidhe, the option will be gone." He paused. "So, will you tell your friend?"

"Eventually. But I need to figure out how and when. It's going to be a hard conversation. She took her mother's illness hard. And then her mom committed suicide. We were eighteen. It was almost like she'd been waiting until Arial was old enough to take care of herself."

I shifted to a more comfortable position, remembered the dress, and shifted back. If my knees brushed against Ronan's leg with both movements, it wasn't really my fault.

"You look uncomfortable," Ronan remarked.

"You don't think this dress looks good on me?"

He gave me a small smile. "I think you look gorgeous. But that's not the same thing as comfortable."

"I can never figure out how to sit without showing off more than I want to."

Our entire conversation had been quiet, so no one else could hear. The other people at the party weren't close enough, anyway. However, a bunch of them had stopped trying to hide their stares. I quirked an eyebrow at them and they turned away quickly, but one glanced back almost immediately.

"We seem to be drawing attention," I said.

"I see that."

"You want to go upstairs?" It was not at all my intention to try to sleep with him, but I'd be lying if I said the thought didn't cross my mind. My heart thudded painfully as I waited for his answer.

His gaze slid down my body like a caress and I watched as he swallowed, then gave a shallow nod.

We left the beers we hadn't been drinking and climbed the stairs. Ronan offered me his arm to hold, and I took it, wondering if he wanted to touch me as much as I wanted to touch him. I held his arm as we ascended and led him to the only bedroom that didn't have a bed in it and left the door open. I would not try to sleep with this man at my best friend's birthday party. Even if I did have my own room.

"This is Arial's hobby room. It used to be her mom's bedroom." I moved into the room, trailing my fingers along her sewing desk and then the bookshelf. "I would always come over here if we were going to hang out. I was here so much that the guest bedroom became my bedroom. I was in foster care and Arial's mom was thinking of becoming a foster parent so I could just live here with them. But then she got her diagnosis and that couldn't happen." A fresh wave of pain swamped me for just a second before I was able to push it away. It didn't make sense that it would still hurt so much that I'd never really had a home. Even this house, the closest I'd ever come to one, didn't quite feel right. I finished my circuit of the room and ended next to where he stood at the open door. I shifted so that he leaned against one side of the door frame and I leaned against the other.

"Do you think whoever changed me would have done it if they'd known what my life was going to be like?"

"I think you are a lot stronger than you give yourself credit for, little changeling. And it is your past that has made you that way. I also think the only reason anyone would create a fae changeling, given the consequences, is if they had no other choice."

He reached up and tucked a stray hair behind my ear, his fingers tracing my jaw before his hand fell away. He'd moved closer to me, so only a few inches separated us. I drifted closer still, my eyes closing. His pine and ice scent surrounded me and I breathed it in deep.

No sooner than I had started to reach for him, he was gone. I opened my eyes and he was standing a couple of feet away out in the hall.

"I can't," he said.

"Can't what? Kiss me?" I felt my cheeks heat in embarrassment. "You can sleep with all the other female fae in Vancouver, but you can't kiss me once?"

"No. It's a bad idea."

"Ugh." I set my teeth together and stalked away from him into the hobby room, creating more distance between us. When I was as far as I could get, I faced him again. "Maybe I am stronger than I realize, but you know something. I'm tired too. I've had to fight for my life three times in less than a week. And that's not including the time the Dark broke into my house and would have killed me in my sleep. And then there's you. You're silent when I need you to speak. You come toward me and then back away before you give me anything. You say it's a bad idea, but you don't tell me why."

I crossed my arms over my belly, feeling exposed in the dress.

"We're no closer to figuring out who killed Meriel or who's trying to kill me. So tell me, Ronan. What is the point? What reason do I have to keep doing this?" I met his gaze and waited.

Ronan stared at me, silently, for what seemed like forever. After a while, I realized he wasn't going to say anything.

"Well, I guess that's my answer then."

I stalked out of the hobby room and brushed past him to get to my room, where I closed the door firmly behind me. I leaned against it and felt it when his magic began to move away, down the stairs and then further. I took the dress off and put on my regular clothes. I couldn't stay here tonight, not with the memory of him in the hall outside, his pine and ice scent lingering near my bedroom. I pulled the pins out of my hair and gathered it back into a ponytail that probably looked horrible. I grabbed my helmet and my leather jacket and went to find Arial to say good-bye.

I found her in the living room with Sam. He seemed to be in the middle of saying something when I came down the stairs, but stopped when they saw me.

"Where's Ronan?" Arial asked.

I said a quick hello to Sam before looking at Arial. "He left."

"You got in a fight?"

"Why does that surprise you so much? He's impossible and arrogant. He thinks he knows everything."

Arial smiled. "You've never been in a relationship where you've cared enough about someone to fight with them before."

Realizing she was right did not make me happier. "Well, it's over. It's a long story and I'll tell you all about it later. For now, I just want to go. Forgive me for leaving?"

"Of course. And Calynn. Tonight, you're angry at him. Don't make any final decisions while you're angry."

I gave her a hug and a kiss good-bye, waved to Sam, and then went to my bike. I tried to think everything through rationally, but it was hard since so many things lately were so irrational. I rode up and down streets at random, making my way toward the highway in a circuitous way.

After riding for about half an hour, I thought I had calmed down a bit until I felt the pressure of the dark Queen's gaze settle on me again.

"For fuck's sake! Leave me alone!" I yelled over the sound of my bike's engine. I don't know when I made the decision—if it was because of the Queen or Ronan or something else entirely—but I made it onto the Number 1 and headed toward North Vancouver.

When I got to his house, Jeremy already had a glass of Bushmills Irish Whiskey poured.

Jeremy was really hot. He was good and kind and he cared about me. I knew he did, even though we hadn't talked about it. I stared at him for a moment, drinking in the sight of his gorgeous body. I could choose this. Instead of all these creatures trying to kill me, instead of Ronan and his lack of communication, instead of the questions I was afraid of, I could choose to be human. I could choose to be with Jeremy. I cared about him. Maybe one day, I could even love him.

Somewhere in the back of my mind, something screamed this was a horrible idea. I shut down the voice and took a step toward him.

"How are you?" he asked.

While I was grateful for the drink, I didn't want to talk. I stripped my leather jacket off and draped it on the back of the couch. Then I took the whiskey from him and downed it in one shot.

"That good, huh?"

I shrugged one shoulder and held out my glass for more. While he poured another shot, I said, "Long story."

I threw back the second shot and immediately dropped the tumbler on the table and wrapped my arms around his neck. I began kissing him and I could taste a protest on his lips. He wanted to keep talking. I did not.

The protest died quickly as he kissed me back. His lips were hungry on mine and we shed our clothes. When we were both naked, he lifted me up onto his hips and started carrying me upstairs to his bedroom. I broke the kiss long enough to say, "I thought you'd never shut up," before he laughed and spilled me onto his bed.

CHAPTER 26

This was the last time.

The thought flashed through my mind as I lay naked in his bed the next morning. He was snoring quietly, tangled in his sheets, one arm trapping me next to him.

I moved his arm as quietly as possible, trying not to wake him as I slipped from his bed. It had been wrong to come here after everything that had happened. After everything I had learned in the last week. In the cold light of day, I knew I couldn't choose to be human. I had another life. I had questions that needed answers, even if the answers weren't what I wanted them to be. I couldn't spend the rest of my life not knowing. I had just needed to feel in control of something and not have someone pull me close just to push me away. Now I would have to push *him* away and I felt like a piece of shit for having to do it.

I started sifting through our clothes scattered in his living room and pulled on my jeans. I'd just found my shirt and was about to put it on when Jeremy said, "I hope you're just going to get breakfast."

I took a deep breath before turning to face him. His brown hair was tousled from sex and sleep and his broad chest sported a few new scratches from my fingernails. He was leaning against the wall at the bottom of the stairs, arms crossed, completely naked, completely at ease. A part of me wanted to crawl back into bed with him. But the look in his brown eyes stopped me. He wasn't looking at me with lust, but with tenderness. It made me supremely uncomfortable.

"I gotta go into the office," I told him, hoping I didn't have to deal with his feelings right now, hoping I could push this conversation off just a little while longer.

"It's Sunday. You don't usually work Sundays. And I have a couple hours still before I have to head back in to the station."

"I know. I have this big client right now and she really needs me to get this thing done. She's already paid me a retainer."

"Will I see you tonight then?"

"I don't think so."

He started coming toward me. I allowed my eyes to travel over the beautiful length of his naked body for what I vowed would be the last time. He wrapped his arms around me. "Okay, but call me when you're free. There's something I think we should talk about."

I disengaged from his arms, knowing I couldn't let this go on any longer.

"Jeremy."

He stopped smiling and said, "That wasn't a good tone."

"Maybe you should put on some pants."

"If you're going to break up with me, maybe I should get completely dressed."

He went upstairs to get fresh clothes, metaphorical armor. When he joined me downstairs again he was wearing pants, a shirt, even socks.

We sat on the couch.

"I don't know where to start."

"Why don't you start with why you came over last night, if you're just going to break up with me now?"

"Fair enough. I was mad. There's some things happening in my life right now that have me really stressed out. I wanted to get away from them and I used you to do it. It was wrong."

"It gave me one more night with you. Fair trade off."

"I care about you. I just don't think I'll ever be able to feel more. You deserve someone who will be able to really love you. That person is not me."

"It might be. It took me a few years to realize I could love you. Maybe it'll just take you a bit longer to realize the same."

My first thought was Ronan. Last night I had thought that Jeremy was good and kind and that was true. But Jeremy looked at me like he was falling in love.

Ronan looked at me like he knew my soul. That gave me the answer I needed. If I would one day be able to feel for Jeremy what I currently felt for Ronan, it would have happened already.

"There's someone else," Jeremy said.

"I—how..."

"I can see it in your eyes. You're thinking of someone else right now."

"It's not what you think. I just met him a few days ago. We haven't... done anything or even started a relationship. We fight more than we get along. He's been helping me with a case. And last night, I was here, with you. I wasn't thinking of him. I swear."

"But you think there could be something."

"I don't know what it is yet, but there's something there. And that made me realize..." I didn't want to say it. It was too harsh. Jeremy said it for me.

"There's nothing here for you."

"Not nothing," I protested, wanting to lessen the blow.

"Just not enough. It's okay, Calynn. I've had this same conversation with women all my life. I've just usually been the one where you're sitting. It's about time it happened to me."

An ice cold dread flooded me. I had also had this conversation with several men. What if it was my turn to be on the receiving end with Ronan?

It didn't matter. I still had to finish this with Jeremy. I still had to answer a lot of questions. I could never really go back to my old life knowing what I did now. In the end, I left Jeremy on his couch and rode my bike out to Ronan's ranch.

When I got there, I found him in the field working with Evander on a tractor. He stood up and faced me as I walked toward him. He looked so fucking good. His magic felt familiar and welcoming, even as it made me shiver. When I reached him I wanted to wrap myself in that strength and magic and let it wash away all the confusion. But he would just push me away again if I tried. So I pushed first this time. Or rather, I threw all my weight behind my arm and punched him in the jaw.

"That's for being an asshole."

He spat blood on the ground. "Finished pouting, I see."

"Don't make me hit you again."

I turned around and stalked back to his house.

"Where are you going?" he called after me.

"To look at my notes."

***

I sat in Ronan's office looking over the notes I had brought with me. I knew we would train again today, but I needed a bit of space from him before we got to that. Aelwyd smiled at me as she came into the office with a cup of coffee. I took it and closed my eyes, inhaling the aroma. Aelwyd told me she had brewed a full pot, and she was leaving to help her mother. Then I was alone with my notes and my cup.

Every instinct I had told me, to find the answers I was searching for, I needed to leave this world and go to the Sidhe. Call me a coward, but I wasn't ready for that yet. I still had three good reasons I could legitimately put off going there. I still wanted to talk to Angor to see if Meriel had told him anything about the woman who had spoken to her. I still had to get Meriel's skin from her house so I could bring it with me. And I still wanted more training with the sword. I figured with the amount of times someone had attacked me in this world, I should expect a lot of attacks in that world as well.

I wrote a list of things I needed to do before I left. As I was writing out a note to contact Bidina to find out if she had gotten the selkie skin, the phone in Ronan's office rang.

I looked around, wondering if I should answer it, but Aelwyd and Ronan were both outside. I should probably let it to go to voicemail. It was Ronan's phone, after all.

I picked it up.

"Ronan's office," I said.

"H-hello."

"Bidina?"

"Yes. I am calling for Ronan."

"Bidina, this is Calynn. I spoke to you with Ronan the other day."

"Right. The changeling. I couldn't get any of Meriel's possessions," she told me. "The police won't release anything. They didn't even want me to get the clothing for her funeral at first."

"I understand."

"You have to bring her skin back to her family."

"I will. Don't worry."

Then she hung up.

I stared at the phone for a moment before hanging up myself and crossing Bidina off my list. Then I tore it out of the notebook and grabbed my jacket, heading outside to find Ronan.

I found him where I'd left him working on the tractor. Another fae had joined them and Evander introduced him as Carrick.

"You brought my bike back after Deegan attacked me."

He didn't smile at me. He barely looked at me, focused on what he was doing.

I turned to Ronan. "You ready for some training?"

We made our way to the arena where we'd been practicing and he switched out my sword for a heavier one again and we squared off. Ronan was intent on drilling self-defense into me. We spent most of our time practicing a single move: removing my sword from its scabbard and into a block position while Ronan tried to strike me. We practiced the motions for half an hour until he was content with my abilities and I was so angry at his detached comments I was ready to brawl.

I switched back to my own sword for a sparring session and went at him, holding nothing back. Of course, I was a lot more sloppy than I should have been and he blocked every strike.

"You're not focused," he said.

"Oh, you noticed." I thrust at him and he easily parried the strike away.

"You're telegraphing your movements. I can see what's coming ages before you strike. Keep your emotions in check."

He came toward me with a few strikes I could tell he slowed down for me to block and that just made me angrier. And then my sword began to glow. Ronan didn't stop. He came at me again with a sideswipe I hadn't seen before, but I blocked it since he was still moving at a slower speed.

"You're frustrated," he said. "You're using your magic."

"Shouldn't that make you nervous? You know what my magic can do." I cut my sword toward him, stepping in close.

He caught my sword on his own and used his free hand to trap me close to him. "You won't hurt me."

His emerald eyes stared down at me without even a hint of concern.

My heart pounded against his chest as the flames of my anger threatened to engulf me. I wanted a reaction. How could he always be so calm while I was spinning out of control? How could he be so sure that I wouldn't hurt him when I couldn't stop hurting myself? He'd known me for a handful of days. How did he see me so clearly?

"I slept with Jeremy last night," I blurted.

He blinked twice and dropped his arm, taking a step back. It was the strongest reaction I'd gotten from him all day.

"Okay," he said.

"I was so angry at..." I stopped myself from saying I was angry at him because it was more than that. It was the attacks, the enemies I hadn't known I had, the parents who had sent me here and left me with nothing. "At everything. And I did something stupid."

"That's so unlike you." He said it with a completely straight face, only a hint of sarcasm in his voice.

"I'm reckless and impulsive and I do stupid things sometimes. But I broke up with him this morning. I should have done it a long time ago. It's over now. I'm not going to see him again."

"You don't owe me any explanations, little changeling."

My sword tip rested in the dirt, the glow drained from the metal just as my anger had drained from me.

"I think I'm done for today," I said, not meeting his eyes. "I'll call you tomorrow about setting up a meeting with Angor."

I walked away from him, back to my bike, slipping my sword into my backpack. He was right; I hadn't owed him any explanation. He'd pushed me away every time I'd tried to get close. He'd kept the distance between us. I owed him nothing.

But the entire ride back to Vancouver, I replayed his reaction over and over in my mind. He'd said I wouldn't hurt him, but I had.

CHAPTER 27

I returned to Arial's house, where we ate dinner together in the living room. She chose a movie. Something about a zombie falling in love she swore was based on Romeo and Juliet. It was entirely lost on me. I confessed I'd gone to Jeremy's the night before and broke up with him in the morning. And she made me love her a little bit more when she didn't judge my bad decision-making skills.

I didn't tell her about Ronan's reaction, but I thought about it all night when I should have been sleeping.

The next morning, Arial made me a coffee and asked what I was doing for the day. I smelled the strong brew and took a sip before answering her.

"I was going to go to my place and get a few things. I should also get my rent cheques ready for the next couple of months if I'm going to be going on a trip."

I'd told her already about going to the Sidhe, but it felt weird to say *going to another world*.

"Good plan. And with the money from... that job, you have plenty."

"Yeah. And if I need more, I can apparently get it from this corporation dedicated to helping fae in the human world that I'd never heard about and would have been supremely helpful years ago."

"You want some help today? We could take an Uber and then bring the stuff back here for some lunch."

I agreed and we ordered a car. When we arrived at my office, I went up to my apartment to get the things I wanted, including more clothes and the vial of Faerie Sea water from my safe. When I got to my door, I took down an envelope taped there and we went inside. I set it on my table and went to my safe.

"Aren't you going to open this?" Arial asked.

"Go for it," I called, gathering the things.

"Uh, Calynn? You should take a look at this."

I went back into my kitchen and did not like the look on her face.

"What is it?"

"It's a ten-day eviction notice for non-payment of rent."

"What?" I took the papers from her and started scanning them. "But I paid my rent this month." And then my heart stuttered for a second and I could feel the blood draining from my face. I looked back at Arial. "Fuck. I didn't. With everything that's been going on, I haven't even been here lately."

I pulled out my cell phone and called the property manager's number. Greg's phone went straight to voicemail. I hung up and called the building management company directly. When the lady answered, I gave her my name and address.

"Oh yes. It says here you didn't pay your rent for November. They left the eviction notice attached to your door on November 1st, so the effective date is today. If you're able to pay, you have five days in which to do so. Otherwise, you will need to be out by November 14th."

"I understand what the notice is telling me. Where is Greg? I tried to call him and it went straight to voicemail."

"Greg is no longer with the company."

I almost dropped the phone.

"Was he fired or did he quit?"

"I am not at liberty to divulge that information. Unfortunately, all I can tell you is you have five days to pay your rent or dispute the eviction. If you do neither, you have to be out of both the apartment and the office by November 14th. If you have any other questions, feel free to call me back."

I hung up the phone. Arial watched me. Waiting for me to say something. I lowered myself into the chair at my dining table, staring at the eviction notice, not really seeing it.

I was being evicted. My actions had possibly led to Greg being fired. I could pay the rent and be allowed to stay, but they wanted to do renovations and re-rent the space to someone at a higher rate. They wouldn't stop looking for a way to evict me. I felt so tired. This was supposed to be my home. The place I was supposed to feel safe.

Then again, I hadn't felt safe here since the Dark had broken in a few days before. And it hadn't really felt like home in a long time. Maybe ever.

"Are you going to pay it?" Arial asked, sitting in the other chair across from me.

I took a deep breath in, ready to nod, to sort it out the easiest way possible so I could move on from this moment. But as I let the breath go, I said, "No. It's time for me to move out."

"You can move in with me for real," Arial said. "You know I'd love to have you."

I lifted my eyes to hers and nodded.

She came around the table and hugged me. I held on tight.

"It's going to be okay," she said.

"It's just so much. All the times I've had to fight for my life and I still haven't even gotten any answers. And now this?"

"You always said you hated this place, anyway."

"I know. But it was mine." I leaned back and looked around the kitchen at the things I kept there. I really didn't have much and the possession that was most important to me was my motorcycle. That didn't stop me from feeling bereft. "I can't help but think if I hadn't gone looking for answers, none of this would be happening. Maybe I should have just left it alone."

***

We spent the day packing, Arial focused and me in a state of shock. I didn't have a lot, so it didn't take me long to fit what I needed to into the boxes Arial insisted we buy from the hardware store. It was well after lunchtime when my phone rang.

"Hello?" I answered.

"Are you all right?"

"Ronan?"

"You sound upset. What's wrong?"

"Nothing," I said automatically. "Why are you calling?"

"You said you would call today about interviewing Angor."

"Oh. Right."

"Calynn, what's wrong?"

I stared around my bedroom. At the boxes stacked in the corner. There were only three, but the bed was large and so was my dresser and safe.

"Can you come out to Vancouver with your truck?"

"I'll be there in an hour. Where do I meet you? Do you need anything else?"

"I don't think so."

He took a breath and I knew he was annoyed with me. He was always annoyed with me. "Where are you, little changeling?"

"I'm at my apartment. I'm being evicted."

I remained in a state of shock until he arrived. Arial let him in, and he came into my apartment like he was ready to do battle. An odd thought occurred to me. He could probably slay all my demons if I let him.

Aelwyd and another brownie followed him. A woman, older than Aelwyd, but clearly related to her. Ronan introduced her as Faline, Aelwyd's mother. Arial took the brownies downstairs to finish packing up my office and Ronan sat down in the chair across from me at my kitchen table.

"What do you need me to do?"

With that simple offer to help, no questions asked, the tension in my chest eased. And I found myself spilling all the thoughts out that were circling in my head like vultures.

"I forgot to pay my rent. It was just a mistake, but I think it got Greg fired. And now I can't get in touch with him and I'm worried. He's a nice guy. And I don't want to be a burden for Arial, and she'd never say I was, but I'm a lot. I know I'm a lot. *You* know I'm a lot. And she doesn't need all my shit at her house. And I have to go to the Sidhe, and I don't know how long I'll be gone or what I'm going to find there, so I don't even know if I'll need any of this stuff anymore, anyway. I could always see my future. It was horrible and boring, but I understood what was coming and now, I have no idea. I can barely see past what tomorrow is going to look like."

I paused for a breath and Ronan took the opportunity to stand and pull me into a hug. My heart was beating so fast from the anxiety threatening to cripple me.

"Faline and Aelwyd can take care of things here. They'll have you moved out by tonight. We can bring everything you don't need to the ranch. I have plenty of places to store it. And if you don't need it again, I can use it. I will have someone find Greg and make sure he's okay. If he's not, I'll make sure he is. As for the future, you'll get through this and you'll figure it out. It's bleak now, but it can't be forever."

I closed my eyes and let the rumble of his voice beneath my ear soothe me as he solved all my most immediate problems. I let the scent of pine and ice engulf me and refused to question why his presence seemed to calm me. Why his steady strength gave me strength. After a few moments, I took a final steadying breath and stepped back far enough to look at him, but not so far that I had to let him go.

"You're not angry at me?" I asked.

The slight tightening of his eyebrows was the only thing that showed his confusion. "Why would I be angry at you?"

"Where should I start? For dragging you into my problems. For needing your help so much. For my stupid decision-making." I didn't say for sleeping with Jeremy, but I thought it really hard.

"You are reckless and impulsive. Sometimes you do stupid things. You are likely going to give me a heart attack one day. And I would not change a single thing about you. I'm not angry." He lifted a hand as though to touch my face, but stopped himself before he made contact. Instead, he took a step back. "Figure out what you need to bring to Arial's house. We'll get it loaded into the truck and I'll take you there. Then I'll come back for the things to go to the ranch."

"I should stay and help."

"No, you shouldn't. The sun is going to set soon, and the Dark has already found you here once. You need to go where you'll be safe."

I groaned in frustration because I knew he was right. What's more, if the Dark showed up here looking for me, anyone with me would be in danger as well.

"If I'm not here, will you and Aelwyd and Faline be safe from him?"

"Yes. He doesn't kill without a contract."

"What if he tries to hurt one of you to find out where I am?"

"We'll be okay, little changeling. We'll finish quickly and be on our way back to the ranch. You've never seen a brownie work."

"What about Arial? Will she be safe if I'm at her house?"

"She has a rowan tree in her front yard."

I blinked, not sure how that answered my question.

"Rowan trees are the best conduits of fae magic. They can give or bolster any magic we can create. That one has protective magic woven from its roots to its leaves."

"Arial's father planted the tree. Or so her mother said."

"I'm not surprised. Find the boxes you need, little changeling."

I set two aside and brought them down the stairs for Ronan to load into the back of his truck. Then I went into the office and found another two. When we were ready, we said good-bye to Faline and Aelwyd, then Ronan drove us back to Arial's house.

"Are you sure—" I began, but Ronan cut me off.

"I'm sure." He lifted a box from the bed of his truck and handed it to Arial. "You get some rest and come out tomorrow. We can do some training and then go see Angor."

He handed me a second box and carried the last two himself into Arial's house and up to my room. I followed him back down the stairs. We stopped by the front door and Arial came over as well.

"I know I'm not supposed to say thank you, but I feel like I'm in your debt for the help you've given Calynn lately."

"There is no debt," Ronan replied. His eyes flicked to mine for just a second before he focused on Arial again. "It is my pleasure to help Calynn in any way I'm able."

"Hm." Arial scrutinized him for a moment before she nodded and then went into the kitchen.

I walked Ronan outside to his truck. We passed by the rowan tree in the front yard and I reached up to touch a leaf, noticing the magic now that Ronan had told me it was there. "I'll see you tomorrow," I said.

He opened the door of his truck and then turned toward me. "Everything will be all right, little changeling. I don't know how or when. But I am certain it will be."

I laugh humorlessly. "Right. I just need to not die before then."

His jaw clenched for just a second and I regretted the quip. But I didn't apologize or take it back. I went inside when he drove away. Arial was already sitting on the couch with a glass of wine in her hand, her legs tucked underneath her, a tumbler of whiskey on the table with the bottle next to it.

"If there was ever a night to get trashed, I think it's tonight."

I sat down and tossed back the shot and poured myself another, which I sipped more slowly.

Arial spun her glass in her hand, staring into the golden depths. "So. Ronan."

"What about him?"

"He's in love with you."

My heart hurt and I couldn't have said why. I covered the feeling with a scoff. "Yeah right. We've known each other for what? A week? I believe he's attracted to me. Fuck. I'm attracted to him. But love? No chance. It's way too soon for anything more than attraction and respect."

She lifted her gaze. "Okay. You're right. You want to order some food? We can watch a show or a movie or something. Maybe something with Meriel Jones in it."

I searched her face for a moment. It wasn't like her to give up on something like that so quickly. But she looked unconcerned about the previous conversation. I wanted to push it. I wanted to know what she thought she knew. But I also didn't want to know. Didn't want to be able to prove her wrong.

"Sure," I said.

She started scrolling on her phone, looking for a restaurant to order from. I considered her statement again. It was ridiculous. Attraction yes, but love? Absolutely not. The fact his presence calmed me was probably just the magic.

CHAPTER 28

A rial had to work in the morning, so I went out to Ronan's house right after she left. I'd tossed and turned all night. Another dream of shattered glass had woken me before dawn, and I hadn't been able to fall back asleep. So when I arrived at his house, I felt like a zombie.

Ronan opened the door before I could knock.

"I heard you coming. Come in. Are you sure you want to train? You look like you could use a nap."

"Maybe just a coffee first?"

"Aelwyd made a pot when I told her you would be here this morning. She also mentioned something about needing a new coffee maker. And a grinder?"

I blinked as I sat at the island and he poured me a cup of coffee.

"A new coffee maker?"

"Yeah. I guess she thinks we need something special. I can't remember what she called it." He set the cup in front of me and I wrapped my hands around it, letting it warm my fingers. "A pour something."

"Pour over coffee maker?"

"That's it." He leaned on the island and watched me take the first sip of coffee. My eyes closed as the taste of the hot brew touched my tongue. "She said something about it making better coffee. But if we get one, we need to *get* better coffee and would need a grinder."

"She's not wrong. But did she say why you need something like that if *you* don't care?"

He shrugged. "She said you would."

I was about to ask why Aelwyd would care about how I like my coffee when someone knocked on the front door. Ronan went to answer it and then led Bidina inside, pulling a suitcase behind her.

"Um. Hello," she said.

"Hi, Bidina."

She stopped in the kitchen beside the island where I was sitting. "I didn't tell anyone I was coming."

"That's okay."

Ronan motioned toward the living room and then pulled out his cell phone. He moved back toward the front door and I stood up with my coffee.

"Why don't we have a seat on the couch?"

I wandered over and sat down in the corner. Bidina sat beside me, her side flush with mine, ignoring the rest of the space on the couch. I figured she needed the contact, so I put my arm around her slim shoulders. She leaned her head on me and I could feel her trembling.

"Everything is going to be okay."

Her eyes found mine and I could see the hope in them before she rested her head on my shoulder again.

Ronan went to the back door and let Evander and Faline into the house.

"My heart," Faline cried as she rushed to Bidina and embraced her.

"Momma. I've made so many mistakes."

"Hush, my heart. You're home now, and everything will be right."

I watched the embrace and Evander standing a little apart as if wondering if he should join in. But it only lasted a moment before he, too, was embracing his daughter.

"I've missed you, Papa."

"I've missed you also, my Bidina."

I stood up and went to where Ronan was standing. Watching the family hurt something deep inside me I tried to keep buried. "Maybe we should give them some space," I said.

"They don't require it."

I looked at him and said something I never say. "Please."

I hated the desperation in my voice, but he listened without hesitation, leading me out the back door. The tears I had felt threatening me for the last few days finally started. I couldn't hold them back anymore. But refused to let the pain out any other way.

For once, Ronan's silence was helpful. It was more helpful when he wrapped his strong arms around me and just let me cry. I clutched his shirt in the back and held on, willing myself not to make a sound that might disturb the happy moment inside. Ronan's arms held me together.

Finally, I took a deep breath and nodded against his chest. He let me go and I spent another moment pulling myself together and wiping the tears off my face.

"Twice in as many days. I don't usually fall apart so easily."

"You don't need to make excuses for what you feel."

I bit my lip. "My parents never wanted me. My human parents, though maybe my fae parents didn't either. I found the human ones once. When I was sixteen. They'd moved on without me. Together. They had a family, other kids, they just hadn't wanted *me*. They told me they never understood it, but they had to get rid of me. My words, not theirs. But I never really understood why they didn't want me."

"Because you're a changeling."

I paced away from him, ready to cling to the frustration rather than the pain I had been feeling. "Why do you say that like it's supposed to explain everything? It doesn't explain anything."

"They could tell you were different, that you were not their daughter. It happens when the fae are changed. Humans know you are not human, and they can react with extreme prejudice. In Ireland, there were people who were killed because someone thought they were a changeling. Sometimes they were, sometimes they weren't."

I turned back to him, but stayed where I was. "What about the girl who was changed with me? Would she be treated like one of the beloved pets you mentioned before?"

"Likely not. When a fae is changed, the human who is brought into the Sidhe is treated the same as the fae who is living in the human world. The fae are all about balance. You've heard the term 'an eye for an eye.'"

"That's ruthless. And unfair."

"Ruthless, yes. But unfair? If humans had treated you well, the girl who lives in the Sidhe would also have been treated well. There is beauty in the balance. The same way there is beauty in a snowstorm or the sun. Both are ruthless. Both can kill. But both have purpose and are beautiful."

"It's unfair because neither of us asked to be changed. That decision was made for us. And the decision was made by the fae who then treated her bad."

"That's true. But the fae are bound by the laws of balance. They could no more have treated her well given your treatment here than a snowstorm could be warm. It's something you will have to learn if you are going to travel to the Sidhe. The laws there differ from here. Each action has a consequence, sometimes ones that are far more terrible than doing nothing at all."

I sighed. "The more I learn, the more I wish none of this had happened."

Ronan started walking toward me, slowly, giving me time to move away. "Whether you learned about it now or later does not change who you are."

He stood in front of me, close enough to touch, but not touching. "And who am I?"

"I can't answer that for you."

We stood there for a moment, and then I closed my eyes. "No. I guess you can't." I started walking to the arena where we'd been practicing. "Let's go exercise before we meet Angor. I feel the need to hit something."

***

After an hour of showing Ronan some krav maga, he called the training session and said it was time to meet Angor. They had set up the meeting at a park near Ronan's house. The weather had been grey and drizzly all morning and I wished it would just open up and rain already. We got to Campbell Valley

Park after Angor. Ronan led me to the picnic table where the other man was watching a few birds fight over some seeds someone had left on the next table over.

When he lifted his head, his eyes were red-rimmed and he looked beaten down, despite his expensive clothing, nice haircut, and manicured fingernails. The scent of the sea and sunshine rolled off him and I would have been able to tell, even if I hadn't known, that he was the male equivalent of Meriel.

Ronan and I sat down across from him. "Angor," he said by way of greeting. The man nodded.

"This is Calynn. She's looking into Meriel's death."

"Have you gotten her skin back?" he asked, driving home to me how important it was. Almost everyone had asked about that first.

"Not yet," I said. "But we're working on it."

"I just can't believe she's gone. I thought maybe there had been a reason for my exile, you know. If I hadn't been exiled, we never would have met. I thought I might be... But it doesn't matter now. She's gone."

"My condolences," Ronan said. "You didn't..."

"We made no vows. Meriel was always so focused on getting back to the Sidhe. I tried to convince her to give up the search. We could have been happy together. I was sure we could."

"There's still a chance you could find someone else, Angor."

The look he gave to Ronan was so bleak it broke my heart. "I think I may have gone past that point, Ronan. I think it is too late for me."

Ronan reached out and put his hand over top of the other man's. They didn't say anything for a few minutes and I didn't break the silence. I felt like I was missing something, but I didn't want to make it worse for Angor by asking about it.

Finally, Ronan said, "If you're up for it, Calynn would like to ask you a few questions about the last time you saw Meriel. You went for dinner at Gotham in Vancouver?"

"Yes. We fought." His voice broke over the last word and I thought he was going to cry, but he held himself together and continued. "I accused her of seeing you right before she came out for dinner with me. I know we hadn't made vows, but I thought it was awful she would see us so close together. She claimed she hadn't seen you in several weeks and she had been thinking we could... But I knew she had done something. It was more than when she would drink a drop of the Muir. I wanted to believe her. I tried to let it go and enjoy the rest of dinner. But when I dropped her off at her house, I didn't go in."

"Did she give you any other reason why she was acting the way she was?" I asked.

"She said she didn't remember. All she could remember was a tip to visit someone who could help her get back to the Sidhe. She said when she got back, she would get me back in as well. I told her I didn't want to go back. I wanted to have a life here, with her. One where we didn't have to worry about what might happen if our exile were to be enforced."

"She didn't remember who she spoke to?" I asked.

Angor shook his head. "She said it was a tip from a reliable source, but she couldn't remember who had told her."

"That seems weird." I looked at Ronan for confirmation.

"If someone had come from the Sidhe, they could have used glamour to disguise themselves or make her forget. It's difficult to do. Only those with incredibly powerful glamour can do it."

"Could a human who lived in the Sidhe do that?"

Ronan frowned and shook his head slowly. "None I had met could control glamour like that. Humans do sometimes gain some magical abilities when they live in the Sidhe for a long time. I suppose it could be possible."

"So she was telling the truth?" Angor asked. "She really hadn't seen you in weeks?"

"Not since September."

Tears rolled down Angor's cheeks. He didn't bother to wipe them away. "So the fight was for nothing. I didn't get to say good-bye." He closed his eyes and more tears seeped out.

I looked at Ronan and he nodded and stood.

"I'm sorry for your loss, Angor," I said as I started toward the parking lot.

Ronan stayed behind for a moment. When he came back to where he had parked his truck, he said, "Angor is going to stay on the ranch for a little while. If you think of anything else you want to ask him, he'll be there."

We got into his truck and I said, "I think that's all the information he has for us that will be relevant. I have a question for you, though. What was the talk about vows and why is it too late for him?"

I could tell from the look on his face he didn't want to talk about it. I wondered again about the conversation we had when he mentioned he could never have feelings for Coira.

"Before we fall in love and make vows, the fae are rather promiscuous. Sex is fun. It is an act that has little to do with love. Though I hear when it is with the one you love, it is... magic." He paused as though he was trying to imagine what that would be like. Then he shook his head and continued. "When we fall in love, though, we become completely monogamous. Forever. If our anam cara dies, we never get over it. We never find another. It is the true definition of soul mates. In fact, anam cara means soul mate. There is one soul mate for each fae out there. And only one. Angor believes he found his anam cara and now she has been taken from him. If he is right, he will never love anyone again for the rest of his life. And it could be a couple thousand years long."

My heart broke for Angor all over again. Ronan brought me back to his house, and I told him I was going to go back to Arial's house for the night. It was still early by the time I got to there, so she wasn't home from work. I paced her living room, thinking. I had learned a lot about the fae in the last few days and something Killian had told me was bugging me. *Her magic still lives. It lives in her skin. It is possible, if her skin is returned to her family, for a new selkie to be reborn from her magic.*

If that was true, and if we were magic, like Ronan said, maybe it was possible for her to be reborn in a form that could allow Angor to have his love back. If it was even slightly possible, I knew what I needed to do. I grabbed my jacket and left the house.

CHAPTER 29

I t was a bad idea to go back to Meriel's house for her skin. Possibly the worst idea I'd ever had. But I also knew it was the right thing to do so I could get it back to her family. And something inside me told me I had to get it myself. I brought my emergency flashlight from my riding pack since I didn't have the small case with my mini mag light. It was brighter than the other flashlight, anyway.

I parked under the no parking sign again and found the path I had cut through the overgrown empty lot the first time I'd been here. I walked along the beach to Meriel's yard and then to her bedroom door. Of course, the door was locked. I was about to search for another way into her house when I felt the pressure in the darkness change. I knew I was already too late.

"You foolish child. Of all the places where I could find you, this place is the easiest."

I spun around, trying to find him in the darkness. "Why is that?"

"Because it is the first place I found you. I will always be able to find you here."

"I'll keep that in mind."

I still hadn't seen him, but from what I now understood about his magic, he could be anywhere. Or everywhere. I didn't want to turn on my flashlight, partly because I knew it could draw the police's attention. But mostly I knew I would have only one chance to use it against the Dark and I had to make it count.

"Well, why haven't you killed me yet, then?"

"You have caused me a great deal of trouble for one so young. My employer punished me for missing my target. I am not sufficiently healed to kill you with my magic, and that is how I want to do it. It will be so much more painful for you to die slowly in the darkness."

"I see. So you want revenge because I made you work for this kill?"

I reached out with my own magic to try to locate him in the surrounding shadows. I could feel his magic everywhere, as though he wasn't just standing in one spot but was all the shadows. I concentrated and found where the magic was heaviest and prepared to make my move.

"If that is what you want to call it, yes. Revenge is a good enough word."

As he finished talking, I turned on my flashlight and shone 1800 lumens in the center of the mass of magic I had felt to my right. I heard him scream as I took off running. I didn't stop for anything. Didn't look back.

Maybe that's why I was so surprised when I felt the bullet rip through my left shoulder. I stumbled for a moment, but I also knew he would be right behind me, so I got my feet moving again and ran for my bike. I got on it and started driving. The pain stretched from the left shoulder throughout my whole body, but I gripped my handlebar, refusing to give in to it.

I couldn't go to Arial's house. She wouldn't be able to heal a gunshot wound. And if I went to the hospital, they'd ask too many questions. The only place I would possibly be safe and get the help I needed was Ronan's. It would be a long drive and I could feel the blood seeping out of my shoulder, but I had gone numb in most of my body and I could feel the Queen's gaze on me and it kept me moving. If she could see me, so could the Dark.

I wasn't sure if he was following me still. I couldn't feel his magic anymore. Somewhere in the back of my mind, I wondered how I had defeated him so easily with just the flashlight. The first time, he'd recovered quickly after I dropped the light from his eyes. An answer came but I couldn't quite grasp it, like my magic understood what happened, but I hadn't learned yet how to turn the volume up to hear it.

I rode for what felt like hours, but was only about one. Most of the ride passed without my notice as my body took over and rode on autopilot. My shoulder burned and my left arm was all but useless, laying limply on my leg unless I needed to use it to grip the clutch to shift.

My bike ran out of gas about a kilometer from Ronan's house. It might have been for the best since I felt woozy from the blood loss. I could barely grip the clutch anymore. I rode the bike off to the side of the road and climbed off.

I checked behind me to see if the Dark was still following. I couldn't feel him, but that didn't mean anything. I pulled my flashlight from my pocket and started walking.

My helmet made it hard to see in the dark, but I wasn't going to take it off. It wouldn't save my life from a direct hit, but it couldn't hurt. The darkness hid the blood as it seeped from the hole in my left shoulder down my arm, but I felt it dripping off the tips of my fingers. My right arm dangled as limply at my side as my left, though it sustained no similar wound, holding the flashlight as if it weighed a hundred pounds. I wouldn't turn the flashlight on unless the Dark caught up with me.

A walk that should have taken me ten minutes seemed to stretch forever. My legs felt like lead and it became difficult to lift my feet. I wasn't sure if the night was getting darker or if I was passing out. Maybe the Dark had caught up to me after all.

When I made it to Ronan's driveway, I would have sobbed from relief if it hadn't taken so much energy to do so.

I started trudging up the gravel and spun sluggishly when I heard a noise to my right. I lifted my arm and turned on the flashlight, pointing the beam toward the sound. In that moment, I knew I was going to die. I couldn't fight the Dark anymore. He had won.

Until I saw a small brownie and I collapsed to my knees.

"Miss Calynn?"

"Aelwyd," I gasped. The flashlight fell from my fingers and I dropped my head to make it easier to take off my helmet.

She moved toward me slowly. "Miss Calynn, are you okay?"

"We need to get to the house," I said as my helmet also fell to the ground. "The Dark is coming."

That got her moving. She ran to my side and lifted me under my right arm. She was much stronger than I had expected and I was moving toward the house at an alarming pace. I didn't think my feet were keeping up with the small girl as we raced down the driveway. She swept me along beside her, calling out as we ran.

"Master Ronan! It's Miss Calynn. She's hurt."

The lights in the house came on and I knew the darkness was closing in on my sight, not the world. The house was not as bright as it should have been. My vision was fading at the edges and I heard a rushing sound in my ears, blocking out all the other sounds. I couldn't hear Aelwyd anymore even though I had a feeling she was yelling for help still.

Ronan came out of his house and toward us. He somehow picked us both up and whisked us inside. He was faster than Aelwyd, and I wasn't sure how that was possible.

He slammed the door behind us and deposited us in the kitchen. He pointed to Aelwyd and she ran off on some errand.

He shook me a couple times, but I couldn't hear him. The last thing I saw was his terrified face as the world went black.

Chapter 30

The sun woke me up. I opened my eyes only to immediately close them. The brightness in the room made my head throb. I felt dizzy even though I wasn't moving. And when I tried to move, I felt like my muscles were made of lead.

I heard someone come into the room and I tried opening my eyes again. A brief glance showed me Aelwyd, carrying a bowl of water and a cloth.

"Good morning, Miss Calynn. Master Ronan has asked me to take care of you. He's gone to fetch some help."

"Help for what?" I asked. I didn't recognize my own voice. It was scratchy and my throat felt like I had been screaming for hours.

"For you, of course. You're in a bad way. We kept you safe from the Dark last night, but he may return tonight. It's no secret he knows where you are now. And the house has additional protections besides the threshold, but the Dark is the strongest assassin in the whole Sidhe."

"I've put you all in danger."

"Nonsense. You were right to come here. If one of us is in danger, we all are. We have had to band together out here."

"What do you mean?"

"Back home, we are very divided. If you were a brownie from Summer, you only associated with brownies from Summer. If you were a dwarf from Winter, you only associated with dwarfs from Winter. But here, it doesn't matter. No matter what part of the Sidhe you were from, you are still Faerie. That's all that counts."

"But I wasn't exiled."

She laughed like a rock skipping across soft ground. "Neither was I."

I didn't have a chance to respond because just then the front door slammed and Ronan come pounding up the stairs into the room. I was surprised at how clearly I could read the emotions on his face, fear followed by profound relief.

The relief swiftly changed to anger. "You little idiot. You could have been killed. I told you not to go out after dark."

"I know. But I have to get Meriel's skin back. The only time I can do that is after dark."

"Her family's peace of mind is not worth your life."

"Maybe it is." I looked at Aelwyd, who stood in the corner of the room.

Ronan turned to look at her as well. "Aelwyd, will you fetch your father? After that, you can get some rest. I will continue to watch over Calynn."

She bobbed her head in assent and rushed out to find Evander.

When she was gone, Ronan took the bowl and the cloth and started cleaning my wound, focusing on what he was doing and refusing to meet my eyes. That's when I noticed I wasn't wearing a shirt, only my bra. Sometime last night, it had been removed to allow access to the bullet hole in my shoulder. Maybe Ronan was right. I should have listened to him about not going out. How many times did someone have to try to kill me before I realized I was truly in danger?

I cleared my throat and started coughing because of how scratchy it felt.

Ronan finally looked at me again, concern on his face.

"My throat hurts," I told him after I finished coughing.

He nodded and reached for a glass of water on the bedside table, helping me drink from it. "You screamed a lot last night. I'm surprised you have any voice at all."

"I did?"

"When we removed the bullet. You were pretty out of it. You passed out almost immediately after I got you inside. I was afraid you had died. But Evander came in and reminded me you wouldn't still be bleeding if you were dead. He saved your life. Him and your own magic, which kept the bleeding slow. You could have bled out on your way here, otherwise. Anyway, you screamed a lot even though you were passed out. Evander believes it was the pain of your magic being wounded by the Dark's bullet."

"How am I awake now? I figure I should be out of it for a few days."

Ronan reached over to the bedside table and pulled out a vial of water.

"I told you this stuff is useful."

"Is that more sea water?"

"Yes. It's Evander's. He was able to bring some out with him when he left. After we pulled out the bullet, we used a drop of this to restore some of the blood you lost. Then Evander made his poultice, which sealed the wound."

"And I've brought more."

The man in question stood at the door, a small pot in his hands. "I spent all day cooking this batch, so it'll be more potent than what I used last night. Move, Ronan. I will take over."

Ronan stood and went to the corner of the room as Evander settled next to me.

"You've been very kind to help me so often, Evander," I said to him as he started working.

"We all look out for each other here. And you... Well, we can't lose you after only just finding you."

He took out a small knife and cut the left side of my chest about an inch below where he'd extracted the bullet. Then he opened the vial of water and spilled a couple drops into the cut. I couldn't see what he was doing, but it felt warm and eased some of the ache I'd been feeling. Not a lot. But enough that I noticed. Then Evander smeared the poultice onto the wounded area. He poured a drop of the sea water into the bowl Aelwyd had brought up earlier and stirred the water with his knife.

"Ronan, will you help me lift her?"

Ronan came back to the bed and gently lifted me so I was sitting up away from the pillows and Evander could reach my back. Everywhere Ronan's skin touched me, my skin tingled. I didn't want to look at him to see if he felt it, too.

I felt Evander wiping a small area and applying the poultice.

"It works better if you can leave it to the air, but it won't do any good if it all comes off on the bedding. At some point, we'll have to have you lie on your stomach to let the entry wound breathe, but for now, you can remain as you are."

When Evander finished, they laid me back down.

"If this poultice and the water are working so well, why am I so tired?" I asked, fighting the pull of my heavy eyelids.

"It is the same as when your hand was broken. They are working because they are using your energy, your strength, and your magic. I've never seen them work so quickly on such a dire wound. It shows just how strong you are." Evander looked from me to Ronan, who hadn't moved away after laying me back down. The small man smiled and set the pot down on the side table. "I'll check back on you in a few hours. I have some work to do before dark. We will all be back before sundown."

Ronan nodded again as Evander left. He stayed next to me, sitting on the edge of the bed, but he didn't touch me again.

"Why is Evander coming back before sundown?"

"I can't guarantee their safety after dark. The Dark is hunting you and you are here. I believe he knows it. I've told everyone who lives here to be at the house before sunset. I can keep them safe in the house."

"I'm putting everyone in danger by being here. I should go." I moved to sit up, but I could barely lift my good arm, let alone my whole body.

"No. You're in no condition to go anywhere. You need to rest."

All of a sudden, a thought occurred to me. "Arial! She doesn't know where I am. She'll be worried."

"I called her this morning. She will likely be here before long. I told her you were okay, but she said she needed to see for herself."

"My bike ran out of gas a bit down the road."

"Evander sent Carrick to get it earlier today. It didn't run out of gas."

"Then why did it stop?"

"I don't know." He stood up to go. "Get some rest."

I reached out and snagged his hand before he could move away from me. He could have easily broken the contact if he'd wanted. I could barely grip his fingers. Instead, he squeezed my fingers in reassurance.

"What is it, little changeling?"

"I've turned your life upside down and I've brought danger to everyone you're supposed to protect."

I must have been really out of it because my eyes hurt from unshed tears.

"It's okay. I wouldn't have it any other way." He squeezed my hand again and offered me a smile. As he walked away, I swallowed the tears and fell asleep again with the knowledge he had lied.

Chapter 31

I couldn't say how much time had passed, but when I woke again Arial was lying in bed snuggled in on my right side, her eyes closed. It was dark outside, but in November that could mean early evening or the middle of the night.

On the table to my left was a glass of water and, given my throat felt like the Sahara desert, I reached toward it. I stopped when my shoulder protested the movement.

Arial woke up and said, "Calynn. You shouldn't be moving."

"I'm thirsty."

"I'll get it." She got out of bed and brought the glass to my lips. I reached up with my right hand and could drink without too much help. She put the glass down for me and that's when I noticed the tear tracks on her face.

"Arial," I began.

She shook her head. "I need to talk first. I know how much this new stuff means to you. You need to solve a puzzle. You need to stand up for the girl who was killed because no one else in her world will. I get it. I've been beside you for the last twenty years. But Calynn. I'd also like to be beside you for the next twenty. Don't take chances with your life."

A huge weight of guilt settled over me. She was right. I don't know what I would do if something were to happen to her. It was rather selfish of me not to think of it the other way around. Arial had already lost her mother too young. She didn't need to lose her best friend as well. "You're right. I need to get something from Meriel's house, but I should be more careful. I *will* be more careful. Are you going to stay?" I asked.

"For as long as you want me here. I told my boss I wouldn't be coming in for a few days. A family member was sick and I had to be here."

"Do you know where Ronan or Aelwyd are? I'm really hungry. And I have to go to the bathroom."

"They're downstairs with the rest of the people who live here. I'll help you to the toilet and then we'll let them know."

When we were on our way back to the bedroom, Ronan was already waiting for us. "You shouldn't be out of bed."

I rolled my eyes as Arial helped me back into the bed. "You would rather I pee here?"

He didn't respond to that. "Killian is here. He and Evander agree you'll be fine in a few days with some rest. Aelwyd is downstairs. She'll bring up food for you shortly."

I nodded.

"I'll be downstairs if you need anything else."

After he left, Arial said, "You still don't think he loves you?"

I rolled my eyes again.

"At the very least, he cares about you."

"You could have fooled me."

"Calynn. You know he does, too. You just don't want to admit it."

"Why wouldn't I want to admit it?"

"Because if you do, and you let him in, you could get hurt."

Her words hit home, just like she knew they would. Just like she'd intended for them to. She knew me better than anyone in the world. She was the only one I really let close, so she would know when I was keeping someone else away.

"I'll think about what you said."

Aelwyd arrived with a couple plates of food.

"So, who are all these people?" Arial asked as we ate.

I told her who and what everyone was. Or at least the ones I had met. I was sure there were more fae on Ronan's property who I hadn't met yet. By the time finished eating, she knew as much as I did about the Sidhe and the creatures in it. I considered telling her about what I knew of her father, but I still wasn't sure if it was the right time. I still didn't know who her father was or if he would want anything to do with her.

I was too tired to make a decision, so I laid back against the pillows on the bed.

"You should go to sleep," Arial said.

"Ronan doesn't have a lot of places in the house for everyone to sleep. What are they all doing?"

"I think most of them are on pillows and such on the floor in the living room. There are a few on the couches, little ones. Ronan said Killian was going to sleep in his bed and he would be in the loft."

"In one of the chairs? It's not the greatest place to sleep."

"Calynn, sweetie. I don't think he intends to sleep tonight. From what I understood, the Dark shouldn't be able to get in here, but he was going to stay awake to be sure."

I felt the guilt settle on me again. I had caused a lot of trouble by coming here. I should have gone somewhere else and not brought so much danger to this place that was supposed to be safe. Then again, where else could I have gone?

"It's not your fault," Arial said, and I wondered if I had spoken my thoughts out loud. "I know that look on your face. You believe you brought the danger. But it's not your fault someone wants to kill you. You don't even know *why* he wants to kill you."

"He lied to me today," I said, not sure why it mattered so much.

"The Dark?"

"Ronan. I said I brought the danger here, and he said he wouldn't have it any other way. But he lied. I could tell."

Arial knew about my ability to sense lies and so she didn't question how I knew. "You know better than I do, lies aren't always hiding something worse. If he lied about the fact that he wouldn't have it another way, maybe the other way he would have it is you not in danger in the first place. You may be able to sense lies, but I have this feeling Ronan, and everyone else, would prefer you to be here where they can help keep you safe."

"But why? They don't even know me."

"You're one of them. It's like you're part of their family."

"I'm part of *your* family."

"Can't you be both?"

***

I woke again in the middle of the night. Arial slept beside me. I closed my eyes and reached out with my magic. It felt like everyone was asleep. Except above me. I felt the cold water flowing over that frozen stone. I tried to get up and found I could this time. It felt good to move. Managing to get up without waking Arial, I left the bed and climbed the stairs to the loft where he was sitting, looking out the window as I had done that first day. Was it only a week ago?

He didn't turn to face me as I came up the stairs, but he said, "What are you doing up, little changeling?"

"I'm not used to sitting still for so long. And I've been sleeping pretty much all day." I moved toward him and had the strongest urge to sit on his lap and snuggle into his chest. I sat in the other chair. "But climbing the stairs was a lot more work than I thought it would be."

"You're feeling okay?"

"My shoulder is a little stiff, and I'm tired still despite all the sleep. But yeah. I think I'm okay."

He opened his mouth as if to say something and then hesitated. Finally, he said, "You scared me."

I wasn't sure what to say, so I said nothing. We sat for a while, watching out the window.

"Do you think he's out there?"

"Maybe not here. Maybe not close. But somewhere. He won't stop. Not until he completes his contract."

"Something about last night isn't sitting well with me."

"The fact you were there at all and put yourself in danger?"

"Besides that. I reached out with my magic and felt for his to find out where he was. He was all around me. He wanted to kill me with his magic. But he couldn't. I shone the light of my flashlight on his face and it allowed me to get away. But he should have recovered and come after me. I was on the road for a good hour, maybe even an hour and a half."

"I've been wondering about that as well."

"As I was driving away, I thought I knew what was wrong. But now I don't know."

"It was probably something you felt with your magic. You haven't gotten accustomed to using it, to knowing it. You may have felt something and not known you had. What did you feel?"

I closed my eyes, trying to remember. "The darkness was suffocating. That's how he can kill with it. He smothers his victims. It was spread around me. I could feel his magic everywhere, surrounding me, but most of it was in one spot. That's how I knew where he was."

"What else?"

I thought about it, trying to recall what I had noticed in those few moments before I ran and was shot. "It was thin. There was something wrong, like it had been stretched. Who could have done that?"

"I can think of only one person who could manipulate the Dark's magic."

I opened my eyes. "The Queen of Air and Darkness."

Ronan nodded.

"But why? He said his employer punished him. Is the Queen trying to have me killed?"

"It does sound that way."

"But why?" I asked again. "What reason would she have to want me dead? I've never even met her. Have I?"

Ronan was silent and we went back to staring out the window.

I thought for a bit longer and realized something else. "The cu sidhe and Deegan were both from Summer."

He looked at me again.

"So if the Winter Queen sent the Dark, and I already figured the Summer Queen sent Deegan, at least two people are trying to kill me. Maybe three if someone else sent the cu sidhe."

I felt so overwhelmed. My throat and my eyes hurt from holding back tears. I hated crying. I wouldn't do it. I only wanted to now because I was so tired. Instead, I sat with my eyes closed, afraid of what would happen if I opened them.

"Come on," Ronan said. "I'll help you back to bed." With no warning, Ronan lifted me and carried me down the stairs. I laid my head on his shoulder, working up the courage to ask something that had been plaguing me since I woke up that morning.

"I need to ask you a very serious question. Don't sugarcoat the answer for me. I can take it."

"What's the question, little changeling?"

I took a deep breath. "What happened to my leather jacket?"

His shoulders shook with silent laughter before he lay me gently next to Arial and smoothed the hair out of my face. "Your jacket is fine."

"Fine? Like... fine?"

"Yes. Bidina fixed it."

"How? I was shot."

The small smile changed to a scowl as his gaze flicked to my chest. "I know." His eyes found mine again. "But it's just fabric. I'll bring it to you in the morning so you can see for yourself. Sleep now. You're exhausted."

"You may not be wrong about that."

I thought I heard him whisper something, but I was too close to sleep to know what it was. All I knew for sure was, whatever he said was the truth.

CHAPTER 32

By the time I woke up in the morning, Arial was already downstairs and almost everyone had left the house. The only ones there were Arial, whose magic I could feel now I knew it was there, and Killian. I started down the stairs slowly, holding tight to the railing as I was overcome with a bout of dizziness. I wasn't paying attention to anything except not falling down, so I didn't notice Ronan come in from outside and come up to meet me.

"I'm okay," I said.

"Just let me help you down," he said with a bit of a growl.

I linked my left arm through his right and held the railing with my other hand and we went down together. He saw me to a seat at the table where Arial and Killian were drinking coffee and handed me my leather jacket. As he went into the kitchen to get my breakfast, I looked it over.

Bidina had indeed fixed it. She had replaced the padding inside to something more flexible than had been there before and sewn the lining up in a way that made it difficult for me to see where the bullet had come through. But it was the outside that made me catch my breath. Over the tear, she had embroidered a blood red rose in full bloom, the stem stretching down the back with menacing thorns lining it. The other side had a mirrored rose, this one snow white.

"They're beautiful," I said, tracing them with my fingers.

Ronan set a plate in front of me and I laid the jacket across my lap, not wanting to stop touching it. But my stomach chose that moment to remind me pointedly it hadn't received proper food in far too long, so I started shoveling the ham and cheese omelet into my mouth. Ronan poured me a cup of coffee. He put two pieces of fresh toast on my plate and I ate faster than was probably wise, but I felt like I hadn't eaten in days. Then it occurred to me I really hadn't eaten much in the last thirty-six hours.

Whatever conversation Arial and Killian had been having paused as I ate. When I glanced up from my plate, everyone was watching me, except Killian.

"What? I was hungry."

Killian grinned. "It is a good sign. I can feel you have more energy today."

"Yes. I feel a lot more human today. Or... like myself anyway."

Not completely like myself, since I hadn't even touched my coffee yet. I fixed that little aberration immediately.

Arial also took a drink from her cup and then said, "I brought you some things. Clothes and such. Let me know if you need anything else."

"I'm not coming back to your place?"

She grimaced. "Ronan thinks it'll be safer for you, for now, if you stay here. I tend to agree with him."

I sighed. She had a point. And I didn't want the Dark to find me at her place. The rowan tree in her yard might offer some protection, but I didn't want to push it to its limit.

"Okay. I'll stay here for now. I'll take a look at what you brought and let you know what else I might need. When are you going?"

"Evander said he'd be by this morning to check on you. If he agrees with Killian, I think I'll go today. But I want to know when you're going into this Sidhe place. I want to say good-bye."

"Of course."

The back door opened and Evander came in, carrying his case of medical supplies.

"You're sure getting use out of that stuff with me around," I said.

He came to me with a smile. "It's good to have practice." He took his time looking over my wounds, including the older ones, and declared everything was healing well. "Even one of the High Healers would have had trouble getting someone well this fast."

"High Healers?"

"They are the oldest of the daoine sidhe. Older even than the Queens. Two are Summer. One is Winter. I worked with Anstice before I left the Sidhe."

Killian was next. He checked me over, and while he did, I noticed something about his eyes that didn't make sense. It felt like magic surrounded them. The magic wasn't what I was used to feeling, but I couldn't figure out what was wrong. Then he spoke and I stopped worrying about it.

"As I suspected, your magic is healing stronger than before."

"Why?"

He touched my chest where Evander had cut the bullet out. "I've heard of this gun the Dark uses. The bullets are specially made using his magic."

"That's why he was so upset I broke his gun."

"He can't easily get a new one. But the magic in the bullet is not as powerful as the magic he wields. It must be aimed perfectly to do the damage it is supposed to." He moved his hand slightly until his fingers stopped right over my heart. "Your magic comes from your heart, so that is where the bullet must hit."

"That makes sense."

"Because it did not hit you true, it only wounded you. And because your magic has been working so hard to keep you alive these past few days, it has been exercised in a way that doesn't usually happen."

"So what you're saying is it's a good thing so many have tried to kill me lately," I said, arching an eyebrow.

He laughed. "Perhaps. There is still much you must face, child. You will need to be strong for it."

"Well. Now that everyone has checked me over and declared me healing, I've decided to go back to Meriel's house and get her skin back."

Everyone had an opinion on that and started speaking at once.

"Absolutely not—"

"I wouldn't advise—"

"Sweetie, I don't think—"

I held up my hand to stop them. Surprisingly, it worked.

"I don't mean today. But, somehow, I know it's my responsibility to get it and I intend to. I have a plan, though. Ronan, do you think you could ask Jeremy to do something?"

"I could ask. I'm not sure what he could do. He won't be able to go into the house and take anything out without breaking a lot of laws."

"I know." I took a deep breath, knowing I was about to start an argument. "If I'm going to the Sidhe, I have to get the skin before I go. I'm not sure when I'm coming back to this world after I go in there. I might be in there for months and her family should have her skin."

"They should," Ronan agreed. "And they will. But you don't have to get it."

"If I don't, who will?"

"The police will release it eventually."

"And who knows how long it will take for them to release it. It could be months. Maybe longer. Who will bring it to the Sidhe then? If I'm already there, I won't know when it's released. Everyone in this world is here because they can't go back. I'm the only one who knows she's dead, cares at all, and is willing and able to bring it back." I thought of Angor and my hope that Meriel's magic could be reborn into a new selkie who could love him. I kept the thought to myself, but it solidified my resolve. "I have to get it. And you can't stop me."

Ronan closed his eyes and took a deep breath. Everyone else seemed content to let us hash this out.

"Calynn, don't do this. If the Dark finds you again, he'll kill you."

"I'm going," I said.

Ronan looked at Arial for support. She looked at me.

"You have a plan this time?" she asked.

"I do."

"That's better than what you had the other night," Ronan said.

"Is it a good plan?" Arial asked.

I felt a smile spread across my face. "Actually, I'm pretty sure it's a bad one."

Arial smiled back at me and shook her head. "Okay. I won't stand in your way."

"You can't be serious," Ronan said, pacing away from the table just to pace back.

"I have some advice for you, Ronan," Arial said, standing. "When Calynn has a bad idea, there's really nothing you can do about it other than try to help minimize the damage." She came around the table and kissed my cheek. "Be careful," she warned.

"I will."

Killian stood as well. He said good-bye and then he and Arial left through the front door together. Evander picked up his case and escaped through the back door, leaving me alone with Ronan, who still paced.

I ignored the restless movements. "I thought you could call Jeremy and tell him what we need and see if he can help by leaving her bedroom door unlocked. Maybe also have a shift change while I'm supposed to be there. I'll go just before sunset, so the Dark won't have time to reach me. I'll sneak in, get the jacket and leave. Hopefully before the Dark can even get there."

Ronan stopped pacing. "It's not a great plan."

"But it's better than no plan at all."

I could tell he wanted to keep arguing. I could see he didn't want to let me do it, but he couldn't think of a way to stop me.

"You know I'll go back again even if we don't call Jeremy. So much has happened and I need to feel like I'm in control of something in my life. This one thing I can control. I can do it. I know I can. And I stand a better chance of not getting hurt again if we ask for help."

"I'll call him and set it up."

"After I get the skin, I want to train again with the sword."

"You've barely healed from the gunshot wound."

"We don't have much time to train before I go to the Sidhe. I want to be at least a bit more than a novice."

Ronan looked like he didn't want to help, but I knew he would. Whether he liked it or not, I knew I could count on him.

CHAPTER 33

Ronan called Jeremy in his office and put it on speakerphone so I could listen to the conversation. I didn't want to deal with Jeremy knowing about me, so I kept quiet.

"This is Detective Lopez."

"Detective. This is Ronan."

"Did you think of anything I should know about Meriel Jones' death?"

"No, Detective. I'm actually calling for something else. Though it is related."

"What can I do for you?" He sounded wary.

"Meriel was a selkie. I assume you know what that means?"

"Yes."

"She kept her seal skin at her house, and we have someone who is willing to return it to Meriel's family in the Sidhe. But we need your help to retrieve it."

"I can't take something from an active crime scene."

"I wouldn't ask you to. I'm merely hoping you could go to her house one day this week and forget to lock the door in her bedroom that leads to her patio. And perhaps schedule a shift change in the officers posted outside her house an hour before sunset."

Jeremy didn't respond right away. After a few moments of silence, he said, "You know what you're asking me to do?"

"I'm asking you to grant the final wish of a dead fae and allow her to return home."

"Way to twist that knife."

"It's what we're good at."

Jeremy was silent again. I knew one thing that worried him was someone coming in and messing up the crime scene, moving things, taking things that shouldn't be taken. I wrote a note on the nearby pad of paper and showed it to Ronan.

"If it helps, Detective, the person who is going to retrieve the skin understands police procedure. She won't disturb the scene at all except to take the skin. She has also been to the house before and knows exactly where Meriel kept it."

"She'll be in and out? She won't touch anything but the skin?"

Ronan glared at me. "That is correct." I knew he was telling me as much as he was telling Jeremy. I rolled my eyes and nodded.

That was the whole plan, after all. Get in and out before the Dark could even notice I was there.

"Okay. What day do you want me to do this?"

I wrote another note on the paper.

Ronan glared at me and I knew he thought it was too soon. But I tapped the paper with my pen and glared back at him.

"Tomorrow," Ronan told him through clenched teeth.

"I can make that happen. You said an hour before sunset?"

"Yes. She'll be out again before darkness has fully settled."

"All right. I'll make sure the door is unlocked and the house is empty before then. But Ronan. You'll owe me for this."

Ronan's eyes locked with mine and I could tell he wanted to say something to me.

"Are you sure you want one of the daoine sidhe to owe you? Our bargains are notoriously double edged," he said to Jeremy. Then he motioned for the pad of paper and wrote something.

"I'm certain I do."

I read his note. *The debt will be yours. Do you accept?*

I nodded.

"If you're going to play with fire, Detective, be sure you are prepared to be burned. A single favor of equal or lesser value."

They hung up and Ronan said, "Are you sure tomorrow isn't too soon?"

"I want to get this done. I feel good today. We can do some training tonight and tomorrow morning. After I get back, I'll decide when to go to the Sidhe."

My heart pounded as I laid out the plan to leave this world behind. It still scared me. I didn't know if I really wanted the answers to the questions I had. After I had found my birth parents, or the people I thought were my birth parents, I vowed not to ask questions if I wasn't sure I could handle the answers. Now, here I was again, asking questions, terrified the answer would be something awful, but asking them anyway.

I was sure I was going to regret something.

***

We trained in the evening and after my shower, I persuaded Ronan to give me another massage, claiming I needed my muscles loose if I was going to use them to defend myself. He didn't take as much convincing as I thought he would. He also didn't follow me into my bedroom like I'd hoped he would either.

The next morning, we ate a large breakfast and followed it up with some more training. I'd showered and changed before we sat down to lunch and told Ronan I thought I was getting better.

"You are," he confirmed. Then he ruined it by saying, "Not that it will do you any good against the Dark."

"What do you mean?"

"He's not going to give you a chance to use the sword. You've defended yourself against him three times now. He'll try to stay away from you and kill you with his magic. The only way to defend against that is with your own magic. You would need a significant amount of light magic to try and would have to know how to use it."

"Why didn't you say so before now?"

"Would it have made a difference?"

I thought about it while his emerald eyes bored into me, waiting, perhaps hoping, for an answer. I knew what answer he wanted, but he was right. It didn't make a difference. I thought of Angor and asked Ronan a question that had been brewing in my mind for a while.

"If I bring her skin back to her family and her magic is reborn into a new fae, is there a chance she could come back as a fae who Angor could love?"

I could tell he knew where I was going with this, but he told me the truth, anyway. Maybe because he knew I would know if he lied. "There is a chance. Yes."

"Then no. It wouldn't make any difference. I have to bring her skin back to her family."

"It's reckless. You know how dangerous it is to go back there."

"Have you never done anything reckless in your life?"

He hesitated. "I did once."

"And what happened?"

"It led to my exile."

That shut me up. He'd never mentioned his exile willingly before. I searched his eyes for more information. Something in them brought another question to my lips.

"Would you do it again?"

He stared at me for a long time, and I could see the determination, the resolve, the resignation.

"A hundred times over," he said on a sigh.

We finished lunch and I got ready. I packed my sword into my backpack, even though Ronan said it wouldn't help. I also made sure my emergency flashlight was where it was supposed to be. Then I went out to my bike. I had checked it over earlier and nothing seemed wrong with it. Killian offered a potential reason it had stopped working the other night. He believed my magic had stopped it to prevent me from falling off and causing my body more damage. I wasn't sure how comfortable I was with my magic working without my conscious decision to use it.

"Be careful," Ronan said as I was pulling on my leather jacket.

"I know. I'll be careful."

He stepped closer to me. "It should be me going."

"We've been over this. Unless the police have moved it, I know exactly where the skin is. I can be in and out in a matter of minutes. Besides, my instincts are telling me it has to be me. I won't start ignoring them now. I'm going."

I could tell he still wanted to argue, but he stayed silent as I put on my backpack. I got onto my bike and he came closer still. I held my helmet in one hand, waiting to see what he was going to say next, but he didn't say anything. He just stared at me for so long eventually, I said, "If you don't want to get run over, you should step back."

Instead, he came closer and lowered his face to mine, slowly, like he didn't think he wanted to but also couldn't stop himself. When our lips finally touched, the kiss was tentative, asking permission. I lifted my free hand to touch him, but I was afraid to make contact and break the spell. Instead, my hand floated near his face, only our lips touching. I wanted to melt into the kiss. I wanted to open to him. But Ronan kept it soft, a feather-light touch, and then he was gone. I felt cold where his warmth had been and all I wanted was to pull him back.

He stepped out of my reach like he knew what I wanted and said, "Please don't die."

Then he turned and went into the house like nothing had happened.

I fought to keep my hands from trembling as I put my helmet on and started my bike. I had two hours before the sun was going to set and I needed to get to the house early. As much as I wanted to follow him and demand an explanation—or another kiss—I left Ronan's house and started toward West Vancouver.

Of course, an accident on the bridge had slowed traffic to a snail's pace. I sat on my bike, practically vibrating with anxiety before I got past the accident and the vehicles flowed again. I arrived with only minutes to spare, so I parked quickly and made my way to the beach and down to her house at a run. The police cruiser had not been parked in front of Meriel's house. I shouldn't have any problems as long as I moved fast.

I checked the time. The sun wasn't supposed to set for another ten minutes, but it was already dark. Fucking November. I arrived at Meriel's bedroom door and, as Jeremy had promised, it was unlocked. I hurried to the closet and took the strange jacket off the hanger. I paused for just a moment to marvel at how soft it was and the smell of the ocean coming off it. So, I was still in Meriel's closet when the Dark entered her house.

I checked the time again and felt completely ripped off. I should have another eight minutes. Yet, his magic reached out to find me, and I knew he had fully healed. He would kill me with his magic if I couldn't find a way to stop him. I turned on the light in the closet, but it wouldn't offer protection from him for long.

"Changeling," he called. "You cannot hide from me. Come out. Meet your fate like a true fae."

"If coming out to die is being a true fae, I'd rather be human."

He was coming closer, but he didn't seem to be in any kind of rush. I could feel amusement sweep through him as he listened to my response.

"You've been a worthy quarry, changeling. Much more than I suspected you'd be. Especially for one so small and young. Let us end this."

I was sure I didn't want to end it. But he was reaching toward me with his magic and I could feel it start to suffocate me.

I was going to die. I thought of Ronan's simple request. *Please don't die.*

I set my teeth together as I pulled my sword out of my bag even as the pressure of the darkness kept building. As soon as it was in my hand, my head felt a bit more clear. I knew the sword would not save me, but its magic was helping. It helped enough to clear my mind and allowed me to remember when I'd reached for Ronan's magic that first day and had almost physically pulled him toward me. I'd been trying not to reach so hard since then, but now, in a last, desperate attempt to stay alive, I reached out to the Dark with my own magic as hard as I could. The darkness enveloped me and I could no longer see my surroundings. I pulled harder.

"What are you doing?" He sounded confused and I could tell his steps paused. I kept pulling and I felt him fighting me.

"Stop. What are you doing?" Panic replaced confusion.

My sight cleared and I could see his magic all around me, no longer suffocating me, but living darkness inside the Dark himself. There were scars, deep and ugly ones. I reached out with my hands and took his magic in them. The Dark kneeled in front of me and I wasn't sure if he was really there, or if this was all in my head.

"Who did this to you?" I asked.

"My mother. She was trying to heal me. My latent magic would not manifest. She said I was sick and she wanted to make me better." He spoke like the child he had been and not the centuries old assassin he was.

"Kai. That's your name. She took it from you when she couldn't bring forth your latent magic."

He hung his head. "Are you going to destroy it?"

"What do you mean?"

He touched my hand. "I can feel your magic just as surely as you can feel mine."

For the first time, I felt a black slimy magic and realized what he meant. The magic felt oily and would strip his darkness from him. It would save my life, but it felt wrong to even think of using that magic, let alone actually do it.

"No, Kai. I won't destroy it."

As soon as I made the decision, my latent magic pulsed within me and realized what I could do with it. I'd been doing it for myself a lot lately and now I understood how. I found the deepest scar, focused all of my energy, and it heated and smoothed out. It was much more difficult than destroying his magic would have been, but then destruction is always easier than creation.

I could tell Kai was in pain, but he knew what was happening. He didn't try to stop me and I healed one scar after another. When I came to the last one, I noticed the magic in my hands was not all that was here. I healed it and felt for the rest of the magic. It called to me and I knew it was different from the darkness. It was hotter. The softly glowing coals of a fire almost spent. I tried to bring it forward, to where Kai could reach it, but it burned my fingers to touch it. I considered my options for a moment. I looked back, but I had gone further into his magic than Kai could reach. I couldn't see him anymore. The only way to give him this magic would be to bring it out myself. I rubbed my hands together and picked up the embers. Then I ran. Back to where I could see Kai. As soon as he was in sight, I dropped the embers and let go of his magic completely.

When I opened my eyes, I was lying on the floor of the closet. The Dark—Kai—had turned out the light and wrapped my hands in Meriel's skin. They were throbbing beneath the cool pelt.

"Why did you help me?" he demanded.

I stared into the blackest eyes I had ever seen. There were no whites to them at all, just two shimmering black orbs beneath black eyelids. But in the center of the black was a faint orange glow, like the glow of an ember.

"Did it work?"

He took me by my shoulders and shook me once. I realized I had no strength left to fight him. If he wanted to kill me now, he could do it.

"Why?"

"It was wrong what she did to you. I don't care if she was your mother or the Queen. She shouldn't have done what she did. She could have destroyed your magic completely."

He laughed, a sound bordering on hysteria. "Changeling. You know nothing of what you are saying. Come. I will take you to your protector."

I could barely stand. He picked me up as though I weighed no more than a small child and brought me to my bike, setting me astride it.

"If I can't walk, how do you expect me to ride this?"

"I don't. But I expect you do not want to leave it behind, either."

The bike started to move. "How?"

"The darkness does what I command. I tell it to keep the motorcycle upright and it does. I tell it to move the motorcycle forward..."

"And it does. And quickly. This is how you could always disappear."

He nodded. "I tell the darkness to take me away and it does. It has ever been so. Now, I feel even more control over it."

"Can the Queen control the darkness like this?"

"No. Air is her main magic. Darkness is her latent one. She does not control the darkness as I do."

"Your latent magic. You can reach it now, right?"

"Yes. You gave it to me."

"I didn't. It was there the whole time, just too far for you to reach. I only brought it closer so you could see it."

"I am in your debt."

I was going to refuse the debt. I only did what was right. But then I realized I could use it to help me. "I'd like to ask you some more questions. About who is trying to kill me."

"I will answer what I can, but I will not be forsworn. Already, I am close for not completing my contract."

"What do you mean?"

"My contract is to kill you. To refuse it calls my oath into question. I have learned over the centuries to always allow myself an out in any contract. But that does not mean I will be able to answer your questions without becoming an oath-breaker."

"That's fair. I won't ask you to do that."

"But these are discussions for another night. I will return tomorrow and you can ask your questions. For now, we are here."

The hour and a half long drive, much longer in rush hour, had only taken about fifteen minutes.

He brought me to Ronan's front door and when we arrived there, Ronan was standing on his porch, already waiting for us. He stepped toward me as Kai lifted me from my bike.

"What happened?" Ronan asked as he got closer and took me from Kai, a wariness in his eyes.

I might have protested being treated like a child if I hadn't been so tired. Again.

"She used her magic."

I held up my hands, still wrapped in Meriel's skin. "He caught up to me. But I think I convinced him not to kill me."

Ronan looked from me to Kai.

"She healed me."

"I didn't know you needed to be healed."

"Nor did I. But I now have access to my latent magic."

"That's not possible."

"It is. Look at my eyes."

I knew when Ronan realized it was the truth because he almost dropped me. "There is fire in your eyes."

"I am no longer simply the Dark. But Kai, once again. To help me, your changeling has burned her hands. You will want to heal them."

"Where will you go?"

"I do not know. I cannot return home for now. I have refused my contract. I must take time in safety to learn my new magic." He looked at Ronan. "Perhaps I will ask the protector of this region for safe harbor until I can decide my next move."

"I will grant you what safety I can as long as you swear not to harm anyone under my protection."

"I swear to you upon my magic I will not harm any under your protection unless they first try to harm me."

Ronan nodded and was about to turn when Kai said, "I know what she means to you, young Ronan. But consider what she will mean to us all."

Between one moment and the next, he was gone, disappeared into the night. "What did he mean by that? What do I mean to you? And to everyone? What..."

His lips found mine in a much deeper kiss than before. This one was filled with relief. I couldn't wrap my arms around him like I wanted since they were tangled in the selkie skin, but I still leaned in, kissing him back. The kiss swiftly changed from one of relief to one of passion and I shifted in his arms to try to get my body closer to his.

Before I could, he ended the kiss, touching his forehead to mine. "You didn't die."

"You asked me not to."

Evander was inside, waiting for us. I wasn't surprised. Aelwyd stood next to him, wringing her hands as we came in the door, a look of worry on her face. "Oh, Miss Calynn," she exclaimed as Ronan set me down on his couch. "We've been so worried for you. We thought the Dark had killed you."

I shook my head. "No. And his name is Kai."

Evander's quick glance told me he understood at least some of what had happened. "Aelwyd, you go fetch me some more towels."

"But, Papa. We already have so many."

"Aelwyd. Go. Tell your mother there is nothing to fear from the darkness this night, and bring me some more towels."

The young brownie looked between her father, me, and Ronan and then stomped away.

"You gave the Dark back his name?"

"I healed his magic. He said his mother had tried to heal him and allow him to reach his latent magic. Instead, she scarred him. I healed his scars and found his latent magic. It was just out of his reach." I paused, something occurring to me for the first time. I looked at Ronan. "I could do the same for you."

We stared at each other for a brief moment and I was certain neither of us were breathing. But then Ronan closed his eyes and shook his head.

"No, little changeling. You're too tired. Maybe you can do it, but you won't try tonight."

"But I could do it. I know it. That's what my latent magic is for. Or at least part of what it's for."

"Ronan is right, Miss Calynn," Evander said. "You do not have the strength to bring another daoine sidhe to his full strength. You've also wounded yourself helping... Kai. You must heal before you can help another."

With that, he uncorked the bottle of fae water he had waiting—like he knew I would return wounded or something—and placed a drop into the bowl of salve already on the coffee table. Ronan unwrapped Meriel's skin from my hands and I saw them for the first time. The skin was red and black, charred as though I had stuck them into a fire. Of course, that is basically what I had done.

"Calynn," Ronan said when he saw them.

"His latent magic is coals and embers. It was hot, but the only way to bring it back to him was to carry it. I didn't know it would actually burn my hands."

Evander spread the salve onto my wounds and then wrapped them in soft bandages. Then he took the water and told me to open my mouth. He placed a single drop on my tongue and it tasted sweet, like syrup. It was warm as it rolled down my throat and into my belly. I could feel the drop as it settled into me. "She must sleep," he told Ronan.

"One more question," I said.

Ronan rolled his eyes. "It's never just one more."

"Who is Kai's mother?"

"No one knows," Ronan said. "Fae pregnancies are not like human ones. It is possible to never know a person was pregnant at all. There was speculation, of course. But no one ever knew for certain. The only thing anyone would agree on was his parents must be part of the nobility. No one ever claimed him. And he had been kept out of the court's eye for many years. Likely due to the mother trying to heal him, as you say. The parents were likely ashamed to have sired a child without his latent magic. If he could not claim his place at court with them, they would not claim him as their own. I've seen it happen too many times."

"Did your parents do that to you?" I asked him.

"You said one more question. That's a second. It's time for sleep now."

Evander chuckled as he packed up his things and left the way Aelwyd had. Ronan carried me upstairs to the spare bedroom where I had been sleeping and set me on the bed.

"Are we going to talk about the kisses?" I asked as I got settled. "Or are we just pretending they didn't happen?"

I knew what he was going to say before he said it. "It's probably for the best if we pretend they never happened. I wasn't supposed to... I don't want to confuse you."

I arched my eyebrow. "I want you. You want me. What's confusing about that?"

He sighed. "You don't know enough yet about who you are to make decisions like this."

I wanted to argue, but the exhaustion of the last few hours seeped into me and started dragging my eyelids down. I fought to keep my eyes open, but I knew it was a losing battle.

"This conversation isn't over," I said. "But I think I need to sleep now."

I heard him laugh softly, but couldn't see him anymore. "Of course, little changeling. Whatever you say."

I thought about telling him off for patronizing me, but was asleep before I could say the words.

CHAPTER 34

K ai arrived as the sun was setting the next day. I was out on Ronan's front porch, getting some fresh air after having slept all day, when he appeared out of the dusk.

"Hello, changeling."

"Kai. You came."

He came up the steps and sat in the chair next to mine. "I told you I would."

"I didn't think it would be so early in the evening. The sun is still out."

And it was. The clouds had broken up while I was asleep. They were supposed to roll back in this evening, but for now, the last of the sun brightened the western horizon.

"I am not as hindered by the sun as I was. I am able to move about at dawn and dusk. Perhaps when I have learned my new magic more, I will be able to be out in full sun. For now, I am happy with the limited amount I am afforded."

"I see. So, how do you want to do this?"

"Ask what you will. I will answer or not as I am able."

I nodded. "What I want to know is who sent you. I think I know, but it would be helpful if you confirmed."

"I knew that would be your first question and you know I cannot answer it."

"Yeah. But I figured I'd give it a shot. Okay. Something that's been bugging me. Why me and why Meriel? We don't seem to have anything in common."

"Who said you would have anything in common with the selkie?"

"You were sent to kill us both days apart from one another. Obviously, we have to have *something* in common."

"Do you?"

"If not, why would someone want to kill us both?"

"That is a fair question. But again, not one I may answer. Instead, let me ask *you* a question. You are an investigator. Why would one person want to kill two people with nothing in common?"

"Isn't that what I just asked you?"

His white teeth flashed in a grin. "Is it?"

"Ugh! This is frustrating."

"It can be unless you know how to listen."

I glared at him for a minute before I turned back to the yard. The sun had fully set, and the stars were blinking into existence. The moon brightened the night and a light shone out of the windows behind us, but otherwise, we sat in the dark of the shadows.

"Okay. So there's an answer in that question, I just have to find it. Why would one person want to kill two people with nothing in common?" I thought for a moment and the answer started to come clear. "They wouldn't. If one person wanted to kill two people, the two people would have to have something in common, unless they're a psychopath looking for easy victims. But these two jobs are targeted killings, so that's not the case." I took a breath. "If the two victims had nothing in common, one person wouldn't have wanted to kill them. Two people would have. You had two contracts from two different people." I looked at him for confirmation.

He smiled but didn't say anything.

"Two contracts. One person wanted Meriel dead and then a different person wanted me dead. I know the contract are connected. I just assumed it was because the same person wanted to kill us both."

He shrugged. "I don't ask why someone gives me a contract."

"But they both sent you. That seems a bit of a coincidence."

"Not so much. I am the best assassin in the Sidhe. I get many contracts."

"The best also means you're expensive. Both employers have to be rich. Can you tell me anything about them?"

He was silent for a moment, considering. "You know little of our world. I can answer questions about that. And I may answer general questions about my work."

"And if they also answer the questions about your employers, so much the better. Do you always talk in circles?"

"Most fae do. We keep secrets as a way of life. It is in our nature."

"Ronan doesn't."

"Does he not? Has he never dissuaded you from an answer by changing the subject or saying you'll come back to it later? Has he never offered answers that are vague and almost no answer at all? You are right to have faith in him, but let it not be blind."

I considered this for a moment and could easily think of a dozen times Ronan had acted exactly as Kai said, the moments when I was almost certain he had omitted something but couldn't quite catch the feeling of an outright lie. "That's something to consider for another time. For now, I other information from you. Okay. Do you ever work for anyone but the daoine sidhe?"

The look he gave me was answer enough. "Gotcha, no other fae. So do you work for Winter or Summer?"

"I work for those who can pay. Though I mostly work for Winter."

"And how many daoine sidhe can pay for your services?"

"Only the nobility."

"I'm confused. I thought all daoine sidhe were nobility."

"All daoine sidhe are nobility to the lesser fae. But there is still a hierarchy within our ranks. Ronan and I are lower because we have only one gift. Though we were both born to the nobility. Others are lower because they were born into lower ranking families. Those families are lower because their magic is not as strong."

"Ronan was born to the nobility?" I shook my head. "No. Don't answer that. It's not relevant right now. So your two employers have to be part of the nobility, most likely Winter. How likely is it the nobility know one another?"

"All the nobility know one another."

"That's not very helpful."

Kai shrugged.

"Okay. Let's change direction, then. Do you know who I am and why I was changed?"

"Yes."

"Can you tell me?"

"No."

"So who I am has something to do with why you were sent to kill me. Here's the series of events as I know them. Someone changed me when I was a baby, reason unknown. Twenty-nine years later, Meriel finds me. A day later, she's killed. A day later, someone," I look pointedly at Kai, "tries to kill me for the first time. These events have to be related. They're too close together not to be."

"Your logic is sound."

"But I'm missing something. The person who wanted Meriel dead is not the same person who wants me dead. Not to mention there seems to be at least two people trying to kill me. And based on my investigations, I think they're both Queens. But why? You can't tell me why Meriel was killed and you can't tell me why I'm on the chopping block. You also can't tell me who I am and where I came from. Thus, this has to be involved in why these people want me dead. That's the thing that's missing. Why was I changed? I figure out this answer, I figure out them all."

"Your puzzle is almost complete. What will you do next?"

"The only thing I can do," I said with a shrug, to try to hide the nervous energy filling me. "I have to go to the Sidhe and figure out who I am."

He nodded. "I thought that may be your answer. In that case, for you." He stood and reached into his pocket and pulled out a necklace. He placed it around my neck.

"The key."

"Aye. Return it to the Queen of Air and Darkness and she must grant you safe passage in her and in her sister Queen's domains."

"You had it all the time."

"With the key, I can come and go from anywhere without anyone noticing."

"You mean you can use it to enter or leave the Sidhe without going through a Way?"

"Even so."

"Was it ever missing?"

"Not that I am aware. Good-bye, changeling. I must leave you here. Good luck on your puzzle."

"Wait. I have one more question."

He waited.

"She is the Queen of Air and Darkness. Your gifts are darkness and coals. How do daoine sidhe get their magic?"

"Magic manifests because the Sidhe and the Ancient Mother will it so. But most times, a child will have gifts similar to or the same as the parents. My latent magic I received from my father's lineage. The other I received from my mother."

He was gone barely before he had finished saying the last word. I took the quick departure as confirmation I was on the right track. Kai was the Dark Queen's son.

Chapter 35

Ronan was waiting for me when I went back inside. If I didn't know better, I'd think he looked nervous. I thought about what Kai had said about Ronan keeping secrets from me. I wished I could discount it, but I knew he was right. The question was, did it matter to me?

"Did you get any answers?" he asked.

"A few. I know Meriel and I were two separate contracts from two separate people. Which makes sense if the Winter Queen is one of the ones after me. She has no reason to kill Meriel. I still don't know who would want her dead, though, or what it has to do with me. But I also know Kai only accepts contracts from the daoine sidhe nobility. So that narrows it down at least a bit." I took a deep breath. "So it looks like I managed to piss off the two most powerful daoine sidhe in the whole Sidhe. Pretty good, hey?"

Ronan didn't look happy with my knowledge. I couldn't say I was particularly happy about it, either.

"Did he tell you anything else?"

I thought about the conclusion I had come to about Kai's mother, but it really wasn't my place to say. "Nothing else relevant, but he gave me this." I took the key from beneath my shirt and took it off my neck, uncomfortable with jewelry.

Ronan stilled, staring at it for a long moment before he tore his gaze away and motioned to the kitchen island. "Put it away and have a seat. I'll get you something to eat."

"Where's Aelwyd?" I asked as I sat down.

"She made chicken salad for lunch this afternoon. I told her to make enough for dinner and to take the evening off. She's helping her mother with Bidina. She's been having trouble adjusting to life here again."

I was curious about Bidina and why she left and why she would have trouble, but I knew Ronan wouldn't answer. It wasn't his story to tell, just as Kai's parentage wasn't mine. Instead, I sat quietly as he unwrapped a dish from the fridge and set it on the island along with some wraps and some shredded lettuce. I scooped the creamy chicken mixture onto a wrap and ate. I was grateful the food didn't need to be eaten with a fork. My hands felt a lot better today than they had last night, but I didn't think I would be able to grip a utensil for more than a few minutes.

After a while, I said, "So. Going to the Sidhe. What should I know?"

"More than I could possibly tell you over dinner." He sighed and ran his hand through his hair. "You'll be entering the Sidhe in the Winter territory."

"Why Winter?"

"The Way to the Sidhe that is closest takes you to Winter. Plus, the Winter Queen is in power at the moment. It's right that you see her first. You'll just have to be extremely careful."

"Yeah. We all know how good I am at that."

He smiled but didn't laugh. "You'll be okay if you remember to pay attention to what is going on around you and never let anyone know what you don't know."

"What do you mean?"

"Never look surprised. Never show emotion. It can be used against you so easily."

"Well, you can remind me if I'm about to make a mistake."

He looked at me. "I can't come with you."

I set my wrap down and stared at him. "But..."

"I can't enter the Sidhe without either the key, an invitation, or a pardon from the Queen. I won't get past the Guardian."

I took the key out of my pocket. "You return it then," I said, holding it out for him to take.

The look on his face as he stared at it told me he wanted to. I'd never seen anyone look at something with such longing and desperation before. Like the key was water and he was in a desert. Like it was the sun and he was freezing. Like he could live with whatever came so long as he could have back the home it promised. He was hungry for it. Starving even. So I was confused when his hand reached for the key, but instead of taking it, he closed my own hand around it.

"No," he said, eyes shut to the temptation.

"Why not? I don't need it. You said it yourself, I've never been exiled so I can go in and out as much as I want."

"Can you put it away?"

His tone held a note of begging, so I shoved it back into my jeans pocket. It was as if he could feel it being taken from him and he opened his eyes again as soon as it was gone without being told.

"You're right," he said. "You don't need it to get in. But it can still help you. Also, it can do things to a fae who hasn't earned the right to touch it. Bad things."

"Like what?"

"They can lose their minds. Some even lose their magic."

"Then why do so many try to find it?"

"Those who look for it believe the price is fair to be allowed back into the Sidhe. I don't believe it is."

"But I have the right to touch it. Why?"

He shrugged. "Could be a number of things."

"Like what?"

"Possibly because you don't need it. Or because it was given to you freely."

"Okay. If you won't take it, how can you come with me? Can I invite you?"

"Why am I going with you?"

"I need you there. I don't know what I'm doing. I need someone I can trust to stop me from making a fool of myself."

He stared at me for a long time and I waited while he thought. I could see an argument going on behind his eyes.

Finally, he said, "I'll come with you."

"You look rather unhappy about it. I thought you'd be thrilled about being able to go home."

"I will only be able to stay as long as you allow me to. The only ones who can rescind my exile are the Queens. Just because I have an invitation doesn't mean I can stay."

"Will it be dangerous for you?"

"It could be. But you make a good point. You need someone you've worked with before. Someone who knows what you do and do not know to help guide you through court politics. I will go with you."

My relief surprised and annoyed me. I didn't like relying on other people, but I had no idea what to expect in the other world. As much as Ronan could tell me, nothing would really prepare me for what I was going to face. I was literally going to another world. I was worried and scared and I hated feeling that way.

"I think we should go tomorrow."

"What? Why so soon?"

"The longer I stay here, the more people are going to try to kill me. I've got all the answers I'm going to find here. The rest are in the Sidhe. What's the point of waiting?"

"You're still healing, for one."

I had taken the bandages off my hands earlier and they were pink and scarred from the burns but healing quickly. The bones in my hand were fully healed by now. And my bullet wound no longer ached.

"If I bring the key back to the Queen, Kai said she had to grant me safe passage. So, people should stop trying to kill me for a bit while I finish healing. If I stay here, that won't be the case and I could end up hurt worse."

"All right."

I wondered why Ronan seemed so unhappy about going back to the Sidhe. I would have thought he would be much happier. But I also knew they hadn't treated him well there and so that might have something to do with it. I also knew once we were there, he would put more distance between us than he did now. If I wanted to be with him, now was my last chance.

I stood up with the guise of putting my plate in the sink, my leg brushing against his as I did. I moved to the living room and Ronan followed me, sitting in his chair while I took the corner of the couch. I wished he would sit on the couch with me, but I knew he wouldn't. If I wanted anything to happen between us, I would have to make all the moves. And there was nothing I could do while he sat so far away.

We talked for a while about what it would be like in the Sidhe and what we needed to bring with us. I paid attention, but a part of my mind plotted a way to get him closer. There was really only one thing I could think to do. So after he'd told me about a few things about going into the Sidhe, I stood up and stretched.

"Well, I'm going to bed," I said.

"That's a good idea. You're still healing and we have a long way to go tomorrow."

Not exactly what I was hoping his response would be. But the response I had expected.

"Are you going to bed?" I asked.

"I will be."

I could tell he was wary of me. After the two kisses we'd shared, I knew he wanted me. I just didn't know why he wouldn't give in.

I went upstairs alone, but it was merely a tactical retreat. I changed into my over-sized shirt that I liked to wear to bed and brushed my hair and teeth. Then I waited. In Ronan's room.

I heard him start up the stairs and pause at the top. I knew he knew where I was, just as I knew where he was. I heard him take a deep breath and come toward the bedroom.

"Calynn." The warning in his voice was unmistakable, but I ignored it as I moved toward him.

"You kissed me, remember? Or was that a hallucination?"

"I did. But Calynn. I don't want to..."

"Confuse me. I remember." I grabbed his face and kissed him before he could stop me. It didn't take him any time before he held me and kissed me back. I continued to hold him, and he pulled me to him until we were standing, bodies pressed together. The scent of pine and ice enveloped me. My arms moved to wind around his neck and shoulders as his hands splayed against my back, holding me closer sending heat racing through me. I never wanted the moment to end. But I needed him to accept this before we went any further. So I ended the kiss and said, "Did that feel confused to you?"

He shook his head and leaned his forehead against mine. "You make everything so difficult, little changeling." But he didn't let me go.

"Always." I thread my fingers into his hair, just to feel the softness. "Tell me you don't want this and I'll leave right now. Look me in the eye and tell me."

His eyes found mine, but he didn't say anything. He held me still, but I wasn't sure if he was going to keep me close or push me away.

"Your move," I said. "Kiss me."

"The problem is, if I kiss you now, I don't think I'll be able to stop."

"Who said you have to?"

He stood there without saying anything. I knew him well enough now that I could see the emotions waging war behind his eyes even though he kept them hidden enough I wasn't sure what those emotions were.

He wanted me. I could feel it in the way he held me, in the way he looked at me. But wanting something wasn't the same as allowing yourself to have it. I had to let him go if that was what he needed me to do.

"Do you want me to leave?" I asked softly.

His arms tightened around me and I knew his answer before he said it.

"No. But this is still a bad idea."

I smiled. "I'm really good at bad ideas."

He lowered his head toward mine but stopped just shy of kissing me.

"I really shouldn't. There's so much you still don't know."

"Nothing I learn will make me want you less. I've wanted you since the moment I saw you. And it has nothing to do with magic or power or being fae. It has to do with you being the sexiest man I've ever seen."

Something in what I said must have been right, because he didn't hold back any longer. His lips touched mine, tentatively at first and then with a desperation I had never felt in someone before.

I kissed him back just as hard, pulling him with me as I backed up until my legs hit the bed. I pulled at his shirt, breaking the kiss only long enough to tug it over his head, and then sliding my hands down to work on his pants. His hands roamed over me just as feverishly, skimming up my back inside my shirt and then back out just to remove it from me entirely.

My hands ran over ridges in the skin on his back that my brain told me I should investigate, but I was too hot, too starved for his touch to stop now. And wasn't that something? To be starved for someone you've only known for two weeks. When we were both naked, I sat on the bed and he came with me, refusing to remove his lips from my skin.

"Just promise me one thing," I said as I lay back.

"Anything."

"Promise you won't regret this in the morning."

He lifted his head to look at me, his emerald eyes finding mine in the darkness. Then he leaned down and pressed a soft kiss to my lips. "Never."

Chapter 36

*T*he window needed to be cleaned. I couldn't see through it.

   There was something on the other side I needed to see. I needed to understand. I lifted my hand to try to clear a spot. Just as my fingers touched the glass, it shattered beneath them, particles as fine as sand fell to my feet. I jerked away from the window and as I did, I saw a figure coming toward me. I knew it was a woman, though I couldn't see any of her features.

   "I was trying to clean the glass. I didn't mean to break it," I told her.

   "Sometimes the only way to clean something is to wipe it away and start again."

I woke up from the dream, gasping and covered in sweat. As many times as I'd had the dream lately, the woman still scared me. I glanced around an unfamiliar room and remembered where I was and who I was with.

Ronan was already sitting up, watching me with concern, waiting for me to calm down.

"What's wrong?" he asked when my breathing was finally under control again.

"I've been having this dream lately. Almost every night since you told me what I was."

"What is it about?"

"A shattered window. I'm standing at it and it's dirty. I try to clean it, but it shatters under my hand. There's also a woman with me. She doesn't seem too upset that I broke the window, but I am. I don't know what it means, but it scares me. And I don't know why."

I leaned against him, savoring the strength he offered and I could accept in the darkness of his room at night with no one around to see. He held me and didn't ask any more questions.

I only leaned against him for a moment before I pulled back and looked into his eyes. I could see how green they were, even in the darkness.

"So, that happened."

"It certainly did. Calynn, I…"

"Don't. You promised you wouldn't regret it, so whatever you're going to say, I don't think I want to hear it right now. Can't it just be fantastic sex? No complications?"

Something passed over his expression, there and gone too quickly for me to read, even though I was looking right at him.

"That would be for the best. You may be attracted to me now, but when you get to the court, you'll meet many others who you may find more attractive than I am."

"I doubt it."

"I'm the only daoine sidhe you've met so far, other than Kai, who spent the last few meetings trying to kill you. You don't know how powerfully attractive strong magic can be."

"You have strong magic."

He looked away from me and, for the first time, I realized what one of the emotions he kept hidden was. He felt ashamed.

I placed my hands on his face and made him look at me.

"Just because you can only reach one of your gifts doesn't mean you're not strong. Once my hands have healed a bit more, I'll get you your latent magic and you'll see what I already know. Whoever made you believe you were less because of your magic was wrong."

The desperate hope in his eyes broke my heart. I wondered for a moment how many other fae were like him and Kai. Broken, not because of their inability to access their magic, but because of the people around them. I kissed him, lightly at first, and then deeper, pulling him toward me. I wanted to bring him into me, fuse us together, give him the comfort he needed, and take the comfort I needed in return. I couldn't do it in a permanent way, but at least we had tonight.

***

I woke the next morning with Ronan's arms around me and for the first time in my life, I didn't feel like I had to escape from such an embrace. I lay there for a moment, surrounded in his scent, and considered the calm I felt. It was like I had found a sheltered spot from the storm that always seemed to rage around me. He still slept, so I moved closer to him to take advantage of that feeling. I wished for a moment the day didn't have to begin. I knew it was a bad idea to leave this world. The answers I was looking for weren't going to make my life any easier, and would in fact likely heighten the storm. But I also knew I could never live without knowing. I was a sucker for punishment.

I felt it when he woke up. My initial instinct was to pretend I was sleeping, but since I knew he was awake, I figured he also knew I was. Instead, I turned to face him.

His eyes glittered in the morning light. I studied the different shades of green and could see how content he felt. He always kept his emotions off his face, but if I looked close enough, I could see how he was feeling in the emerald depths. I was so busy studying him I didn't even realize he was doing the same until he said, "I could spend hours watching the colors change in your eyes."

It wasn't something he would normally have said. I knew he hadn't meant to say it out loud because his face immediately shuttered and became the impassive mask it usually was.

"No, don't go," I said, reaching out to touch his cheek.

"What?"

"You shut down again. I can't see you when you close up like that. I like when I can see you. But it's like you put up this wall to keep me out. Why are you fighting so hard to keep us apart?"

"I've already let you closer than I should have."

I rolled my eyes and got out of bed. "Oh, don't start that *we shouldn't sleep together* bit again. It's too late for that. Like I said last night, I don't need an emotional commitment, but I like to think we've at least become friends. And you promised you wouldn't regret it."

I stood to snatch my shirt from the floor, but he grabbed my hand before I could put it on.

"I will never regret a second we're together. I'm worried *you* will. You don't know what it means that you have both of your gifts and I only have one of mine. And you can't know how much higher you are in the courts because of that."

"I wasn't raised in a court where position means everything, Ronan. I was raised as a human in foster care. *You* don't know what *that* means. I don't care what position you have in the court. I don't care what position *I* have in the court. All that matters to me is if you're there for me when I need you to be. And so far, you have been."

I pulled my hand from his and put my shirt on. It covered me from shoulders to mid-thigh so I still showed quite a lot of skin, but it was all I had. "You're not the only one who's had a rough past that makes it difficult to trust people. I figure you had a lot of people in the Sidhe thinking you're less and so you started to believe it yourself. Well, people literally threw me away my whole life. My human parents, a dozen foster parents at least, teachers, people who claimed to be my friends. Now I find out my human parents weren't even the first ones. My fae parents also threw me away. That kind of thing makes a person think they're worthless. So I understand what you feel." I stood and turned toward him, keeping some physical space between me and the bed. "Now, I've never felt this way about anyone before. I understand I haven't met any other fae until now, and there was just no way for me to fall for a human. But I still feel like we could have something one day. You're right that it's way too soon to think about that, and I've got a lot on my plate right now. But that doesn't mean we couldn't have a bit of fun while I try to get this shit sorted out."

"I don't want to confuse you."

"I know that. You've said that already." I shrugged. "It sounds like an excuse to me."

He stood up and came toward me, completely at ease with his nakedness. And when you looked like that, why wouldn't you be? He stopped in front of me and took my hands in his and stared down at them. They looked a lot better today than they had yesterday.

"You have no idea what you're asking of me."

"Then tell me."

He was silent so long I thought he wasn't going to answer again. Finally, he found my eyes with his and said, "I can't."

He let go of my hands and turned toward his dresser. When he did, I finally saw what my brain had told me about the night before, but I ignored.

"Son of a bitch," I breathed, moving toward him before he could put clothes on and cover the scars crisscrossing his back. Ridges of scar tissue lifting where wounds had not healed properly. I touched the worst one, a large scar that ran from his right shoulder to his left hip.

"Who did this to you?" I asked, needing to know so I could plan my revenge.

He didn't say anything at first, just stayed turned away from me. I moved in front of him and found his eyes cast down at the ground. "Ronan. Who did this to you?"

When his gaze finally met mine, I could see shame in them. "Before I left the Sidhe, I was in liege to two people. First the Queen. Then her brother. Both punished me for..." He shook his head. "One thing or another." His mouth twisted into a disgusted grimace. "The Queen likes her guards to be beautiful, so she always ensured I was healed after. Her brother, however..." He shrugged and then he took a breath. "So you see—"

"Don't you dare finish that sentence. What they did to you is not who you are. It has no bearing on what kind of relationship we may or may not have."

He pulled out a shirt, and I stepped out of the way to let him put it on, even though I knew he was just trying to hide from me again. I adjusted the list of people I would need to deal with. It had already included both Queens, but now it included the Dark Queen's brother. I had no idea how I was going to deal with them, but I knew I would. Even if it took me a hundred years. I apparently had the time.

Ronan pulled me from my considerations when he said, "You're right. There could be something between us if we both allow it and decide to explore it. You're also right that it is not an easy thing for me to allow, and part of the reason is because of how people treated me before I was exiled. Another reason is because of fear. You will learn things in the Sidhe I cannot tell you while we are here in this world. But once you have learned them, and if you still want to explore whatever could be between us," he turned toward me, fully dressed, "I am willing to explore it with you, little changeling."

I wanted to wrap my arms around him, kiss him, and tell him there was nothing I could learn that would make me change my mind. I set my hands on my hips instead.

"Why do you keep calling me that? Is it just to tease me?"

"I would never do such a thing."

If my internal lie detector hadn't told me he was lying, the gleam in his eyes would have. I arched an eyebrow at him and waited.

"I call you little changeling because of how very small you are." His eyes traced my body from the top of my head to the soles of my feet. I wasn't sure how he made his looks feel like caresses, but it wasn't something I wanted to stop. "I told you how physical size correlates to magical power. And you have so much, but you are so small."

The wonder in his voice took any sting from his words. I'd always hated being short, but how he looked at me, with awe and reverence, made me feel like the most beautiful woman in the world. I took a first step toward him.

"I want to explore a relationship with you, Ronan. But I'll wait until you're ready. Ground rules between now and then?"

"No more sex."

I rolled my eyes. "Fine. But it was good, wasn't it?"

He crossed his arms over his chest and scowled at me. It was answer enough. I moved toward him again.

"No more kissing, either," he said.

"Amendment: No kissing once we're in the Sidhe. In this world, it's okay."

His eyes dropped to my lips, and he swallowed. I smiled and stepped a little closer. I was almost toe-to-toe with him.

"Once we are in the court, I will walk behind you. I am not there as your equal, but as your protector and guide."

I hesitated before I reached for him. "Once we start to explore, will that change?"

He shook his head.

"I don't like that."

He shrugged. "It is not something that can be changed."

I considered that for a moment. I already hated the place for what it did to Kai and Ronan, for exiling so many fae, casting them out of their home forever. I had a feeling Ronan had nothing to worry about when it came to me finding someone I liked more than him. How many people could I like in a world with rules like that one and with people who tortured the ones they were supposed to protect?

"Enough rules. We don't have much time left before we leave." I wrapped my arms around his neck and his hands came to my waist almost as if they had always been there.

"You are going to make this difficult, aren't you?"

"Always."

Finally, his mouth came down on mine.

CHAPTER 37

We were ready to leave faster than I thought we would be. It was surprisingly easy when you had a brownie pack for you. I sat on the front porch with my pack while I waited for Ronan to give Evander some last-minute instructions. Evander would take care of the day-to-day stuff, while Killian took care of the Diaspora representative things until Ronan returned. While I waited, a car pulled up in front of the house and Arial got out of the passenger side. Carrick shut the car off but didn't get out.

Arial approached the porch. "Ronan sent Carrick to pick me up so I could say good-bye."

She came up and sat in the chair next to me.

"I asked him to send someone. I didn't want you taking a taxi or Uber again. That's a lot of money."

"You're coming back."

It wasn't a question, so I didn't answer it like one.

"And you'll remember what I said about being careful. And if you make me come into that Sidhe place to get you out, don't think I won't do it."

I laughed. "I have no doubt."

We were silent for a while and I acted like I didn't notice the tears she was trying to keep from falling. She kindly did the same for me.

"I mean it, Calynn. Even if you decide it's the place for you and you want to make it your permanent home, you need to come back and tell me. I don't want to worry about you forever."

"I don't think I could make my home anywhere you aren't."

"How long do you think you'll be gone?"

"I don't know. A few weeks to a few months. Shouldn't be longer than a few months."

We sat together without talking for a long time and then Ronan came to the front of the porch and said, "It's time."

I stood up and turned toward my best friend.

"Be safe," she said.

I nodded, not trusting myself to speak.

She wrapped me in a tight hug. "I love you, Calynn."

"I love you, too. I promise I'll try to be safe." This time, when I felt the weight of the words, I understood what it meant. I had just made a vow to my friend and the magic that governed me would make sure I kept it.

"You don't need to be everyone's hero. It's okay to be the bad guy sometimes if it means you stay alive. You don't have to be the bad guy in your own story just to be the good guy in someone else's."

I let her go.

"You know I'm good at being a bad guy in my own story. I'm very good at..."

"Bad ideas," she interrupted. "I know. But something you don't know, you're also capable of some pretty good ones."

We hugged again, and I stepped off the porch with my pack in one hand and my short sword in the other. I followed Ronan deeper into his property and didn't look back at Arial.

I didn't want to see her tears any more than I wanted to show her mine.

***

The trees grew in a perfect circle. Too perfect. Nothing grew in the middle of the circle except grass. The trees were different ages and heights, the smallest was barely taller than I was, while the tallest was at least fifty feet. In addition to the trees, other little bits of flora grew in a circle, flowers that were wildly out of season, mushrooms, ferns.

"This is it," Ronan said.

"No kidding. We just walk into the circle?"

"You have to open the door first."

"Why can't you do it?"

"I'm exiled. I may not enter the Sidhe without an invitation. I can't even open the door. But you've never been exiled. You can open it."

"How?"

"You'll know. Close your eyes and focus."

I did as he said and as soon as my eyes were closed, I could feel what I hadn't been able to see. The magic coming from the circle stretched from tree to tree. The door was all of it and none of it, and I reached my hand out to push it open. The magic that spilled out from behind them made me catch my breath. I was about to walk toward that magic when I felt an ice-cold grip on my arm. I turned around and opened my eyes.

Ronan was holding me back. "Do not enter this place with your eyes closed, little changeling. It is dangerous in there."

"I can handle it."

He smiled a quick, fierce smile. "I am certain you can." Then his smile disappeared and he stepped closer to me, sweeping a stray hair from my face back behind my ear.

I knew him well enough by now to see something was troubling him.

"What's wrong?"

"Things will be different in there. You will hear things. Things about me."

"This is about why you were exiled."

He nodded. "I've never lied to you, Calynn. But I haven't told you the whole truth either."

"Ronan..." I didn't know what to say. So I touched his face and gave him a soft kiss. Then he pulled me closer for another. It was unlike any kiss we had shared before. It was hot and desperate, like he wanted to fuse us together. He held me tightly to him and when he finally broke the kiss, he didn't let me go right away.

"I wish we had more time," he said, his forehead resting against mine. His eyes were closed, like he was praying. Then he opened them, stepped away from me, and said, "But we don't. Come on, little changeling. It's time to go home."

I took a breath. This was my last chance to turn back. Once I did this, I would never be able to choose a human life again.

"Ronan," I said, "I invite you to accompany me into the Sidhe."

The words were apparently important. I walked through the door, into the circle, and at first, I thought nothing happened. But then I felt the magic.

It filled me up. It started in my heart and spread to the tips of my fingers and the soles of my feet. My skin tingled, but it didn't hurt. It felt... right.

It seemed like we were still in the same set of trees we had just left, and then I saw the cat. It was the largest cat I had ever seen—easily forty pounds, with beautiful, thick golden fur and bright yellow eyes.

"The Guardian of the Space Between," I said, remembering the voice on the dock by Cardero's.

The cat nodded as it watched me, unblinking.

The memory of the other Guardian's warning had me reaching for Ronan's hand and pulling him with me. I took another step and the leaves under my feet crunched on the frosty ground. I took another step and stood in two feet of snow. The wind picked up and bit through the leather of my motorcycle jacket, making me shiver for a second before I acclimatized to it.

"Where are we?"

"Winter," Ronan answered as he stepped in beside me. "I am Winter and so the door on my property opens to Winter."

"That seems awfully mean, having a door to your home on your property you can't open."

"It is balance. The Sidhe is supposed to always have balance."

His voice sounded strained and so I turned to look at him. His eyes were closed, and he braced himself on a tree. He looked like he was in a lot of pain.

"Ronan? Are you okay?"

He didn't open his eyes. "I will be. The magic is so strong here. You don't know..."

"How safe are we by the door?"

"We should be okay."

I found an evergreen tree that had large branches. The snow underneath it wasn't as deep and so I cleared it away as best I could before setting down the backpack and taking out the blanket Aelwyd had insisted I bring.

I had asked her why I would need it and she said because it was cold in Winter. She also packed me a sweater, some gloves, and a hat. When I asked how she had got it all in, she just said, "I'm a brownie."

I went back to where Ronan still braced himself against a tree and led him to the spot I had made. He leaned back against the tree and said, "I'll be fine in a minute."

"Why am I not affected the same way you are?"

"Because..."

"Wait. Let me guess. Because I'm a changeling."

He laughed and then he opened his eyes. I was relieved he was starting to feel better.

"What does it feel like?"

He took a moment to answer me. Then he said, "It's like I've been living at the top of a mountain where the air is thin. I've gotten used to it, but now... suddenly, I'm back at the base of the mountain and I can take a full breath again. Once I get over the initial shock, I'll be able to breathe easier than I have for the past thirty years."

"Is that how long you've been exiled?"

"Nearly."

"You've been exiled about as long as I've been alive."

He nodded slowly, his emerald eyes searching mine. I knew he was telling me something. Kai's words came back to me. *You're right to have faith in him, but let it not be blind.*

"I can walk now," Ronan said, interrupting my thoughts. "Come on. We have a bit of a distance to go."

I stuffed the blanket into the backpack somehow and we started in what seemed like a random direction. I had no idea how to orient myself. At home,

I knew which way was north because of the North Shore mountains. I knew which was west because of the Rocky mountains. Here, I had no such frame of reference. I was overwhelmingly glad Ronan was with me.

"When I first entered, the trees looked the same as when we were in BC. But then, as I took a couple of steps, it changed. The snow appeared."

"The doorway is long. The steps you took where it seemed like we were still in BC were neither here nor there. That space is both and neither."

"The Space Between. The Guardian is a cat."

"You saw him?"

"Didn't you?"

"No. The cat sidhe don't show themselves often. But yes, they are the Guardians of the Ways."

"So you said we were in Winter, but you didn't say where we are exactly."

"We are just north of the Winter city, Glacia. It should take us an hour or so to get there. To the west of us is the Winter river, the Ogir." He pointed to his right. "It flows from the Fréimhe of the Sidhe in the north through the city and into the Muir."

"The Muir is where I'll find Meriel's family."

"Yes. But they are Summer selkies. You'll have to go east to Summer to find them. North of here are the wild lands, also called the Fréimhe. It's not part of either Queen's domain and the fae who live there do not belong to either Winter or Summer."

"Tell me about Glacia."

"In a moment."

We walked in silence for a bit until we came to the crest of the hill we had been climbing. As we reached it, I looked down and saw the city. The river came from my right and wound around the base of the hill, flowing down into the city in the valley below. The city was contained within a circular great wall, but little towns had popped up here and there around the outside and up the hill. In the center of the city, an island sat in the middle of the river. A road ran east to west, straight through it. On top of the road was a castle I could see clearly from here. The roads in the city looked like a giant spider web except where they were truncated by the river.

"Is it…" I tried to look closely, but it was too far away to be sure. "Is the city made from ice?"

"Yes. It is Winter."

"What is the Summer city made from? Sunshine?"

"I don't know. I've never been there." He pointed toward Glacia. "We go to the Queen's castle first. You can see where that is. She doesn't understand the meaning of the word subtle. We'll come in from the east. When we get there, I will walk slightly behind you and to your right." He faced me forward and stood slightly behind my right shoulder. "Like this."

"Why?"

"I told you. I am not your equal here, little changeling. I am here as your protector and your guide. Nothing more."

"But as my guide, shouldn't you go first?"

"The route to the castle is simple. Don't turn and you'll get there."

"And after we get there? How will I know where to go if you're walking behind me?"

"If you need direction, I will tell you where to go. We will pass through one of the towns first. Be careful in the town. The fae who live there won't hesitate to steal from us if they think they can get away with it."

"Who lives in the town?"

"Mostly daoine sidhe who cannot afford to live in the city. The closer to the center, the more expensive it is. But also some of the lesser fae who sell their goods or services to the daoine sidhe."

We started down the hill toward the town on the far side of the wall. As we walked, he took his sword from its scabbard and cradled it in his right arm so his hand rested at the top of the hilt and the blade lay flat on his shoulder. When we got close to the town, he took his place behind me and to my right.

"I just go straight through the town to the city and then straight to the castle."

"That's right. Keep your head up. You belong here. Make sure everyone you pass knows it. If anything happens, I'm right here."

His left hand reached forward and squeezed my right one briefly before we got to the first building of the town. I knew how to act like I belonged somewhere. Rule number one of breaking into a place was to act like you had a right to be there. I could do this.

Before I had passed the first building, a kid of about fifteen ran straight into me. I caught him before we both fell to the ground. His eyes were so dark brown they looked almost black. Something in those eyes hooked into me.

His face was smudged with dirt and his hair had been cut ragged and was so dirty I couldn't tell what color it was. Maybe blonde. He was just as shocked as I was by our encounter, and it took us a second to shake it off. In that time, the people he had been running from caught up.

A group of three men in guard uniforms came to a stop in front of us. "You caught him. Good. Come on, boy. Queen Mab doesn't tolerate thieves in her city."

I looked down at the boy. I had indeed caught him. His thin shoulders were between my hands. Ronan had acted the moment the kid stumbled into me, his sword pointing at the young boy's neck. He couldn't escape if we didn't want him to.

But I pictured the scars on Ronan's back in my mind.

"What did you steal?" I asked him.

He held up a bright red apple in one hand and a loaf of bread in the other.

"That's it?"

He hung his head.

"Cough it up," I told him.

He stuck the apple in his mouth and pulled a small purse from the pocket of his pants. He handed it to me and I checked inside to see a few of the gold coins Ronan had shown me before we left. I tossed it back to the guard who had spoken to me.

"If I pay for the apple and the bread, will you let the boy go?"

The guard shrugged. "I suppose so. But why would you do that?"

If the idea of him being hurt for stealing food wasn't reason enough, something else tugged at me about this boy, though I couldn't articulate what it was.

I also knew if Ronan was less than me here, so were these men. "I don't have to tell you my reasons. Ronan. Pay the man what he needs. Then you three can return the money to the vendors where the things came from."

Ronan settled his sword on his shoulder again and gave one of the guards a gold coin for the food, and they left. Then Ronan returned to me. "Calynn, we have to move along. It's important we meet with the Queen immediately."

I nodded, but I was still looking at the boy. "What did you learn from this, kid?"

He bit down on the apple before taking it out of his mouth to speak. "Don't get caught?" he said around the apple he was chewing.

"Smartass. Ronan. Give him some of our money."

Ronan pulled out five gold coins and gave them to the boy. "You know, there are a lot of kids on the streets of these towns. If we give them all money, we'll have none left."

I shook my head. "This one is important."

I was already looking in the boy's dark brown eyes, so I saw the surprise followed swiftly by the fierce pride as he felt them. He obviously hadn't learned yet how to hide his emotions the way Ronan had.

"How do you know?"

I closed my eyes. My hands were still on the boy's arms. I felt for his magic. I could tell he was a pure daoine sidhe, and he was strong. But something blocked me from the magic. I opened my eyes.

"Why are you living on the streets?" I asked him.

"My mother told me to leave until my magic manifested. She wouldn't have me bring disgrace to the family."

"I have to go to a meeting. But we'll meet again. Until then, remember what you learned."

He grinned. "Don't get caught."

"And spend that money wisely."

I let him go and he ran off.

"I don't understand," Ronan said as we started again for the city.

I gave him a somewhat bewildered look. "Neither do I."

Chapter 38

We continued down the road toward the gates of the city. People stopped and stared as we passed.

"Why are they all staring?"

"Glacia is a small city. Everyone knows everyone. But no one has ever seen you before. At least not since you were changed."

The weight of the stares pressed down on me. For just a second, I wanted to turn around and go back to Vancouver with Ronan. Forget this whole stupid thing. My life at home was fine the way it was. I could be with Ronan. My family hadn't tried to find me for the last twenty-nine years. Why did I need to find them now?

The key turned to ice around my neck and my backpack seemed to gain five pounds, reminding me of the selkie skin I had to return. There were things I needed to do here. I couldn't go anywhere yet.

Still, I asked, "This is going to change everything, isn't it?"

Ronan gripped my hand again for a second before saying, "Yes."

We made it to the first crossroad where the beautiful homes behind me become mansions in front of me.

"A little obvious."

"The point is to show your power and wealth."

We continued down past mansions and shops. The second block was much longer than the first and there were a lot of mansions. Many more than I expected. Finally, we came to the last crossroad before the bridge. In this spot, the mansions had become estates, one to my left and one to my right. The one on my right was obviously owned by the more powerful of the two. It competed with the Queen's palace for size and prestige. And since the palace was directly in front of it, the comparison was easy to make. I stopped to look at it for a moment.

Ronan stopped behind me. "The Queen's brother's estate."

"The Queen's brother. He's the one who hurt you."

He didn't respond. But then, he didn't need to. The Queen and her brother would answer to me for what they'd done to Ronan. Maybe not today, but eventually.

"This is the block where the high nobility live," I said, still staring at the Queen's brother's estate.

"Here and on the other side of the river."

I took a deep breath and started for the bridge again.

The road ran through a tunnel underneath the castle. Guards lined both sides, each one holding a spear in their right hand. In the middle of the tunnel, two sets of double-doors faced each other.

Ronan sheathed his sword and draped it over one shoulder again, like he had in the forest.

I looked at him.

"It's impolite to bring a naked weapon before the Queen."

"Of course. We wouldn't want to be impolite. What do I say to get in?"

"The truth. They'll know soon enough."

"Which side do we go in?"

"To the right."

I walked up to the guards that stood by that door.

"I require an audience with the Queen of Air and Darkness."

One continued to stare straight ahead. The other turned his glance to me, sizing me up, finding me wanting. I was used to it.

Then he looked behind me. He blinked for a moment, as though he was coming out of a fog. "Ronan?"

"Hello, Linden," Ronan said.

"Haven't seen you around in a while."

"Been busy."

Linden returned his attention to me. "Huh. So the rumors were true."

Then he allowed us into the castle without any other fuss.

"What rumors is he talking about?"

"I don't know what rumors were spread after I was exiled."

My breath caught in my lungs as Kai's words came back to me: *Has he never offered answers that are vague and almost no answer at all?*

I could almost feel a puzzle piece click into place, but I was already worrying about too many things to see what picture was forming.

We wound through the labyrinth that was the Queen's castle. Ronan directed me through it, and I worried about getting out again. We made it to a set of double doors that stretched about fifteen feet high, all the way to the ceiling. They were decorated in etchings of snow-covered trees and snowflakes. I was about to push the doors open when Ronan grabbed my hand.

"Whatever she says, you need to act like you knew it already. Whatever anyone says, act like you know. Knowledge is the highest priced commodity here."

His emerald green eyes bored into mine.

"She scares you."

"She scares everyone who knows her."

"Meriel called her Mad Mab. Is she crazy?"

"Oh no. It's far worse than that. She's completely sane. And completely ruthless. She has no conscience."

I didn't want to do this anymore. I wanted to go home. Unfortunately, I had a small problem of not knowing exactly where that was anymore. "What are we doing here?"

"Getting the answers you seek. Just act like you already know them."

"I'm not sure I want them anymore."

"We can go back right now. But I don't think you could really live without ever knowing."

I nodded. He was right. I knew that. Had known it last night when I thought about not coming. Had known it this morning when I thought it was better to stay in the world I knew. Had known it when I entered the Sidhe and almost immediately wanted to turn back. I was here for a reason. I thought of the last time I had tracked down my "parents." It had turned out badly then, but I had survived. This would turn out badly also, I was certain of it. So maybe, if I was already prepared for the worst-case scenario, it wouldn't hurt quite as much this time around. I turned back to the door, took a deep breath, and pushed it open.

I immediately felt under-dressed. The room was filled with fae nobles in beautiful dresses and suits. There were about thirty or forty people who looked at me when the doors opened. The amount of magic in the room engulfed me, likely similar to how the magic in the world had engulfed Ronan when he stepped through the door. It took all of my control not to show how it affected me. I knew without Ronan telling me, you could not show weakness in front of these people. Predators every one.

The crowd parted until I saw the Queen sitting on her throne. Five steps led up to the chair. A naked man kneeled on the floor by her feet, a collar around his throat with the leash clipped to the arm of the throne. I remembered what Ronan had said about humans being beloved pets. Though that man didn't look very beloved.

I walked toward her, keeping my gaze on her and nothing else. She was even more beautiful than in the pictures. Her wild black hair seemed to float around her face, like she was sitting in a soft breeze. She wore a silver lace dress similar to the red one from the picture. It reached the ground and covered her toes. The sleeves reached her wrists. It might have been my imagination, but the dress looked like it was actually made from spun silver. Her black eyes stared right at me as I made my way toward her. And she did not look happy to see me.

"You have made it to my court, I see."

"Yes, your majesty." I dropped to one knee and bowed my head like Ronan had taught me to do. Then I produced the key. "I have brought you the key back."

I moved toward her to give her the necklace and noticed her fixation on my hip. No. Not my hip. The sword that hung there. I guessed, when you were the queen, you didn't need to learn to control your features, because if anyone in the ballroom couldn't see she was pissed, they were blind. I remembered the story

Ronan had told me about how Mab had offered to let Killian stay in the Sidhe instead of being exiled, if only he gave her this sword.

After a moment, her eyes came back to mine. She seemed to have controlled her anger.

"You did not use the key to enter the Sidhe."

"No, your majesty. As I'm a changeling, I've never been exiled. I do not need the key to enter."

"Indeed." She held out her hand, and I stepped forward and dropped the key into it, fully aware this woman had tried to kill me no less than four times.

As I did, a man stepped forward. He was taller than Ronan, but only by about an inch. His hair was as black as the Queen's, but his eyes were softer. They were gray instead of black and held none of the anger. In fact, he almost seemed happy to see me.

"And her reward, my Queen?"

"Do not push me, brother."

The Queen's brother. The man who had hurt Ronan. I looked between them. They both had.

"I merely ask you to grant her the reward that all receive when they return the key of the courts."

She stared at the man like she would kill him with her gaze. I wondered if that was possible here.

Apparently not possible for the Queen, anyway. She turned back to me. "Welcome, my changeling niece. In exchange for the return of my key, I grant you safe passage in my and my sister Queen's domains. Have a care you do not cause me to revoke that gift."

I couldn't breathe. I was her niece. That meant the man who had spoken, her brother, was my father. He smiled encouragingly. I swallowed past the shock and said, "You are gracious to grant such a gift, your majesty."

The Queen's gaze had shifted past me. The anger had melted from her face and she looked almost gleeful. "Ah, Ronan. My pet. It is so nice to see you again."

I shifted my body, putting myself between him and her, and felt Ronan shudder at the same time as the man at Mab's feet whimpered. She tugged on the leash, and he fell silent again.

"You must be careful, too, my pet."

"Yes, your majesty."

Ronan's voice was hoarse, and I wondered if he'd been having trouble breathing as well.

Then Mab stood up. "Feel free to continue, my friends. But I must retire. An urgent matter has come to my attention."

The way she looked at me before she swept from the room told me, and everyone else, *I* was the urgent matter.

The crowd mingled again, and the man who was apparently my father started toward me.

"It's not over," Ronan whispered next to me.

"That's my father. My aunt and my father are the ones who hurt you."

"Yes." He turned me to look at him. "You need to be on your guard still. You can't trust anyone in this room."

"You're in this room."

The look on his face scared me. Guilt.

"Morna! My daughter!" The man had reached us and held out his arms for me. I looked around the room, but he was staring at me and I realized Morna must be the name I would have had if I'd grown up in the Sidhe. It was a stupid name.

I wasn't much of a hugger, but I figured it would be rude to not hug my father who had just made the Queen swear to keep me safe and thus stop trying to kill me. I stepped into his hug and out again as quickly as I could.

"You have finally returned. I would have hoped you would have come a few months from now, but no matter. You are here now. And you have two gifts." He seemed proud.

Behind him were two women. One was about my age and glaringly human among all these magical creatures. Looking at her felt like looking into a mirror that somehow dressed me up way fancier than I was ever comfortable. I knew who she was immediately.

The other woman was fae and looked like she wanted to melt into the floor to avoid people looking at her.

"Nialas. Come. Meet your sister."

The human stepped forward and I could see she did not want to meet me.

"She is not my sister," Nialas said.

"What else would you call her? She is my daughter. You are my daughter."

"She is a changeling."

The word sounded dirty coming from her.

"So are you," my father pointed out. "Quinn."

The woman behind Nialas flinched so hard at the sound of her name, her long dark braid twitched behind her.

"You will be Morna's maid now. You will get her dressed appropriately for a party. I will host it tomorrow night to celebrate your return."

"Father," Nialas protested. "Quinn is my maid."

"Bah," he said. "You have a dozen other maids. Morna can have one. Besides. Quinn is the only one of your maids who has not sworn allegiance yet. She can say no and stay with you if she wants."

My father and Nialas turned toward Quinn and waited for her answer. She was petite and seemed to get smaller right in front of me. I felt sorry for her. With her dark skin and small stature, she reminded me of Aelwyd, though I could tell she wasn't a brownie. If I wasn't mistaken, she was half human. I wanted to help her, but I wasn't sure what I could do. Her large brown eyes found mine, and she seemed to swallow some of her fear and nod.

"I will do as you ask, Prince Queran."

Queran nodded, pleased. "Wonderful. Your mother will be overjoyed to have you home. Even if she cannot be here to welcome you herself." He clasped my hands and kissed my forehead. "Ronan, come. You must tell me everything."

"Sir, should your daughter not have an escort through the city?"

"Quinn will suffice."

"But, sir, do you not think she needs a guard?"

I could tell Queran was losing patience. "The Queen has offered Morna safe passage. No harm will befall her. Now come."

Ronan looked at me. I didn't want him to go. How would I know anything here?

"Father. I've come to rely on Ronan. Will he be able to return to me after you have finished speaking with him?"

"I will consider it. But there are many who could serve in an honor guard for you, my sweetling."

"It's just that I know Ronan. We've developed a communication. It would be difficult to train a whole new guard."

Queran seemed to consider this. "If it would make you more comfortable, I will make it so. Now, go with Quinn and start to prepare. Tomorrow night, there will be a feast in your honor."

CHAPTER 39

As soon as Ronan walked away, I felt exposed. Despite what he said about not trusting anyone in the room, I still trusted him to answer my questions and have my back. Instead, I stood there, in the middle of a few dozen people I didn't know, all who had powerful magic themselves, and who were glancing at me every few minutes. A few were openly staring. Like Nialas in front of me. Though I could tell by her stare, she was not happy to see me.

What do you say to the girl who you were switched with? If anyone could possibly understand what my life had been like, it would be this woman. Though we were also different because she had known she was a changeling. She had known she had essentially been kidnapped. All I had known for most of my life was my parents hadn't wanted me.

I was saved from saying anything to her when Quinn said, "Shall we go to your suite at your father's estate?"

"My suite?"

"Yes," Nialas sneered. "It's been set aside for you since you were born. The golden child. The prodigal daughter. Waiting for your return."

I understood then why Nialas seemed to hate me on sight. But Quinn didn't let me respond as she gently took my arm and made me walk toward the doors. She stayed a step behind me and to my right, just as Ronan had on the way in.

"Quinn," I whispered. "I don't know where I'm going."

"I will make sure you do not get lost, Princess."

I almost stumbled at that word. "What did you just call me?"

"Princess. You are the daughter of the Prince of Winter and the Princess of Summer, after all."

Princess of Summer. My mother. She couldn't be here, Queran had said. I ran through what I knew of the courts in my mind. And I remembered what Ronan had said about the Sidhe being about balance.

"Right. My father is the Winter Queen's brother. My mother is the Summer Queen's sister."

I phrased it as a statement. Like this was something I knew all along. But inside, my head was reeling. Princess. How the fuck was I a princess?

I kept walking, paying close attention to Quinn's whispered instructions. She was even better at guiding me from a step behind than Ronan had been. I wouldn't be surprised if people watching us, and there were a few, thought I knew exactly where I was going.

We made it to my father's estate, and I got to the suite Quinn said was mine. The first thing I did when I got into the room was close the door and lean against it.

"Can anyone see us here?" I asked her. "Can anyone hear us?"

"No, Princess. We are alone. No one will hear us."

I could tell she was frightened. I didn't know why, but I couldn't get my brain to work to try to come up with a reason. I slid down the door until I was sitting on the floor, trying desperately to control my breathing. I was hyperventilating, on the verge of a full on panic attack.

"Why did I come here?" I said, not really asking Quinn. "What was I think-ing? We could have stayed in the human world. I didn't need these answers. Not really. We could have been together and I would never have known...."

Quinn crouched down in front of me. "Are you okay, Princess?"

I looked up into her eyes. They were a beautiful deep brown, shining with concern and a generous amount of fear. I felt immediately calmer, knowing I had to focus so I could keep us both safe.

"I'll be okay in a minute. I'm just a bit overwhelmed."

"If it makes you feel any better, you would always have had to come back," Quinn said.

"What do you mean?"

"I've heard things. Things some of the more powerful fae don't realize I've heard because they forget I'm there. Your father had planned to retrieve you from the human realm after your thirtieth birthday."

"Why then?"

"That is when a daoine sidhe's gifts manifest and are fully mature." She shrugged. "You would be harder to kill."

After taking a deep breath, I stood up and looked around the room. The first thing I noticed was the lack of a bed. Because it wasn't a bedroom. It was a small apartment. A bigger one than my old apartment, but still small. Next to where I stood at the door, a bar held a platter of food and a weird-looking contraption with a coffee cup set underneath it. On the other side of me was a desk and chair, both carved from ice. On the other side of the desk was a living room area with a sectional couch and table and a glass door leading out onto a patio.

"This is all mine?" I asked.

"Yes, Princess. The door ahead of you is a wardrobe. I believe it's empty at the moment, but we will fix that. And the door in the sitting area leads to your bedroom and withdrawing room."

The set of rooms was bigger than my apartment had been. I went to the glass doors to look out. I could see the entire east side of Glacia and the town beyond. I stood there for a moment, and realized I was looking for the boy I had met, even though it was ridiculous to think I'd be able to see him from up here.

Finally, I turned back to Quinn.

"What do we need to do?"

***

Quinn and I spent the rest of the day getting me a dress for the party my father was going to be throwing the next day. I felt stupid wearing it, like a blue cupcake.

"It's an excellent color for you," Quinn said, and I knew she could tell what I was thinking. "It brings out the silver of your eyes."

"It's too big," I said.

"It fits you perfectly."

"I don't mean the fit. I mean the skirt."

It was a real princess dress, huge and poofy. I had never been into dresses, and this kind in particular was a certain brand of evil.

"Can't I choose the style of my dress?" I asked as Quinn played with my hair, holding it up and then twirling it around to see a curl.

"Prince Queran asked for this dress specifically. He's having several dresses made up for you. He sent a message that he didn't want to ever see the pants you wore here again. If you really prefer pants, I think we can persuade him to have some new ones made for you."

"Where are my old clothes?" I asked, alarmed.

"I was told to get rid of them."

I turned to her. "Quinn. If you value working for me at all, you will disregard that order."

She swallowed, paling and seemed to literally shrink. I felt bad for scaring her, but I wouldn't have my old clothes, especially my leather jacket, taken from me.

She nodded quickly. "I am not required to follow your father's orders. I won't throw them away. They'll be safe."

"I shouldn't have been so harsh. What does he have against my jeans, anyway?"

"They're too common."

"Excuse me?" That was not the response I had been expecting.

"Cotton is for the lesser fae. The ones who work. Not for the nobles."

"You're serious."

"Your father is."

I closed my eyes and held on to my temper, not wanting to scare my maid for a second time. Who was this man to tell me what I could and could not wear? He was my father in name only. He had no right to dictate to me.

"Have you heard when Ronan is coming back?"

"No, Princess Morna. I can inquire if you wish."

"Don't call me that. My name isn't Morna. And yes. But after we get this stupid dress off. How did they get one so quickly for me?"

"It was your mother's dress. They only had to make a few adjustments. You're about the same size as she is, though much shorter."

"My mother?" I had so many questions about her. Who was she? What was her name? Why wasn't she here? When would I be able to see her? But I didn't ask Quinn any of them. I wasn't sure I could trust her.

Quinn offered some answers without my asking. "Yes. She is only here once every year for the week of the fall equinox. Your father goes to Summer to be with her for the week of the spring equinox. She doesn't care for the dresses she must wear while she attends the Winter court, so she will not miss this one."

So she was told what to wear as well. I wondered what she wore while she was at the Summer court. Would I have more freedom there? Or would it be a different kind of dictatorship?

"Wait. They're only together for two weeks in a year?"

"No. They have country estates in both Winter and Summer. They spend most of their time at one of them when they are together. But the Prince is required at court for much of the weeks leading up to the Winter Solstice. I assume your mother is also required at her sister's court for the same time in the summer."

While I was considering this, Quinn helped me put on a simple silk night-gown, something else I would never have chosen for myself. Just then, someone knocked on my door.

Quinn answered it and Ronan stood on the other side.

I wanted to run to him and hold on to the one familiar thing I had. But I stopped myself and said, "Quinn, why don't you go to bed? I'm sure we have a lot we need to do in the morning, so you should get some rest."

She curtsied and then left. Ronan stayed just outside the door.

"The Prince has allowed me to be part of your honor guard." He handed me a slip of paper. "I've given this list to him as well, and I hope he will choose from it to fill out the guard. You can trust any person on this list. I will be outside the door tonight."

"You can't come in for a minute?"

He shook his head.

"You work for my father?"

He hesitated for a moment. "I am in liege to the Prince, yes."

A cold dread seeped into my body, but I forced it away. Whatever my subconscious mind had realized, I wasn't ready to look at it yet.

"Still? Even after what he did to you?"

"Yes."

"But you were exiled. I didn't think you were in liege to anyone anymore."

"I couldn't rescind my fealty before I left the Sidhe. It stands until I do so."

"Then do so now."

"It's not that simple."

Another one of those things I didn't understand. I wanted to ask him about it, but his face was that closed mask I had gotten used to seeing past. Except he held it even tighter here, as though it was a literal piece of armor.

"Will you be at the party tomorrow?"

"I will be there as your guard. Good night, my Princess."

He closed the door, leaving me alone in my room. Despite being in Winter, practically in the middle of a fucking glacier, I hadn't felt cold until the moment Ronan called me princess.

CHAPTER 40

I woke up and immediately felt for Ronan's magic—and found it just outside my suite. But even as I felt it, I noticed it was moving away. I got up and ran to my door, throwing it open to see Ronan walking down the hall.

"Where are you going?" I said before I noticed the other guard standing at my door.

Ronan turned. "I'm off shift. Finian will be your guard for the morning. I'll see you tonight at the party."

I watched him walk away and felt a weight press down on my chest. It eased a little when Quinn walked toward my room. She hurried toward me.

"Princess M—" She stopped, her eyes widening with fear.

"Yes, Quinn?" I prodded gently while I watched Ronan's retreating figure until he turned a corner.

"We must get started. We have a lot to do and little time."

"If you say so."

I spent an awful morning and early afternoon having my hair pulled, curled, and pinned until I could barely recognize it. Compared to Arial, Quinn's hair-styling left a bit to be desired. But I couldn't deny she made it look good.

"What glamour do you feel comfortable doing?"

"Glamour?"

We stared at each other for a while until she must have realized I didn't know what she was talking about.

"Glamour is a magic that allows you to alter your appearance."

"Oh, right. I'd forgotten what it was called. I can't do that."

Quinn laughed. "Every fae can do glamour."

I continued to stare at her.

She stopped laughing and paled. "I'm sorry, Princess." She dropped into a low curtsy and refused to look up at me. "I didn't mean to cause offense."

"You didn't. Quinn, stand up. I'm not mad at you for laughing. I'm going to trust you with a secret, okay? But you have to swear not to tell anyone."

She stood up and I could tell she didn't think she was out of trouble yet.

"I don't know much about this world. Ronan could only tell me so much before I came. I might say things or do things differently from everyone around here. Can I count on you to help me?"

"Of course, Princess. I'll do whatever you need."

"Well, first. Can you stop calling me Princess?"

"Oh, that wouldn't be proper."

I grimaced. "I figured that would be your answer. But maybe just when we're private, you can call me Calynn? When no one else is around?"

She nodded. "I can try."

"Good. And if you hear me say something that doesn't make sense, correct me. I swear I won't be angry. But I need someone who will tell me when I'm making a fool of myself."

"I can do that."

***

I'm not sure what I had expected when I got to the Sidhe, but spending my first full day getting a complete makeover and then attending the most lavish party I could imagine hadn't been on the list. I guess what I had really been expecting was more attempts on my life. Despite Kai telling me the Queen had to offer me safety, I hadn't really believed it. I didn't think for a second they were just going to stop trying to murder me, but I guessed I had a small reprieve while they found a loophole in their own rules.

Another bonus to coming into the Sidhe that I hadn't anticipated was my magic was working even faster to heal me. My hands had almost completely healed from the burns, though the skin on them was still pink with new growth, and my shoulder where I'd been shot still ached when I used my arm too much.

The party was in full swing by the time I entered. I was announced upon entering Queran's ballroom, almost as big as the Queen's and just as luxurious despite the furniture all being carved from ice. Of course, I was introduced with the wrong name.

"Introducing Princess Morna, daughter of the Winter Prince Queran and the Summer Princess Eilidh."

Finally, I learned my mother's name. I wondered how often fae from Summer and Winter got together, but I hadn't seen Ronan yet and so had no one to ask. Quinn had promised to keep my confidence, but I still wasn't sure how much I should rely on her. Who did she really work for? My father had said she hadn't sworn allegiance to anyone, but I didn't know what that meant either. I felt completely lost and needed to find Ronan before I did something that could get me killed.

Before I could find him, my father found me.

"Morna, my sweetling. I trust you had a good day."

"It was fine. I wondered though if I could be called Calynn. Morna doesn't feel like my name."

He stood there and blinked at me for a long time without speaking. "Why would I call you Calynn?"

"Because that's the name I've had for the past twenty-nine years, and I rather like it."

He didn't look entirely happy at my request. Then he said, "Tonight I will introduce you as my daughter. And my daughter's name is Morna. We will discuss this other name at a later date." Then he turned on a smile that looked fake and began introducing me to what seemed like the entire Winter court. For all I knew, it was.

At first, I thought I'd be able to remember some of them because of the odd skin colors. Some were blue, purple, or green. Others were white or black, the way Kai was black. After a while, I realized there were too many colors and it wouldn't help me remember anyone. I'd have to ask Quinn for help. About an hour later, I was introduced to a woman who made an impression. She was the only one who stared at me with naked hostility in her black eyes. Her skin and hair were as white as snow. But her eyes looked like two pieces of coal, hard and black. Her skin-tight dress matched her eyes but also sparkled with silver thread.

"Ah, Deardriu," my father said. "Allow me to introduce you to Morna."

The woman didn't look at my father. Instead, she stared at me like she wanted to scratch my eyes out.

"She has both of her gifts, I see," Deardriu said as she measured me with her eyes.

My father chuckled. "She comes from good stock."

Deardriu turned those hate-filled eyes on my father. "And the rest of the noble children do not?"

I gave the man credit. His smile didn't falter, even though I wanted to cringe at the crushing magic radiating out of the woman. But then I felt my father's magic push back against hers and was amazed at how easily he did it. It was like her gifts were nothing more than a feather against his. It scared me.

"I said nothing of the sort, Deardriu. The Ancient Mother has blessed my family at long last. Eilidh and I have waited over a hundred years to have a child who did not die. Perhaps the Ancient Mother thought we had already suffered enough."

Deardriu bared her teeth, which I was shocked to see were black, contrasting sharply against the pale pink of her lips.

"It was quite a tragedy when your youngest died so young," my father continued. "I would think you understood some of our pain."

Her snarl seemed to get even bigger before she turned on her heel and stormed away.

I wasn't sure what I had just witnessed, but I felt like I had an enemy in that woman and I wouldn't be forgetting her any time soon.

"Well, dear," Queran said, turning to me, "I believe that is all the introductions. You'll forgive a doting fool. I just want to show you off to everyone."

"Uh. Yeah. No problem." I tried to offer him a smile, but wasn't sure I completely pulled it off.

He kissed my forehead, and I fought not to rub it away immediately after. I didn't know anything about this man other than that he had beaten Ronan and not gotten him a healer after. He hadn't spent any time with me today other than at this party, and so I couldn't help feeling like that beloved pet Ronan had mentioned before. I recalled the naked man sitting at the Queen's feet the night before and suppressed a shudder.

"Go," Queran said. "Mingle. Get to know some of the ladies and gentlemen here. You never know, you might find someone you want to get to know better."

I walked away from him and noticed Quinn was following me. I waited until she was right behind me then whispered, "Does he want me to make friends or find someone to fuck?" He'd made a few suggestive comments during the introductions, but I had tried to ignore them.

"Both? Either? I don't think he cares as long as it's with the right crowd."

"The right crowd. So only the men I was introduced to."

"Or the women."

"I'm not gay."

"I don't understand what you mean."

"Gay. As in a homosexual. I'm not physically attracted to other women."

"Oh. There is no such word for that here. Sex is just sex and love is just love. If you are not attracted to women, then you are not." She shrugged.

I scanned the crowd, looking for Ronan. He said he'd be here, but I hadn't seen him yet.

"I guess Ronan doesn't count as part of the 'right crowd'?"

"Oh no. He may be from a noble family, but he only has one of his gifts. He is not one of the ones your father would recommend."

"Someone else mentioned that. Which noble family is he from?" I wanted to turn to look at her, but that would draw attention to us.

"You haven't met his parents. They took a trip to the Muir last week. But you met his uncle Anant. He is possibly the oldest daoine sidhe in the whole Sidhe and is the best healer in Winter."

I vaguely remembered one old man, but there had been so many people it was hard to keep any of them straight. It didn't really matter right now, anyway.

I reached out with my magic, searching for Ronan. I found him in a moment. The familiar frozen stone beneath the water. I went toward his magic and found him standing at the doors.

"I thought you were going to be guarding me," I said when I reached him.

"I am."

He didn't look at me. Instead, he watched the crowd as it ebbed and flowed behind me.

"I thought you were going to be guarding me a bit closer."

"The Prince told me to stay by the door until you were ready to leave and then man the post outside your suite."

"I see."

I didn't feel like I could ask any of my questions here where anyone could hear us, so I just stood there for a moment and wondered what I should do next. I didn't want to mingle the way my father had suggested. What I really wanted to do was go to my room and take this stupid dress off. I was about to ask Quinn how much longer I was expected to stay when the doors opened and the herald announced the next guest to the party.

"Announcing Her Royal Majesty, Queen Mab of the Unseelie fae."

She stepped in and it sounded like everyone in the hall gasped. Her dark hair floated around her head like it had the night before. She wore a beautiful, floor length blood red dress that clung to her curves and showed off her body while still being demure.

She scanned the crowd, waiting until all eyes focused on her. Then she gave everyone a small smile and said, "Don't let me stop you. Enjoy yourselves. Revel."

It was as if it were her party and not Queran's. I found him in the crowd. He had a good poker face, but I could see a slight tightness around his smile that hadn't been there earlier.

Because I was by the door already, the Queen turned to face me.

"Leaving so soon, my dear niece?" She glanced at Ronan, who didn't look at her. "Or were you just playing with the toys?"

Quinn had me practice curtsying today in the massive skirt, and I was glad for it. I moved in front of Ronan, putting myself between him and the Queen, then dropped like I had any idea what I was doing. "Good evening, Auntie. It's a pleasure to see you again."

She laughed. "Oh, you don't have to lie to me, my sweet."

I stood again and nodded. "Fine. I admit to having a couple of questions for you."

"I am feeling generous this evening. I will answer two questions. What would they be?"

I was already certain I knew the answers I was about to get, but I wanted to ask them anyway. Especially if she was going to give me straight answers. "Were you the one who had Meriel killed?"

"Who is Meriel?"

"The selkie in Vancouver."

"Vancouver." She said it like it was some disgusting thing she wanted to wipe off the bottom of her shoe. Then her face changed. "Oh. You mean the exiled selkie from Summer. Why, in the name of the Ancient Mother, would I have *her* killed? I have no reason to even look at a *selkie* from *Summer*, much less kill one."

"Why do you want to kill me?"

"You're far too powerful for your own good. It was nothing personal." She smiled at me, and I felt like taking a step back. "But I can't try to kill you anymore. Not since you returned my key. Now, that is a story I would love to hear, how you obtained it." She stepped closer to me, and I fought the urge to cringe. Then she lowered her voice and whispered, "What did you do with my Darkness?"

At first, I thought she meant her magic. Then I realized she was talking about Kai.

"Oh," I said. "He hasn't come back? What a shame. If you'll excuse me, my father requested I mingle."

I didn't turn my back on her. I figured only a fool would do such a thing. Instead, I strode past her, my back to hers, and into the crowd, Quinn following close behind me.

CHAPTER 41

I stayed at the party for a bit longer, but as soon as Quinn told me my duties were done, I retreated to my room. It was a few hours later, and I was almost asleep, when someone knocked on my door. I jumped up to answer it, knowing who was there.

When I opened the door to him, I wondered for an instant if Ronan wanted to come in, but he ruined it by saying, "The Prince requests your presence in the hall."

I nodded and he followed me there.

Except for my father, the room was empty, all the revelers having partied enough for one night. Queran was sitting on a throne that matched Queen Mab's, even if it was slightly smaller.

"Well, my dear. I'd say it was a successful introduction."

"I guess so. I'm not really interested in parties."

"I'm sure you will be in time. You'll be attending many over the next few weeks. Especially with the Solstice approaching. Now that you are home, you must be seen by as many as possible. Your mother and I have missed you terribly. Nialas was a comfort, but she wasn't *you*, dear. You could never be replaced in our hearts."

Something inside me cracked open. Years of feeling inadequate because my parents hadn't wanted me melted. But I still had so many questions.

"If you loved me so much, why was I changed?"

"The Queens never approved of your mother and me. You had a brother, about a hundred years before you were born. Maybe a bit more. They killed him before he was more than two months old. After that, you had a sister. She survived until she was six months. Your mother did not want to try again. She refused for years. But then she had you. I knew our sisters would eventually kill you as they had killed your brother and sister. They'd already tried. So I had you changed. Secreted out into the human world where the Queens couldn't find you. Ronan switched you with Nialas when you were about a month old. Mab and Titania were displeased. They wanted to kill Ronan, but he had gone back to the human world before either could find him. Instead, he was exiled. And then Titania placed a glamour on Summer—and Winter, at Mab's request—to ensure no one would remember you being here."

There was a lot to process in that statement, but one thing resounded louder in my mind than anything else. "Ronan changed me?"

I looked at Ronan, standing slightly behind me. His hands behind his back, his gaze settled on everything and nothing. He didn't speak.

That icy dread that had swept through me before settled in again. Everything clicked into place. His evasive answers. The lies of omission. Fuck, even the times when he seemed relieved for something I couldn't figure out. Or didn't want to figure out.

"Yes. Did he not tell you that?"

"No. He didn't."

"He changed you and then I ordered him to protect you. In any case, with the humans, you were safe. Until that stupid selkie found you. I'm not sure how she did it. But I had to take care of it. So I sent the Darkness for her."

I whipped back around. "You killed Meriel."

"Of course. I had to keep you safe. You're still so young. And you're so small. You don't have the strength to protect yourself. I feared Mab would see you with the selkie and send the Darkness for you. And I was right."

"That's what she meant."

"What? That's what who meant?"

"Mab. When I asked her about Meriel, she said she had no reason to look at a selkie from Summer, much less kill one. She didn't see Meriel with me. She had no reason to look at her at all. She sent the Darkness after me because *you* had him kill Meriel. If you had left her alone, if you had left it for Ronan to deal with, *which was the job you gave him*, the Queen still wouldn't know about me. This whole thing... It's all because of you."

"Be careful what you say to me, daughter. I am still your father."

"You had an innocent woman killed. A woman whose only wish was to be allowed home. You don't even care that she died because she was a lesser fae. You probably wouldn't care if Ronan was killed for the same reason. Anyone less than you is just a tool."

That part of me that had begun to thaw toward him sealed itself back up.

"I am going to leave you now, daughter, before you say something you cannot take back."

I opened my mouth to say something more, but then Ronan stepped forward. "Sir, before you leave, there is something I would say."

"What is it?"

"Have I fulfilled all my duties to you as you set them forth to me?"

Queran looked between Ronan and me, frustration marking his features. "You have," he said curtly.

"With my duties complete, I am leaving your service."

"Oh? And what will you do? You know what this means, boy."

"Yes, sir. I mean to offer my pledge of fealty to your daughter, sir. If she will accept it."

"She's still a child. Look at her. She's barely taller than a brownie. She's not strong enough to protect herself, let alone someone like you."

I blinked, certain he had just insulted me.

"She is strong enough, sir. She can handle it."

My father's face turned from skeptical to completely stony. "I see. You've finally done it then." He turned and started toward the doors, throwing one more quip over his shoulder. "You are freed from my service, boy. I hope you know what you're doing."

The doors closed behind him and Ronan and I were alone. I walked a few steps away from him toward the throne my father had vacated. I didn't turn to face him. My thoughts whirled as I tried to sort out the new facts I had obtained. Queran had Meriel killed in some misguided attempt to protect me.

It was because of me Meriel was dead. And the man I had come to trust, who had become my friend, my lover, was the one who changed me.

"I knew. I didn't want to believe it, but I knew. Kai knew, too. He said not to have blind faith in you. I should have opened my eyes."

I couldn't look at him. I'd let my attraction to him distract me enough.

"Will you accept my offer of fealty?" he asked cautiously.

"I don't know what that means."

"It means—"

I turned, filled with anger, and held up my hand to stop him. "I don't care. You lied to me."

He shook his head. "I didn't lie. I told you everything I was able to tell you."

"Everything? Like how *you* were the one who changed me in the first place? You brought me to a different world and brought a little girl back here. Neither of us will get to be what we were meant to be because of that. He ordered you to change me and you just did it."

Ronan swallowed hard. "He didn't order me to. I volunteered."

"You what?"

He spread his hands in what was probably supposed to be a placating gesture. "You don't understand—"

"I understand, all right. You made me believe you cared about me. When all along, you knew *exactly* why I was changed. You knew who had sent Kai after me. You knew it was the Queen. You probably even knew the Summer Queen was also trying to kill me. *And* it was my own father who had Meriel killed."

"I suspected, yes. But I couldn't—"

"I don't want to hear it. If you had just told me, I wouldn't have needed to come here at all. I wouldn't have lost my home. I could have done things differently and maybe not had quite so many people and creatures try to kill me."

"You're mad. And you should be. But our worlds are different. There are laws—"

"Yeah. They are different. Because of what you did. How can I ever trust you again?"

For a moment, we were both silent. My question seemed to echo through the cavernous room. My heart was pounding. I felt like I'd just thrown down a gauntlet. I wanted him to apologize, to explain, to make everything right again. But I also didn't want to hear a word he said.

"You're right," he said after a long time. "It was because of me. And I will have to pay for that. I just hope one day you will find a way to forgive me."

Then he left the way Queran had. As I watched him go, I felt the first tear slip free. I had been so angry at first, I didn't even realize until he left I hadn't been as mad as I thought. I was hurt. The mountain of anger had been hiding a crevasse as big as the Grand Canyon. That one would leave a scar. I sat down on the steps in front of my father's chair. I closed my eyes, struggling to control the pain that threatened to overwhelm me. He'd had all the answers I needed and didn't offer them to me. He knew what I wanted to know. He made me come here. He also made me leave here so long ago. Would I be able to trust him ever again?

"Princess?"

I looked up to find Quinn standing in front of me. She had been so quiet, I hadn't heard her come into the Great Hall from the other side.

I wiped away the tear, but she had already seen it.

"Princess." She glanced around the empty hall. Then whispered, "I mean Calynn."

I smiled at her and wanted to hug her, just to feel a little less alone.

"I heard what just happened. Are you okay?"

I nodded. Then I shook my head.

"Is there anything I can do for you?"

"No. I don't think so."

"Okay."

She stood there for a few minutes.

"Calynn. Maybe." She stopped, twisting her hands together.

"Go ahead, Quinn. You can ask me anything."

"Well, I know you just declined Ronan's offer. But I... well, I was hoping. Maybe you would accept *my* offer of fealty?"

She looked so scared and hopeful. I had no idea what I was doing.

"How would I go about accepting it?" I asked her.

"You simply say yes."

"And if I accept it, what does it mean for you?"

"It means I am loyal to you. I must do what you ask of me, for the length of the fealty term. In return, you offer me your protection."

"What's the term length?"

"Thirty years."

I swallowed hard. Thirty years was a long time to be responsible for someone. "What would I protect you from?"

She dropped her gaze to the ground. "From the other fae. Lesser fae, those who are not strong enough and who have no protection, can be used in terrible ways. Especially the mongrels like me."

I didn't ask what terrible ways. I had an imagination. I'm sure the noble fae did as well. "Have you not already offered your fealty to someone else?"

"There has been no one I have wanted to follow, and thirty years is a long time to be pledged to someone you dislike."

"How have you stayed safe?"

She looked up at me and I knew. She hadn't. She was a beautiful woman with her smooth brown skin, long black hair, and deep brown eyes. And so timid it would be easy to take advantage of her.

"Why me?"

She bit her lip and twisted her hands together. "You aren't like the others. You have treated me well since you arrived, even when you didn't like what I was saying. And I can tell you're strong enough to protect me. Even now, before you reach maturity, you are already stronger than half the noble fae."

"I am?"

She nodded.

"How do you know that?" Queran obviously didn't.

"I pay attention."

I considered her offer. On the one hand, even if she was sure, I didn't know if I could really protect her if I needed to. But on the other hand, having someone who I knew would be loyal to me would be helpful now that I couldn't trust Ronan anymore.

"How old are you?"

"Fifty-seven years."

Fifty-seven years old. She had been on her own, with no one to protect her, for fifty-seven years. There was only one answer left for me to give her.

"Quinn. I accept your offer of fealty."

She smiled and ran and hugged me tightly. I couldn't help it. I smiled, too. Until she suddenly backed away, another look of fear on her face.

"Hey," I said. "You can hug me whenever you want. And you can tell me anything. Even if you think it will make me mad. Just tell me the truth. Not what you think I want to hear. We have to trust each other."

I didn't mention to her I would know if she lied. I wanted her to tell me the truth for its own sake.

"I can do that."

I stood up from the step. "Come on. Let's get ready for bed. Again."

Quinn followed me through the halls, back to my room. When we got there, I said, "You go to bed. I don't need anything. I'll see you in the morning."

She curtsied and left, and I stood in the middle of my living area. There were dresses laid out on the couch to be sized over the next few days. Fancy food, and that weird contraption that was apparently used to make some fancy coffee, laid out on the bar by the door. In my bedroom, there was a huge bed with lots of blankets and pillows. All things I was supposed to enjoy now that I was a princess. I noticed the paper Ronan had given me with the list of people I could trust. I'd set it on the table in the living area to look at later. Despite what he'd done, I knew I could count on those people.

I was exhausted, but I knew I wouldn't be sleeping for a long time tonight. And I craved something that would make me feel better. I went to the bar and fiddled with the weird thing until I had a cup of coffee. I held the cup up to my nose, breathing in the steam and the scent, trying in vain to make this world feel like home. But the coffee was infused with magic, and I could barely smell the brew beneath that scent.

I found my backpack and pulled the blanket out. I wrapped it around my shoulders even though I wasn't cold. Despite the estate being built from ice, it was a perfect temperature in the room. I hadn't noticed the cold at all since arriving in the Sidhe. There was nothing I could ask for I wouldn't get. I trailed my hand along the silver inlay on the table and made my way out onto the patio and set my cup of fresh coffee down before I accidentally shattered it.

It wasn't going to make me feel better. Neither was the scent of pine and ice that infused the blanket around my shoulders.

As I watched Glacia glitter in the moonlight, I whispered, "Little more than a cage."

To Be Continued...

If you enjoyed *Truth in the Smoke*, please consider leaving a review. Reviews help indie authors like me gain exposure which helps sell books. Which helps me create more books.

Did you love Ronan as much as I do? How did he volunteer to change Calynn? What was his first thoughts when she showed up on his doorstep? Sign up to my newsletter to find out in *The Other Side of the Fire Vol. 1*. It's a collection of scenes from this story written from his point of view.

www.18streetpress.com/getintouch

But what you're really asking now is when do I get to read the rest of Calynn's story? She's going to continue her adventures in the second book of *Glamour Blind: **Destiny in the Flames** coming November 2023!

Turn the page for a sneak peak at the first scene.

DESTINY IN THE FLAMES

I don't think I'd ever thought of what a luncheon was before I came to the Sidhe. Now that I'd been to a few, I realized it was just a fancy word for lunch. And while most of the ones I'd been to lately had been set up by my father, Queran, today's luncheon had been at my request.

I entered the mansion and the butler or whatever he was offered to take my jacket. I passed him my leather motorcycle jacket, the one piece of clothing, other than my boots, that I refused to stop wearing. The butler eyed it warily like he thought it was going to bite him or make everything in the closet worth less just by its proximity.

I ignored him. I was getting pretty good at ignoring people who annoyed me. There were a lot of them in the Sidhe. I'd been here for two weeks now and was still having trouble adjusting to life here. I thought every day about going back to the human world, but there were things I needed to accomplish, one of which was today's meeting.

The butler hung up my jacket and then led me to a room that I had learned was called a drawing room. My host was waiting with a tray of tea set out. I fought the grimace when I saw the tea, but there really wasn't much good coffee in the Sidhe anyway. It was all infused with magic.

Egan stood up to greet me.

"Princess Morna, it's such a pleasure to have you here."

I gritted my teeth at the name. I hated it more than the title of princess, but almost everyone insisted on calling me Morna, the name I was supposed to have if I'd lived in the Sidhe my whole life. But Queran insisted and the only one who could stand up to him was his sister, the Queen.

"The pleasure is mine, Egan. I was hoping to get to know you a little better, and perhaps some of the members of your family."

Another thing I'd learned in the last two weeks was how to talk pretty. How to say things I didn't mean to make other people feel better about themselves. When people felt good about themselves, they were more likely to give me the answers I was looking for.

"Most of my family is away at the moment, I'm afraid. Idris is with our youngest child, Ryleigh. They are practicing for the Solstice challenge. And our oldest child is at his estate in the country. He is going to set up his own house this Solstice."

"You must be very proud," I said, though I had no idea what he was proud about. I could just hear from his tone that he was.

He handed me a cup of tea. "Indeed. So I'm afraid the only one available today is me. But I'm honored to have you here."

I never knew what to say when people said stuff like that to me, especially when I felt the ring of truth in their words. I just smiled and sipped the tea. Then I set it on the table.

"I thought there was one more person in your family. A changeling. Bridget Cleary."

"Ah, Bridget. Yes. She is here. Though she keeps her own schedule. She may join us, she may not."

The butler returned and announced that lunch was served in the dining room. I followed Egan to the room and we began to eat and exchange pleasantries. He talked about how his family had been some of the strongest earth wielders for the past two centuries and he had high hopes that Ryleigh would continue that tradition. He told me about how his oldest son, Sruthan, would be starting his own house. Egan and Idris had been helping him get ready for the past few years and Sruthan finally felt ready to make the leap.

We had moved on to the final course of the lunch and I was starting to think I wouldn't get the meeting I'd been hoping for after all, when a woman came into the dining room.

"Hello, Egan," she said, going directly to the sideboard and filling a plate with food.

"Bridget, my darling, we have a visitor."

She turned to look at us, pausing with her hand extended over the food. "Oh, hello," she said.

"Hello, Bridget. I'm—" I cut myself off before I said my name.

Egan took up where I'd left off. "This is Princess Morna. She has honored us with a visit. Unfortunately, everyone is out today. Come join us."

Bridget finished filling her plate and then sat down across from me. When I looked at her, I saw a human, the difference between her and the rest of the fae who lived in the Sidhe was stark and I finally understood what Ronan had meant when he'd told me it was easy to see another fae in the human world because I was looking at the opposite now and there was no mistaking her. She looked like she was around fifty years old, but I knew that she was about three times that age. Humans lived longer in the Sidhe than they would in the human world. And Bridget Cleary had lived here longer than any other human in the Winter domain. She had her long dark hair caught up in a simple style that kept it all out of her face. Her dark eyes watched me and I wondered what she saw.

"What have you been working on today, Bridget," Egan asked.

She smiled and launched into a description of the dress she was making for a sweet leprechaun she had met a few weeks before.

"Bridget came to us," Egan looked at the woman, "how long ago, Bridget?"

"Over a century, to be sure. But of course, you don't notice the passing of time as much in the Sidhe."

"I heard the story," I said. "Your husband was going to kill you and the fae took pity on you and brought you here instead."

Bridget laughed. "He thought I was a changeling. I've always found the irony delightful. I didn't become a changeling until after he tried to kill me for being one."

"But you were changed with an inanimate object?"

"Yes." She looked at Egan. "It was a piece of driftwood, wasn't it?"

"It was. Of course, no one would have known until after it was buried." Egan turned back to me. "Bridget's mother was a good friend of mine. When I saw what was happening to Bridget, I wanted to step in. Idris agreed and we brought her here to live with us. She is an excellent seamstress, you know."

Bridget blushed. "I'm sure the Princess has plenty of seamstresses to help her with her wardrobe."

It was true. Not that I liked any of the clothes I had gotten so far. Which gave me an idea.

"I do, Bridget. But I would love to see what you could do for me. Prince Queran has generously offered me anything I need."

"Show her your workroom, Bridget. Maybe she'll commission something from you."

She didn't need a lot of convincing. We finished eating and I followed her to the next level of the mansion where there was a large room with fabric strewn everywhere.

"It's quite a mess in here," she said.

"Helps with the creativity," I said, looking around.

She showed me the dress she had been making for the leprechaun. It was lovely, but not really my style, then again, most dresses weren't my style.

"I have a confession, Bridget," I said, as I moved to another piece she was working on, an emerald green shirt that looked more like something I would consider wearing. "I was hoping to speak with you, actually. I've been doing some research on changelings and everything I've found said that you're the oldest one in the Winter domain."

"I believe that's true," she said, cautiously.

I lifted the sleeve of the shirt to better look at the white embroidery along the front panel.

"I'm looking for information about changelings."

"You know I'm not a changeling like you are. We're very different."

"A bicycle and a rocket ship," I said quietly, fingering the snowflakes on the shirt.

"What was that?"

I turned back to her. "Nevermind. I'm wondering what kind of magic you have?"

"Magic? Why would I have magic?"

"You've lived in the Sidhe for the last hundred and twenty years. Eventually, the magic here is going to sink into you."

She looked scared, casting her eyes around her workshop as though wondering if anyone else was listening.

"Are changelings not supposed to have magic?" I asked.

"I don't want to risk my place here. I know how some of the other changelings are treated. Little more than slaves."

I remembered Ronan mentioning beloved pets before. Clearly what Bridget was in this household. She was allowed more freedom than I was in Queran's home and I was a full daoine sidhe.

"I don't want to get you in trouble, Bridget. I'm trying to learn more about myself." I hesitated for a moment, considering. But if I wanted Bridget to trust me, I would have to give her some trust in return. "I'm also looking for a changeling. A few weeks ago, a changeling left the Sidhe and sent a selkie to me. It resulted in me coming here and the selkie being murdered. I want to find the changeling who did that."

"Why?"

I tried to think of something that would make sense to her, even though it barely made sense to me. "The selkie hadn't done anything wrong. I need to figure out who was responsible."

"Once you figure it out, what will you do with the information?"

I had no idea. There didn't seem to be anything I could do about Queran's involvement in Meriel's death. I wasn't sure there would be anything that could be done about the changeling's involvement. Eventually, I said, "The changeling responsible owes a debt. It should be repaid."

"What do you know about this changeling?" Bridget asked.

"They were able to leave the Sidhe, so they couldn't be too old. They have enough magic to make a selkie forget who she had spoken to."

Bridget moved around her room, touching a piece of lace here, a ribbon there. "There are very few changelings I can think of who might be able to accomplish that. Give me some time to consider and I will come up with a list for you."

"What would you ask as recompense?"

She looked up at me, a dark green ribbon wound around her fingers. "You remind me of a human so much, but you still aren't one, are you?"

"I don't know what I am."

She huffed a little laugh. "Nor do any of us. No longer human, but neither are we fae. Perhaps we have more in common than I thought. Before I came here, my husband always tried to stifle me. He hated that I had two businesses, I made dresses and I sold eggs. He believed it made him less of a man that his wife didn't rely on him."

"Your husband..."

"Michael."

"Michael. Do you think he tried to kill you because he thought you were a changeling or because you were so independent?"

She smiled sadly. "That is something I have wondered nearly every day for the past hundred and twenty-five years. If you can figure out a way to answer the question, I'd love to know the answer. Perhaps that could be my recompense. How would I learn this answer?"

"He's long since gone. I don't know that you can. But you can decide it's not worth the energy to dwell on it anymore."

She gave me a nod. "I will have the list for you as soon as I am able. It was a pleasure to meet you, Princess Morna."

"My name is Calynn, not Morna."

Her smile this time held more mirth and I glimpsed the independent woman her husband had such a problem with. She was a woman I'd like to know.

"Perhaps you know who you are after all."

Acknowledgements

Everyone thinks that writing is a solitary endeavor. However, I would never have finished a single draft if it weren't for my community of friends cheering me on and keeping me accountable.

First I need to thank my Team Hikes and Games: Krys, Steph, Jenn, Meagan, and Kim. Thanks for answering all my polls, for reading my books before they were ready, and for all your support.

Thank you to all my writing friends at The Urban Fantasy Bookstore, The Creative Academy for Writers, and Author Ever After, especially Danika Bloom. If it weren't for the accountability meetings, this book would still be an unfinished draft.

Last but not least, thank you to Sean and Ryan for all of your patience and tolerance when I'm spending too much time at my laptop.

About the Author

Sarah has always been a storyteller. From when she was a child telling stories to her parents in the back seat of the car on long drives until today, she has always loved to tell stories. She tried not being a writer for a long time and then decided there was no stopping the people talking in her head so she might as well let them have the voice they seemed to crave.

When she was deciding what she wanted to write, she at first decided on Urban Fantasy. That's what she liked to read the most, so it made sense. But as time went on, she realized she also loved to read Contemporary Romance and suddenly had an idea for a story in that genre. After spending a lot of time ignoring the voices, she knew how futile it was, and so decided to have her cake and eat it too. Now here we are with two genres.

Will there be cross-over? Only time will tell.

Follow Sarah on Facebook and Instagram @sarahneesonwrites

Made in United States
Troutdale, OR
07/30/2023

11678831R00192